New York Times bestselling author Jeff Long creates riveting suspense and chilling scenarios—in novels that are "terrifying and exquisite in a single breath" (Dan Brown).

THE RECKONING

"Gripping . . . menacing. . . . A neatly tied, portentous thriller about a mission to find the remains of American soldiers—a mission that uncovers a lot more than their mortal souls."

—*Kirkus Reviews*

"Packed with satisfying shocks."

—Scripps Howard News Service

"Long's considerable knowledge of Cambodian folklore and history is put to good use as he superbly depicts the war-scarred country, its people and its beautiful, hazardous landscape."

—*Publishers Weekly*

"An adventure thriller that takes its characters on a haunting trip beyond the boundaries of human endurance and into enemy territory."

—Vince Flynn, *New York Times* bestselling author of *Memorial Day*

"Jeff Long's books have always been must-reads for me. . . . He's the best thriller writer you've never read. Rectify that by picking up a copy of *The Reckoning*."

—*Rocky Mountain News* (Denver)

YEAR ZERO

"Jeff Long writes with poetry, style, and pace . . . crafting his twists and doling out his delectable details with exceptionally gratifying results."

—Dan Brown

"Wow! There's no other word for *Year Zero*."

—CNN.com

"Fast reading . . . just plausible enough to make readers queasy."

—*Rocky Mountain News* (Denver)

"The sum of this complex tale is more than its parts of medical thriller, archeological fiction, action/adventure and doomsday scenario, as Long thrills with an intricate puzzle. Long mounts one nearly impossible escape scene after another and doesn't miss a step as he builds a no-win scenario, then pulls it out. The shifting terrain is vibrantly portrayed, the religious fallout is deftly handled and the characters engage completely as they face a gruesome end to civilization in this dashing, exciting thriller."

—*Publishers Weekly*

"[A] clever, apocalyptic thriller. . . . Long writes stylishly and tells a good yarn."

—*Kirkus Reviews*

"Long . . . makes the fantastic seem real."

—*Booklist*

THE DESCENT

"Jeff Long has written a remarkable novel, an imaginative tour de force that somehow succeeds both as sober-minded allegory and nail-biting thriller. A page-turner for thinking people, *The Descent* is equal parts Ray Bradbury and Robert Stone, Michael Crichton and T. C. Boyle. It is a rip-roaring good read."

—Jon Krakauer, author of *Under the Banner of Heaven: A Story of Violent Faith*

"Absolutely bone-chilling—every bit as good as Stephen King at his best."

—Charles R. Pellegrino, author of *Dust*

"This flat-out, gears-grinding, bumper-car ride into the pits of hell is one major takedown of a read. Jeff Long writes with force and unearthly vision. . . . It is one page-burner of a book."

—Lorenzo Carcaterra, author of *Sleepers* and *Gangster*

"Jeff Long keeps the pages turning at a feverish pace and creates a world so vivid that we are compelled to follow him to the gates of Hell."

—Jonathan Rabb, author of *The Overseer*

"Reminiscent of early Stephen King. . . . Compelling . . . difficult to put down."

—*Library Journal*

"A dizzying synthesis of supernatural horror, lost-race fantasy, and military SF. . . . Long's novel brims with energy, ideas, and excitement."

—*Publishers Weekly*

ALSO BY JEFF LONG

FICTION

Angels of Light

The Ascent

Empire of Bones

The Descent

Year Zero

NONFICTION

Outlaw: The Story of Claude Dallas

Duel of Eagles: The Mexican and U.S. Fight for the Alamo

THE
RECKONING

JEFF LONG

POCKET **STAR** BOOKS

NEW YORK   LONDON   TORONTO   SYDNEY

A Pocket Star Book published by
POCKET BOOKS, a division of Simon & Schuster, Inc.
1230 Avenue of the Americas, New York, NY 10020

Copyright © 2004 by Jeff Long

Originally published in hardcover in 2004 by Atria Books

ISBN: 0-7434-6301-3

First Pocket Books paperback printing July 2005

10 9 8 7 6 5 4 3 2 1

POCKET STAR BOOKS and colophon are registered
trademarks of Simon & Schuster, Inc.

Cover art and design by Tony Greco

For information regarding special discounts for bulk purchases,
please contact Simon & Schuster Special Sales at 1-800-456-6798
or business@simonandschuster.com

Manufactured in the United States of America

For Emma, my wild love went riding. . . .

THE
RECKONING

PROLOGUE

They fish him from the Mekong like a long, pale dragon, shouting and prodding him with bamboo poles, full of dread. He thinks his white skin scares them, or his loincloth made from the last strips of his American uniform.

Babies cry. A dog won't come close.

A village. He laughs at his good fortune. *Home free.*

"Food," he demands. "America."

They scatter at his voice. Their fear gives him heart.

He is mostly blind by now. His legs are too heavy to move. He can barely lift his head. He lies there like Gulliver in the gray rain.

After a while some brave soul sneaks close enough to tie his ankle with a vine. They leave him in the mud on the bank above the flood, tethered like an animal. This sobers him. He must appear very weak or they would bind him properly. But he seems to have some value or they would kill him or feed him back into the river.

As a Boy Scout, he was taught when lost to follow

water downstream. And so for over a week he has been on the move, fording creeks that became muscular tributaries, climbing down around waterfalls and rapids, swimming, and finally drifting on a huge gnarled ship of a tree down the river. Evading and escaping, he'd thought.

He remembers emerging from the forest and its dark shadows, and working through seas of grass, following the water. He expected to descend into light. But as the waters mounted, so did his darkness. When it wasn't raining, monsoon clouds covered the sun. Day by day, his eyesight has decayed. He blames the water. The river is filled with parasites. Or the rain is driving him blind.

Before losing his compass, his course was reliably west by southwest, away from the savage borderlands. Away from the lotus-eating madness infecting his comrades. Deeper into Cambodia.

But the farther he traveled, the more things seemed to melt from him. His paper map dissolved the first day. His clothing flowered with fungus and blue moss and fell apart. His web gear and rucksack vanished. Possibly animals stole his boots in his sleep. Thinking it was his rifle, he carried a tree limb for miles. The illusions nibbled him away. Now they have him.

The men sit at a distance, out of the rain, watching him. He can hear their whispers and smell their tobacco pipes. Raindrops patter on his eyeballs. He can't shut his lids anymore. It should hurt, but it doesn't. He stares into the rain drumming on the bones of his head.

Like every prisoner in a foreign land, he clings to his exceptional circumstances, his singularity. He is young, just nineteen. If he could stand, he would tower over his captors. He has a girlfriend waiting for him. He can throw a football, do algebra in his head, and play "House of the Rising Sun" on the guitar. His folks have the Chevy he rebuilt parked in their garage. If only he could explain. Coming here was not his doing. Somehow the currents brought him to this point in time. The war was somebody else's idea.

At last his captors feed him. Out of caution or because of the rain, they don't light a fire, so there is no rice or cooked food. They give him a little fruit, plus insects and water creatures. By this time, after so many weeks subsisting in the forest, he knows some of the tastes and textures. Crickets have a nutty flavor. The beetles crunch more. The shrimp still wiggle. He is so hungry.

They can't bring enough over the coming days. As his sight fails, he grows more ravenous. He chews grass, tree buds, even clay, anything to slake the hunger. While he can still crawl, they let him forage, moving his tether when he has consumed everything in a circle.

Floating on the great tree in the river, he dreamed of being carried out to sea. Peasant fishermen would find him, or sailors or pirates who would ransom him. Or the U.S. Navy would gather him in. He would be saved.

On the third day, guerrillas arrive. With the last of his vision, he realizes that he has traded one set of shadows for another, the shapes in the forest for these gray phantoms. The world has blurred, but he can still see that they wear black. He recognizes the banana clips in their rifles. The only mystery is their red-checkered scarves. They are a whole new species of enemy to him.

They speak in whispers above him. He can't understand a word. They seem afraid and uncertain of what to do with him. He lies among their legs, stranded in the tonnage of his body. He despises them. He despises himself. In their place, he'd waste him. But all they do is wait.

The men in black pants and red scarves are the last sight he sees. Soon after their arrival, his blindness completes itself. He can't tell day from night anymore. Time slows. The rain comes and goes, thick and warm as piss.

Maybe two more days go by. His limbs grow heavier, heavy like the earth. He listens to the river. Occasionally someone touches his eyes with a twig. That and the rain, like flies he can't kill. He is losing his mind.

Then one day, or night, a man speaks to him in English. "Are you awake or asleep?" he says. His voice is close to the soldier's ear.

The soldier thinks it must be a dream. He hears men murmuring nearby. "Hello?" he calls.

"Look at you," the voice says, clearly shocked. "How has this happened?"

The young soldier fills with hope. "Thank God," he says. He would reach for the man's hand, but can't lift his arms. "I prayed. Who are you?"

"A passenger, like you. They sent for me. I came to help." He sounds like a Frenchman. He could be a colonial, maybe a doctor or a priest.

"Can you save me?"

"I will do what is possible. But time is short. You must tell me everything."

Like holy confession. A priest, he decides. The soldier calms himself. He has to play this right. "Whatever you want, Father. I'm blind. My arms are like stone. I'm eating dirt. What's happening to me?"

There is a pause. "Let us talk."

"Something's wrong with my eyes, Father."

"Yes, your eyes. Can you see?"

"Not really."

"Something, surely."

"Nothing real. Only a dream, the same one. I'm in the forest again. There are giant heads, and spires with monkeys. I need medicine, Father. Can you get me to the Americans? They'll pay you."

The stranger evades his plea. Not good. Whose side is he on? "Where did you come from?" the stranger asks.

"Chicago, Father. America."

"Yes." The man is patient with him. His voice is kind. "You mentioned a city, where this curse began."

A curse, exactly. That's what this was. "You mean the ruins?"

A silence, then, "You found the city?" The ruins excite him. He seems to know them, or of them.

"On a mountain, Father. Right when we needed it. An old place surrounded by walls. Wild, you know, unreal."

"The wars have not injured it?"

"It's untouched, like a thousand years ago. There was no sign of anybody. It was empty."

More silence. The man asks, "Do you remember the way?"

What way? Water flowing into water? But this could be his ticket home. "Absolutely. I can show you once I'm better."

"And the rest of your men?"

The soldier could deny their existence. He could hide them. But now he has mentioned "we," and he is desperate. "They're still there, all of them. I told them to come with me. But they chose a fool over me. We followed him onto the mountain. He led us wrong, then told us to stay. So he died for his sins. And the rest of them will, too."

His interrogator is quiet a minute. He doesn't ask how many Americans are left, nor their unit or any military information. His only interest seems to be the ruins.

"*Âme damnée,*" the man finally murmurs.

The American has no idea what that means. "Yeah," he says, "like that."

"Fallen angels," the priest says. "And yet you escaped."

The soldier grows wary. "I warned them. We were coming apart at the seams. Everyone was afraid. We were lost. There were voices at night. No one knew who to trust or what to do. It was every man for himself. Finally, I left to get help. They won't last long up there. I followed the water. The water brought me here."

"Are they fossilizing as well?"

The young soldier can't cut through the accent. "What?"

"Your eyes," the priest says.

The soldier grows quiet. "What about them?"

"You have not touched them?"

A hand hoists his heavy wrist and guides his fingers to his face. He feels the familiar shape of his cheekbones and forehead, but avoids his eyes. He doesn't want to know.

"Touch them," the voice says.

"My eyes?"

"I, too, am maimed," the priest tells him. *Mayhemed*, it sounds. "There was a bomb. This was a year ago. For a time, I could not bear to see what was left of my body. But at last it was necessary. I had to touch the wounds. Do you understand? We must accept our fate."

The soldier feels his dead eyes. "Oh lord, help me." The lids are peeled back in wide round circles. His eyes are as hard as polished jade. He knows from the ruins what they look like, the green jade eyes. They don't belong in his face.

His hand is returned to his side. It settles upon the mud, like an anchor. His fingers sink into the earth.

"Father? Don't leave me."

"I'm here."

"What will happen to me?"

"The people are afraid. They want you to go away."

"Put me on the river. I'll go. Far away."

"I will put you on the river," the man promises.

Relief floods the soldier. Even blind, he has a chance. "Thank you, Father. Tell them thank you."

"Don't come back to their village, that's all they want. Put this place out of your mind."

"I swear."

"But remember the city. It is punishing you. I think you must return to there someday."

Not in a million years. "Yes, Father."

Then the soldier hears a sound he knows too well, the drawing of a knife. It is done softly, but there is no mistaking the linear hiss. The murmurs stop in the distance. "What are you doing, Father?" he whispers.

"Releasing you," the voice answers, "so that you can finish your journey."

The soldier's heart thunders in his chest. He waits for a tug at his ankle, for the vine tether to be cut. Instead a hand grips his forehead. His throat is bared.

From the start, he knew this was no priest. But he couldn't help but hope. He still can't. "Forgive me, Father," he says. "I was only trying to go home."

"Be brave." The voice is kind. "The dream goes on."

1.

CAMBODIA, 2000

She arrived on the remains of a big American deuce-and-a-half left over from the Vietnam War, its black and olive camouflage peeling. Rust gored its flanks. The beast had no brakes, or if it did, the driver—plastered with burn scars and missing three fingers—had some superstition against touching them. They began their halt a mile out, a matter of patient downshifting and calculation.

"Here?" Molly had to shout her disbelief over the engine noise.

The driver shook his head, not here. He gestured farther ahead.

Through the cracked windshield, the land lay flat and checkered with rice paddies. The mop-topped sugar palms bent at wacky angles and the far-off villages perched on tall, skinny stilts reminded her of the illustrations in a Dr. Seuss book. In every direction, the horizon melted into haze and heat mirages.

Molly thought there must be some mistake. There was no sign of a dig or a camp. And it was so hot. The heat drove at her. It disowned her. She shoved back at it, trying to belong.

The New American West was her gig, not Asia, especially not the part with dead souls from the baby boomers' war. Her writer friends were baffled. They already thought she was made in the shade. She was the get-girl for photo features about ski country plutocrats, gang bangers on the rez in Navajo country, crop circles in Nebraska, and psychotherapy for brain-damaged Everesters who would be king. She had a regional following and a cute Victorian town house in Boulder. Why risk her place in the universe? To them, Cambodia was like some weird fit of hubris. Molly could barely explain it to herself.

She had first learned of the existence of an official grail quest for soldiers' bones at a gallery opening in Taos. The artist's brother was a navy kid full of tales. Something in his mention of a circular, never-ending bone hunt funded by taxpayer dollars had triggered her instincts. The *New York Times* had gone for it. Now she was here.

A white rag hung from a bamboo pole, and she decided that was their landmark. Her sense of relief as well as her misgivings welled up all over again. She wanted the forensics team to see in her a kindred spirit. Like them, her job was to lay bare old secrets. And she was jet-lagged and Cambodia's furnace heat had sapped her pluck.

Let them be kind, she thought, *or at least not hostile. Let me get a foothold.* They were U.S. military. They were their tribe. She was hers, a professional outsider forever working her way in. She knew better than to count on the kindness of strangers, yet found herself praying for it anyway.

It shouldn't have mattered. The story was her mission. She'd moved heaven and earth to land this assignment with the *Times* Sunday magazine, and she meant to make it work. She could freelance for the Rocky Mountain region until doomsday. Or she could make her grab at the brass ring. The same week she turned thirty, Molly had cropped her black hair and gotten the last of her hep-A shots and flown off to the dark side of the moon.

The truck finished its long drift, coming to rest precisely beside the white rag. They sat idling. The driver stared ahead with both hands on the wheel. Molly squinted into the white light, searching for some sign of Recovery Element 1, or RE-1, as this particular recovery team was designated. Their concealment aggravated her. She did not want to take them on blind faith.

Finally, she reached for the rope that served as a door handle. Climbing down, she hurried to the back to drag her big black mule bag from between stacks of wooden Coca-Cola boxes. The truck departed with an intricate clattering of gears.

She was a week late, a matter of finishing other assignments, and of course no one was waiting to greet her. By now they had probably given up on her. Molly turned in a slow circle, one hand shading her eyes. The sun was high and her shadow was barely a splash underfoot.

She felt tiny and vulnerable standing there in her mountain-biker T-shirt. "Vicious Cycles," the slogan said. She'd saved it for this very moment, to make a macho debut with the GI Joes, to show she had some pedigree. *Some pedigree,* she thought, panting for air. Heat rash bubbled on her bare arms.

She unlocked her mule bag and rummaged for a loose white shirt with long sleeves. She had Irish skin that instantly freckled and burned. Vampire skin, a boyfriend had once called it, the ruin of a body built for the thong. Naturally, she'd forgotten a hat. But she was sure the soldiers would swap or sell her something, if she could only find them.

She walked to the far side of the road, hoping to find them toiling away in a large hidden pit. Instead, to her dismay, she looked out upon a labyrinth of emptied paddies, and heaps of dirt, and footpaths branching off this way and that into mirages.

She refused to call out. She couldn't possibly be lost. It was broad daylight and the immense floodplain lay flat in every direction. An orange pin flag marked one of the paths. The flies flocked to her sunscreen, and they had a bite like bees. Cursing in whispers, she set off along the path with her camera bag swinging.

At the end of ten minutes, she spotted a figure quivering in and out of sight on the far side of a drained lake. Molly wiped the sweat from her eyes. Through her longest lens she decided that with his blond hair and long jaw he had to be one of the American soldiers. He seemed to be looking right at her, but didn't return her wave.

Take the bull by the horns, she thought, descending from the footpath. By the time she unraveled their trail system, he might be long gone. She was about to start directly across the dried lake bed when a man spoke behind her. "I wouldn't go out there," he said, "not if it was me."

Molly turned. The man was tall and thin and tidy, with a red-and-white-checkered Khmer scarf hooded over his head. Dirt smudged the knees of his baggy Levi's. He was clean shaven and wore a T-shirt emblazoned with the movie-star face of Che Guevara. A mason's trowel hung from one hand. On the ground behind him, a dented and scratched steel briefcase sat neatly upright on top of two sticks, obviously his work kit. And something else, she noticed. He was not sweating. In every way, he seemed to govern himself, even in this climate.

"I didn't see you," she said.

"The place is littered with leftovers. War junk. Nightmares," he said.

UXO, he meant. Unexploded ordnance from thirty years of killing. Ordinarily she would have rolled with the sermon; it was gentle enough. She was new to the territory, and as a journalist she valued the early guide. But she was tired and pissed off by the heat and this strange flat maze, and was in no mood for wisdom.

"I've had the lecture," she said. "The orange flags mean the area's cleared. Red means stop. But the lake bed is empty." It was a silly thing to say. Just because you couldn't see the danger didn't mean it wasn't there.

"Ever seen them fish?" he said. "Take one grenade, any vintage. Remove pin. Throw in water. It's easier than a net. The problem is, the stuff is old. Half the time it just sinks into the mud and waits." He paused. "What I'm saying is, Molly, let it not be you. You're much too pretty."

He knew her name. And he was hitting on her? *In this heat?* She fanned furiously at the flies.

He leaned down to offer his hand, and reading her race, affected a brogue. "Duncan," he said, "Duncan O'Brian, descended from kings. As for you, Miss Drake, there's no mystery. Everyone's known you were coming."

She thought he only meant to shake, but he took a good grip and lifted her from the lake bed. He was simply not going to allow her to be stupid. She desperately wanted to sit, but it was too soon to show weakness. It showed just the same.

Before she knew what he was doing, his scarf was draped over her head like a veil. "There, that should help," he said. "It gets brutal out here."

The scarf was a marvel. Immediately the air felt cooler. The blinding sun became bearable. The flies disappeared, and with them the feeling of assault. To her surprise, the cloth smelled clean, like rain, not sweat. The small bit of shade heartened her. She had a place to hide. All of that in a stranger's gift.

"I'm fine, thanks." She started to lift away the scarf.

He brushed aside her pride. His hair came to his shoulders, streaked with gray at the temples. She could not tell his age. A very weathered mid-thirties, or a young fifty.

"It's called a *kroma,*" he said. "The Khmers use it for everything you can imagine, a hat, a shawl, a fashion statement, an umbrella, handcuffs, a basket for fruit, a sling to carry their babies. The checkered pattern represents the cosmic tension between life and death. Or knowledge and ignorance. Your pick." There was a touch of the hermit to him. He loved to talk.

The strength was coming back into her. "I only wanted directions," she said. She pointed at the man across the lake bed.

"From our gypsy child?" He had a farm-boy smile. "Not a chance. He never comes close, and you can't get within two hundred yards of him. We've put food out for him, in case he's American. But he leaves it for the dogs. We're not sure who he is or why he's like that. He just showed up one day. The first time I saw him I thought, Ah, boy, you've reached the end of your magical mystery tour. Look at him, all borrowed together. Peasant pants and Vietcong sandals made of old tires. We know the sandals, we've found his tracks, tire tracks. Probably Michelin rubber, from the old Michelin plantations to the east. And no hat, you notice?"

It took Molly a moment to catch his teasing, the "no hat." "I thought he was one of you."

"One of us?"

"A soldier."

Duncan smiled. "In that case, I'm not one of us either."

"Come again?"

"I'm just a visitor like you. One more civilian."

"You're not a soldier?" Her eyes flicked down at the Che shirt.

He flashed her a peace sign. "Ever heard of Kent State?"

She connected the dots. He was talking about the event, not the place. "You were there?" she said. It dated him, though she couldn't remember the date. Before her time.

"On the grassy hill, on the very day," he said. "May 4,

1970. I heard the bullets cut the air. I saw the blood on the lawn. It took me all the rest of the spring and summer to come out of hiding."

Some other time. "But I thought they only used their own people for recoveries," she said.

According to the information officer, Joint Task Force-Full Accounting and the Central Identification Lab based in Hawaii deployed their own military investigators, linguists, anthropologists, and assorted other experts. At a cost of tens of millions of dollars per year, JTF-FA and CILHI were the official forensic archangels of Vietnam and other foreign wars. They were very territorial about it, she had come to learn. The bones were holy relics. "Sacred Ground" was her working title for the piece.

"They have their rules," Duncan said. "They make their exceptions. I'm not the only one. You'll meet the other soon enough, John Kleat. The captain took us in. We like to think we're of some small use."

"You came together?"

"Kleat and me? Nope. I just happened to be in the neighborhood, an archaeologist down from the jungles. My specialty is temple restorations. But I know my way around grid strings and a hole. I help where I can. And I try to keep my place."

"And Mr. Kleat?"

"Kleat," said Duncan, "has come searching for his brother."

Molly pricked her ears up at that. "His brother was the pilot?"

"No, we know that much. But Kleat, he's philosophical about it. The digging season is like an annual pilgrimage for him. He believes one of these years his brother's bones are bound to surface."

"Have you done this before, gone digging for them . . . the others?" She fumbled, unsure of what to call them. The dead? The fallen heroes? They would have their own lingo.

"The boys, you mean?"

"The boys," she repeated.

"Oh, I keep my eyes open when I'm out with my temples. Sort of a professional courtesy, don't you think?" Duncan looked off across the labyrinth, then back at her. "And what about you, miss?"

"Me?"

"Camp is on the far side of the road. I can take you there. Or if you like, we can go on to the dig site."

She told him the dig site. They started walking. He carried his steel briefcase in one hand, the trowel in his other.

"They're all waiting for their fifteen minutes, you know," he said. "They think you're going to make them immortal."

2.

Duncan led her along a succession of paths toward a surf roar of men's voices and clattering tools and the drumbeat of earth being chopped and a generator snarling to pump away water. They arrived at a small army of locals pick-and-shoveling through more paddy walls, raising a cloud of orange dust. Molly curbed the impulse to reach for her camera, waiting to meet the head honcho and get the inevitable ground rules.

Duncan called "Captain" at two Americans on a dike above the toil, but neither heard. They were busy consulting a map with a wiry village elder, or a Cambodian liaison officer. The old man had a dark brown moon of a face with burr-cut white hair and one pink plastic leg. Somehow he heard Duncan over the din. He lifted his head abruptly and looked at Molly as if he'd been waiting for her.

"Samnang," Duncan told her, walking closer. "He's the work boss. In the old days, before Pol Pot, before Nixon, he studied at the Sorbonne and taught music and math at the Royal Academy in Phnom Penh. That was then."

The two Americans noticed her now. Molly figured the taller one to be the mission leader. He looked commanding with his sun-bronzed skull, photogenic as hell, a seamed scar looping across his throat. He wore black cargo pants bloused in his boot tops, a close second to the American uniforms that were forbidden on these military excavations.

But it was the squat younger man dressed in a Hawaiian-print shirt, Gargoyle sunglasses, and a baseball cap who descended to them. Molly took in the cap, the veins, and the wedding band. The captain was an Orioles fan, a gym rat, and married. And a hopeless legs man. Even the Gargoyles could not disguise his stare.

"Welcome to the kingdom, Ms. Drake." The young captain didn't mention that she was badly overdue. He didn't try to own her. She liked that. His eyes flickered at Duncan's *kroma* on her head, and he did not begrudge Duncan's first contact with his guest of honor. "You plunge right in," he said to her. "Already out meeting the natives."

"Mr. O'Brian saved me. I was about to go off chasing phantoms."

"The gypsy kid," said Duncan.

"Some poor mother's son," the captain said.

She had not meant to apologize, but since all seemed forgiven she saw only merit to be gained by it. "The week got away from me," she offered.

"No problem."

She looked around at the mounds of dirt. "I was praying I wouldn't be too late."

"If you mean have we found the pilot, we have not."

She tried to read his tone. Was he optimistic? Dis-

couraged? They had been here for nearly three weeks.
Generally their digs didn't go longer than a month,
which was a blink of the eye compared to other digs
she'd covered. At Canyon de Chelly, Yellowjacket, Little Big Horn, and elsewhere, it took years and even
decades to lay bare the past. Coming over on the plane,
she had worried about their quickness. She had sold
her editor on a find, not a hit-or-miss process. She
needed bones for her story. But she could not say so,
not to these bone hunters.

Duncan seemed to read her mind. "We'll find him,"
he said.

"If he's here," the captain qualified, "we'll find him."

"He's waited long enough," Duncan said. She
sensed a subtle tug of war between the captain, under
deadline, and this long-haired middle-aged archaeologist who did not even wear a wristwatch.

The captain didn't take it personally. He clapped
Duncan on the shoulder. "A true believer," he said.

"They're talking about the July Fourth issue," Molly
said. She offered it as information, but also motivation.
The captain needed to understand she was under deadline, too. She didn't volunteer that the next big patriot
slot wouldn't come until Thanksgiving, and no one at
the magazine wanted to wait that long. This was just
another Vietnam rehash with a short shelf life, less a war
story than a nostalgic nod to the Rolling Stone generation. And she needed bones. It came down to that.

The captain said, "We'll be long gone by July. Once
the wet season starts, we close shop."

"When does the monsoon come?"

"Every year's different. Sometimes May, usually mid

to late June. The meteorologists are forecasting a late arrival this year. That gives us a little more wiggle room if we need it. But there's time for all that later. First let's see to you. We've got another three hours left to the workday here, but let me suggest you get squared away at camp. Rest up this afternoon. Drink lots of water. Wash the dust off. I should warn you, the shower sees a lot of action around seventeen hundred hours. I'll make the introductions at dinner."

She was more grateful than she allowed herself to show. Her body was still operating on mountain standard time, as in 2:00 A.M. And this heat. Three mornings ago, she'd scraped frost off her windshield. Now she couldn't seem to take a whole breath. It felt like slow suffocation.

"Just point the way," she said. "I'll find it."

"You're new to the territory. I'll get someone to run you through mine awareness tonight, and assign you an escort."

It was exactly what she didn't want, a keeper hemming her in. But she smiled gracefully. "I'll learn my way around," she told him.

"Until then," the captain said, "I think Mr. Kleat was on his way back to camp." He waved at the big American.

"I'll see you later," Duncan said.

"Your scarf," she said.

"My gift, Molly." He touched his trowel to his forehead and walked off into the dust.

Kleat came down the slope of the dike in big, clod-busting strides. Molly took in his details. Here might be her centerpiece, this brother of a missing soldier searching through the years. He was not so tall as he had seemed up there. His head was large and his neck surprisingly thick, as if it carried a great weight of ideas. His steel-rimmed glasses flashed in the white sun. He did not cover his baldness. He looked ambitious.

"We were starting to think you'd given up on us," he said to her.

"You said you were heading back to camp," the captain said to Kleat.

"Sure," Kleat said, taking his cue. "I'll show her in."

The captain started back up the dike, then turned to Molly. "One other thing," he said. "When we find him, no photographs. Don't shoot the remains."

They'd told her already. "Absolutely," she said.

Kleat led the way. Molly followed him away from the noise. After a few minutes' walking, he said, "Boulder."

She heard the scorn. You got it all the time. "The People's Republic," she confessed. "What about you?"

"Angeles City."

"L.A.?"

"Christ, no. The Philippines. There's a nice colony of vets live there. We live like princes. Beers cost twelve cents. Like that."

"What do you do?"

"When I'm not here? I'm a contractor." He didn't volunteer what kind of contractor.

"They say you come to Cambodia every year."

He didn't answer. "I thought there'd be more of you," he said. "A crew of assistants. Helpers."

"I like working alone."

"I've read some of your articles on the internet. That fisherman who cut off his own leg. The

Columbine murders. Those peace-scam artists. And your piece on the Super Max inmates, 'A Season in Stainless-Steel Hell.' "

Molly didn't know if he was trying to flatter or control her. They knew her better than she knew them—where she lived, what she wrote, her photos. She noted that he didn't say if he approved of her work or not. "It's a job," she said.

"Why give them personalities, though?" he asked.

"The inmates?"

"Just kill them, I say."

"It's a matter of what we do with evil," she said. "That was my point."

"And now you're working for the big dog. The *Times*, right? Moving up in the world." He was testing her, she realized. Deciding if she was good enough.

Humility. "They're trying me out. I'm a very little fish in a very big pond."

He gave a small grunt, but still had reservations. "Cambodia, though. Why chase the dead?" He gestured at the trenches and square holes along the trail. "Why come after these guys?"

"Memory," she said. "Memory is flesh. As long as we remember, they're still alive, don't you think?"

He didn't answer. She followed the sleek, gleaming prow of his head as they zigzagged along the maze of footpaths above paddies and between heaps of red dirt. Finally Kleat began to open up.

"It looks like a jumble," he said of the dig. "But this is how it's done. There's a method to the madness. Our metal detectors have found pieces of the plane scattered to kingdom come. But you can see the general east-west line of our digging." He showed her his topo map with colored-pencil markings. "Here's the crash trajectory."

The site was vast and complicated. He described how the dying warplane had ricocheted across two linear miles of rice fields, disintegrating in leaps and bounds. Afterward, local peasants had patiently rebuilt their paddies over the gouged earth. Then the Khmer Rouge had come, erasing whole villages, and, along with them, all memory of the buried plane. Later the Vietnamese army swept through on their "liberation" of Cambodia. Then the United Nations entered, determined to jump-start the devastation known as year zero. Not far behind them came the men and women of U.S. military forensics teams. Ever since, they had been resurrecting American warriors from the Cambodian hinterlands.

"Sometimes the locals show up with a bone that has no story. In this case, we have a story but no bone, not yet," Kleat said. "We know exactly who we're searching for and when he disappeared. All we need to do is find him."

The "we" jarred her. According to Duncan, he and Kleat were outsiders. But to hear Kleat, he was a full-fledged member of the recovery team. She glanced at him. Was he out to steal the captain's thunder?

He stopped by a trench surrounded by torn sheets of metal lying across the mounded earth. Some had been fitted together in puzzle pieces. Red and black and green cable and wire stretched like bunches of fried snakes. A collection of digging tools was stacked in the trench below.

"It's weird in a way," he said. "When the refugees got relocated to this area twelve years ago, they inherited the tools left behind by dead villagers. Talk about memory, there was no memory here, just the land and a bunch of strangers. But then it turns out the tools had a memory of what happened in this place."

He bent and pulled up several of the shovels and examined them. He found what he was looking for and handed it to Molly. The head was wider and blunter than on an American shovel, and the metal was brighter and silvery. The edges looked crudely cut and you could see where a local blacksmith had hammered it to fit the wooden shaft.

Kleat scratched away some of the dirt. "Can you see it?"

There was a number stamped in the metal, and beneath that the inscription "Made in the USA." She took out her camera and started getting shots.

"It comes from a section of the stabilizer flap of a Cessna O2 Skymaster," Kleat said. "It was a slow, twin-prop airplane used for forward air control. The pilot would mark targets with white phosphorous rockets, then the bombers would come. This one left from Ubon Airfield in Thailand on January 3, 1969, to scout the Ho Chi Minh Trail, but he never came home. After the plane crashed, the peasants beat the sword into the plowshare, literally."

He explained how military investigators had found plow blades made of cut-up propellers, wooden ox bells with bullet shells for clappers, and handmade sickles and pots and pans still bearing telltale serial numbers. The recovery teams always deployed with a database called Brite Lite.

"The pilot and his plane just vanished into the abyss.

All signs of the plane, even the crash scar, disappeared. Thirty years of farming devoured every trace. Even the satellite photos showed nothing. We knew the plane was out here somewhere. We've known for years. We just didn't know enough." *We*.

"So you've got farm tools left by ghosts, and a plane without a pilot," she said.

Kleat cut a look at her full of suspicion. "There's nothing supernatural about this," he snapped.

Molly was taken off guard. "Of course not," she said.

"I've done this before," he declared. "An air crash isn't rocket science. The physics are simple. The path of impact is known. We have his trajectory. We're unearthing his wings. It's a matter of time. He'll answer to us."

That was a curious way to put it, even imperious, as if the dead pilot were a fugitive or a truant. Molly gently slid the shovel back among its brothers.

They continued along the path. It was past noon, but the sun only seemed to reach higher in the sky. The light would have been painful if not for the checkered shawl draped across her head and shoulders. They walked in silence for another half mile or so, the straps of her camera bag creaking. The air smelled of water and sewage. The trail seemed to go on forever.

Then, far off in the sheets of heat, Molly caught sight of the gypsy man. By now she had no sense of direction, no idea where the road was or—looking back—where the excavators were harrowing the earth. She fastened on the gypsy as if he were a magnetic north. It felt like she was traveling in circles around him.

"There he is again," she said, pointing.

Kleat squinted across the fields. "Him," he said.

"Who do you think he is?"

"There are always stray dogs around the bones. I told the captain it was a mistake encouraging him. This is a recovery, not a lonely-hearts club."

"Duncan said he might be a drug addict or the son of a missing soldier."

An expression came onto Kleat's face, as if she were joking. "But that *is* Duncan," he said quietly.

She brought her camera up and telescoped the figure through her lens. There was the mane of brown hair and the sparkle of his steel briefcase. Duncan was walking along the top of a paddy wall with a long stick in one hand, poking at random.

She lowered her camera. "I didn't know." She couldn't think what else to say.

A stray dog? Kleat didn't make any attempt to apologize. She didn't say anything. Suddenly she didn't know whom to trust. In this flat land that seemed incapable of hiding anything, everything seemed concealed.

3.

It was a story to sweat and bleed for, and she did both over the coming weeks, down in the trenches, under the sun, earning her way into the family of them.

She was a photographer first, a writer second. The lens was her habitat. It was her sanctuary. Prose came more slowly. It always came after the picture.

The afternoon the *Times* editor called to assign her the story, Molly had gone straight to Mike's Camera and maxed out her credit card on a digital Nikon with all the bells and whistles. She had wanted it forever, but could never justify the sticker shock, over $10,000. Now that she was going national, though, she figured the camera would pay for itself.

With digital you could edit the image and change the look, even turn color into grainy black and white, as she'd contemplated, to evoke a '60s 'Nam-scape. It would give her the ability to mimic the great war photographers, Henri Huet and Tim Page and Larry Burrows and Kyochi Sawada and Robert Capa, all without lugging blocks of Velvia and Kodak through the tropical heat.

The camera was unlike any she'd ever owned. It was more than the usual sum of lenses, filters, and film, more than a boxful of memories. Its instant recall made it both a tool and a communal event.

On a hunch, she had brought a pair of five-inch barber's scissors. Her dad—her stepfather—had been a barber. *Never underestimate the value of a free haircut.* The scissors paid in aces with the recovery team. People flocked to her tent in the evenings. While she trimmed their hair, they talked about music, sports, movies, and home. She shared anything they wanted to know about photography, from the rule of thirds to underexposing one f-stop for the midday glare. Also she showed them her camera, and that was the real icebreaker.

With a flip of a switch, they could see themselves the way she saw them. She flipped the switch. The display lit up.

Here was their dig, and in the distance nut-brown children wrestling on water buffalo, *National Geographic* country as far as the eye could see.

Here were the faces of RE-1, black, white, and brown, all rendered one color, the color of Cambodia's dirt, the color of blood oranges. Here they mined the earth, here they shook it through screens with quarter-inch mesh.

Here was the captain in repose, toasting her with a bottle of warm grape Gatorade while he smoked his evening Havana and read one of her *Vogue* magazines. He was smart and freethinking, a postmodern soldier who reveled in not carrying a weapon, and lived to raise the lost souls from the dirt.

There was Kleat, a dead end. The brother angle

would have been so sweet. But after the first week of him, she knew there was no way around his hatred of the people and the land. Kleat treated Cambodia like a curse or a disease. There was no way she could turn his bile into nobility, and so Molly had dropped him from her story and started framing her shots to exclude him.

And here was Duncan, who was not part of her story either. But she could not keep her camera off him; there was something she liked. Here he stared into a dark square hole covered with grid strings, like a scout about to leap into the underworld. Here he stood among the laborers, head and shoulders above them, spinning some hilarious joke in fluent Khmer. Here he sat on his briefcase with his sketchbook on one knee, drawing faces and scenes and artifacts that no one was allowed to see because of his shyness.

She peeked into his tent one afternoon, and was startled by its austerity. It was bare except for a black Ace comb and a toothbrush tucked in the wall pocket. He slept on the ground without sheets or a sleeping pad or a mosquito net. He owned nothing but the clothes on his back and whatever he carried in that briefcase.

Here was their base camp, a hodgepodge of wall tents, pup tents, and her North Face dome. They had pitched their camp where a village once stood, not knowing that for some reason the locals thought it haunted.

They used a clothesline strung between trees for their occasional volleyball games. Barbecue ball, she called it. Roasting the weenies. Almost six feet tall, she played like a gladiator, six-packing the ball into the faces of husky trash talkers. She bloodied noses, made kills, tooled them mercilessly . . . and they loved her for it.

Not unnaturally, so far from home, they began to court her. It was nothing personal. After she sliced herself on a piece of the wreckage, the special forces medic who stitched her thigh proposed marriage. Another Romeo braved the mosquitoes and recited Shakespeare to the wall of her tent at night. One morning, Kleat caught her shooting him. He rose up from his washbasin, the water dripping from his salt-and-pepper chest hair, and opened his arms to her.

She felt like a hypocrite, keeping them at bay. After all, day after day, she stalked them intimately. But that was the way it was. Molly didn't tell them about one bad night in Oklahoma long ago. She just gave them her policy: no hookups on a shoot. And went on seducing them for her camera.

Each night, she downloaded her day's harvest into a digital wallet, a portable hard drive, and cataloged her shots and watched her story grow. While the soldiers listened to Dr. Dre or Beethoven, read paperbacks, or played Game Boys, she lay on her back in the dark of her tent and the images lit her face. The wallet became her dream box. Some nights she couldn't tell if she was awake or dreaming with the crickets going wild outside under the Cambodian stars.

Among professionals, the purists argued that digital wasn't pure. The geeks argued that there were still bugs in the machine, and there were, in hers at any rate, some serious gremlins in some of the shots. She became aware of them gradually.

Within a week of arriving, Molly had gotten their

labyrinth memorized, and made a habit of waking first each morning, before dawn, to visit the dig site. Every day the site grew longer. There was nothing much to do at this hour. Night still pooled in the holes. It was too early for the teams to work and too dark for her to shoot. But it was cooler then, and she had her best privacy. She wandered along the cut-open earth, alone with her thoughts in the gray mist. But not quite alone, she began to realize.

Ghostly figures ambled across the fields, distant and only half visible above the ground fog. She supposed they were villagers. Some wore *kromas* over their heads or around their necks. Some carried mute babies.

By five the sky would start to gain color. Roosters crowed far away. She could practically taste the wood smoke of breakfast fires in invisible villages. Then, just as the sun broke the horizon, a faraway temple bell would ring once, just once. Each dawn broke that way, with the bell's single gong. The early morning wanderers would fade off and she would return to make her breakfast.

On a whim one morning, Molly lugged along her tripod and snapped a shot of the villagers in the dim light. She didn't expect much, and when she downloaded the camera into her wallet at the end of the day, there was next to nothing. The camera had captured the fields and haze, though none of the wanderers.

But a few days later, in scrolling through the JPEG files, she discovered that her morning shot was populated. The wanderers had been buried in the pixels somehow, and the camera was finally letting them rise to the surface. Not only that, every time she turned the display on again, the image changed. Like spirits, the villagers came and went. There might be five people when she turned the device off, and ten or dozens when she turned it on again.

The photo became something of a freak show, attracting a small audience of soldiers who would drop by to see if the digital figures had moved around or vanished back into the mist. Duncan joked that her camera was possessed.

A navy explosives specialist diagnosed the ghosts as faulty software. Digital noise, he called it. In getting compressed and decompressed, the image apparently altered itself, as if peeling away layers of reality.

One morning she noticed one of the hooded figures trailing her in the muggy gloom. She stopped. He stopped. "Hello?" she said, approaching him.

It was old Samnang, wearing a blue-and-white *kroma* like a shawl, and under that a headset for his tape recorder. All but buried in the mist, his prosthesis had a blue sandal glued to the pink foot.

"Ah, *bonjour,* Molly," he said. *Maw-lee.* His accent, so beautiful.

"Samnang, what a surprise," she said without surprise. It was so clear. "Did the captain tell you to follow me?"

"The captain? Not at all."

"This was your idea," she said.

Samnang sniffed at the air. "The hour is so fresh, don't you agree?"

She could have been rude and insisted on her privacy, but she liked Samnang. He was as honest as a monk, and the American recovery teams hired him year after year to run their crews. He jokingly compared himself to a chicken scratching in the dirt for a living. She had never heard him speak about his past. He never mentioned the loss of his leg, never said a word about any family. Following Duncan's example, she made a point of calling him by his full name, not Sam like the others did.

Finally she said, "So what are you listening to?"

During the wet season, when excavation was pointless, Samnang used his U.S. dollars to go around the countryside collecting folk songs. *Before the water washes them away.*

He laid the *kroma* along his neck and handed Molly his headset. He pressed the button. Expecting folk music, she was amazed to hear Margo Timmins singing on *The Trinity Sessions*. "The Cowboy Junkies?" she said.

He smiled sheepishly. "An old vice of mine."

After that there was no way she could refuse his company. They started walking together.

"Duncan told me about your photograph of the morning people," Samnang said. "I thought to see them for myself."

It occurred to her that he had come to protect her. Did he fear they might resent her presence? But they seemed unaware of her. For that matter, they seemed unaware of one another.

"They're harmless," she said. "They never look at me. They never come close."

"Are there any out there now?"

She counted a woman with two children in the fog, and a man standing in place, looking off. "Just three," she told him.

"But some mornings, more?"

"Many more. I wonder if they're studying the damage. You know, figuring out how to repair the paddy walls before the rains come."

"What are they doing now?"

She glanced at Samnang and his black eyes glistened inside the lips of his shawl. He was watching her face, not even trying to look for them. Was he testing her, or were his eyes too old? She turned her head. Several more had appeared a hundred yards to the side, motionless or nearly so. One drifted along some hidden dike path. "Nothing," she told him. "They're just standing out there, like they're waiting for a train or something."

Samnang nodded his head slowly, intent on her face.

"My other thought was that they might be foraging," she said.

" 'Foraging,' " he repeated.

"Like a cargo cult or something. Salvaging the plane's wire and metal. Getting a little treasure before the day starts and the Americans show up. This is their backyard, after all."

"Have you seen them taking anything? Reaching into the ground? Digging?"

"Never. They never do anything. They don't even talk to each other."

He had risen early for her. He could still be sleeping. She felt responsible. "You shouldn't worry about me," she said. "I can take care of myself."

"The villagers are quite frightened by them," Samnang said.

She frowned. These *were* the villagers. "I don't understand."

"They complain to the government. They want them gone."

She was trying to keep up with him. "So these people come from another region," she tried. "They're poaching the metal."

"No, it's not that."

"Then what?"

"It is a local matter."

What a strange battle. A trespass each morning before dawn, and with babies and children, too. But never a confrontation.

"You said the villagers complained. Why don't the soldiers make them leave then?" she asked. The Cambodian government had posted a dozen troops to guard—or contain—the American forensics expedition. They did little except lie in hammocks, or squat above the dig and gossip in the sun.

"They are just as brave as the villagers at this hour," Samnang said. "No one comes, except you."

"And you," she said.

He smiled. "Anyway, it wouldn't help. You find these morning people all through the country."

That was the second time he had said it that way. "Morning people?"

"Now you have made me one, too," he joked, growing even more elliptical. She decided to drop it. A local matter.

Just then the sun cracked the night. The haze lit like fire. In the sudden flare of color, it was hard to see. The figures began to dissipate. That distant bell rang across the fields. Its single note vibrated in the air.

Molly felt the heat against her face. "I have to see that bell someday," she said.

Next morning, he was waiting for her again. It was

clear. Since she was going to persist in these morning walks, he would accompany her. Their walks became for her the high point of every day.

When Kleat heard about her new friend, he advised her to dump Samnang. "Ditch him," he said. "The old man's KR. Or was."

KR was a universal phrase, part of every language spoken in Cambodia. Khmer Rouge, a French label, the Red Khmers, red for Communist, red for blood. "That's crazy," she said. "He was a professor at the university. How could he be KR? They killed people like him."

"Open your eyes. You haven't seen him with the men? He never raises his voice, and he's a cripple. But they always do what he tells them. One word and it's done."

"That's how it's supposed to work, Kleat."

"But they're *afraid* of him."

It made no sense to a guy like Kleat how this gentlest of men was able to control the pent-up tempest of the workers. Born and raised in violent refugee camps, many of the local Khmer men were semi-wild. At night some got drunk in their villages, gambled, beat their women, and bloodied each other with knives and axes. Molly had pictures of that, too.

But even the worst toughs obeyed Samnang without question. "They respect him," she said.

"He has a power over them," Kleat argued.

"Like voodoo?"

"Laugh. He's KR, I tell you."

"The KR don't exist anymore."

"Tell that to the workers. They have their memories."

"If he was KR, what's he doing here?"

"The same thing you're doing," Kleat said to her. "Making a buck. Doing penance. I don't know."

Duncan was sitting there. He said it was none of Kleat's business, even if Samnang had been KR. "Everyone has secrets they'd rather forget."

"Not secrets like that," Kleat said.

"Let up," Duncan said. "Survival always has a price tag."

4.

At the end of her third week, Samnang approached Molly. "I have something to show you."

They rode in a Land Cruiser hired from three brothers who lived in Samnang's hometown, Kampong Cham. The driver, a heavily tattooed boy, drove them to a nearby village. The village was built on stilts for the rainy season. There were even bridges between some of the huts, and a dock with canoes lying on the dirt. It seemed inconceivable the land could ever be flooded. Water was their faith, a phantom thing, nothing Molly could believe in. All she'd seen since arriving was dry, cracked earth.

On a slight hill beyond the village there was a shack with a corrugated tin roof and no walls. Inside sat a cheap cement Buddha, like a garden gnome. To one side, hanging from the rafters, was the bell.

Samnang took a small hammer and rang it for her. The pitch was perfect.

She was delighted, and went closer. "But it's made from an old bomb shell," she said.

"Yes." Samnang was pleased by her surprise. "It is inescapable, don't you think? That the rubble should be turned into order. Even into beauty."

"No," she answered. "I would think it was the other way around. Beauty fades. Civilizations grind to dust. I would say loss is the norm. Chaos. Noise. Not music."

Samnang touched the bell with his fingertips. "But you see?" he said. "They have restored themselves from the horror."

On May 29, a dog brought a human femur to the site.

Molly got a picture of the dog just before one of the Cambodian soldiers shot it, the bone still in its mouth. The Americans rushed over, excited that this might be evidence of their missing pilot. But one glance told them it was another false lead. The thighbone didn't come close to matching a six-foot Caucasian's. It could not belong to their pilot.

Very possibly the bone had come from a mass grave somewhere in the region. Killing fields hid everywhere, even around here. After every rainy season, bones cropped up, often no more than tiny white fragments. In the beginning, Molly had mistaken the crushed bits along the outer paths for bleached seashells. Then she'd spied checkered fragments of disintegrating scarves mixed among them and realized she was walking on the dead.

Curious to see what would happen, Molly followed the bone. The forensic anthropologist with RE-1 judged the femur to be Southeast Asian Mongoloid. He wrapped it in bubble wrap and turned it over to their Cambodian liaison officer. The liaison officer kept the bubble wrap and gave the bone to a soldier, who tossed it into a distant ditch, dog food again.

She watched it all through her telephoto lens. Then she saw Samnang go over. Looking around to make sure no one saw him, he took the bone and buried it by a tree. He lit a stick of incense, and she realized that Kleat was right.

Samnang was guilty. He probably had been KR. Finding the dead was his way of doing penance.

One of the Cambodian soldiers, or a villager, perhaps, must have seen Samnang ministering to the bone and drew the same conclusion. There were eyes everywhere, factions and subfactions and jealousies. For one reason or another, KR or not, Samnang was dismissed from the dig that evening.

The purge was swift. Molly heard about it at the last minute. She rushed to the road to say good-bye, but the truck carrying him away was already leaving. She caught his face in her camera, and he turned his eyes away from her. She figured that was the last she'd ever see of him.

As the red dust settled, Molly saw a figure watching the departure from out in the fields. At first she thought it was the gypsy kid standing in the ball of the sinking sun. But when she shaded her eyes, he turned into Kleat, and she realized who had gotten rid of old Samnang.

5.

By then the dig was nearly done. Their dead reckoning had failed. The crash site looked like a carcass—rice paddies breached, dirt piled by the sifting screens, holes collapsing, and grid strings let loose—and still the pilot eluded them. After a month of brute labor, RE-1 had pulled up hundreds of pieces of the cockpit and fuselage and wings, seemingly everything but the bones that were their quest.

As they reached the end of the crash trajectory, the Americans sensed their failure. They took it personally. Their high hopes came tumbling down. One night, at the beginning of June, two of the youngest marines got into a fistfight over a stolen *Hustler* magazine. They fought like jealous teenagers, and everyone was embarrassed by the display.

After the captain got the two fighters separated, it turned out that others, including Molly, had suffered petty thefts, too, mostly letters and snapshots from home. Whoever it was had snitched her barber's scissors. The culprit, probably some desperately poor

Khmer—though Kleat made sure to accuse the roaming gypsy—never was caught.

The stealing was almost beside the point. What mattered about the fight and the thefts was that it suddenly became clear their losses outweighed their gains. Their daily miseries—the spiraling heat, the snakes and bugs, the dust of dried paddy sewage that festered in their sinuses, and a hundred other small things—could no longer be sustained with hope. Whether the pilot had ejected or been cast loose of the jet or dragged away, it was plain they were not going to find him.

As if to hasten their departure, they received news that a typhoon was building to super class in the South China Sea. With winds in excess of 150 miles per hour, it already equaled a class 4 Atlantic hurricane. The navy meteorologists could not say when and where it might strike land, in four days or six or ten, in Malaysia, Thailand, or Cambodia. But it was sure to usher in the mother of all monsoons. The rains would come. The roads would turn to grease and the paddies would fill. Rivers would run backward. The villages would turn into islands.

On the evening of June 7, the captain invited Molly, Kleat, and Duncan to a private gathering inside his wall tent. He had lawn chairs for them and coffee mugs for the last of his Johnnie Walker Black.

"We're terminating the recovery," he told them. The search was over. He had already broken the news to his team. "I wanted to tell you separately. To thank each of you for your hard work."

Molly sat back, stunned. Her shock was a curiosity to her. For at least a week now, she had been trying to invent a story that glossed over the fact that she was essentially writing about empty holes. "It's over?" she said.

"Can't you hear?" said Kleat. "It's done."

Duncan tried to rally the captain. "You don't give up on the good ones," he said.

"We're not, Duncan," the captain said. "But at a certain point you say, enough."

"A few days more," said Duncan. "Where else could he be?"

For Molly's sake, the captain said, "I'm disappointed, too."

"There will be other seasons, other excavations," Kleat said. He was adamant.

Other chances, she thought, but not for her. The *Times* had not sent her to write about barren dirt, not after a pitch entitled "Sacred Ground." The bottom line was that without the bones for a climax, her story was not a *Times* story at all.

"We start redeploying tomorrow," the captain said. "I'll arrange transportation for you."

Molly went through the motions of the captain's farewell celebration. Afterward, she meandered through camp, dealing with the letdown. She could hear soldiers through their tent walls. They were excited to be going back home.

The paper was covering her travel expenses, and she'd get a kill fee for her trouble. Maybe one of the airline magazines would take a condensed version, and she could spin off a travel piece for the *Denver Post.* She'd never recoup the cost of the camera, though. Ten grand. She'd gambled big, and lost.

On a whim, she took a few pickup shots of the camp. Wasting battery juice just to waste it, she paused by a hole that had once been the village well and fired her flash into the darkness, not even aiming. There was nothing to see with the naked eye. The hole was deep and the flash too quick, and when she kicked a pebble, it plunked on water so stagnant it smelled gray.

She didn't bother looking at the image on her camera display, just turned it off and returned to her tent. She began packing some of her things, but that only made her feel worse. Lying down, she held the camera overhead and flipped on the display.

The bones were waiting for her.

She gaped at the illuminated image. How could a camera see through water? Actually it was possible with a long enough time lapse. But she'd used a flash. The light would have bounced off the water.

There was a hint of poorly focused white sticks beneath the water. Garbage, she decided. Twigs tossed in by children or the wind. More digital noise. She turned the camera off, then on, to see if the image corrected itself. This time, there was a rib cage and a long tail-like spine.

An animal, she thought. Then saw the skull.

6.

First thing the next morning, filled with excitement and disbelief, they lowered one of the marines on a rope, by his ankles, headfirst. He took a deep breath. They dunked him into the water, gave him sixty seconds, and then hauled him, soaking wet, back up the shaft and into the sunlight. He held a handful of human vertebrae. There was more, he said, much more.

Things got noisy fast. They snaked hoses down the well shaft and the pumps roared. They rigged a klieg light over the hole, and fired up another generator. As the water drained off and small glittering shrimp writhed in the mud and water weeds, the brown tips of bones jutted up like driftwood.

They lowered a man again. This time he brought up two skulls.

"What in God's name," a soldier muttered.

Their forensic anthropologist examined the skulls. Neither was Caucasian. One belonged to a child. The nuchal crest at the base of the skull was rounded, the forehead smooth, the wisdom teeth not yet descended, the whole aspect gracile. Probably female, he said, probably eight to ten years old. He laid it on the ground and went to join the others peering into the hole.

"The fucking KR," Kleat said.

It was a mass grave, not fifty feet from their camp.

Duncan knelt down and took the skull. "Look at you, poor bug," he whispered.

"What?" said Molly, not sure she'd heard.

He looked up at her, and there was a streak down his mask of red dust. Through her lens, at first she thought it was sweat. But it was a tear for the nameless girl. She got the picture.

The find staggered them, the enormity of the murders. They were familiar with the killing fields. All had seen the displays of bones in places like Phnom Penh. But this was slick and shiny. The event of death seemed unfiltered, unprocessed. It could have been yesterday.

Just the same, it was not their pilot. They switched off the pumps and cut the light. Their eleventh-hour hope went as dark as midnight.

The captain turned away. "That's that," he said. "Let the Cambodians have it. This isn't ours."

But Duncan would not give up. "He's down there," he told them. "I'd stake my life on it."

The captain turned to him. "Duncan," he said softly, "the cockpit is two miles away."

"The well was used for burial once, why not before?" Duncan said. "Think about it, the morning after the plane crashed. There's metal and wire lying everywhere, a windfall of riches. But also there's this body of a stranger, and not just a body. A ghost."

"Ghosts," Kleat scoffed.

"A serious liability in these parts," said Duncan. "These are peasants straight out of the tenth century. I've spent time among them. They see spirits everywhere. Tiger spirits. Forest spirits. Witches flying in the night, drinking people's blood. They've already got their hands full with ancestors. Now suddenly a body falls from the sky. What would you do? Conduct a respectful Buddhist cremation? For a stranger? Waste a week going off to find the authorities? Authorities, by the way, who might try to lay claim to your plane parts. The body was a nuisance. A pollution. So they dumped him here."

"Into their drinking water?" said the captain.

"It's an old well in an abandoned village. And the tradition could have carried over. Years later, when the Khmer Rouge needed a dumping ground, some villager might have led them to the same well."

"There's no way to be sure the pilot is underneath the rest of them."

"There's only one way to be sure he's not," Duncan answered.

"We've never encountered a situation like this," said the captain. "Never."

And yet Duncan had planted the possibility among them. Suddenly it seemed that week after week, they might have been digging farther away from what they were looking for. And now the dead from one era could be hiding the dead from another.

But they could not simply dredge up the bones to see what lay at the bottom. The Cambodian liaisons suddenly became officious and prickly. There were problems, it developed, diplomatic, jurisdictional, archaeological, and cultural. Molly loved it. With a single, giant twist, her story had not only been saved, but was taking on dimensions she'd never dreamed of.

Among other things, as a matter of policy, American bones were supposed to be separated from Southeast Asian Mongoloid remains at the site of excavation rather than at the central lab in Hawaii. The Department of Defense had learned the hard way how difficult it was to repatriate Asiatic remains. The Vietnamese government, especially, regarded any bones found in the proximity of American remains as those of *ling nguy,* or South Vietnamese puppet soldiers.

There were also issues of territorial authority. This might be a shared underworld, but it happened to lie within Cambodian soil. Who owned the dead? Should the Cambodian authorities be the ones to oversee the excavation of the well? Did that place American soldiers in the role of undertakers for Cambodian citizens? What if there was no American pilot beneath the layer of Khmer Rouge victims? Did the Cambodians even want the mass grave to be exhumed? The competing interests created a tension that made her story at once international, delicate, and highly emotional.

The captain ordered the area around the well ringed off. There was a process to be observed, channels to go through. Cambodian soldiers were posted around the camp to keep away the locals. The men on the labor crew were told to return to their villages. The captain, the forensic anthropologist, and their Cambodian counterparts all retired to a tent and began placing satellite calls to their headquarters. Instructed to stay away from the site, Molly and the others waited in whatever shade they could find. Hours went by.

The team members couldn't get over it. They treated Molly like a seer, as if she had a gift for this. "How did you know to look down there?" one asked.

"I didn't," she said.

"But you went right to it."

"Yeah, after four weeks, right to it."

As the day dragged on and they still sat idle, Kleat stewed. "What are they doing in there? We could be down clearing the hole."

"It's not that easy," Duncan said. "They're on to us by now."

"Who?" said Molly.

"The locals. These are the dead they inherited their earth from, literally, the original owners of the land they're farming. The villagers could demand to cover the bones over or burn them to ash. One way or another, they'll have to exorcise the spirits."

"Screw their boogeymen," Kleat said.

Molly began to worry. The captain emerged from the tent with a frown on his face, took a long breath, and returned inside. Plainly, he was getting nowhere fast. Once more she felt her story slipping away. They needed proof.

While the rest of the team nodded off in the heat or waved away flies, she got to her feet, ducked under the tape, and stood beside the well. It was darker than ever down there. Expecting nothing, she snapped another blind shot of the depths, then pulled up the image on her display.

"What you got this time, Molly?" someone called to her.

She looked up from her camera display. "You need to see this," she said.

They stirred and came out into the high sun and crowded around. The display was full of muddled bones . . . and something else. They all saw it. Mixed among the skulls was a flight helmet. "You've done it again," Duncan whispered.

At 1700 hours—Molly had acquired military time— an American helicopter landed on the road, bearing a colonel and two Cambodian government officials wearing sunglasses. Molly went out with the others to photograph them, and was surprised to see how many villagers had flocked to the area. The Cambodian soldiers were keeping them at a distance from the camp.

The colonel was not pleased. "Quite the circus," he shouted to the captain as the rotors wound down. Dust flew everywhere. He gestured at Molly. "Who's this?"

"She's the *Times* journalist I told you about," the captain said.

The colonel did not shake her hand or thank her. "You were shooting the bones," he said.

"I didn't know what was down there," Molly told him. His unfriendliness confused her. Hadn't she just provided them with proof?

The colonel looked away from her. He noticed Duncan and his long hair and Che shirt. "And him?"

Molly saw the captain's throat tighten. "A local archaeologist," he said.

"All right," the colonel declared, "let's get this thing under control." The captain led him and the officials to the mess tent. An hour later the colonel and the officials departed on the helicopter.

The captain announced that the excavation would resume in the morning. They had been granted a week—seven days—no more. After that the site would be returned to the kingdom of Cambodia. "We've got our work cut out for us," he said. "If he's down there, we'll find him."

There were high fives, and Duncan whistled through his fingers. The captain did not smile. He asked Molly and Duncan and Kleat to join him.

There was no Johnnie Walker Black this evening. The meeting was brief. He was grim. "Due to the sensitive nature of the mission," he informed them, "your presence is no longer expedient."

Molly's mouth fell open.

" 'Expedient,' " said Kleat. "What the hell does that mean?"

The captain's lips pressed thin. Clearly he had argued. Clearly he had lost. "I have been advised to compress the operation to essential personnel only. We're letting go of the work crew." He added, "And you."

"You can't do that to us," Kleat said. "I've paid my dues. Year after year—"

"Be ready to leave at 0700 tomorrow morning," the captain said.

Duncan appealed, not for himself, but for Molly. "Without her, you'd have nothing," he said.

The captain looked ill. He lowered his eyes. "That will be all," he said.

7.

"Like outcasts."

The words poured with smoke from Kleat's mouth.

Molly was sitting with him and Duncan at a window table overlooking the Mekong River. It was a brand-new restaurant to go with the brand-new Japanese bridge leading east. Sunset lit the water red. Fans spun overhead, politely, enough to eddy Kleat's cigar smoke but not rustle the pages of Duncan's *World Tribune*. The starched white tablecloth was immaculate.

None of it seemed real.

"We find their pilot for them," Kleat said, "and like that, *adios, pendejos.*"

"For the record, he's not found yet, only his helmet," said Duncan. "And one other thing, it was Molly who found him. Not us." He raised a toast to her.

Molly gamely lifted her glass. Kleat passed.

The ice-cold Heineken was like culture shock. She sat there. Her farmer tan torpedoed the dandelion-yellow sundress she had been saving for just such an evening. It jumped up at her, the sunburn and freckles to her upper arms, then the shoulders as white as moons. She looked half naked to herself. And her hair, like something chopped to Goth with surgical scissors, which was what she'd resorted to. She lifted her chin. Nothing to do about it tonight. Beauty, skin deep, all that.

The sun went on sinking. Only this morning, the sun had seemed like a peasant disease, breaking them down all day, leaving them sore and weary by night. Now, with a drink in hand and the fans cooling the air, she did her best to see the sunset as a thing of great beauty. She tried to savor her postexpedition daze, to relinquish the heat and dust and insects. She put off thoughts of whatever came next. The day was ending. The month. A full month she had spent grubbing after the dead.

Kleat started in on her. This last supper was his idea. Molly had actually hoped they could part friends. Dumb.

"You were told," he said. "Day one. Their first commandment. I heard the captain tell you. No shooting the dead. Anything but them. So what do you do?"

The scar at his throat turned purple. He never talked about the scar. He seemed to think it spoke for him. Most of the people on the dig thought it came from a sloppy thyroid surgery.

"We've been through this," Duncan said quietly. "The camera was just their excuse." He was still holding his *World Tribune,* five days out of date, devouring every word.

"We got pulled down with her," Kleat said.

Molly sighed. He couldn't help himself. She only wished he could have waited until after dessert. The waiters hadn't even arrived with her salad. The restaurant was known for its salad Niçoise. For a month, she had been waiting for it.

"A deal was struck," said Duncan. "They were given a week to recover the pilot. However they're getting through those bones, it's not for public consumption, American or Cambodian. They don't want outsiders to see it."

"Get this straight," Kleat said. "I'm not one of you."

"I don't mean this harshly, John," Duncan said, "but that's all you are. One of us."

The veins stood out on Kleat's burnished skull. He leaned in. "I belonged."

"I'll say it again," Molly said. "I thought the well was empty."

"You knew. Somehow you knew."

"She has a gift," Duncan said. "Leave it at that."

It was useless talking about it. The captain had been ordered to make a clean sweep. His three guests had been loaded into a Land Cruiser and sent away.

She looked from one man to the other, each freshly showered, their whiskers scraped off. The dig had thinned them. Their clean shirts hung on their shoulders like stolen laundry. They looked like sticks of hard driftwood among the last of the Europeans at the tables around them. The package tours had all but shut down. The monsoon season was almost here, and the typhoon was circling in the South China Sea.

"It was never your brother down there anyway," said Duncan. "We knew that from the start. You said he went missing along the border. That's a hundred miles to the east. And this was a crash site. We were looking for a pilot, not a soldier on foot."

"You don't get it." Kleat was plaintive. "They'll never have me back again."

The sunset trembled. Thunder, too low to hear, vibrated the window in the frame. The glass buzzed like locusts.

The typhoon qualified for a name, an Asian name for a change, Mekkhala, Thai for Angel of Thunder. It was only the coming monsoon's daily grumble, but everyone tied to it the angel's thunder. The restaurant owner had sheets of wood ready to protect his expensive windows. The glass vibrated again. It would come soon.

"I'm sorry," Molly said.

Kleat wasn't prepared for that. His eyes seemed to crouch. "Tell it to the captain."

"I mean about your brother," she said.

The stub of cigar flared.

"I hope you find him someday."

"Because you know how it feels?"

"Yes."

"Not your orphan story," he said. "Again."

This was a mistake. "Forget it," she said.

"No, really. Sharing losses while you gave them haircuts? You think that made you part of the team? We came to locate soldiers."

"I know."

"Molly," he said. "Your mother was just some hippie chick."

"Enough," Duncan muttered.

"Why?" said Kleat. "I'm curious. You make me wonder, both of you. We didn't come together by accident. We draw up the dead for a reason. It was a rough, dirty, hot toilet of a month. You suffered for this."

"We all suffered," said Duncan.

"But the thing is, you didn't have to. I need to be here. And the captain and his team, we have a duty to perform. Not you, though."

Duncan shrugged. "Just lending a hand."

"The boys have waited long enough."

"Something like that."

"You talk like it was your war."

"Wrong address, friend." Duncan flashed a peace sign.

"Tell me, sitting on your campus back then, were they all just fools to you?"

"Not a single one of them. I'm only saying that it wasn't my war. I wasn't here."

"And yet here you are," said Kleat.

"In the flesh."

"Of all places."

Duncan gestured at the glorious river. He took a deep lungful of the air, and Molly smelled it, too, the scent of bougainvillea as thick as hash smoke. "It grows on you," he said.

"I didn't mean the territory in general. I was talking about our little dig. Where you had no real business. Professionally speaking."

"Professionally speaking," Duncan agreed, "no business at all."

"Getting right with God? The old pacifist burying old warriors?"

"That must be it," said Duncan.

"And you?" Kleat said, turning to Molly. Duncan wouldn't fight him, maybe she would. "Do you mind me asking?"

How could she mind? She was an inquisitor herself. "Go ahead."

"Just to connect the dots, you know. We've got a soldier, my brother," he opened one hand, then the other, "and your mother. A suicide."

She blinked at his malice. "I never used that word."

Kleat considered his cigar, one of the captain's Havanas. "She parks her baby with a friend, leaves twelve bucks and a week's worth of cat food. Then takes a hit of LSD and wanders off into a blizzard. That is what you told us."

"Not like that, I didn't."

Not until it came time to fill out her college application forms had Molly learned that she was adopted. She had taken it hard. She'd actually made her parents—her stepparents—apologize. Then she'd run off to hunt for her birth mother. Over the coming years, she had changed to her mother's maiden name, and her sleuthing skills led to journalism. That was her point in telling the soldiers on the recovery team, to identify where she came from, not to infiltrate them with a sob story.

"So you found her, and it made you whole," Kleat said. He wanted blood.

"It took me three years to find a picture of her," Molly said. She had it now, in her passport wallet, a Texas driver's license issued in 1967. But no way was she going to share that with them, at least not with

Kleat. "It took another two years to find her grave." She did not describe the miner's cemetery in Breckenridge, altitude 9,600 feet, wildflowers everywhere.

"At least she got a grave."

Molly stared at him. From the start, he had treated her like treason waiting to happen. She'd thought it had to do with her occupation, but it was both more and less personal than that. He was one of those troubled souls in constant need of a scapegoat, and for some reason, she'd been filling the role for a month. Going along to get along, maybe. Not anymore. The story was stone cold. Let the bastard go find another punching bag.

Molly looked out the window. The river was on fire with red. Small boats ferried back and forth, the far shore going dark.

The cocktail hour was dying. Soon the waiters would bring their dinner. The evening could end.

A tiny desperation crept in. Tomorrow was almost here, and her future was in tatters. She'd banked everything on the *Times*. From this piece others would flow, then book deals, and film options. But the world was no longer her oyster.

Kleat was making a quick escape, back to his twelve-cent beers and five-dollar wives. He'd already booked a flight out of Phnom Penh, two hours to the south, for tomorrow afternoon.

Duncan had decided his restoration work in the north could wait until the rainy season passed. He was going to the big city. Though he must have resupplied in Phnom Penh countless times over the years, he acted like Marco Polo about to enter the marvels of Xanadu.

He couldn't wait to investigate its streets and markets and temples.

In short, one of them was going, one was staying, and Molly was torn. Nothing waited for her at home, no obligations, no cat, no boyfriend, and no deadline. It had been too early to plant her herb garden on her little deck before leaving, and it would be too late by the time she returned. There was a friend's wedding in July, a half marathon for breast cancer in August, her yoga classes at the Y, and an astronomy class up at the university. And bills to pay and work to scare up.

But she was here. Asia no longer intimidated her. After a month in the field, she was toughened and road ready, and Duncan had caught her eye. He was an islander, of sorts, solitary and curious and uncomplicated.

She was going to ask him to guide her through Angkor Wat. Not tonight, but once Kleat left, she meant to propose a short adventure before the storm. It was a whim, one that hadn't occurred to her before an hour ago. She suspected it might lead to other things between them, other cities, maybe another life, a bend in the road.

She wasn't quite sure how to handle their age gap. Kent State was ancient history, though Duncan didn't seem old enough for it by a decade. She had tried to imagine him thirty years ago. He would have had a little more meat on him, and fewer creases around the eyes. But he would have had the same sweet calm. A keeper. Thirty years ago.

She'd never tried a winter-summer relationship,

never even thought about it. On the other hand, he wasn't exactly winter and she wasn't exactly summer. She told herself it shouldn't matter. If things didn't work out, the typhoon was all the excuse she'd need to flee.

The glass trembled again.

8.

The restaurant grew quiet.

Kleat looked at his watch. "Six sharp," he said. "Send
in the clowns."

Molly turned as the entrance lit with the color of
tangerines. Three old monks filed in, led by a child. Bits
of the sunset seemed caught in their saffron robes.

She had heard of them. They were blind. The
owner let them in each evening.

All around, tourists hushed reverently, even the
Germans at the bar. Chairs creaked as people twisted to
see. A woman started to applaud, and stopped herself.
This was not like on the sidewalks where the amputees
and widows leaped out at you. The monks were well
washed and stately, a taste of Cambodia to go with your
umbrella drinks. The waiters backed against the wall
and bowed, theatrical with their white gloves pressed
together at their foreheads.

"*Tanto quiso el diablo a sus hijos que les sacó los ojos,*"
Duncan said.

"What?" said Molly.

"It's an old saying. 'The devil loved his children so much that he poked out their eyes.' "

"Only it was the KR, not the devil," said Kleat. "And they used spoons."

She was reminded of Brueghel's painting, the blind leading the blind, stumbling among the rabble. No rabble here, though. Nor stumbling. The young boy's head was shaved to the skin, a novitiate. They wove among the tables with serpent grace, gathering their alms, American dollars mostly. Molly saw one couple sign over a traveler's check. The man and woman pressed their palms together in an awkward *sampeah,* but of course the monks could not see them.

"The waiters will be taking a cut," Kleat observed.

As the monks approached, Molly saw old scars glistening at the center of their wrinkled foreheads. Their third eyes had been ritually mutilated. They held their heads high, each connected by a few fingertips to the shoulder ahead of him.

"What, no sins to pay for?" Duncan asked Kleat. He was opening his steel briefcase to get his wallet.

"At these prices, I'd say it's already built into the menu," Kleat said.

Molly stood to get a dollar bill from her pocket.

That was when she noticed the gypsy from their dig. He was standing in the doorway staring straight at them. She jerked with surprise.

"What's he doing here?" she said. The two men looked up at her. "There," she pointed.

Just then the line of monks passed in front of the doorway, blocking her view. When they had moved on to the next table, the opening stood empty.

"Never mind," she said.

He'd never come within two hundred yards of them, so why would he be here? His place was in the mirages, along the horizon, in the ball of the rising or setting sun.

She started to sit down, but he had moved, and was watching them.

"There," she said, startled all over again.

He had maneuvered across the room and was standing by a table with a French couple. He had gray peasant pants and a green and black camouflage T-shirt with ragged holes. He was barefoot. The French pair was not pleased by his presence.

They all saw him now. It was as if he'd stepped out of her camera.

"Incredible," said Kleat.

The baggy gray pants had once been black. The cuffs stood at his knees, shredded by dogs. His shins were crisscrossed with bite wounds.

Some of the soldiers back at the dig had thought he might be a freelance journalist down on his luck, way down. Or, as Kleat had suggested, a heroin addict lost in inner space. Duncan wondered if he might be the son of an MIA, shipwrecked by a lifetime of hope. There was even the possibility that he could be an actual, living MIA, though no one on the dig really believed that. It was a powerful piece of MIA mythology, the POW who was still out there, or the defector who'd decided to stay into infinity. One such man, a marine named Garwood, had in fact surfaced in Vietnam years after the war. Ever since, Molly learned, the Garwood factor had become red meat for the MIA movement. They fed on it endlessly. The official military forensics teams viewed themselves as an antidote to such wishful thinking. Their only prey was the bones, though they tipped their hat to the MIA movement.

The stranger didn't nod at them. He was gaunt. A hundred twenty pounds, Molly guessed, no more. Duncan had said he must eat weeds and insects, like John the Baptist. "He must have followed us from the dig," she said.

"Impossible," said Kleat. "It took us five hours by car to get down here. We would have seen him behind us."

"One way or another, here he is."

"He's stalking us," Kleat said.

It did feel like that. But which of them was he after?

The man began walking toward them. The boy. He was much younger than she'd thought. His blond hair was almost white from the undiluted sun. He had a cowlick and reminded her of Dennis the Menace, on smack. All he lacked was a slingshot in his back pocket.

Kleat placed one hand on the table. Molly looked twice. His hand was covering his dinner knife.

"Relax," said Duncan. "He probably just wants some of our peanuts and beer."

The fans loosened the countryside from creases in his clothing and his hair. The sunset lit the fine dust into a fiery nimbus. The French couple covered their food.

Molly expected bad smells, the reek of old urine and feces and sweat, but he only smelled like dust. He came to a halt behind the fourth chair at their table, with the window—and the sunset—behind him. It was hard to see his eyes. A thin corona of red dust wafted from his shoulders.

"What are you doing here?" Kleat demanded.

"I see you out there," the man said. "Going through the motions. Wasting away."

"Is that so?"

"Like starved hogs. All that dust for nothing, Jesus."

For all his raw bearing, he had a voice like the breeze. Molly had to strain for it. He was American, no faking the West Texas accent. Twenty years old probably, going on a thousand, one of those kids. He'd seen it all.

"It don't work," he said. "You can't hide."

"It worked. It took a while. But we found our man," Duncan said. "Molly did."

"Who?"

"The young lady," said Duncan.

The stranger didn't waste a glance at her. "What man?" he said.

Kleat lifted his chin. It showed his scar like a second smile. "A pilot. He's found. It's done."

The stranger stretched his fist to the middle of the table and opened his fingers. Molly looked for track marks on his forearm, but there were none. Then she remembered that the poppy was so cheap here, people just toked it. A clot of hard black dirt, as hard as cement, fell from his hand onto the tablecloth.

"Quit pretending," the man said.

The thing looked worthless, an animal turd, nothing. A chain protruded from one end.

Kleat lifted the chain with his dinner knife. "Jewelry?"

"You could say that."

It was a fistful of mud grabbed from the earth and dried in the sun. Molly saw his finger imprints. Then she saw an edge of flat metal at one corner. With that and the chain she could guess what it was. She took it from Kleat and scratched at the crust with her fingernail, but it was baked on hard.

"Here," said Duncan. Without ceremony, he sank it in his water glass. He stirred with his spoon and the water clouded dark gray, then black.

While the clot dissolved, Molly spoke. "We left food for you. You never ate it."

The man didn't say a word to her. He just stood waiting, infinitely tolerant. Flying on junk, she thought. But his eyes were too bright, too present in the shadow face.

"We know what it is," said Kleat, "if it's even real."

"Real as you or me," the man answered. "Real as anything."

"Three possibilities then." Kleat issued a thick stream of smoke. "You bought it. It's your own. Or you looted it. Is that what you did?"

Duncan scooped out what was left of the clot and crumbled it over his dish. What emerged was a small, flat metal plate, a dog tag, just as she'd suspected. Her heartbeat quickened.

If this really had been stolen from the well, then it was a possible proof of identity, perhaps their only one. She'd learned that the forensic labs wanted teeth, preferably an entire mandible, to match to dental charts. In addition, DNA testing could work, though only if a maternal relative had stepped forward over the past thirty years to offer blood. Without the benefit of primary, organic identifiers, the agencies had to rely on circumstantial evidence: a wedding band, a class ring, an engraved pocketknife. Or a dog tag.

"It's a message," the gypsy said. Deep gone, that face. *Lost in the arms of Asia,* thought Molly.

"Excellent," said Kleat. "What's it say?"

"Quit your pissing around."

Kleat, the searcher, flushed. "That's the message?"

"I'm still waiting," the boy spoke.

"What it says," said Duncan, washing the tag in his water and wiping the embossed letters, "is Samuels, Jefferson S. There's a birth date. His blood type. Protestant. And a serial number."

Molly knew everything about the pilot RE-1 had been searching for, from the date of his shoot down to the root canal in his left molar. And his name had not been Jefferson Samuels.

"Nothing," Kleat said to the man. "You have nothing."

The man dropped two more clots on the white tablecloth, two more tags.

Duncan cracked them open like eggs, black dirt all over the white tablecloth. He read the second tag, and the third. "Sanchez, Thomas A. Bellwether, Edward P."

"Who the hell are you?" Kleat demanded.

Molly tried, more gently. She pointed at his arm, at the tattoo like a ghost beneath the dust. "Is that your name? Lucas Yale?"

"Luke," he said.

Molly looked at Duncan and Kleat, and the name meant nothing to them. It defeated her, the uselessness of the name. She had nothing more to ask.

"Where did you find these?" Kleat said.

Luke looked at Molly for the first time. "I come to show you. Let's go."

"Just tell us," said Kleat.

"It's not so easy," the boy said. The red sky bulged behind him, a great final burst of coloration. Night was falling.

"You're playing a dangerous game," Kleat said, "kidnapping the dead."

In fact, the practice was as common as despair in this fertile green country. Peasants trafficked in human bones all the time, trying to prize money from the Americans even when the bones weren't American.

"How much do you want?" said Molly.

The stranger smiled at her suddenly, and he was missing significant teeth on the right side, upper and lower. What teeth still remained lay green in there. Duncan was right, the boy must have been eating grass and weeds, rifling the land. But then Molly saw that it was moss, actual moss, growing between his teeth, like something out of a movie. The tropics had taken root in this young ancient. It showed in the leather of his face. It peeked from his mouth.

"No charge," he said, "not for you-all."

"Show us on a map," said Duncan. He took a map from his briefcase. He suspected the stranger even more than Kleat did, and that put Molly on alert. His instincts were telling him something.

"Never mind that," Luke said. "It's off the map."

"Come on, this is the twenty-first century. There's no such thing as off the map. They have satellites."

"Well, if it was on a map, they wouldn't have ended where they are," said Luke.

"How far away is this place?" Molly asked, trying to cut through the mystery. The key was to get your source talking.

"It's a ride. We need to leave."

"A ride. Does that mean an hour? A day? Two days?"

"One night's ride. Tonight."

It sank in.

"You're joking," Kleat said. "Leave tonight? We've been on the road all day. I have a flight to reschedule. We need to rest. Prepare."

"There's six more," Luke told them.

That shut Kleat up.

"Six more dog tags?" Molly was incredulous.

"Bones, weapons, whatever it is you need." Molly could see his tongue in the gap of missing teeth. "It's all there. All yours."

They were quiet for a minute. Nine soldiers? Molly felt something like rapture. She was saved. Here was her *Times* story, minus the scolds at the Pentagon.

"And all we have to do is follow you?" said Duncan.

"I can't make you do a thing."

"They don't belong to you," Kleat said. "These tags, the bones, the relics, whatever you found."

"What more do you want? I'm saying come on. They're all yours."

"Sit down," Molly said. He could walk out as easily as he had walked in, and then where would they be? "Eat with us. We've ordered our supper. We can talk things through."

Luke stayed on his feet.

"There are proper channels for this kind of thing," Duncan said. Molly could hear his turmoil. The boy confused him. Molly had never seen this side of him. Things were moving too fast for him. "You could have told the captain at camp. You could go to the embassy. Why here? Why tonight? Why us?"

Luke said, "Because you want it so bad."

It was true. He had them cold. Week after week, he'd been watching them. He couldn't know their individual appetites, but he'd seen their hunger.

The possibility grew on her. An American drifter circling through his own tropical dream world, stumbling upon relics from the war, why not? And it was perfectly conceivable that a drug addict, or schizophrenic, whatever he was, would trust three civilians over the captain and his soldiers. Uniformed or not, the military would represent an authority that might take him away. An authority that had rejected her and Duncan and Kleat.

Luke pointed at the new bridge. "I'll wait on the far side there. You have two hours."

"Two hours?" Kleat snapped.

Molly spoke to Luke. "It's just so unexpected. There may be a serious storm coming. We can't afford to be stranded in some godforsaken place. Is there a village nearby? How many days will we be gone?"

He was backing away from the table.

"You've waited this long, and there's so much to be done," she said. Slow him down. Keep him here. But he was leaving. "We have to arrange transportation, find food, get our gear."

"I told you," Luke said, "I can't force a thing. You have to make up your own minds." Then he turned and walked off. The doorway swallowed him.

Duncan was the first to speak after the boy left.

"The poor kid belongs in an asylum," he said. "Or in Cambodia."

"You don't think it's real then?" said Molly. *But we can make it real.* The story held that kind of childlike potential. You just had to believe in it.

"We'll know soon enough," Kleat said. He stabbed his glasses tighter against the bridge of his nose and produced a small dog-eared notebook. It was his bible, an index of all the American soldiers who had never returned from Cambodia, including his brother. He had copied it from Brite Lite, the team's database of the missing. He leaned over the first dog tag and thumbed through the pages.

Just then the waiters arrived with dinner. Seeing the dirt and mud, they wanted to change the tablecloth and bring clean napkins and silverware. Duncan instructed them to set the various plates wherever there was room. Determined to have their ceremony, the waiters lifted the lids from the dishes with a flourish. Molly's Australian lobster steamed. Kleat's steak ran bloody, the way he'd ordered it. A hamburger sat in a croissant—a makeshift bun—for Duncan. No salads.

Kleat grunted at his index and picked up the second tag.

"Even if he was telling the truth," said Duncan, "he's withholding information. And if he isn't telling the truth, we'd be fools to rush off into the night with him. They have gangs out there. He could be part of them. This is a desolate country."

"You think he might be bait?" said Molly.

"I don't know. There's something about him. He's too much in love with his own mystery."

"How's that make him different from any of us?" said Kleat. "We're creatures of our fictions, every one of us."

His mood had shifted. He was suddenly in high spirits. And Molly noticed that he was speaking once again in the plural, "us," not "me." It was no accident. He was, she realized, team building. He needed them. Not an hour before, he'd been ready to damn them for spoiling his place with the captain. Now he was trying to recruit them.

"I've had enough make-believe in my life," Molly said. "I agree with Duncan. The boy is up to something. But what if he's also telling the truth?"

"It would be a coup," said Kleat. "The search-and-recovery agencies average twenty finds per year, at a cost of close to a hundred million dollars. Per year. Here's our chance to take home nine sets of remains, paid for with the spare change in our pockets. Imagine that, three civilians, on their own."

His excitement verged on lust, and Molly felt it, too. For Kleat it would mean sweet revenge for his eviction from the dig. It wasn't in her nature to live for payback. The story was its own reward. This could translate into a book deal, maybe even Hollywood.

She started constructing it in her mind, a brief history of the misbegotten war and then the tale of discovering nine of its lost children. She would keep herself out of the story, but at the same time make it deeply personal. Once she had names for the whole bunch of them, she would dive into the soldiers' pasts and weave the story of their nexus in the jungle.

The sunset died. Its vast light winked out. Kleat finished by candlelight, grinning, knowing.

"What?" said Molly.

"Private First Class Edward Bellwether," he read to them. "Master Sergeant Jefferson Samuels. Private First Class Thomas Anthony Sanchez. They're real, or were. All three of them are listed as unaccounted for. And get this. They were part of the same platoon, an armored cavalry unit with the Blackhorse Regiment. All three were last seen embarking on a reconnaissance along the Ho Chi Minh Trail inside Cambodia on June 23, 1970." He paused. "I'd say we have ourselves a mission."

Molly drew in a breath, all the aromas mingling, firing her hunger. She looked out the window, but darkness had turned it into a mirror and she saw only herself. Her world felt reversed. On the verge of leaving, they were returning. Instead of being driven out, they could go back in, deeper, to greater reward, all on their own terms.

"What about the other six men?" asked Duncan. "What does it say about them?"

"There's no way to cross-reference names and events. We could try calling the Department of Defense; it's seven in the morning in Washington. But that might only tip off the captain, and we already know what he thinks of us. No, we have to go with what we have."

"I still don't like it," Duncan said.

"We're talking about just a few days more."

"You don't know that. And if the typhoon makes landfall . . ."

Kleat bent to his steak. "We can do this thing."

"In the middle of the night, though," Duncan pondered. "What's his game?"

"The kid's full of demons. A psycho. So what. He's found something."

"He wants a sense of control," said Molly. "I say let him have it. Let him run the show his way. Soon enough we'll have what we want."

"And then he can go back to prowling around the moon," said Kleat.

"I was going to say, then maybe we can take him home, where he belongs."

Kleat's jaw muscles bunched. He was ravenous. "That's your business."

"Your mind is made up then," Duncan said to Molly. It was a question.

She looked at him. "I want this," she said.

He looked at the window turned to mirror. "Then I'll go, too," he said.

9.

The idea of the journey hijacked them. This was a quest of their own making. It had the effect of making the last month with RE-1 nothing more than preparation for a much larger voyage.

Mindful of Luke's petulant deadline, driven by it, they nevertheless forced themselves to stay at the table for fifteen precious minutes. They devoured their meal with the haste of thieves stealing someone else's dinner, knifing the meat to pieces, tearing open the lobster, going for protein. Between bites, they made lists, compiled a budget, created a treasury of $458 American, and assigned each other tasks. Then they cast off through the town.

It was simple, really. Having just come off one expedition, they knew exactly what was needed for their next. Also, they didn't require so very much. They agreed that the search would last no more than one week, round-trip. The remains were either real or they were not. A quick look, a quick retrieval, then they would race back to the city. At the first raindrop, whether it fell from the monsoon winds or was driven by the typhoon Mekkhala, they would all obey reason.

Kleat was sent back to their hotel to collect their clothes and other possessions, while Duncan took a taxi with Molly to try and find old Samnang.

Kampong Cham was not a large city. A few inquiries led them to Samnang, getting ready for bed in his cement-floored apartment. He graciously invited them in. His plastic leg was propped to one side. Incense was inking up from a little shrine in the corner.

Like Duncan, Samnang questioned the midnight ride. But like Duncan, when he saw Molly's resolve, he agreed to join them. They were doing this, she understood, to protect her.

With Samnang's involvement, the expedition metamorphosed from an idea into reality. He immediately knew where to obtain everything they required. He gravely fitted on his leg, then locked his door, leaving the incense to burn itself out.

By taxi they drove along the river to a small, walled compound, the home of the three Heng brothers. Molly knew them, or at least their faces, from the dig. One had driven her, Duncan, and Kleat from the dig that very morning, which gave a promising symmetry to tonight's venture. It was almost as if she were being delivered to her proper destination.

The brothers owned a white Land Cruiser from the UN days, along with an antique Mercedes truck dating back to the French colonial period. Once the expedition was presented to them, they pounced at the chance for more work. Driving into the night didn't bother them at all.

It now unfolded that the Heng brothers owed their relative wealth to the black market. Molly marveled at their hoard of military rations, fuel, tents, medicines, weapons, and digging tools stolen from various UN armies, USAID, the Red Cross, and, she recognized, the RE-1 dig. There were enough provisions here for five expeditions.

With Samnang's help, Duncan bargained the brothers down to what he called their "all-inclusive rate." With fuel, the week of driving, supplies, and "equipment rental," their fee came to four hundred and twenty dollars. Shouting back and forth, the brothers dashed around the courtyard with boxes and bags and jerry cans of fuel, loading the truck and wiping the dust from the seats for their passengers.

It was not quite eight-thirty as their little convoy crossed the bridge leading north.

Luke was waiting for them where he'd said, sitting on his haunches at the far side of the bridge in a globe of yellowing electric light. The bats were rampant here. Molly had seen them before, hanging from the highest branches like leathery fruit, but now they dove from the shadows, cutting swaths through the clouds of huge moths drawn to the lamp.

As they approached, he stood in their headlights and Molly noticed the dogs. There were twenty or thirty of them, skeletal orange and tan things, circling Luke, keeping their distance. Until Cambodia, she had never given two thoughts to the expression "dog eat dog." Hungry enough, they really did. She had pictures of puppies being carried away in the jaws of mongrels, of a dog gnawing at a dog skull. Her shock had amused Kleat.

He stood without a wave or a greeting, holding not one thing in his hands, not even a cigarette. Under the road dirt, his skin gleamed in the headlights. The dog bites and thorn cuts on his shins had the plastic gloss of old scars.

For a moment, a terrible moment, Molly saw her mother in him, crazy as hell, ricocheting from the kindness and torment of strangers, lost to the world, surrounded by dogs. A chill shot through her. For all the smothering wet heat, goose bumps flared along her arms and legs.

The sight of him made Molly fear for herself as she had been long ago, for the half-forgotten infant in her mother's arms. How many animals had circled them, too, waiting for a meal? How many lamplights had her mother sheltered beneath? The miracle of that baby's survival flooded Molly, not with awe, but with terror.

Had flies billowed around the smell of breast milk on her mother's blouse? Had truckers ejected the roadside Madonna and child when they caught a whiff of unchanged diapers? Molly had floated through a gauntlet of loathing and dangers that she could never precisely know. But the sight of this stranger, this walking suicide, threw her into a panic.

Molly's hands went to her stomach, her womb, as it were, and felt the passport wallet hidden under her sundress. Inside it were her passport and money and one other thing, perhaps her most valuable possession, the driver's license issued in 1967 to a teenage girl named Jane Drake. The image came to her, Molly's same black hair, Molly's same green eyes. Molly had three inches on her, and outweighed her by ten pounds, but they were still the same woman. She closed her eyes and drew up the sweet optimism on that face, and it was nothing like the harrowed madman in their headlights. Her alarm subsided.

She snapped a picture of Luke through the cracked windshield, mostly to return to herself. The big Mercedes pulled alongside. Kleat looked down from the cab. "What are we waiting for?" he said.

Molly was sitting in the front seat of the Land Cruiser. Luke took the backseat, next to Duncan. He was thin as a willow wand, but when he climbed in, the vehicle sagged under his weight. She thought the shocks must be worn out.

"Please fasten your seat belts and place your trays in an upright position," Molly said to him. She was excited. A great discovery was about to unfold. Then she glanced back, and Luke's face was joyless.

10.

Highway 7 lunged at them. No neat white lines. No mile markers. No speed limit. No warning signs. Speed was their only safe conduct, or so she gathered from the way their driver drove. They didn't slow even when they passed through darkened villages or swerved for potholes Molly could not see.

She had never ridden at night in Cambodia, and so help her God never would again. To conserve their headlights, everyone drove with their lights off. Trucks, cars, buses, all hurtled at them from the darkness. Only at the very last instant would their lights spring on, then off, blowing her night vision, leaving her—and presumably their driver—more sightless than before.

The boy hunched in the darkness, like a reptile, his chest to the steering wheel, his forehead pressed to the glass. He was the youngest of the brothers, maybe nineteen or twenty, with wrists little thicker than the plastic steering wheel. Born and raised in refugee camps, they had come up through misery she could only imagine.

He was wearing a blue-checkered *kroma,* and his arms and neck were crosshatched with tattoos. He kept humming Smashing Pumpkins tunes learned from the RE-1 soldiers.

She wished Duncan would tell some of his jokes and stories, but he was mostly silent beside the stone lump of their guide. The boys weren't having fun. It was a road trip, not a funeral. She tried to prime the pump. She handed out little Jolly Rancher cinnamon candies from her bag, offering one to the driver.

"His name is Vin," said Duncan.

"Vin," she said. The boy smiled.

"Heng Putheathvin," Duncan amplified. "Among Khmers, the surname goes first, though it varies from child to child depending on the parents' whim. It can get confusing. They might use the mother's surname for one child, and the father's for another. It's like a gift they decide upon at birth. Sometimes the father will give his surname to a favorite child. Sometimes he gives it to a bad luck child just in order to protect him. Or her."

"A bad luck child?"

"It's a curious custom, a kind of fetal scapegoat. While the baby is still in the womb, he or she bears responsibility for any bad luck that lands on the family. Say a mother goes into labor and sends her son for the midwife, and along the way a dog bites the boy. The infant is held responsible. From then on, you're marked. Everyone around knows you brought bad luck from the womb. But the father can help deflect it by giving you his family name."

"That's so unfair," said Molly. "To blame an unborn child."

"It's that destiny thing," Duncan said. He spoke to Vin in Khmer. The boy responded shyly. Duncan laughed. "I asked him, and Heng is their father's name. He said he and his brothers are all bad luck children."

"Ask him about his tattoos."

Duncan and Vin went back and forth. Vin seemed quite proud.

"They're called *sak*," said Duncan. "It's warrior magic. The tattoos protect him from knives and bullets. He has them on his arms, legs, and chest, even a little one in the part of his hair. He got them because his brothers have them. His oldest brother has the most elaborate ones. That's because he was actually a soldier with the government. His brother has killed men. Rebels. Vin wants to get a tiger done on his legs, the tail down one leg, the head down the other. That way he'll be safe from the land mines."

"Jesus, man." It was Luke, staring at Duncan in dismay. "You talk like a believer."

"We're not in Kansas anymore," Duncan said to him.

"And what's this?" Molly asked, pointing at the most unusual marking. She'd seen it earlier. Duncan shined his light on Vin's neck. At the upper tip of a series of welts lay a reddish image of George Washington.

"That," said Duncan, "is an American quarter. In reverse."

"He had a quarter tattooed on his neck?"

"Not tattooed. It's folk medicine. *Koh khchal*, 'coining,' in English. It's not so different from medical philosophy in medieval Europe, the idea of ridding yourself of bad humors. A healer, or it can be a parent or a friend, dips a coin in kerosene to get a good grip, then they rub like hell, usually on your back or chest or arms."

Duncan asked Vin a question. "He has a headache. One of his brothers gave him a good, hard session. The coin can get pretty hot. His brother pressed it on his neck, like a signature. George Washington was here."

"Tell him I have a tattoo," Molly said, "a butterfly."

Duncan told Vin. "He said he'd like to see it someday."

"Oh, it's in kind of a private place."

"In that case, I'd like to see it someday."

Molly's eyes flicked up at the mirror, but she could see only Luke's dark face. Duncan laughed and told the boy. Vin tucked his head, mortified.

"You didn't have to embarrass him," said Molly.

"He'll survive."

"Listen to you." It was Luke, his voice hard.

"Yeah?" asked Duncan.

"You're losing yourself."

"No harm in connecting with the culture. It is their country."

"Maybe," Luke said, "you should stick with your own kind."

"And why is that?" said Duncan.

"It's all tricks, you know," Luke said. "You're only fooling yourself."

Duncan's smile faded.

Molly turned to Luke. Talk about bad luck children.

"What about you?" she tried. "Where do you come from?"

It was like talking into an empty pipe. He said nothing more. The Jolly Rancher candy sat in his hand. After that the talk died. The miles went by.

A small light flipped on and off as Duncan periodically marked their position on a map spread across his legs. She guessed they must have covered two hundred miles, though it was impossible to know with the gauges broken or unhooked and the dash light dead.

For years the American embassy had been warning against travel into the distant provinces, especially at night. Rogue soldiers and war cripples were epidemic, with a nasty habit of highway robbery. The wars were over, she told herself. Those days were done. But she knew they were not really. Violence lay just beneath the skin here. Rebels still came together for various causes, and the countryside held more land mines per square mile than even Afghanistan or Bosnia.

But mile after mile there were no roadblocks, no highwaymen, and Molly tried to relax. Apparently the bandits had exploited the road too efficiently. It seemed they'd driven themselves right out of business.

During one stop to put more oil in the smoking truck, Kleat came up to them.

Molly made some remark about the wild night driving.

"You're afraid? Good," said Kleat. "Fear is a gift. It purifies us. Listen to it and you can see right through the night." He was exultant. "And how's our guide? How are you doing, Slick?" he said to Luke.

Luke looked at him. "Johnny Hollywood," he said, like he knew him.

It startled Kleat. He flinched, almost as if it meant something. He spit on the road. "Do we have some problem?"

"Are you really sure you want to be here?" Luke asked him.

Kleat glanced suspiciously at Molly and Duncan to see if they'd been talking among themselves. Molly shook her head at him and frowned. She didn't know what this was about.

"I'm helping pay for your ride, aren't I?" Kleat said to Luke.

"That don't make it your party. Slick."

"How's that?" Kleat said.

But Luke only trained his eyes back on the road. He had nothing more to add. Molly couldn't make sense of it. Neither one of them played well with others. But hell if she was going to be the mommy. Let them sort it out.

Kleat let loose his grip on. He returned to the truck and climbed up into the cab. The convoy started off again, back into the flash of metal giants roaring by in the night.

The moon broke from the clouds, and the paddies bracketing the road jumped to life. The highway became a dark strip sandwiched between hundreds of reflected moons. The land turned dreamlike, a world of harbored water arranged in honeycombs. The clouds sailed over, returning them to darkness.

Molly checked her watch. Barely eleven. A long night of the soul still ahead. Thankfully, whether because of the deepening night or their growing remoteness, the traffic grew sparse. They passed more villages, more paddy fields with their thousand moons.

"Mamot," Duncan noted. The map rustled. A little later, he said, "Snuol, is that where we're going?"

Molly could see Luke in the rearview mirror, his face yellow in the penlight. He tapped his dusty head. "I haven't forgot. It's all up here."

"Up there," said Duncan. "Is that like a state of mind or something?"

Molly listened. It wasn't like Duncan to taunt.

"What's to worry?" said Luke.

"It's just that you seem to be making it up as we go along."

"And you're not?"

Molly wanted Duncan to leave it alone. If the night was a bust, it was their own fault. Luke wasn't duping them. They were duping themselves. He had whispered to their expectations, and they had run with it. The man wasn't about to give up his secret, and that was that. Their destination, real or not, was the only currency he had. She wished Duncan would quit worrying with the maps and turn off his light. It glared on the windshield and made the road that much harder to read.

"Run it past me again," Duncan said, "how you found this place."

"It seemed like the place to go," said Luke.

Duncan persisted. "You were just out knocking around? Slumming in the provinces?"

"Like that."

"Except you don't have the look of a tourist. More like a runaway."

That had been another conjecture among RE-1, that the gypsy had escaped from some Asian jail. It would explain why he stayed at a distance, but always stayed. According to the theory, he was scared and homesick and needed their proximity. He didn't sound scared or homesick tonight.

"There's things you can't run from," Luke said. "You're here, aren't you?"

"Not really. You can thank Mr. Kleat for our presence. He's the one so hungry for it." Duncan didn't mention Molly, even though she was his real reason for coming along.

"The big appetite." Luke seemed amused. "What's he think is up there?"

Up where? Along the road or higher? Molly was listening intently.

For a month, Kleat had been slandering Duncan behind his back, calling him a liar, a sad sack, a fraud, laboring to get him tossed from the dig. Duncan wasn't stupid. Molly knew he knew. Now was his chance to strike back.

Instead, Duncan said only, "Redemption."

It was gracefully said, and Molly was glad for it. Somewhere in the complicated knot that was John Kleat was a human thread. It would take a good heart to see it so cleanly, and Duncan was saying he'd seen it. She was glad, not because she cared about Kleat, but because Duncan was a rock. Maybe she could trust him.

"Redemption?" said Luke.

"He's been looking for his brother for years."

A noise came from the backseat, startling Molly. It sounded like an animal—a monkey, a jackal, something with sharp teeth—a single, feral bark. A hoot. Vin jerked his head to see in the mirror.

It was a laugh, but not like anything Molly had ever heard. "He says that?" said Luke. "He says his brother?"

"I'm missing the joke," said Molly.

"What brother?" said Luke.

"He went missing in the war. It's unfinished business."

"You sure you want to be sticking up for him?"

"I'm just telling you."

"He wants back in," Luke told her. "That's how come he tracked you down. He thinks he found a ride. He thinks he's going home."

Molly had no idea what he was talking about. "He didn't track me down. He was there at the dig when I arrived."

"Waiting for you," Luke said. "We knew you were coming."

We?

"Sometimes there's no second chances," Luke said. "He wants to belong so bad. He won't ever belong."

"Belong to what?" Duncan said. "Who's this 'we' you're talking about?"

"The boys," Luke interrupted. Molly frowned. That was Duncan's term. Had the man sneaked up one night and overheard them? It wasn't impossible.

"Whatever," said Duncan. "I take it you belong."

"Same as you."

"And me?" said Molly. He was like Job, this raving prophet, but without a god to blame for his misery and ugliness. She wanted to hear what he would say.

He looked at her. "Who else do you think we come for?"

A huge dark shape—a truck—thundered past, lights out. The Land Cruiser rocked in its wake. Her thoughts scattered. It was a relief, she decided, to quit the conversation.

11.

They came to a town, or what was left of it. The moon made a brief appearance, and the destruction leaped out at Molly, the dirt as red as Mars. Here and there lone walls stood scored by thousands of bullet holes, the rest of the houses chopped away. Otherwise the place was a shantytown floating on stilts between the rubble.

"Snuol," Duncan read from his map.

"What happened here?" Molly asked.

"I'd say the United States Army paid a visit," Duncan said. He had taken the red and white *kroma* from around his neck and draped it over his head, like blinders almost.

"Birth is death, brother," Luke said. "Somebody has to feed the machine. This was their turn."

The destruction fascinated Molly. The war had erected an architecture so grotesque, it verged on beauty. And the people let it stand, that was the strangest thing. They chose to live among the ruins.

"We're getting there now," said Luke.

"North to Kratie," Duncan guessed. "From there, it's not so far to Sambor."

"You know the country?" Luke was amused.

"I came this way years ago," Duncan said. "I was retracing the footsteps of the great Dutch explorer Van Wusthoff. He was making his way to Vientiane. This was back in 1642. He was the first Westerner to set eyes on the supposed ruins of Sambupura, the capital of a pre-Angkor civilization in the sixth century. Sambor, it's called now. The locals stripped it clean centuries ago. They took away the building stones to make dikes. There are a few foundation stones left in the ground. Some scholars doubt the Sambor stones mark the real Sambupura. They think the stones are just traces of a satellite city, that the capital must have been somewhere else. Skeptics say Sambupura never existed, it's just the local version of Shangri-la."

"More tricks," Luke said. "You and your folklore and history."

Duncan was quiet for a moment. "It's what I do. Temple restorations. My specialty is the pre-Angkor period."

"Let's say that's so," said Luke. "What's that change?"

Duncan looked stricken. His little light hovered above the map. Molly didn't know why he let the crazy gypsy get to him.

The road forked ahead. "Tell the boy to go right here," Luke said.

They exited Highway 7 onto a side road that actually improved. The ripped asphalt of Snuol smoothed into compacted dirt. Duncan's map rustled. "East to Mondulkiri," he said. "This is an old logging road. The Ho Chi Minh Trail branched all through these parts."

"History," Luke said.

Night spilled over the windshield. Molly felt vaguely seasick. Since leaving the dig site at seven that morning, she had been on one road or another for over sixteen hours. She was tired. Her head ached. She was thirsty from the lobster, and her mouth tasted sour. She prayed Kleat had grabbed her toiletries kit when he'd gone to the hotel. She was going to want a toothbrush, a T-shirt, and a tent, in that order.

The moon came and went. Molly found herself nodding off in short bursts.

A hand slapped the top of her seat. Molly started.

"It's coming," Luke said. "Tell him."

"We're there?" She peered out the window. "How can you see anything?"

"Are you going to tell him or not?" Luke reached over the front seat and stabbed at Vin's ribs. It hurt, Molly could tell. Vin bared his gold teeth and stepped on the brakes. A swirl of dust enveloped them.

"Did I say stop?" said Luke. "Go off up there."

"Sit back," Duncan said to him.

Luke's arm withdrew. The backseat creaked under his weight. Vin gripped the steering wheel, angry at being prodded. At last he flipped on his one good headlight.

There was only the red dirt of the highway and high, green grasses. The grass enclosed them. Slowly Molly made out a dark mass in the distance, the sloping hip of a mountain, or an upward march of trees. In either case, nothing but wilderness.

"We keep going," said Luke.

"Going where?" said Duncan.

The truck arrived behind them in the moonlight. It approached with the immensity of a shipwreck, its tattered canopy flailing like a torn sail. Bald car tires wired to the prow served as a bumper.

Vin went on sucking his golden front teeth, making up his own mind.

A fingernail tapped at her window. Molly cranked the handle, and her reflection became Kleat. "Lost?" he said.

Samnang's round face appeared behind Kleat, a creased brown melon with white hair.

"There's a road," said Luke. "It goes through the grass."

"An invisible road," scoffed Duncan.

"What are you saying?" Kleat asked.

"Turn around now," said Duncan, "we can be back in Phnom Penh for breakfast."

"Turn around?" said Molly.

"Look for yourself, there's nothing out there." He wiped his hand across the map.

Luke didn't argue. He had switched off, tuned out. It was their decision.

Kleat fumed. "If it was in plain sight, they would have been found already. Sometimes you have to dig a little further, that's all."

Molly didn't see Samnang slide away. He simply appeared in the light beam, moving up the road, hitching his false leg ahead. One by one they all quit talking.

His shadow reached in front of him, long black lines

like puppet strings tied to each limb. He followed the edge of the highway, peering into the overgrown ditch. Fifty yards ahead he stopped and began parting the grasses.

Everyone got out and went up the road, all except Luke. He sat in the car, knowing whatever he knew.

Samnang was working deeper into the tall grasses, feeling along with his one good foot. "A track for oxcarts," he announced to them. "It hasn't been used for many years."

The three brothers descended from the highway and joined Samnang, chattering away, eager to continue. They wanted a week of wages, not taxi fare for a night ride. They churned through the grass, trampling it flat and tying bunches at their tops as landmarks.

Abruptly the night detonated around them. A clamor filled the air. It sizzled and crackled like wild voltage, loud, almost tangible.

The suddenness and volume startled Molly. She whirled around, searching for a source, but the noise pressed in from every direction. Cicadas, she realized, thousands of them.

She'd never heard such a massed voice of insects. She registered it as anger, but that was only because it was so alien to her. She stepped back from the grass.

That suddenly the noise stopped.

The silence had a slight sucking vacuum to it. Molly felt pulled by it. "What was that?" she said.

The men had frozen. They were staring at the grass on all sides of them.

Then Kleat waved at the night. "Bugs. Nothing."

The clouds opened to the moon, and the distant

mountain revealed itself as a pile of low hills crowned with dense forest.

"Okay?" Kleat said. "It's there. The man said it was there. There it is."

Molly gazed up at the mountain.

"An oxcart path," Duncan said, dismissing it. "A mountain."

Kleat was having none of it. He grabbed a handful of grass and gave a fierce yank. It was a foolish gesture. The roots were deep and this was saw grass, with firm, sharp blades. His fist slid up and came away empty. Kleat snapped his teeth in pain and opened his cut palm. When he shook his hand, drops of his blood spattered into the dust like petite explosions.

They followed the oxcart path. The convoy climbed through grass growing higher than the doors. The grass stroked the windows like fingers of seaweed. Behind them, the truck's headlights swam through an ocean of brilliant green lines.

Their pell-mell highway dash slowed to a crawl. The path was rutted and winding and hard to see, but it rose gently. The shovels and jerry cans piled in the rear quit clattering. They merely rustled at the curves. Molly could practically feel the grass slithering along the undercarriage.

She relaxed, grateful for the quiet and the sinuous path. With each looping turn, the moon shifted in the sky. It seemed to have grown to twice its normal size, as if they were rising off the planet.

"We're farther north than I thought," said Duncan. "We're reaching into the Annamite range. The mountains run all the way to China. It's wild country. The lowlanders stay clear of it. The hill tribes live up here pretty much the way they have for ten thousand years, taking animals, throwing down a little corn between the trees."

"History," whispered Luke.

At three-thirty they crested a ridgetop and stopped. Ahead stood all that remained of a bridge, a single stone pillar rising from the wide riverbed. Beyond that, higher up, a tall forest took over the grassland.

"Now where?" said Duncan.

They got out, except for Luke, who once again left them to their own conclusions. Molly faced back the way they had come, expecting their path to be flattened by the tires. But the grass had folded shut behind them. They would have to hunt their way down just as carefully.

To her surprise, the logging road lay far below them. Winding back and forth, they'd ascended hundreds of vertical feet. From this height, you could see moonlit paddy fields far to the west, and curious rows of ponds. They were not ponds, she realized, but bomb craters.

Kleat paced along the riverbed rim like a trapped tiger. "We're close," he said. "It's right there in front of us."

"It's just a forest," said Duncan.

"It's cover," said Kleat. "It makes sense. We're looking for the remains of an armored cavalry unit."

"How do you know that?" asked Molly.

"Who do you think the Blackhorse Regiment was? The Eleventh Armored Cavalry. They were famous,

George Patton's men. 'Find the bastards and pile on,' his orders. Nine men, Luke said. That would have been enough to crew two tanks or armored personnel carriers. That's what we're looking for. Anything that large, left in the open, would have been spotted by plane or satellite years ago. I don't know how these guys got lost. But those trees are where they went."

"Not across that bridge, they didn't," Duncan said.

"Why not? Bombs were falling like rain all through this area. Our pilot was returning from a run along this very borderland. Sometime after the Blackhorse soldiers crossed over, the bridge must have caught a bomb. That would explain why they never got out."

"Except the bridge is too primitive," Duncan said. "See these stones? It was a cantilever design. That dates it to a thousand years ago, or earlier. A bridge like that couldn't have taken the weight of a tank. And look at how the building stones have been shoved downriver over time. Some of them are huge. No, this fell to pieces centuries ago."

"The closer we get, the less you care," Kleat said. "Or are you afraid of something?"

Molly stood away from them. The night air was a joy to breathe. She actually felt cold in her sundress.

"Even if they got across thirty years ago, it doesn't mean we should follow them," Duncan said. "Look at the width of that riverbed. It carries some major water. Once the rains begin, we'll never be able to cross back. We'd be stuck over there for the next six months. And that, not a bombed bridge, would explain why they were never seen again."

"I don't see any rain."

"It's coming."

"June 23, 1970," Kleat said to him. "That's the day they went missing. They were part of the Cambodian incursion. Nixon sent them. That's what Kent State was all about."

"I remember."

"Somehow these nine soldiers got separated from the main body. Maybe night was coming on. The enemy was out there. They couldn't stay in the open."

"And you think they drove this far north? We're halfway to Laos."

"Maybe they were going for the high ground. Maybe they saw the trees. Maybe they were being pursued."

Molly left them arguing. The night, the dark morning, was too fine to spoil. Venus stood bright. The constellations beckoned. For a month, swamped by haze on the plains, she had missed the stars. Down there, in another couple of hours, the dawn people would be plundering the site, dodging through the mist. Up here, she felt free. She clutched her arms across her chest and meandered along the broad rim.

At first she didn't notice the strange ribbing under her shoes. It rose out of the ground only gradually. At last the notches threatened to trip her. She bent to run her fingers across the imprints and they were as hard as ceramic.

"Duncan," she called. "Kleat."

They were arguing. She called louder.

"What?" said Kleat.

She showed them the marks on the ground.

Kleat had a six-battery bludgeon of a flashlight. He

shined it on the rows of corrugated imprints, each the same fourteen or fifteen inches wide, leading off like dinosaur footprints. The track marks ran a hundred yards before sinking back into the earth. The clay had captured the passage of vehicles. The sun had baked it and made it impervious to three decades of weather.

"Blackhorse," Kleat said. He identified the prints as the marks of two armored cavalry assault vehicles, ACAVs, both the same size, one following the other.

"They came this way, up the hill, along the river, chasing a way to cross without the bridge. What more do you need?" he said to Duncan. "They're over there. They're waiting."

12.

They came to the pass where the stream spread across the wide riverbed, and the Eleventh Cavalry strays had left more prints in the clay. The water, at the deepest point, came axle high to the Land Cruiser, though it built against Molly's door on the upstream side, slapping and gurgling. The moon made a skin of silver on it. Dangling her hand out the window, she found the water had the temperature of blood or bathwater.

"It's got to be one of these drainages," Duncan muttered at his map. She could hear him back there, twisting the paper to try to fit it to the terrain. Couldn't he see the handle of the Big Dipper, the stars skipping up to the North Star? They weren't lost, only in motion.

She closed her eyes and, midstream, they seemed adrift on a raft. Her feet were wet, and she saw an inch of water on the floor. She laughed.

"You're happy," said Duncan.

She didn't turn. "Yes," she said.

It pleased him. That pleased her.

She didn't try to explain her joy. After all these weeks, she felt released. The tension of searching for the pilot, the pushing and pulling of tool against earth, of man against man, civilian against soldier, of Kleat against Duncan, all of it seemed left behind. Her trespass upon the pilot, with her camera, was a thing of the past. The highway and its dark menace were forgotten.

The sun would find them somewhere. That was the heart of it. The farther they got from the main road, the more it felt like she was finally reaching a center. When the time came, one way or another they could always retrace their journey, and eventually she could return to writing her words, publishing her photos, and promoting her name, the maiden name—the only name she knew—of a woman who had forsaken her. For now, she just wanted to keep going.

The river—or her happiness—changed Duncan, too. His anxieties fell away. He put aside his map, and she thought that now they could cast themselves into the journey. They had made their crossing. Their hellbent midnight ride could slow. She could start to know Duncan without the background noise and her urgency to catch the recovery team's story. They were on their own now, threading up a path across a river that was just a stream upon a mountain that was just a hill, wandering off the maps. Two searchers, that's who they were.

The bones were an excuse. That divorced her and him from Kleat, who was so bound to his dead and his duty. She hadn't come to resurrect soldiers any more than Duncan had. The missing pilot had drawn them as a novelty, an opportunity, nothing more. Now they could enter a territory of the heart.

They had never talked about what preceded Cambodia for him. For a month, they had worked and lived within inches of each other, but she still didn't have a real handle on him. For all his tales of high school football and a dog named Bandit and his summer-long Harley solo to Anchorage and special barbecue recipes and favorite old movies, she had no idea why he'd landed here, or even when. The one time she'd asked, he'd dodged. *Sometimes it feels like I was born here,* he'd said. *Like I'm like some dusty thing out of a Kipling novel, just one more relic of the empire.*

Not Kipling, she thought. Conrad. And not Kurtz, not *Heart of Darkness,* but *Lord Jim.* Duncan had secrets, maybe dark secrets or sad secrets or old guilt. One does not go to the jungle out of innocence. He never talked about a wife or children or another woman, never crouched over snapshots of a lost family or a lover who had chosen a different man or died a tragic death. He never mentioned where that part of his life had gone. Survivor guilt, she guessed. Maybe that was what attracted her to him. He seemed to carry her same sense of a past best unrepeated, of a voyage without anchors. Like an orphan, he acted never quite worthy of love. They were perfect fodder for a grail quest, the two of them.

They passed worn blocks of stone in the river wall, evidence of ancient channels. That perked him up.

"Incredible," he said. "We're looking at water control that predates the Angkor kingdom by centuries, and on the opposite side of the country. A massive hydraulics system in the mountains, for Pete's sake. You need to understand, water is everything here. There's not another country like this on earth. For the Khmers, the world is water. When the monsoon comes, almost half the country vanishes under water. The Tonle Sap River reverses course. Great battles were fought on inland boats. Their civilization was founded on wet rice cultivation. The Angkor empire rose and fell based on their ability to control water. The Angkor kings captured the rain in huge pools and would dole it out in drought years or choke their enemies with thirst. But where did the Angkor genius come from? What sparked their greatness? Who passed to them the divine mandate? Who came before them?"

Luke would have muttered "history" had he been conscious. But he had gone to sleep or was traveling in his head. His eyes were shut. Perhaps his delirium had cycles, or the loss of his secret had emptied him. Hibernation suited him, Molly decided. He looked younger without the junkie eyes. Asleep, he looked resigned to himself.

Trailed by the hulking Mercedes, they wound higher along the contour lines. The moon spun left to right across the windshield, a moving target. Molly let go of the urge to orient herself. There was no longer any question of where they were headed.

The prow of the forest seemed to descend to them. White mist leaked from the throat of the trees. Early morning fog was part of the Cambodian clockwork. But tonight it looked to Molly like a word exhaled, like a syllable spilling downhill to greet her.

To the right and left, creeper vines stitched shut the forest wall. The only possible entry was directly through a break in the screen of trees. She wanted to ask Vin to stop for a picture. But that would have meant setting up a tripod for a time-lapse shot, and it would have been more an emotion than a picture anyway.

"It will be a whole other world in there," Duncan said. "An ecosystem writing its own rules. You'll see. There are species in these mountains that no one knows exist. The *khiting vor,* practically a unicorn, like a myth, part gazelle with curlicue horns. They say it stands on its rear legs to feed, that it eats deadly snakes. There are herds of white elephants, like ghosts. Peacocks. Langur monkeys with two stomachs. Hundreds of species of moths. And the flowers."

Teak and gum trees soared. He knew them by shape, and by their Khmer names, too. They reached the outskirts of the fog, and it turned to brilliant milky smoke in their beams. Vin slowed, feeling his way forward. But they had their bearings now, that gaping hole in the forest.

Something tapped against the rooftop. A leaf. A twig. "What about tigers?"

"These days you see more pelts than paw marks," Duncan said. "The hill tribes and ex-soldiers are trapping them out. It's obscenely easy. They take an old land mine, hide it under a dead monkey for bait, and boom, jackpot. Skin, meat, claws, and penis . . . you can make enough money for a Honda Dream. That's the bike of choice here. The tiger parts go to China for folk medicine."

Another story, another time, she idly thought.

"I wouldn't worry about the big cats. Not this deep. They've never bothered me. This far from people, they don't have a taste for us."

There was another soft pat on the roof, a light rap, an ounce of pebble, less. Then another. Molly glanced at the ceiling. Another. Tiptoes on the metal.

She frowned, wishing the noises away, guessing what they were.

"It can't be," she stated firmly. "Tell me it's not starting."

But it was. Duncan had his fingers against the roof, feeling the minute landings. "The luck," he said.

The season had beat them.

"I don't believe it," she groaned. "We're so close."

They had a deal, though. First rain, turn home. It was all the more imperative now with the river between them and the world.

More soft pats on the roof, little metallic kisses.

"I'm sorry," said Duncan.

A raindrop slapped the windshield. Molly leaned closer to see it. "That's not rain." She put her fingertip on the inside of the glass.

It was blood. Gore. With little webbed feet. Molly lifted her finger away.

"Is that a frog?" said Duncan.

He was right. It was a storm of frogs, little tree frogs. They were falling from the sky. She cranked her window shut.

You read of tadpoles being sucked into the heights and growing into young frogs among the clouds. Was this that? she wondered. Did the monsoon have that power?

Then she saw that they weren't falling. They were leaping out from the forest's high branches. Another struck the windshield. Another, and this one didn't splash to bits like the others.

Dead or stunned, the frog stuck in place. Its red and black bands glistened, backlit by the white mist.

Another hit, this one alive. It took position on the glass, head high. The tiny thing looked majestic, like a creature mounting their world, claiming it. Its miniature lungs pulsed.

"What are they doing?" she said.

"They must be drawn by the headlights," said Duncan. "Or it could be some territorial imperative."

"They're trying to drive us away?"

"I wouldn't make it too personal," Duncan said. But his voice was sober.

They began to patter, like small hail, on the hood and roof and windshield. Now that she knew what they were, Molly could see them in the lighted mist with their tiny legs and arms stretched wide.

"Or it could be the typhoon affecting them," Duncan went on. "Animals are sensitive to change. With the low-pressure cell building, their rhythms go haywire. Lemming behavior. One dives, they all dive."

"This is awful," she said.

The pat of bodies became a rattling, a squall of miniature carnage.

"But at least it's not the rain."

"It's unnatural."

"It's just a few frogs."

"A few?"

The windshield was layered with bits of tissue.

They were casting themselves down by the scores, cat- apulting from the trees. She saw a mother, her back swarming with tiny young. The wiper blades went to work and mangled them. The hood looked like a butcher block. Molly hated it. The death and mutila- tion were senseless.

Plainly, Vin had never witnessed such a thing. He gripped the wheel, and the tattoos on his skinny fore- arms—crude lines and circles and suns, his magic symbols—rippled. He believed in other worlds. And here was this, this curse, a hailstorm of frogs.

Vin drifted to a halt. He craned his head up to see inside the strange torrent. The banging grew louder. He was staring at her. She saw his fear. It made her more afraid.

She put her hands against the roof, as if it might collapse. The metal throbbed. "We can't stay here." She had to shout over the noise.

Like vomit against the windshield, the forest puked its creatures at them. It sickened her. She glanced around.

Luke's eyes were closed. How could he sleep through this? And he was smiling.

Duncan said something in Khmer, his tone calm. He said it again. Vin nodded. They lurched into motion.

Duncan spoke into her ear. "It's okay, we're going inside now. They'll stop, Molly." His hand was on her shoulder.

She could barely see through the plastered glass. Up ahead, like the mouth of a cave, the forest parted its lips. "Faster," she whispered.

The forest yawned open.

13.

Roots and stones rose up from underneath the fog. Vin picked up speed. The Land Cruiser hopped and bounded, tools rattling in the back.

They entered.

Instantly the darkness changed. The moonlight vanished. It was like mercy. The hailstone beating quit. The frogs stopped.

The wiper blades were squealing on dry glass.

Their battle was over, but Vin didn't slow a bit.

Molly hunched over and peered through her side window like it was a porthole. Dark shapes reeled past, trees as thick as bridge pillars. The Land Cruiser lunged over roots like big swells, throwing her against the door.

Duncan barked something at Vin. The boy ignored him, still racing from the animal assault, driving blind. In a way, Molly was relieved by his dread. It validated her own. His fear gave her a fear to settle. She placed one hand on his arm and found he was quivering.

The wiper blades scratched at the crust of frogs. Forward vision returned in streaks. The mist flared in sudden white eruptions. Blackness and light.

Abruptly a huge face jumped up in front of them. Vin braked and swerved. Even so, they banged against it, not ruinously, but with a jolt.

"My God," Duncan whispered.

Molly unclenched her hands from her camera.

The stone head was as large as the car.

The wipers clawed at the rusty glass. Duncan patted Vin's shoulder. The wipers stopped. They stared at the head's tilted eyes.

Molly lifted her camera. Fog edged through the dark trees, sliding in slow, soundless white bunches between the strings of vines brewing up around the stone head.

Time had partially melted its demonic rage. The head had rolled onto one rounded jaw, part human, part animal. Its angry, bulging eyes had eroded over the ages. All around lay more pieces of toppled giant statuary.

"What on earth?" said Molly.

"A warrior icon," said Duncan. "A holy warrior."

"With fangs?"

"A wrathful deity," Duncan said. "A guardian."

"Guarding what, though?"

"That's the question. I don't know. They usually don't appear singly. There must be more like him around here, sentinels to warn the enemy away. But away from what? And look at the style, crude by Angkor standards. Primitive. Old. Molly, this goes back." His mind was churning.

She wasted a shot through the crappy windshield.

"Something's out there, Molly. This is big." His voice grew larger. "Why didn't you tell us?" he said to Luke.

But their guide was deep in REM sleep. Molly could see Luke's eyes darting beneath the closed lids, stormed by dreams.

Duncan rolled down his window for a better look, and Molly braced for the amphibious stink. But the air carried a rich, potent scent full of flowers and fertile soil and, for all she knew, tigers and old rain.

"How can this be?" he murmured to himself. His excitement infected her.

"I need pictures," she said suddenly, and fumbled in the camera bag between her feet, feeling for her wide-angle lens and the strobe flash.

She opened her door. The story quickened in her, morphing, branching off into a completely different narrative. They had set out to find one thing, a few bones from a war, only to discover something monumental. Punt the war, this was Indiana Jones territory.

The story would begin here, she determined, fog swirling, with the blood-encrusted Land Cruiser held at bay by this ferocious head. She backed off to shoot the vehicle, its fender bent around the head. Pieces of hundreds of frogs smeared the grille and hood and rooftop.

She angled right to get Duncan's stunned expression as he approached the beast. Her flash made small explosions. He touched the carved face. He ran his palms over its blind eyes. He peeled off rug sheets of lime- and rose-colored moss.

Vin stayed inside his getaway car, engine idling, as spooked as a thoroughbred.

Light from the headlight beam played up the great flat nose, a ridiculous shot. They'd discovered a nose?

She compensated with her own light, prowling for more shots.

"I know him," Duncan said. "*Ganas,* they're called. He's a kind of Buddhist/Hindi hero, like a Superman for the faithful."

"A fetish," she said, prompting him, capturing his moment of discovery.

"Much more than that," he said, "a destroyer of ignorance, a protector of the Way. A guardian, not just of a people, but of a whole cosmology."

"A hill tribe?"

"Something this large? It's the tip of an iceberg."

She liked that, a tropical iceberg. "A city?" she said. Molly wanted this for him, whatever it was. All his years of humble, anonymous, lonely searching were coming together here tonight.

The truck arrived, adding more light to the display.

Doors opened behind the rank of headlights. She heard a curse, Kleat tripping on a root. Samnang materialized from the rags of fog. She snapped him pressing his hands together in a *sampeah* to the demon head. Then he kept on walking into the darkness.

Kleat joined them, wiping the humidity from his glasses. The circles under his eyes were discolored pouches. Molly had never seen him like this, his bluff vigor drained, that muscular face betraying frailty. He fit the steel rims back onto his face.

Molly lowered her camera. Edit. Delete. Kleat wasn't going to be part of this story.

"Were you trying to have a wreck?" he said. "You took off like a bolt. Now look. You're lucky it wasn't worse."

"The frogs," she said. Now that the danger was past, she tried to make light of it. "We thought it might be a spring shower."

Kleat peered at her from beneath his thick bone of a brow, then turned to the stone head. "It would be a lot easier to go around the rocks, not through them," he said.

"Rocks?" Duncan said. "This could go back to the Funan empire, a thousand years before the Angkor regime. The time of Christ, of Rome. It's practically a myth, like Atlantis or Babylon. Funan wasn't even its real name. That's the Chinese transliteration for 'phnom,' or hill. It was mentioned in early Chinese travel accounts, lost fragments referenced in later accounts. And look, here we are on a hill."

"Save it for the lecture circuit," said Kleat.

Molly held her hand against the bright lights. Vin's older brothers were scolding him for damaging the bumper. Luke lay piled asleep against his door.

"We didn't come for this," said Kleat.

"But this is what we've come to," Duncan marveled.

"Irrelevant." Kleat snapped it like a whip. "They're waiting for us." His dead.

She no longer thought of them as hers. In the holes, working the screens, gathering the facts, shedding blood on the airplane metal, she had felt a contract with the bones. Not anymore. The captain had not confiscated her camera, his way of protesting what his superiors were making him do. But the exile had stolen her pride of place. The bones were meaningless to her now.

There was a movement in the darkness, and Kleat

aimed his big flashlight cop-style. Samnang appeared among the trees in his neat white shirt. He blinked at the lights.

"The boulevard goes on," he announced.

Intent on the stone head, they had failed to notice the road beneath their feet. Even with roots and rocks shrugging up through its surface, it did resemble a Paris boulevard. Paved with stones, it stretched thirty feet from side to side, and extended off into the pit of the forest.

"Where does it lead?" said Duncan.

"Who knows? It goes on," said Samnang.

"Then let's keep going," Kleat said. He clapped his hands. They returned to their vehicles.

"It could be nothing," Duncan cautioned as they drove on. Molly could hear his hope. First the channel stones lining parts of the river, now the carved head and this decaying road.

She reached back and laid a fist on his knee. "But also it could just be something," she said.

He closed his hands around her fist. His palms were wet. He looked dazed and childlike.

Chastened by his accident, Vin took it slowly, steering around big stone tiles tipped up by time. Fog curdled in pools. Enormous trees bracketed the road. Their seeds had taken root with time, and younger trees grew in the middle of the avenue, rupturing more tiles.

"Look how big around these monsters are," Duncan said. "Things grow fast here. But this is old growth. Very old. I can't believe the loggers haven't plundered it."

No spindly, fibrous sugar palms in here. No fields of

grass. No paddies. No sky. The trunks were like columns of skycrapers, red and gray and black and tan. Their massiveness had the look of a great cosmic weight being held aloft. As they crawled over and around the roots and rocks, it was like sliding over immense tendons and slippery bone. She could imagine the ribs of Jonah's whale.

The fog puddled in recesses as dark as side canyons. It hung like linen rags among the branches.

"Look," said Duncan, his window wide open. His wobbling light picked out another carved face watching them. There were more. Half buried among the trees, big stone *ganas*—some with the heads of monkeys and hook-beaked birds of prey—loomed among the branches. Gods appeared, their eyes half shut, their mouths half smiling. The statues kept pace with their advance. They seemed aware. The smiles seemed too serene.

Molly struggled to get a feel for their welcome. Even the times she'd visited Super Max in southern Colorado to shoot portraits of mass murderers, there had been a sense of control. This was different. They'd landed among giants. Giants wearing the masks of good and evil.

"The city wall," said Duncan.

It appeared ahead of them among the complex of vegetation. The closer they drove, the more it took shape, a long, high barrier of mineral colors in the night. It seemed to be forming from their presence, taking on detail out of their expectation of its details. The stone blocks were cabled with vines. The vines had fingers. Ferns grew from the joints.

"It must be twenty feet tall." His breathing had tripped into high gear, Molly could hear it. Then she realized it was her own breathing.

She bent to see through the windshield mottled with gruel, trying to make out the parapets or battlements, whatever you called them. Gaps plunged like missing teeth, muscled open by fat towers of trees with bark as smooth as pigskin. There was no way to tell which was winning, the forest or the dead architect.

"Here we go," Duncan said. "The gateway."

A broad, crumbling tower straddled the wall, a tunnel running through its base. Faces crowned the tower, each staring sightlessly in a different direction. The tunnel lay at the center of their collective chest. One entered through the heart of gods. Vin flipped his light beams from low to high to low. The eyes stared down at them and then away.

Vin inched in.

"It's the perfect traffic control," Duncan remarked. "You could stop any invaders with a few rocks piled inside. In fact, I wonder if this tower's rigged to drop its guts." He cast around with his flashlight.

Molly had never suffered from claustrophobia, but the moment they entered, the walls seemed to close in on her. A sort of nausea gripped her. She felt physically sick. It went beyond that. She felt trapped, as if she were calcifying inside her skin.

They emerged on the far side and the feeling lifted. She cranked at her window handle for fresh air.

"You're sweating," Duncan said.

"No, I'm cold," she said. But her face was dripping.

Duncan laid his *kroma* around her bare neck, and it carried his body heat.

She had expected to drive into a city in ruins, but there was more road. Elevated upon a spine of solid, squared stone, a causeway ran in a straight line, bound on either side by vast pools of water that had degraded into swamps fouled with mangrove trees. Their serpentine roots breached and looped back into the water.

"You're looking at the wealth of kings," said Duncan. "*Barays*—reservoirs—with enough water to feed a whole people. This could be the prototype for Angkor. It could be the genesis for the very idea of Cambodia."

They came to a gauntlet of stone cobras carved along the roadside. "*Nagas,*" Duncan said, identifying them. "Water snakes that figure in all kinds of Asian creation myths. From *naga* you get *nagara,* Khmer for 'The City.'"

There were at least two dozen of the fantastic creatures arranged along the roadway. Some had snapped off at the neck and fallen into the pools. Most were intact, rising higher than the Land Cruiser, their hoods spread open to expose multiple heads with fangs bared.

As they motored slowly through the dangling moss, the water stirred. Molly could hear it down there. On an impulse, she held her camera to the open window and fired blindly, triggering the flash. Her light ricocheted off the black water. The sound stopped. She looked at the LCD to see what her camera had seen.

"Anything?" asked Duncan.

It showed a bulge in the surface, less than that, a shadow, not even a shape. "Not a thing," she said. "It reminds me of the bayous along the Gulf Coast." Just the same, she rolled her window shut.

The causeway came to an end. The broad, flat vein of solid limestone fed back into the earth. Their sculpted road top turned to dirt, and they drove on.

"There are the others," said Molly. The truck was parked at a crooked angle in a clearing between toppled pillars and scraps of fog. The men were busy unloading the vehicles.

She was glad to see them, for a minute. Then she caught sight of their guns. One of the brothers had a rifle slung over his back. Kleat had brought a pistol of his own. He wore it boldly on one hip.

Duncan whispered, looking around. "Where do we begin?"

She made herself part of it. "We'll take baby steps. A little bit at a time."

They had arrived at a terminus. There were no buildings or arches, only the end of the road. From here one climbed on foot. Behind them lay the pools. Before them, rising above their lights on three sides, squared stone terraces formed an arena of sorts. The sheer mass of stone, quarried and hauled into place, promised a kingdom. A set of stairs led into the darkness above. If there was a city, it would be up there.

They parked and dismounted, and, first thing, Vin received a rifle, too.

Kleat was stacking axes and shovels against a fallen tree. Molly stood five-eleven in her bare feet, taller than Kleat, to say nothing of the Khmers. But for a moment, faced with that gun strapped to his hip and all the other firepower floating around, she felt like a child among strangers.

"We thought you'd turned around," he said. She saw

him look at the scarf Duncan had placed around her neck. He made his assumptions.

"We'll make camp here," Duncan announced. He had a tent sack in his hands.

"Sleep?" said Kleat. "The sun comes up in two hours."

"But the light will lag behind in here. That's triple canopy above us. For now, we need to rest."

"I will instruct the men," said Samnang. He had no weapons, Molly noted.

He held out his hand for the tent. It was an important moment. The old man with one leg was anointing Duncan, not Kleat, as their leader. He issued an order to the brothers, who took the tents and hurried toward the ledges.

Kleat carefully laid aside a shovel. Nodding his head, he measured the alliances. His eyes flickered at the brothers moving in and out of the headlights. He studied Molly. "By all means," he said, "sleep."

Molly went to the back of the truck for her mule bag, a huge black duffle made of ripstop nylon, to root for her warmest clothes. For a month, she'd smothered in heat so thick men fell over in it. Now the slight mountain chill had her trembling, even as sweat trickled down her neck. She wished her body would make up its mind, hot or cold. A mountain girl, she knew to layer clothing and find the equilibrium.

There had been no time to sort her laundry at the hotel before their farewell dinner. Unzipping the bag was like opening a dead animal. Bad smells rushed from the interior, and when she thrust her arm inside, the contents were still warm and clammy from the dig. She grabbed the first thing that came to hand, the Vicious Cycles T-shirt, and pulled it over her sundress. It smelled like a hunter's buckskin with her body odor and weeks of soil and Off! Deep Woods cooked into the threads. Deodorant and regular mosquito spray only attracted the bugs, and she'd quickly gone native with the soldiers.

She pulled on a second shirt, then found her Gramicci climbing pants still bloodstained from her encounter with the cockpit metal. The canvas thigh was sewn back together with bright pink thread, prettier than the scar on her leg.

She wasted another minute rummaging for her toilet kit, but it was too dark to find it or, more likely, Kleat had not bothered to pack it for her. She'd have to brush her teeth with a twig. Maybe Duncan would loan her some toothpaste to use with her finger.

The Heng brothers were bustling along the terrace ledges above, farther away than she would have liked. Their lights looked small and moved rapidly up there as they assembled tents for the Americans. Molly guessed they would sleep in the back of the truck, and that would have suited her fine. But Duncan had won his showdown with Kleat, and she wasn't about to scramble the outcome with any complaints.

She returned to the crisscross of headlights looking like a bag lady, the sundress half buried by shirts on top, toting her camera bag, pants, and a neoprene sleeping pad. Heading into the tropics, she hadn't thought to bring a sleeping bag, and her final act before leaving the dig site had been to give her sheets to a Khmer family. She could manage with her own body heat for the next couple of hours. In the morning, she'd see what covering the brothers might spare.

"I'm ready," she said.

Kleat had already started up the staircase to the tent ledges.

"In the morning," Duncan promised, "it will all look different."

14.

The birds woke her.

Her eyes came open.

She found herself curled in a fetal ball on the sleeping pad. In her sleep sometimes, her knees would pull up and she would roll onto her right side like this. It was an old arrangement of her limbs, an occasional habit. It happened in times of stress and signified surrender.

Not moving a muscle, she wondered, *Surrender to what?* What had her ears heard while she lay sleeping?

With her higher shoulder draped with Duncan's red and white *kroma* and her head pillowed on the camera bag, she listened to the birds. She listened closely, but could not connect to their alien song. The whistling and clatters and caws were more like a secret code.

She went on hugging her knees, sifting for a clue. The long ride had pummeled her, that and the hard ground and scant sleep. She ached. Even the image of those ancient stairs rising up through the night could not budge her.

Her plastic Timex said 0730, military time. Kleat was right. Maybe they should have stayed awake. Three hours of sleep felt worse than no sleep at all.

She lay there, assembling the world. At this hour yesterday, they'd been starting into exile from the crash site. Last night they'd eaten dinner in a restaurant. The colors were vivid, the red lobster, the black dirt on the white tablecloth, the sunset. The details crowded in like eager children. The moonlit highway, the green grass, the silver stream, the frogs, the fortress walls.

But none of that explained why her body was afraid. Had she heard something in her sleep? Was there danger out there?

Her fetal curl was like an early warning device. She knew it all too well. There was no controlling it; she'd tried. The trauma posture would seize her in her sleep, a dream signal that something threatened. It stemmed from tension sometimes, or simply vague bad vibes. Usually it was just echo behavior, residue from Oklahoma. Boyfriends complained that they could not hold her at night. She would clench into an animal ball at the edge of the bed, as far from them as possible. It's not you, she would explain in the morning, but then would explain no more. It freaked them out. They felt like monsters. One by one, they always left her.

Lying on her tent floor, Molly did everything in her power to stay in the moment and feel for any real menace. Recycling the past was a dead end. She'd been through it so many times with therapists. But memory has a mind of its own. This morning, spent and dull, with her bones arranged just so, she was too weak to stop it. From deep inside, it rose to the surface. Oklahoma mounted her all over again.

It was April, thirteen years past, the morning after.

I don't want you, she thought. But the memory pinned her.

The playground grass was brittle and yellow and rimed with frost. Like this, exactly like this, on her right side, eyes open, she had watched the town come awake. The cold sun climbed. A man stocked the newspaper box. After a time, a school bus had passed. No one noticed the bundle of rags in the park. It was mid-morning before the lady who owned the stationery store saw her and called the police.

They never did find the guy. They never really looked. He was just another nomad like her. Like her, he'd given up trying to thumb a ride the night before and had walked to the town park to find a little shelter. That's where they'd met.

She didn't have to be bumming rides. Her parents would have given her the money if they'd known how serious she was. But part of the exercise in running away was to hurt them the way they'd hurt her. It was stupid. They loved her more than their own lives. They said that over and over. And yet they had confined her in a fiction for all her conscious life, and how loving was that? In running off to search for her birth mother, she had invited suffering for them all.

They treated her like one more case of the suburban blues. The ER nurses were kind. They swabbed her with Q-tips and cleaned her cuts. One of the cops said that it wasn't what you would call an actual rape. She'd overheard him outside the ER room. These kids, he said, they couple up on the road and then something goes sour and all of a sudden it's a 911. She just doesn't like how it turned out.

His words had made her wonder. After the first few minutes, it was true that she'd just let the attack happen. She had quit fighting and stood off to one side and watched him go at her underneath the swing set. She'd heard of out-of-body experiences. It was true. She'd quit smelling his breath and tasting the canned spaghetti on his teeth.

When he was done, she'd gone back into herself. Her knees had drawn up into her chest like rawhide constricting. She'd hugged herself through the dawn.

She heard her name. "Molly."

She thought it was part of the memory. He'd asked her name. He'd shared his SpaghettiOs before doing it.

When the cop had come in to take a description, he'd asked her for her parents' phone number. In that instant, Molly had realized that her search could end right there. She could return to their sunny fiction, defeated by reality. Or she could accept the ugliness and get on with her journey.

He'd fucked her so hard she could barely stand. But she somehow got to her feet and took the cop's report and crumpled it into a ball to drop at his feet. With blood leaking down her thighs and one eye swollen shut, she told him, sure, she'd made it up. They released her that afternoon.

Only later, years later, did it occur to her that the animal who'd mounted her that night might have been her own father. Not her very father, of course, but a man like him. Because who could say what violence her poor mother had accepted in the name of love? Who could say where she'd come from?

"Molly."

This time the birds fell silent.

She listened. Men were calling her from far away. She clung to the sound of her name. "Moll-lee."

She stirred.

She felt earthbound. It took an act of will to get her hands to let go and her legs to straighten. Oklahoma faded. She sat up in the center of the tent.

It was her home away from home, the same dome tent she'd used to grand-slam Colorado's fourteeners and photograph the Pleiades meteor shower and sleep by high lakes and wake to vistas of light. Only this morning, she noticed, it had leeches.

Their silhouettes showed through the fabric. They were as graceful as dancers waving their bodies out there. She passed her hand underneath them and they bent to her chemical signature or whatever leeches go for. At the recovery site, she'd never seen more than a few at a time. The forest was more abundant. Here they waited for her by the dozens.

Unconcerned, Molly put herself together, what little there was to put together. She pulled off the layers of shirts and quickly shed the sundress and pulled the shirts back on and tightened the belt on her canvas pants. She folded the yellow dress and laid it in one corner. If all else failed, it could serve as her blanket tonight.

Shedding the night, warming up, she rolled her shoulders and tried a simple yoga position. But the voices called her again, dragging the syllables out, like grappling hooks. Did they think she was lost?

"Moll-lee."

They wanted to start their morning, though the day was still dim, with no hint of eastern light. "Coming," she said under her breath.

She tried rattling the tent to shake the leeches loose, but that only agitated them. She reminded herself that they were slow, blind and mindless. A little haste on the exit was all that was needed.

She scooted to the door, arranged her camera bag, and wrapped Duncan's scarf around her head. On three, she pulled down the zipper. Feet first, she slipped out through the opening and, that quickly, her *African Queen* moment was over.

Now that she was standing outside, there were even more leeches than she'd thought. The tent wall was covered with them, glistening and stretching for her, maybe not so mindless or blind after all. She zipped the door as tight as a drum to prevent any bedtime surprises, and made a note to get her hands on a flashlight.

Blue mist had replaced last night's patchy fog. Her tent stood on a wide stone ledge, and below that she could just make out another ledge. The men were invisible down by the trucks, but she could smell their cook fire and coffee and cigarettes wafting up. Oddly, their voices were coming from above. Could they have started exploring without her? Kleat wouldn't care, but surely Duncan would have come to wake her. They were in this thing together.

The stone terrace was cool and slippery under her bare feet. Her shoes were somewhere in the mule bag, a first order of business once she got down. Her flip-flops were set at the entrance to the tent, or at least one of them was. The other had been tipped upside down during the night.

Ordinarily she wouldn't have noticed, but local custom had seeped into her habits. It wasn't just a matter of taking off your shoes or sandals when entering a temple or someone's house. Footwear was always positioned neatly, side by side, and always upright. Even Samnang was superstitious about such things. And so she'd very exactly placed her sandals with the soles flat to the ground before climbing into the tent last night.

The culprit was a thin green shoot of bamboo that had grown up through a joint between the stones. It was three inches high, and she definitely hadn't seen it there last night. There was only one explanation. The bamboo had sprouted through the crack while she was sleeping, tipping her sandal out of its way. She pressed at the sharp nub, charmed in a way. Duncan was right. Things grew fast in the rain forest.

"Moll-lee." They were up there all right, and it was more than one voice calling her to join them. Possibly there hadn't been time to wake her. Duncan could be trying just to keep abreast of Kleat's predation. What were they finding?

15.

Slipping her sandals on, Molly shouldered her camera bag and hustled along the ledge toward the stairs. A red tent materialized on the lower shelf, then atomized in the mist. Giant airborne faces floated off to her right, their tonnage elevated by dharma smiles. Invisible animals shifted in the brush. Dewdrops hung like jewels.

She glanced up the steps, tempted by the pale brightening in the upper forest. Instead she started down into the thick of the mist where coffee was brewing and her socks and shoes waited in the truck. A quick cup of St. Joseph, then the proper footgear, and she'd double-time the staircase. With her long legs and jogger's lungs, she'd overtake the men before the amazement died from their eyes. The mist would bead her lenses, but this green light was gorgeous. You couldn't get more saturated color. She wanted to sprint down the steps, but they were steep and greasy with moss, forcing her to pick her way carefully.

She passed two more ledges, expecting the white Land Cruiser or the truck and the fire to appear, but the mist concealed them. Reaching the ground, she worked across her memory of the clearing. The floor had a slight tilt to it, to drain off the rain no doubt.

Trees bulged up, sudden immense pillars that evaporated overhead. Molly looked up and stopped, not trusting her eyes. Twenty feet above the ground, the remains of a name seemed to hover in the mist. She went closer and it disappeared. She backed away and it reappeared, letters carved into the skin of the tree. Years of growth had lifted them high, and their once neat incisions were stretched apart and rutted and ribbed. The scars were only slightly lighter than the smooth bark, and the wood had absorbed whole sections.

She circled around the base of the tree. "Helen," the letters said. She went a little farther, and found a final *a*. Helena.

The Blackhorse soldiers had been here.

She turned to another tree, and the name Barbara hung in the mist. There was an Ada and an Emma and a Rosita, each upon its own tree. She was in a forest of lovers. The men had taken their knives to the trees and left this much of themselves. It was magical. How much more was hidden in here?

She would have gone on wandering, but after another few minutes, she saw the fire's orange glow. Its heat had melted an opening in the mist.

Vin and his two brothers were squatting on a ledge above the bright orange flames, their eyes bloodshot from lack of sleep or from the wood smoke. They did not look like happy campers. Propped within easy reach against a fallen tree, their rifles gave them the air of bounty hunters.

"Ah-roon soo-ah-s'dai," she tried. But none flashed his

golden teeth for her this good morning, not even Vin. She blamed her awful accent. She was a total linguistic cripple. Some days, faced with her blank screen and a couple of thousand words to crank out, she could barely manage the King's English.

A little distance off, Kleat and Duncan were leaning over a squared foundation stone strewn with rolled maps, and that was strange. She'd heard them calling her from above. Samnang was here, too, hunkered inside the pall of smoke like a gnome, his plastic leg stowed away from the fire. She shrugged. So the forest had wiggy acoustics.

Kleat was stabbing at the forest and the sky and the map. By this point, she would have been surprised if they weren't arguing. Whatever the concern, Duncan appeared to find it pressing, too. He glanced at Molly, then returned his attention to Kleat.

That left Samnang as her official greeter. *"Bonjour, mademoiselle,"* he said, welcoming her. "I have for you a coffee."

"Is that how you keep all your wives so happy?" she said.

Samnang smiled. He had no wife or family. He had no one. The wars had eaten them all, and she knew it. But they could—and did—pretend. She played his saucy American daughter. The light would come on in his brown face.

He reached through the fire for the covered pot and poured the coffee into a white teacup on a white saucer. Probably he'd brought it from his own kitchen, probably just for her. He knew she liked it black, but went through his daily ritual of offering her sugar.

For all its noisy crackling and the billowing white smoke, the fire was a small thing. The wood was green. It was a miracle the stuff had lit at all. Then she saw the jerry can of fuel, their miracle, parked behind a stump.

"Ar kun," she said, thanking him, and sat underneath the plume of smoke by his side. The fire was warm. "I didn't mean to sleep so late."

"No matter," Samnang said. "You see this mist. Duncan said to let you sleep."

Then why, she wondered, *call her name?* "Will the mist lift soon?"

"The forest decides these things." He looked more closely at her. "Be still a moment, please." He reached over.

She knew without asking what it was. The leech clung to the skin of her throat before coming away. She touched the spot, and her finger came away bloody. She looped the *kroma* around her neck to hide the tiny wound.

Samnang held the leech for her to see. It must have fallen on her as she was exiting the tent. The wisp of a worm had bloated to a slug the length of her little finger. What surprised her more than its size and stealth was the speed of its gorging. In ten minutes, such hunger.

She watched to see what came next. Would Samnang throw it against a rock or squeeze it in his fingers? He was contemplative. "She humbles me," he said.

"That?"

"If only I could obey God with such faith." He juggled it on his palm to keep the suckers from getting hold.

"What faith is that?"

"Oh," he said, embarrassed to be preaching.

"No, go on, tell me."

"To exist in the forest with no questions, no doubt. Imagine." He smiled. "Someday, this lowly worm, a Buddha." He gently tossed it to a bed of leaves.

One of Vin's brothers went over and picked it up. He was the one named So, the middle one. He laid the leech on a twig and held it over the fire. The leech began writhing. The man grinned at Molly with yellow hepatitis eyes. She frowned, not so much distressed by the leech's fate—the thing had sucked her blood—as by the man's vandalism. It was pointed, his ruining Samnang's little act of compassion. Something was going on between them.

The oldest brother, Doc, with wisps of mustache hair and geometric suns tattooed on each shoulder, made a joke. It had to do with throwing Samnang's artificial leg into the fire. Vin glanced at Molly and did not join in the laughter. She had no idea what the problem was, but disliked seeing the old man mocked.

Samnang went back to tending the fire. He rested the pot on three neat stones above a nest of embers. The flames were trim, the heat no more or less than the morning called for.

Molly went on sitting by Samnang for another minute, mostly to show her solidarity. Then she stood casually. "Let me see what the lords of the jungle are up to," she said.

"Of course," said Samnang.

She walked to Duncan and Kleat and placed her white saucer and cup at the farthest corner of their

makeshift bench, away from the maps. Like a skin drying, one map was pegged open with chunks
of rock and food packets. Small pebbles on a U.S. military topo marked last night's passage. From Snuol, the
logging road ran east and north, and the pebbles became
bits of twigs—hypotheticals—leading off to nowhere.
You could conjure up a hundred phantom rivers and
streams from the wrinkles and curves, all of them
descending to the Mekong.

"Got us figured out?" she said.

"Not a clue," Duncan said. He seemed frayed. He
gestured at a big, boxy GPS receiver that looked almost
as obsolete as his colonial-scientist compass in its
brown wooden case with oiled hinges. What antiques
stores had these come from? The lighted panel read
"SEARCHING."

"It's like all the satellites fell from the sky," said
Duncan. "We're not getting a single reading."

"Our location can wait," Kleat said. "No more fuss-
ing around."

"You don't understand. These hills may not seem
like much. You can't properly call them mountains. But
they can eat you alive, especially—"

"I know," said Kleat. "I know."

"We're lost," said Duncan. "It matters. We don't
even know if they came in here."

"We know they crossed the river. We saw their
tracks. Where else could they have gone?"

"They were here," said Molly. The two men
stopped. "You didn't see the names?"

"What's this?" Kleat said.

She led them into the mist. After the fire, it seemed colder and darker out here.

Head craned back, she searched for the names. "They were carved on the trees," she said. "The names of their women. Up high."

The names had disappeared, though. There were so many trees, and she must have come in differently from the stairs. "They were here somewhere," she insisted.

"I believe you," Kleat said, though he didn't really. It was simply convenient to his argument. "Once this fucking mist thins out, we'll find them."

They went back to the fire and their maps on the stone.

"The names don't change anything," Duncan said. He didn't question that she had seen them. He took it on faith. "I still say we should backtrack, take a second look from the outside. Get a handle on the risks."

"Leave?" said Molly.

She said it with more censure than she meant. The caffeine was kicking in. But also, his apprehension confused her. He was the archaeologist. His job was to pry open the earth and raise cities from the dead. Forget the Blackhorse bones. Forget Kleat. Even forget the typhoon and the rains. In the back of her mind, they were already trapped—held under house arrest—by the river. Something stood at the top of those stairs. This was their chance to raise Atlantis.

"While we still can," Duncan said to her.

"I keep telling you," said Kleat, "he's halfway to China by now. Burma, Afghanistan, wherever the dope grows wild."

"I don't think so."

"Luke?" said Molly, jolted by the sudden awareness. "He's gone?"

"Unless he spent the night with you," Kleat said. "No one's seen him since we arrived."

Molly looked at the mist. Had he been the one calling her? "He must be here."

"That's what I keep saying," said Duncan.

"Sam took a try looking for him," Kleat said. "If anybody can track a man, it's him."

"We don't need to go through that again," Molly said.

"It's not irrelevant. Your gentle musicologist was also KR."

The brothers were all watching now. They heard the KR and began murmuring among themselves.

"We've been through this," Molly said quietly.

"And you didn't believe me."

"I agreed with Duncan. It's not our business."

Kleat gave her an owlish blink. He called across to the fire. "Tell us what you found, Sam."

"He went this way into the forest," Samnang said. "Then his footprints disappear."

"He's still here," said Duncan.

"Isn't that the direction of the gate?" Kleat asked.

"Yes. The gate is that way," Samnang said.

"He's not finished with us," Duncan insisted.

"He's harmless," said Kleat. "You're making monsters."

"He could be hiding twenty feet away and we wouldn't know it."

"Do you want this or not?"

"Maybe you want it too much," said Duncan. "Think

back to last night when we saw him in the restaurant, your own words. You said he must be hunting us."

Kleat set his knuckles on the map. "Not anymore. Look around. We're the ones with all the guns."

"He brought us here for a reason," Duncan said.

"The reason of a seriously disturbed mind. He brought us here to unload a secret. A big secret. A secret that freaked him out. He found something here and needed to hand it off. Don't ask me why he chose us. What counts is that now he's freed. In his mind, he's released from his burden. We freed him." Kleat grabbed at the wood smoke and opened his hand to the air. "He's gone."

How could she have missed his absence? It seemed ungrateful and wrong to forget someone so easily.

"This was all he had," she said. "Wouldn't he hang on to it for dear life? Why leave?"

"For that, Molly," Kleat said, "you'd need to ask your mother."

Her mother, again. He was relentless, like a jackal after meat. "What on God's earth does *she* have to do with it?"

"You were all she had," Kleat said, "but she still left you. This place was Luke's baby. Now he's thrown it away. You think love heals all. But we're talking about the damned here. Love is a horror to people like them."

Molly slapped him. *The damned.* She slapped him so hard it hurt her hand. His glasses flew off. Coffee spilled across the map.

The brothers halted their low drone.

Molly pulled her hand back. She didn't know what to say. For better or worse, she wasn't wired for conflict, much less a lightning bolt like this. She shouldn't have let him get to her. She shouldn't have slapped him. Then she thought, *The hell with it, maybe she should have slapped him a long time ago.*

Kleat nodded his head, thinking, making up his mind. The bared pouches under his eyes were even darker in the daylight. After a minute, he bent to retrieve his glasses. He fit them onto his face.

"Don't apologize," Duncan said to her. "If you do, I'll have to hit him myself."

"I'm not." She'd hit Kleat too hard for that. He would take any apology as patronizing, and besides, she wasn't sorry. "You know," she said to him, "we could work together here. We came for the same reason."

Kleat looked at Duncan's scarf around her neck, red and white checkered like the KR—and millions of other Khmer people—used to wear. She couldn't tell if he distrusted the scarf or the giving of it to her, again, by Duncan. "I'm not so sure anymore," he said. "I know why I came. But there seem to be other temptations in the air."

That quickly, Molly's anger dissipated. She owed Kleat nothing, not one more emotion, not another thought, and least of all her little flight of fancy about Duncan.

One of them had emptied two MRE packets on the stone top. Molly made a show of pocketing the energy bar. She ripped open the scrambled-egg packet with her teeth and squeezed pieces of it cold into her mouth, wolfing the food down. It took sixty seconds flat. "There, done." She wiped her mouth. "Later." She started off into the mist.

"Where are you going?" Kleat said. She looked back at them. Duncan was rearranging his pebbles and twigs on the map. Kleat stood rooted in place with his hands on his hips. The Khmers seemed content hanging by the fire, waiting for the mist.

"I'm getting my socks and shoes out of the truck. Then I'm going up the stairs," she said. "The light's too fine to waste."

16.

By the time she finished tying her shoelaces, the rest were ready to go. They left Samnang and his leg by the fire to watch over the vehicles, and started off in a bunch.

The three brothers soon sprinted ahead, the slaps of their flip-flops fading into the mist above. Molly wanted to go bounding up the stairs with them, but curbed her excitement and stuck with Duncan and, by default, Kleat.

"There will be one hundred and four steps," Duncan told them. He seemed very certain of it.

"You've been here before?" Kleat said, mocking him.

"I could be wrong, of course," Duncan said. "But the place is monumental, and the statues are like half-breeds, part Buddhist, part animal. My guess is that they built it to a blueprint, one dictated by their gods. They would have dedicated a stair to each of the Buddha's hundred and four manifestations."

They were tall, steep, narrow steps, like those found on Mayan pyramids, the kind that take confidence to climb upright without hands. Greasy with fluorescent green and blue moss, they would need special care coming down. Tourists, someday, would require a handrail or a chain to hold on to. Vendors would sell them warm Cokes from the stone terraces.

"You could bleed the ecotourists white with something like this," Kleat said. "There's room down there for a parking lot and a lodge. Put it on the water's edge. Spray the pools for mosquitoes. Clear out the trees." He pretended only to be tormenting Duncan, the purist. He accused them of giving in to the temptations of the place, and to each other, but Molly heard him warring with himself, the dutiful brother versus the building contractor, the bones versus his visions of development.

"That would destroy everything," Duncan said.

"Do you seriously think you can hold on to this for yourself? The jack is out of the box. There's no stuffing him back in again."

"We'll have to keep it secret until we can get the proper protections in place," Duncan said. "You don't rush something like this. The restoration will take years, even decades."

"First thing," Kleat said, "I'd clear the trees. The quickest way would be explosives. Give me a few pounds of C4, I could open up the sky. Better yet, bring in the loggers. Let the development pay for itself."

Duncan stopped on the stairs. "Kill the trees and you kill the city. Without the trees, it would fall to pieces."

What city? It was all conjecture. But like them, Molly was eager. She craved whatever waited above, in the mist. The stairs were building to a climax. Something was up there, she could feel it.

"After the destruction we saw coming in last night?" she said. "It looked like the forest is ripping the place to shreds."

"I know that's how it looks. But the trees are the only thing binding it together," Duncan said. "It's true, the trees have invaded the architecture, but they're also locking it in place. I've seen this at other sites. The forest is like a living glue."

He started pointing out the phantoms of trees in the mist. "Banyan trees. Giant strangler figs. And that one there, the most common invader, a form of ficus. 'Spong,' the Cambodians call it, *Tetrameles nudiflora*. They can live for up to two hundred years, and all the while birds are scattering more seeds, spreading the forest's skeleton."

Kleat lost interest in his game. "We didn't come for this. The ruins are a distraction. Ignore the city, if that's what it is. Our mission is to find the remains of the Eleventh Cavalry men."

"You need to be prepared to find nothing," Duncan said.

"We know now they were here."

"Were. It's entirely possible they left the names of their women and headed on."

"On to where?"

"I don't know. But there's no sign they stayed. Did you see any of their tracks in the clearing?"

Kleat was quiet for a minute. His boots methodically slugged at the steps. "Our gang of mercenaries will have the place looted to the ground before we even see it," he growled. He accelerated, stumping upward, leaving them behind.

Molly held to Duncan's leisurely pace. They were going to be the last ones up. It wasn't a race, she told herself. If this proved to be half as big as it promised, Duncan was going to be the crux of her story. Let the others disperse into the ruins, out of frame. She would make him a hero. And herself a name. Kleat could find his bones. There could be something here for everyone.

As they passed the ledges leading off to the tents, she could see how the brothers had spaced them apart last night. Knowing the Americans liked privacy, they'd pitched each tent on a separate terrace. She began counting the steps from her ledge to the top so that she could find her own shelter even in the dark, but gave up. She let go. She was not alone. She was with Duncan. The two of them could manage somehow.

"How does it feel?" she asked Duncan. This could be his triumph. If only he would climb a little faster. Then she realized that he was lagging on purpose.

"I'm afraid," he said. "What if it's not what we think?"

"What do you think it is?" In her head the tape recorder was running. She had her camera out.

"I don't know. Have you ever had a dream that wouldn't let go of you? I don't know how to put it. These stairs, it's like I've climbed them before. But I've got no idea what comes next."

"You deserve this, Duncan." *And so do I, whatever comes.*

She'd paid her dues. She'd turned her sweat and blood into black ink, and made her eye the camera's eye, thinking to make the world a little better through her witnessing. But over the years, for one reason or another, she had squandered herself on trivial events and prideful men and women who tried to manipulate her pen and camera. She'd become a cynical hack. A hireling with no faith. That was about to change. The stairs were leading to something larger than life. Every writer should have that.

They worked higher into that netherworld of green mist, and when she looked down, the abyss seemed bottomless. At last she could make out the shape of cobra hoods, poised along the crest like gargoyles. The stairs reached their apex. One final step, and the ruins heaved up before them.

17.

There was no transition from below to above, no sense of arrival. They took a few steps and the architecture seemed to hurry around, enclosing them.

It was a city, a phantom city of buildings and statuary and the tangled network of the forest, a city of hints. If anything, the mist was thicker here, lush and aquamarine. Molly took a deep breath, and the air was so dense she could taste the smell of vegetation growing from its own rich compost, and flowers that were as invisible as ideas. The mist deformed the ancient metropolis. It softened the squared corners, revealing and devouring hints of towering spires, and washing against vast stone heads like a tide.

"God," said Duncan.

She got his astonishment on camera, his blank, plain daze. Every square in the red and white scarf around his neck jumped out from the mist. The background was pure Seurat, tiny dots of color flooding the air. The suggestion of a massive stone head peered over his right shoulder.

That would be the cover photo. This was a book, not an article. Done right, it might stand as a classic. She took a step and it felt like planting a footprint on the moon. They were the first, it seemed, to discover this place.

"How can this be?" she said. "A lost city in this day and age?"

"Why not?" said Duncan. "They're still finding Mayan cities and Incan tombs. There are species in these mountains that scientists thought were just myths. And look at the forest canopy. The ruins have been buried for centuries, not forgotten, just lost."

She was too stunned to arrange her thoughts. *Shoot,* she commanded herself. *Sort it out later.*

"Where did the others go?" Duncan said.

"Who cares?" For the time being, the two of them owned the ruins.

Working left to right for a digital panorama, she shot immense stacks of pyramids and squared monuments with ornately carved doorways. The mist seemed to breathe, blossoming then paling. But she realized it was her own heartbeat she was seeing through the lens, the rhythm of blood through the capillaries of her eyes.

"We need a plan," he said. "We could lose ourselves in here."

"You're driving the bus," she said.

"A basic assessment," he decided. "Yes. Describe the circle's edge, then spiral in."

They returned—with difficulty, a few steps and they were already twisted around—to the head of the staircase. The stairs plunged down into the mist. Somewhere down there Samnang was sitting by his fire.

Duncan set off along the perimeter of the chasm, following a walkway bordered by a fence with *nagas* facing outward. The walkway curved in a great semicircle along the very edge of the plateau. On their left, the architecture seemed to rush at them like a flood ready to spill over a waterfall. The *nagas'* sandstone mantles flared like pink spray.

They came to a fortress wall like the one they had passed through the night before. Standing twenty feet high, it was built of fired bricks. Some of the bricks had loosened and spilled from the top of the wall. Duncan hefted one and noticed a symbol baked into its top. "These are names," he said.

"You can read that?"

"No." He picked up a second and third brick, and they were inscribed, too. "But certain Chinese emperors had a quality-control system like this. These are possibly the names of the brick makers. That way, any defects could be traced to its creator and corrected, or the creator punished."

As they moved on, Molly could practically feel the weight of the names holding up the wall and declaring the inside from the outside. It was like an army of magical symbols, containing the citizens and repelling outsiders.

Where the hillside rose, the wall stepped higher. A deep streambed lined with bricks and bedrock served as drainage, or possibly a moat. *A curious moat,* thought Molly. This one ran along the inside of the fortress. It was dry just now, but during the rainy season, Molly could imagine water coursing down the channel. In the slickrock country of Utah, she'd seen for herself how a small rain shower could turn the arroyos into deadly flood chutes.

The moat ascended in stages, the stone edges polished and worn by centuries of runoff. From the windows of nearby buildings, the sound of water must have been, by turns, sweet or thunderous. She wanted to veer off into the city and look out through those windows. She wanted to wander among the spires and floating heads.

But Duncan stuck to the path beneath the wall, stopping repeatedly to examine flowers and insects or animal prints and scat. They heard dogs barking in the far distance, and Molly thought there must be a village nearby, even within the ruins. Duncan explained that they were rare barking deer. He could tell the difference between one invisible bird and another by its song or even the sound of its wings. They spent ten minutes studying a spiderweb pattern, and another half hour counting the growth rings on the shells of two different species of snails.

It was maddening, almost as if he were avoiding the city. She didn't complain out loud as the wall went on and the minutes turned to hours. It took an effort not to direct his story. It would be a labyrinth in there. She had learned from the recovery team the primacy of the grid. The founding event of every dig is the driving of the first stake, traditionally at the southwest extremity. From that benchmark emanated all the squares spreading to the north and east. That had to explain Duncan's uncertainty. He was hunting for an edge to dub southwest, a corner to the circle from which to begin.

Leaves stirred in the mist. They sounded almost like a child crying very softly. As the sound drew closer, the crying became a little singsong rhyme coming from the trees, and Molly decided it could only be the birds. The sound mushroomed, rushing between the buildings with a blizzard howl. The mist churned open. A great gust of wind broke against them, nearly toppling them into the dry moat. Molly heard shouts and the clash of metal, and screams, an entire battle, all within that blast of wind. Just as suddenly the air was still again.

Molly straightened. "What was that?"

Duncan chewed at his lip, staring at the mist-bound city. "The weather's changing," he said.

But there was no more wind, not even a breeze. They went on.

Molly kept looking for a breach in the wall. Surely the forest had broken it open somewhere, and they would be able to see the far side. But the wall loomed intact except along the very upper sections, where the masonry had come undone in fractions. The path and the wall went on twisting with the hill's contours.

Eventually, a gateway surfaced in the mist ahead. Like the one they had entered through the night before, it had a multiheaded turret with eyes that seemed to watch their approach. In her mind, the shapeless citadel became symmetrical. They'd entered the front door, and here was the back, and this road logically pierced the city from side to side. On the other hand, there could be a dozen more gates, with roads leading into some center like spokes.

The tunnel mouth was guarded—or had been, once upon a time—by a host of terra-cotta statues. They were life-size replicas of ancient warriors, dozens of them. "They have to be based on the sculpture army at Xi'an, in China," he said. "Or, what if the Xi'an army is based on this? Who knows how old it is?"

He kept a curious distance from the terra-cotta warriors, afraid, she thought, of disturbing the artifacts. That didn't stop her. "I'll be careful," she assured him, and moved among them with her camera. "They're so beautiful."

Extraordinary, she meant. Exquisite. But not beautiful. Each had his own distinct face, round or lean, vicious or youthful, some with little shocks of beards or delicate Fu Manchu mustaches. But their eyes destroyed the realism. They were primitive round holes, sockets, some still holding bulging, round jade pebbles.

The crudeness of the stone eyes confused her. Every other detail was so refined and lifelike, and these eyes were horrible. Was that the intent, to cow the beholder? Some still had paint remaining on them. As if the bulbous pebbles weren't frightening enough, the artists had added shocked black circles around each eye. It reminded her of war paint, or a child's drawing of a nightmare.

"Are these supposed to be like glass eyes?" she asked Duncan. "Sight for clay men?"

"Maybe. Or reminders."

"Yes?"

"That we come from the earth. I don't know. Stones for eyes in a city of stone. They could symbolize the all-seeing city. Or the forest."

Guardians at the gate, she thought. Many had shattered, and their shards still bore bits of colored paint. Others lay unbroken, on their backs or chests like store mannequins toppled by the wind.

Some still stood at attention, though these had all sunk to differing degrees into the earth. They looked like quicksand victims, dragged under to their knees or hips, some to their necks, but still vigilant. A few showed only the tops of their heads. Whatever siege—or exodus—they were designed to guard against, here they waited. They seemed ready to spring into action. Some even wore their original armor of jade plates stitched together with what looked like wire spun of gold. Gold, though? Surely thieves would have taken it long ago. Elsewhere, the wire had failed and jade plates lay scattered like pale green dragon scales. Their fists clenched empty holes where the wood shafts of spears or bows had rotted.

"There's a fortune lying here," she said.

"They came this way," Duncan said. He had stopped and was staring at the tunnel.

"Kleat and the brothers?"

"No, our soldiers, Molly. They were here."

"They went through the tunnel?"

"Not through," he said. "But they were here."

She looked into the dark maw. "How do you know?"

He opened and closed his mouth without a word. The answer man had no answer.

Molly stepped closer. The tunnel looked impassable, choked with vegetation. Ugly with it, to be honest. It disgusted her in a strange way, the messy, clenched chaos in there. She felt physically sick, and thought it might be that compressed cold egg she'd eaten for breakfast.

But as she went nearer, her uneasiness—her sense of

outright disease—grew. The walls pressed down at her. The tunnel, this awful hole, made her dizzy. She remembered her repulsion as they'd entered last night, and this was worse. She was on foot. Dread and nausea shackled her. A sudden despair washed over her. What did it take to leave this place?

But she forced herself to the tunnel mouth. Vines and roots clotted its bowels. She reached to part the leaves and something bit her. She yanked her hand back, blood beading on her wrist.

"Molly," said Duncan. "Leave it alone."

Peering inside, she saw the culprit. She took a careful grip and tugged at it, dragging it into view.

"Is that barbed wire?"

"What do you think?" she snapped. Clearly this was what he'd seen.

"Molly?"

A wave of anger rocked her. "You could have warned me."

"I didn't see it."

She yanked at the rusted coil. There was a whole Slinky of concertina wire inside, bound in place by years of undergrowth. "We'll never get out," she said. Fear seized her. Despair. They were prisoners.

"Come away from there," Duncan said.

She let loose of the wire and it drew back into the tunnel like a snake. She stared into the devouring pit.

"Molly." A command.

She turned from the tunnel.

"Come here."

She started toward him, and with each step her terrible emotions faded.

"Are you all right?" He took her arm and drew her farther away from the tunnel.

"I must be hungry," she said. "Or yesterday's still catching up with me." She sat down, emptied out.

"Drink." He gave her a water bottle.

"They closed themselves in," she said. "Why didn't they just leave?" She glanced at the tunnel, and it was just a tunnel now. But she felt scarred by it, not just scratched by the wire, but wounded by the tunnel. She wanted nothing more to do with it.

"Maybe they felt safer in the ruins," Duncan said. "One thing's certain, they didn't exit this way."

"You really didn't see the wire?"

"From here? You didn't see it until it cut you."

"Then how did you know they'd been here?"

He frowned. "It's logical. If they had time to carve names in trees down below, then they would have had time to explore up here. They would have examined the walls, don't you think, secured their perimeter, whatever soldiers do?"

Her watch read just eight-thirty. They'd left camp at eight-fifteen. The second hand was barely crawling. She pressed the stem and the little night-light glowed. The battery was working, but something was wrong with the mechanism. "The humidity," she said. So much for "water-resistant to fifty meters." "What time do you have?"

She'd forgotten that Duncan didn't wear a watch. And yet he carried an antique compass in his briefcase. She'd have to ask about the contradiction another time, one more quirk to slip into her book.

"We left camp hours ago," she said. "We should

think about getting back. Don't you want to take a look at the city?" In her mind, the road leading from the tunnel would be a direct shortcut to the head of the stairs.

Duncan eyed the ruins drifting in the mist, and then the path continuing along the wall. She cut off his thinking. "The wall could go on for miles," she said. Let him connect his circle another day. The mist was thinning. She wanted to see.

"You're right." He nodded, then stepped back. She led them away from the sealed exit, in from the wall and toward the ruins it enclosed.

Only now did she discern that there was a road underfoot. Roots burst up through the ground, as high as their shoulders. The paving stones had buckled in waves, or split open in grassy zigzags. They passed between pyramids and terraced buildings. Strangler figs occupied rooftops and walls, like sea monsters with waxy brown tentacles. The careful architecture looked squashed.

Corridors branched off the main avenue, impassable, colonized from side to side with primordial trees. They crossed a bridge over a dried-out canal with little landing porches leading up to dark holes of doorways. "Like Venice," she said, "a city of water."

Every bend promised a secret. She had to discipline her photography. The Nikon would hold only so many images, and it was a battery hog. She got Duncan clambering across the wreckage of another bridge, this one pierced by a mahogany giant. She shot spires soaring like delicate, baroque rocket ships, their needles pricking the lower canopy and disappearing from view. She took six shots of a Buddha the length of two whales, lying on his side, head pillowed on one hand like a child lazing away a summer day. She could spend a whole week with him alone.

Everywhere she turned, the city offered itself to her, a prehistoric vision. Her wide-angle lens was not wide enough. The place defied her.

Baby steps, she reminded herself. She was intensely aware of the sum of the place, the notion of a grand design. Duncan was right, it would take years to decode. A lifetime.

He found a coin woven into the belly of a discarded bird's nest. Only Duncan, in the midst of a lost city, would have thought to look in a nest that had fallen from the branches.

"Do you know who this is?" He handed the coin to Molly. One side was scaled with verdigris, the other bore a crude profile. "I've seen one other like it, in a book. It's Antoninus Pius, the second-century Roman emperor." He was awestruck. "Whoever they were, these people were part of a trade network going all the way to the heart of the Roman Empire."

They entered a canyon of carved panels. Red, gray, and blue lichen plastered the bas-relief in neon blotches. It was like falling into myth. Monkey gods and human warriors waged war with exotic weapons. Concubines lounged, children played. Dancers' fingers curved like currents of water. A majestic peacock was oblivious of two crocodiles stalking it with wide-open jaws.

She and Duncan moved slowly, like lovers in an art gallery, occasionally admiring a find, then drifting apart to continue their separate investigations. The canyon seemed to contain the germs of every kind of fable and myth. The carving was peculiar in its style and demanded her concentration.

Here was a dragon rising from the sea. Here was a great fire set by invaders with spears, and a murderer stabbing his brother. She tried connecting the stories in order, and realized that every arrangement could be disconnected and rearranged to tell other tales. Was the dragon a storm? Were the invaders possibly saviors? Was the fire renewal, not destruction? Was the killer actually a hero? It went on like that.

Molly gave up with her camera. She touched the carvings. They touched her. It was hard to explain. It went beyond seduction. The walls contained her. They invited her to read herself among the carvings. It was as if she inhabited the stone.

Here was a woman exploring a garden. Here was an infant adrift on a river. Here was a woman about to stab herself. Reverse the order: Here was her mother, here the orphan, here the searcher.

She didn't know she was crying until Duncan laid one hand on her shoulder. He saw what she was looking at. It embarrassed her, and he saw that, too.

"Ancestors," he said. "The place is full with them."

"I don't know why I bother with her," said Molly. "Kleat's right. She was just a hippie chick. A suicide. One more lost child."

"It's not that easy with ghosts," he said.

"I found her, though. That should be enough."

He ran his fingers above the stone, not touching the

lichen, only isolating the story. "You still have questions. What else is a ghost but a question?"

"I know everything I need to know," said Molly. "She showed up in Breckenridge with a baby in her arms. The old mining towns were going through this Neil Young *After the Gold Rush* kick, kids—hippies— settling into shacks, you know, letting their freak flags fly. She knitted hats and made candles with flowers in them. She sold them from a cardboard box. She didn't have the sense to get food stamps, so neighbors brought her meals. People stacked firewood by our trailer in the winter."

"And your father?"

"Which one? It was the Age of Aquarius. I doubt he ever knew I existed. And what would I do with him anyway?"

"You're probably right."

Molly brushed at the lichen, and if she was destroying a priceless carving, Duncan didn't reprimand her. "She would sing sad songs on the streets," she said. "An old priest told me that. She had a beautiful voice. Ballads. Hymns. Dirge music."

"Yes?"

"She died of a broken heart, he said. My poor, crazy mother."

"And so you're crazy, too?"

She looked at him, and he was not Kleat taunting her. He was Duncan. "On bad days, I wonder," she said.

"And the good days?"

"On the good days I sing."

"Sad songs?"

He had her. She could not help but smile. "Maybe."

"Then maybe, if I'm quiet, I'll hear you," he said.

"So you're counting on good days ahead, Mr. O'Brian?"

"Days?" He opened his arms to the city. "I'm counting on years. I could spend the rest of my life in here. I was born for this."

A single gunshot broke their reverie.

18.

At the crack of the bullet, as if the skin of the place had been punctured, the mist drew off in a sudden rush. It didn't burn away; the sun could not penetrate the triple canopy. It simply lifted and was gone.

They were surrounded—dwarfed—by those god heads and demon faces and the dreams of architects raised in stone and by this complicated forest. The canopy stretched overhead like an umbrella with veins. Molly felt made up, as if the giant stone heads among the trees were dreaming them all into existence.

She had forgotten about the others. Hours had passed. She could not read the green twilight. It seemed lighter without the mist, and yet dark for her sense of the time. Could it be late afternoon so soon?

Suddenly she was starving.

They followed the echo of the gunshot out of the canyon. It took some searching to locate the head of the stairs. Molly could barely distinguish between one building and another. She was in sensory overload, drained from too little sleep and too much emotion, way too much. She hadn't experienced so many raw feelings in years, all packed into the space of a single day. The city was like a fuse. One sensation seemed to trigger another in a chain reaction of old fears and repressed memories and anger and wild hope.

Luckily, Duncan had an instinct for the ruins. After a few false turns, he brought them to the rim with its pink sandstone *nagas* and the staircase. With the mist cleared, the terminus sprawled beneath them, a grand cul-de-sac in a bowl of steeply terraced walls. Trees and vines clung to the most precipitous walls.

From this height, the white Land Cruiser looked as delicate as an eggshell. The big Mercedes truck could have been a toy. The rest of them were down there, and when Kleat saw her and Duncan, he gave a big wave with his gun hand, which only made him look more miniature. The expedition suddenly seemed fragile and overreaching. Their discovery was vastly bigger than they were.

As they descended the stairs, Molly saw that Samnang had not been idle during their absence. A bright green rectangle of a hut made of leaves and poles now occupied the lowest terrace, with one side open to his little spark of a fire. The fire gave her a clue to the time. It glittered too brightly for day. Night was nearing.

They reached the ground. As she wove through the trees, Molly kept an eye out for the names of women carved in the bark, but the light had changed or she was among the wrong trees. She couldn't find the marks.

Even before entering the camp area, she saw Kleat grinning, and his reason for it. He was wearing a GI helmet with most of the canvas eaten away. Closer still, she could see fading tally marks along one side where a soldier had been counting down his days.

The brothers were in high spirits, too. A row of green bronze and jade vessels and geometrically painted jars stood along one ledge. She expected Duncan to start in about the plundering, but he only sighed.

"We're on their trail now," Kleat said. He opened his hand carefully, as if it might hold precious jewels, and three empty brass cartridges lay on his palm.

"You found those in the city?" asked Duncan.

"No, right here in the clearing. Sam found them lying over there." He knocked on the helmet. "We almost drove over it last night."

"That's all you have?"

"It's a start. Now we know where to look. Down here. Forget the city."

Molly glanced around at the forest enclosing them. You couldn't see the reservoirs from here, or their tire marks in the leaves. When it came time to leave, they would have to search just to find their way back to the causeway.

"What are those?" she asked, pointing at saplings bent into O shapes. They appeared at various distances among the trees, like animal snares.

"That's Sam's work. Landmarks. I sent him to look for the ACAVs. They have to be around here somewhere."

"Was that your gunshot?"

"No sense wasting time up there. They probably never went up into the ruins."

Molly resented that. She and Duncan had been

crossing the city's threshold, drifting among its stories. And Kleat had summoned them.

"Well, they did, for your information," she blurted out.

Duncan grimaced. She bit her lip. How could she have known that was their secret?

"They were up there?" Kleat said.

It was too late to take back her words. "We found barbed wire in the gate at the back."

"You found wire?" Kleat said. "And you didn't call for me? That was the deal. I told you—"

Molly darted a glance at Duncan. It was true, they had abandoned the evidence in order to go exploring in the city. "We called for you," she lied. "We waited. You didn't hear us."

"What gate?" His eyes fell on her camera. "Show me."

She turned on the camera and showed him her pictures of the tunnel. The camera was quirking out again. The flash glare had blanched white the interior of the tunnel. The vines and roots and coiled wire were thin dark arabesques, but also there were shapes inside, trapped shapes if you wanted to embellish the image. With some imagination, one could almost make out arms and legs.

"What are those things?" Kleat said.

"Ricochet. The flash bouncing off the mist. Maybe I'm wrong about the wire. It looks like vines." Or tendons.

But his curiosity was piqued. "And what about these?" he pounced, as she scrolled through the terracotta warrior series. This was what Duncan had been hoping to hide.

"Statues." She shrugged. The stone eyes stared out from the display.

"There must be fifty of them."

"I didn't count."

"Where is this gate?"

"There's no way to describe it," Duncan said. "You saw what a jumble it is."

"Then you can lead me there tomorrow," Kleat said. "But first thing, we're going to do a line sweep of the area down here. Those ACAVs are somewhere."

She started to object to his diktat. But Duncan was quicker. "Good," he agreed. "There's nothing left of today. It's getting dark. We need rest and food. We'll start fresh in the morning." Not a word more about the city, as if Kleat really might forget it.

The two men went to the hut. Before it got dark, Molly walked to the truck to grab a flashlight and another camera battery from her mule bag. Picture possibilities swarmed through her mind. There had to be a temple or a tree from which to shoot that giant reclining Buddha in its entirety, and she wanted to line up three particular spires so they took the eye to a vanishing point. And there were those sweethearts' names in the forest, so tender, so terribly mortal, the letters deformed by the years.

She was zipping shut the mule bag when Samnang returned through the dusk. He went straight to the ledge with the looted ceramics and bronze and jade bowls, and obviously this was the first he'd seen them. He approached the brothers, crouching by the fire. From the truck, she could hear him chastising them. One of the brothers rose and shouted back, shaking his rifle. Another flicked a burning twig at him. *Bad luck children*, she thought.

She joined Kleat and Duncan in the hut.

"A regular civil war out there," Kleat said. The Khmers' arguing seemed to please him. At last Samnang disengaged and hobbled off into the forest again.

Someone had put a box of MREs inside for them. Molly sorted through the packets, calling out the names of meals. She made her own selection and slit the thick plastic with her Swiss Army knife. People complained about the meals, but she'd developed a taste for them while covering a crew of hotshots one fiery season in the San Juan range.

While her chow mein heated in the bag, she gazed out at the darkening trees, unwinding for the first time in a month. After the muggy central lowlands, the forest felt cool and restoring. Even so, sweat beaded her forehead. She wiped at it.

Soon, inevitably, Kleat and Duncan began arguing. There was no excuse for it. The evening was quiet except for animal noises, and each of the men was occupied, Duncan with his sketch pad and Kleat cleaning his pistol. And it was the same argument they'd had that morning. The only difference was that now they had real artifacts to fuel their positions. They were no longer talking about the hypothetical. Duncan had found a city. Kleat had found war relics.

"We have to retreat," Duncan said. "First thing in the morning, before anything more gets destroyed or pillaged, we need to pack up and leave. We're not prepared for this. The city needs protection. We have to get this right."

Kleat rejected it with a grunt. "Not going to happen."

Molly didn't know what to say. She felt safe in here. She felt found. And yet Duncan was inviting the world in before they even had their foothold.

"But we could lose everything," she said, trying to reason with him. Once word of the find spread, the eight-hundred-pound gorillas—the *Smithsonian*s and *National Geographic*s and universities and celebrity professors and best-selling authors and staff photographers—would descend on the place. She would get cut out, and so would Duncan. That was how it worked.

Kleat picked up the theme. "This is what I've been saying. We're here. It's ours." He dripped solvent onto a patch and pumped the rod down the barrel.

"We'll come back again," Duncan said, "but on our terms, not theirs." He gestured at the brothers. "We can get them to drive us down to one of the towns, and bring us back with supplies to last us through the next six months. That gives us the monsoon."

"And what makes you think they'll keep the big secret down in town?" said Kleat.

"They won't. That's a given. They're human. They're poor. We're in a race against time. Which makes you, Molly, the most important one of us. Everything depends on you. You can document the city before the jackals pick it clean. It's not just these guys. Once the news breaks, the Cambodian army and government will step in. That's when the real looting begins. You're our witness to all the greatness the way it is. It means staying through the rains, though. I'd send the drivers away before the river swelled. After that, we'd be shut inside, alone."

"Yes," she answered him, though he hadn't asked

the question. Yes, she wanted to be here. Shut inside. Alone.

"Get all the snapshots you want," Kleat said, "while we search for the men. They come first. There's not going to be any mission creep here. We came for the bones, not a city. We can beat the rains. Once I have the bones, this pile of rocks is all yours. You two can stay until kingdom come, I don't care." He started assembling the pistol.

"We can spend the next few days preparing," said Duncan. "And the next six months exploring."

"You and your city," Kleat said. He fit the spring onto the barrel. "What about the men?"

"If they're here, we'll find them."

"There's no if. They're here. And we're here. And we're staying."

Molly dabbed at the sweat trickling down her temples. Was she getting sick?

Now was her turn to try reasoning with Kleat. "What if we can't find them before the rain comes? Duncan has a point. It's the difference between having a few days to search or having six months."

"I need this." For a moment Kleat sounded desperate. "Before it's too late."

"I don't understand."

"The captain will come, or someone like him," Kleat said. "Once they hear it's us up here, they'll come to take it over. The river won't stop them, they'll fly right over it and banish us again. And that's not happening. They had their chance."

"Their chance?"

"These bones belong to me," Kleat declared. He fit the barrel into the frame with a metallic *click-clack*.

Molly and Duncan exchanged a look. The bones belonged to him? "John," Duncan said quietly. "That's not right. What about your talk of honor?"

"One buys the other," Kleat said. "These dead buy my dead. It's the only way I'll ever find my brother."

Molly remembered Luke laughing—barking like a monkey—at the claim that Kleat had a brother.

"That's why you're here?" said Duncan.

"The captain sent us off like traitors. Here's their wake-up call. Every year, the missing die a little more. Wives remarry. Children grow up and forget. New wars eclipse the old ones. Soon it will be too late."

"What do you think the captain and his people are doing in the dirt and mud and sun?" said Duncan. "Searching for the lost ones."

"They need to search harder, then. With the bones to shame them, I can make America sit up and listen. That's why you're important," he said to Molly. "You and your newspapers. Shame them. Destroy the old rule. We need fresh blood. New direction. My brother is out there somewhere, and one way or another I'm going to take him home."

The fire crackled outside. No one spoke for a minute.

Finally, Duncan said, "I'm sorry it's come to this, Molly. I'm trying to think of a middle way. But nothing's coming to me. It seems we have to choose between the bones and the city, and I know where I stand. And we know where John stands. Bu there are three of us."

He looked to Molly for the deciding vote, and she

made a face. "What can I say?" She was genuinely at a loss. Kleat had all but persuaded her, and yet the city needed her. "You both have strong arguments." She was about to ask if there was really no compromise to be made, but Kleat spoke up.

"No need to fret over it," he said. He clapped the magazine into the grip and chambered a round. He looked at his pistol, then at them.

"Are you threatening us?" Molly asked.

"Please," he said. "It's just that sometimes we get carried away with this democracy thing. And we shouldn't."

19.

According to her watch next morning, she rose at 9 A.M. the previous morning. It was darker than nine, though. *Six,* she thought, and hurried from her tent.

Gray rags of fog drifted in the mist, as if the morning could not make up its mind which way to blind her. She had her bearings, though. In less than five minutes she found Samnang's bright orange fire and the men all gathered.

She feared that Kleat and Duncan were battling for the brothers' loyalties, the one to stay, the other to leave. But as she quickly learned, the brothers had their own loyalties to attend to. They wanted more money.

"Otherwise, they're leaving without us," Duncan said. He was good-natured about it. "It makes sense. Why stick around? They scored a few thousand dollars' worth of pots, and as far as they're concerned, the city belongs to them. They're bringing some friends back with them."

"What about leaving *with* us?" Molly asked.

"More money."

"Pirates," Kleat fumed.

"We knew that coming in," said Duncan.

"They'd strand us?" Molly looked around. Vin kept his eyes on the ground. The other two brothers held their chins high and their rifles prominent.

The mist was churning. The forest breathed.

Samnang brought her a coffee. "Sugar?" he asked.

"No, Samnang." It was all spoiled. They needed food to stay. Blankets. A generator to recharge her batteries. Umbrellas. More malaria pills. A toothbrush. They needed solitude.

"This is your doing," Kleat said to Duncan.

"It does me no good," Duncan said. "They've got us."

"How much?" said Molly.

"Another five hundred for the ride out. Five thousand to stay through tomorrow. They're not stupid. They keep talking about the typhoon and the river."

"I only have two hundred," Molly said.

"I'm out," said Duncan. What had they been thinking, supplies for six months?

"The statues," said Kleat.

"What?"

"Show them on your camera. The terra-cotta warriors."

"No," said Duncan. "Don't."

Samnang squatted by the fire and blew on it with pursed lips. He had breath like kerosene. The fire leaped.

"They're worth hundreds of thousands," Kleat said. "Tell them you'll show them the location. They'll deal."

"We can walk out of here on foot," Duncan said. The mist was drawing away. Trees appeared around them.

"Show them," Kleat told Molly.

She noticed Samnang watching her through the fire. Was there a right and a wrong to this? She was scared. They were in the middle of nowhere. "No," she decided.

Kleat turned to the brothers. "Statues," he said in English. He pointed up at the city. "Understand? Big money. Statues." They frowned at him.

Tails of fog flickered off through the branches. The truck stood over there, and the Land Cruiser. Molly glanced up. Her mouth fell open.

There seemed no way they could have missed such a thing yesterday.

Eyes fixed to the canopy that was their false sky, she backed away from it.

"Molly?" said Duncan. Then he saw it, too, hidden in plain sight. Kleat swore with surprise. The brothers crouched and raised their rifles.

The rusting hulk of a vehicle hung in a spur of limbs, like a Lost Dutchman, beached in the air. One long metal tread had broken and dangled from its belly. She lifted her camera and, on the flank, in plain view, a faint insignia still showed: a black horse rearing.

20.

The revelation—the relic of the Blackhorse patrol—unplugged them from their wrangling. You could not call what followed a peace. They did not reconcile so much as disengage. It was spontaneous. No one willed it. They simply forgot one another, at least for a time.

They drifted apart, staring up at the trapped war machine, struggling to make sense of it. Sixty feet up, the vehicle looked stranded by some mythical flood, but it was the forest that had lifted it.

"Impossible," Kleat said. "That's eleven tons or more."

Yet there it hung in the crook of massive branches. The helmet and cartridges had fallen from it. No one had bothered to look up. Who would have thought such a thing could happen?

Kleat paced beneath like a starving man eyeing an apple, alternately quiet and then stringing out thoughts for anyone to hear. "The first time the Vietnamese saw an APC, they called it a green dragon," he told anyone who cared to listen. "The army used them for amphibious taxis. M-113s. Armored personnel carriers. The cavalry turned them into gunships on tracks. ACAVs. 'Tracks,' the troops called them. They were fast and mean. There was usually a crew of five. They'd load them full of ammunition and go hunting in columns."

He went on about its armament, travel range, and the thickness—or thinness—of its armored skin. "They were death traps if you hit a mine or caught a rocket." Molly quit listening. She could not get over the power of the trees. Sixty feet, six stories high, in thirty years. Eleven tons.

Duncan, the dedicated scientist, went to one of the terraces and opened his steel briefcase to take notes and sketch on his pad.

The three brothers retired to the staircase in a smudge of cigarette smoke, stricken with superstition or just discussing the possible profit to be made. The market in American bones from the Vietnam era was not something the DOD talked about, Molly had learned, but they paid well for the real thing.

Samnang alone did not seem awestruck. He had unwittingly made their fire under the dead vehicle and now began shifting it to a more suitable place. A few at a time, he carried the logs with their smoldering tips to the base of a broad, flat terrace and blew the flames back to life.

Molly noticed him. His simple act declared acceptance. Everything was changed, and yet nothing. For all their differences, they were staying. He had grasped that fact. They needed a center. The fire was that, an anchor for their camp.

"This is only one of them," Kleat said. "We're looking for nine men, though. There has to be a second track somewhere."

The canopy didn't seem to be hiding any more of them. Molly looked up among the ganglia of limbs and vines, and this appeared to be the forest's sole catch.

She stood back and faced it as if facing the Sphinx. That's how it seemed, like a beast in the middle of the desert. A riddle in metal skin. They had come for bones and found a fortress. They had looked in the treetops and found a chariot. What did one have to do with the other? Some hidden hand had sewn them together, but why?

She drew out her camera and telephoto lens and sighted through the long barrel. The ACAV leaped at her. Tipped slightly downward and canting to its right, it hung up there with its machine gun aimed straight at her. She took the shot and stepped to the side, out of the line of fire.

Meandering, angling for the best shots, she ransacked the track with her high-tech spyglass. The details bounded out at her. A ramp at the rear flapped open like a drawbridge. Beside the neatly stenciled U.S. ARMY, graffiti vowed maximum savagery. There was another gun shield behind the main turret, but this one lacked a barrel in the slot.

A man was watching her from the roof of the vehicle.

It didn't register in the first instant.

She saw him, but didn't see him.

Her mind rationalized the face as a knot of wood, or a distant statue. His eyes were right on her, and she accepted them as bulbs on a limb, or openings in the leaves.

But then his nostrils moved, nothing else, just the center of his watching face, and she realized he was taking her scent.

"Christ," she said.

Her hand jerked. The camera moved, but not before she hit the shutter release. In or out of focus, she didn't know. She lifted the camera back to her eye, searching, zooming, not certain she wanted to see him again.

Duncan was at her side in moments.

Gone, he was gone. Her hands were shaking, next to worthless for holding the telephoto steady.

Kleat came over.

"A man," she said. "I saw him, his face, up there."

"Bullshit." But Kleat's gun appeared. He held it in a two-handed grip, half raised.

"See for yourself." She fiddled with the display. There was the face, or almost a face.

"You got one," Duncan congratulated her. "Too bad he moved."

"One what?"

"A gibbon, it looks like. A pileated gibbon. They're all but extinct east of the Mekong. The hill tribes loved them to death. Good meat, I hear."

Kleat holstered his gun. "A monkey," he said.

She stared at the lighted image. The focus was ragged. The turret details were perfectly sharp, but the face was a blur, barely there at all. It was charcoal gray and, granted, simian in some measure. But it wasn't quite the face she'd seen.

"Let me see," said Kleat. She passed him the camera, thinking he wanted to study the image. Instead he brought it to his eye like a marksman.

"You've done it again," he said after a minute.

"What?"

"First the pilot, now this." He handed her the camera. "That's a skull."

She steadied the camera. There the sloped breastplate, a fading white army star, up higher the snout of the machine gun, and the turret—empty now where the face had been. And behind that, all but hidden along the upper shell, she saw the head, tucked within the shadows, unmoving.

Hard and glossy, it rested on a stubby metal pole. It looked freshly plucked from the battlefield. Through her lens, the eyes gazed down. Kleat took the camera.

"The Vietnamese must have found them," Kleat said. "Or the fucking KR. Those poor guys. There could be more of them inside." The idea quickened in him. "Someone's got to go up there."

"That will be a trick," Duncan said.

"Get one of the boys to do it."

"They'll never go," Duncan said. "Especially with a dead man up there."

"Bargain with them."

"Don't force this, John. I keep telling you, part of them still lives in the tenth century, with curses and evil eyes and flying spirits. The locals give their babies charms to protect them. They stack firewood against the door to keep out the dead. You wouldn't believe some of the stories."

Kleat wheeled around and walked quickly to the brothers. For a moment, Molly didn't miss her camera. Then she realized his game.

"He's showing them the statues," she told Duncan.

They hurried after Kleat, but the damage was done. They were holding her camera and smearing the display with their fingertips. They were excited.

"What have you done?" said Duncan.

"I just gave you and me the world," Kleat said. "Now talk to them. Get whatever you want out of it, all the supplies in the world, just as long as you get us into that track."

"Forget it."

"Sam, get over here," Kleat said. "You tell them. The place is huge. They could search for days and never find these statues. And they don't have days. The typhoon's coming. We know where the statues are. I need someone to run a rope up to that vehicle. That's for starters. They're businessmen. Let's do business."

Samnang relayed the message. Doc, the eldest brother with the full *sak*—the suns and flames and lines and dots from his toes to his throat—glanced up at the ACAV and said, "*Tê.*" No way.

"Come on," Kleat said in English. He pointed at the camera display. "You want these? We'll show you where they are. One of you street heroes, come on. All you have to do is climb up. Tell them, they don't even have to go inside. All we need is a rope to it. We'll take it from there."

Doc said something. Samnang said, "They want your gun."

"My gun?"

"They are saying that. The statues and your Glock."

"Why? We're already outgunned, three to one."

Outgunned? thought Molly.

"What does it matter?" said Duncan. "If the bones are there, you get what you want."

"And if they're not? Tell them no statues until we get inside the track," Kleat said. "Tell them."

"They understand," said Samnang.

Doc spoke. Vin handed the camera to them. Duncan and Samnang exchanged a wary look.

"Here's your camera. They're requesting to look at your gun. An exchange."

"The hell." Kleat's voice flattened out. A vein appeared on his scalp.

Molly took her camera.

"They want me to hand it to them?"

"Just do it," Duncan said.

"You know what they're doing," said Kleat.

"Not necessarily, John. Keep calm."

"They're pirates."

"Don't raise your voice, John."

He was going to pull his gun on them, Molly realized with sudden alarm. They were baiting him to do it. They were waiting for him. Their yellow eyes stared off into the distance. They toked their cigarettes like Marlboro men. But their fingers had shifted on their rifles. They were getting the weight of their weapons, the arc of their descent, the timing, the targets. The signs were all there.

She could almost picture herself lying among the dead.

"I'll go," she said suddenly.

Her voice startled them.

Kleat narrowed his eyes, suspicious of everyone now. "Up there?"

"You don't understand." She smiled large and stepped between the men. "I'm good at this. It's one of the hats I wear. I hang off rocks for a living. Mountain photography. Calendars and magazines. I'm not the greatest climber in the world, but I can manage a tree."

"No," said Duncan.

She smiled at him. "Baby steps," she said.

She took over, chattering brightly, getting them distracted. Samnang began relaying her decision to the brothers. Vin's eyes grew big. She reached for him and brought him down into their midst, rifle and all, disarming them one at a time.

"I'll need a rope," she said. "Do you have a rope?"

Samnang droned on softly. Vin nodded his head and started for the truck.

"And you," she said to Kleat. "Give me your gun."

Kleat backed away from her. "Now you?"

"I'm not going up there without some protection. Who knows what's living in there?"

"Forget it."

"You want me to fix a rope? That's my price. A loaner."

"I'll watch your back."

She held out her hand. "Right now." She added quietly, "You son of a bitch."

Samnang halted his translating.

She could see Kleat's gears turning. He could refuse her. But she was his only hope, and he knew it. They were locked on to his every move, and his one chance at keeping his gun was to give it away. She would take it out of the brothers' reach as well as his . . . for the time being. He handed her his Glock.

"Is the safety on?" she asked, looking at both sides of the gun.

"It's a Glock," he said.

"That's what everyone keeps saying."

"It's all internal," he said. "Don't worry about it."

She tucked the gun into the back of her waist, out of sight, out of mind.

The brothers' hands relaxed on their rifles, just as she'd hoped. "Keep this for me," she said to Duncan, and gave him her camera.

He laid one hand on top of hers, and she was shaking. His touch steadied her. He took the camera. "You want me to get a picture of you?" he asked.

That was a first. None of her subjects had ever bothered to ask if she wanted a record of herself.

21.

Vin returned with a coil of frayed, greasy brown Perlon. Molly walked to the tree and everyone followed. She turned it into a high-wire act, something to lift them from the morning of threats.

Lodged in the middle branches, the ACAV looked like a strange, small fish caught in talons of coral. She circled the tree, running her palms over the tan and white bark. "This will do."

She shook the coil loose and, without looking, tied a bowline around her waist. She shifted the knot around to the small of her back so the rope would trail behind, not between her legs. She wouldn't need it for anything until she got to the vehicle. The brothers squatted down to watch through a cloud of fresh smoke. *Razzle-dazzle 'em,* she thought.

She shucked her shoes and socks and placed them neatly by the tree. The bare feet were for extra grip, but also a bit of theater. Patting the dewlap folds of wood, she hopped up onto a massive root. "Feed me the rope," she said. "Make sure there aren't any knots." Duncan stepped forward. She started off.

The climbing went quickly. The men grew smaller, their heads tipped back, mouths open. Partway up, double-checking her grip, she faked a slip. That got an audible grunt from the audience. "No problem." She pretended to grapple her way past a perilous crux.

It was easy. The tree offered itself to her in phases, its knots and boles and branches forming a natural ladder. A whole metropolis appeared in the canopy, with limbs and looping vine bridges interlocking the great towers of trees.

It felt good to open her wings, good to get away from the men. Things seemed much saner up here. It occurred to her that she could keep on climbing. She could vanish into the upper branches and outwait the gunslingers.

The thought grew into a temptation. Untie from the rope and she could enter the canopy and they'd never get her back. The place abounded with food and niches for shelter. Nuts and mangos and other exotic fruits nestled like Christmas ornaments.

"Molly." Her name, so faint. Like leaves rustling.

The forest was so beautiful, and when she glanced down, her holds had withdrawn into the tree. Pathways led off along the great branches. She felt drugged.

The forest was her answer, she comprehended. But it went beyond that. The message built like a heat. All she had to do was take to the trees. Forget the men, they were deceivers. Forget the rains, they would pass. Forget the past. The forest would provide.

The ACAV broke her fantasy of dancing off into the heights.

More quickly than she'd expected, its squared metal corners and sprockets and pipes and bulldozer tread emerged around the corner. Her temptation snapped. This brute thing—not escape—was what she'd come for.

The metal ramp at the back invited her like a sturdy porch. One step and she would be inside.

"Moll-lee." The rope tugged at her waist. It was Duncan, invisible beneath the foliage. He called again, more insistent this time.

She took a breath. It was like pulling herself from a dream. "I'm good," she shouted down.

She peered at the inside of the thing. An open hatch on top helped illuminate the recesses. Stenciled warnings read DANGER—MONOXIDE GAS. She sniffed the air, and there was only the slight odor of fuel and oil and fertilizer. Dung, she realized. Animal dung. The green dragon had become a nest for forest creatures.

"I'm going in," she called down.

"What?"

She pulled up some slack and made the small leap, landing lightly, barefoot, on the cool metal. The wedged vehicle didn't shift an inch.

The rope tugged again, Duncan fretting.

"I'm off," she shouted, and realized that the climbing lingo might confuse him. "I'm in. I'm up." She untied from the rope and knotted it to an eyebolt on the back of the ACAV. "Come on up. The rope's anchored."

Branches had infiltrated through the open cupola, and white orchids with red pistils grew here. Butterflies spiraled above the war machine, their wings bright blue and the size of her hand. Death and life. She wanted her camera.

She peeked on top, and the head was jammed onto an exhaust pipe. Its eyes and face were aimed forward, and she was grateful for that. Let the others deal with it.

As it turned out, once she'd hung the rope straight down from the ACAV, the line was too greasy and thin for them to ascend. Kleat wrapped it around his fists and hauled himself up a few feet, and the rope creaked, but that was as high as he could get. Duncan had no more luck. The brothers wanted nothing to do with it. Without a climber's Jumars to grip it, the rope was only good for a one-way ride, down.

"You've done your job," Duncan called up to her. "Come down."

"Wait," Kleat shouted. "What about the bones?"

"It's too dark to see," she called out.

"We'll send up a flashlight," he said. "And a bag for the bones."

That was the part she'd been hoping to avoid. "My camera," she shouted down on a whim. Through it she could filter any horrors before having to touch them.

"What?"

"I want my camera. And some water. And a PowerBar."

The burlap sack came to about fifteen pounds. She pulled it up hand over hand, and someone, Duncan, no doubt, had included the bag of M&M's. There were two more burlap sacks stuffed inside. Kleat was expecting a lot of bones.

She sat on the edge of the ramp with her back to the ACAV, her bare feet swinging, and ate the PowerBar and candy and drank the water. Then she stood and turned on the flashlight and went to work inside.

22.

Over the next hour, Kleat called up periodically, impatient. "What's keeping you?" she heard his tiny voice say. "Are they all there?"

Duncan only wanted to know if she was okay.

She didn't answer them. A ripple of thunder sounded in the far distance. That meant it was approaching noon. The monsoon was working up its nerve. Or else the typhoon was nearing. Would it announce itself or just open up on them?

She was thorough, exploring the deepest bay of the ACAV, poking with a stick where she was afraid of snakes. With each discovery, it became more obvious that the armored box held only questions. Their answers hid elsewhere.

She saved the head for last, climbing onto the top through the opening with the machine gun.

After an hour, there was no more to find.

She started to wrap the rope over one shoulder to descend, then had a thought. Untying the anchor knot, she threaded the end of the rope through the pistol's trigger guard, and retied the rope. Then, dangling the burlap sack from her belt, she backed off the ramp and rappelled to the ground.

As she descended from the canopy, she looked across to the top of the terraced walls and saw the city waiting for her. Her view lasted only a few feet, then she sank lower into the terminus.

Kleat and Duncan waited for her at the bottom.

"Well?" said Kleat.

She opened the sack like Santa Claus and handed him the head. "You were wrong," she said.

Kleat held it at arm's length. "What the hell is this?"

"It's a trophy. They had it mounted on their exhaust pipe."

It was one of the terra-cotta warriors' heads, its neck a long, rounded plug with a hole at the bottom. The jade pebble eyes glared up at them. The painted circles had mostly washed away, but the expression was still ghastly.

"Is this some kind of joke?" Kleat said.

The brothers, watching from the fire, saw that the head was safely inhuman. They came over from the fire. Hunkered down by his water pot, Samnang saw it, too. He approached more slowly, his expression incredulous. "Those eyes," he said.

"You've seen them before?" Molly asked. He couldn't quit staring at them.

"Once," he said. "I can never forget."

"The soldiers must have brought the head down from the gate," Duncan said. "Like Molly said, a souvenir to show they'd been here. It means they were getting ready to leave. But for some reason, they never left."

"That's all you found?" Kleat said to Molly.

"No bones," she said. "It was mostly empty. There's a big machine gun, rusted solid. And these." She gave him a handful of rotted currency.

"GI scrip," said Kleat. "They didn't use dollars in the field."

"And these." She pulled out a set of maps in plastic.

Duncan took those. "Nice," he said. "Very nice. These could tell us where they were going and why they came here. And where we are."

"Do you think that's the end of it?" Kleat said. He tossed the currency away. "Funny money and a piece of pottery and some maps?"

"No." She had wanted the city for herself and Duncan. But for a little longer they were going to have to put up with Kleat's hunger and the brothers' ransacking. Somehow she and Duncan could turn this to their advantage, but it would come at a cost. The question was, how much of a cost? "We'll keep looking for the soldiers. That comes first." His departure came second.

Kleat held out his hand. "My gun." He hadn't forgotten.

She reached behind her. She planted her feet. She'd rehearsed it in her mind. He would go ballistic when she confessed, would maybe even hit her, but not if she could help it.

Without a word, she brought her fist around in a long arc. It wasn't a graceful boxer's roundhouse, and it wasn't very fast. His surprise was almost sad. His face turned slightly away. She landed against his ear. The shock of it ran up her arm bones.

Kleat dropped to the ground with a bellow. The terra-cotta head fell from his hands and rolled across the leaves.

The brothers fell silent, astonished. First she'd slapped him, now she'd brought him to his knees. It was so strange to them, the alpha-femme twist. It was strange to her.

"I didn't bring it down." She was breathing hard, wondering how it could have come to this.

Kleat looked at her. His blank expression was changing, the rage getting traction.

"I left it," she announced loudly. "Before someone got killed."

The worm veins surfaced. "Do you know what you've done to us?" he shouted at her.

Duncan came alive, thankfully. He stepped between them, pressing his back against Molly, forcing her back. He faced Kleat. "There," he said, "it's done. Not finished, just changed. I'm with Molly."

"You two." He spat at Duncan's feet. A drop of blood trickled from his ear. She hadn't meant to draw blood. She hoped his ear was okay.

"The gun was a crutch," Duncan said. "You were a threat to us all."

Off to one side, Doc picked up the head and was gawking at the jade eyes. His brothers gathered around him.

"You're going back up that rope," Kleat said.

"No, she's not," said Duncan. "There's nothing more in the ACAV for us. The soldiers went someplace else. We'll do what Molly said. We'll keep searching." He paused, with a glance at Doc. "And plundering."

He offered his hand to help Kleat stand, and of course Kleat pushed it away.

They ate a hurried lunch while the brothers rooted through their truck for sacks to carry relics. Molly could see the terra-cotta head resting on the front seat, a baleful passenger. Duncan studied the map she had brought down.

"You can still see traces of grease pencil," he said. "They went east at Snuol and kept on going. Who knows why? The fog of war. But the interesting thing isn't the map itself or where they thought they were or weren't. It's this little bit of marginalia."

He turned the map for Molly to see, and the old, creased plastic reflected the light. She had to separate one layer of reality from the other, the underlying contour lines and typeset names on the map from the red smudge marks on the plastic. There were four numbers beside a circle on a road.

" 'Oh-six, twenty-four,' " she read out loud. "Map coordinates?"

"It's a date, as good as an entry in a logbook. June twenty-four." She gave the map back to Duncan to give to Kleat. He was brooding over his meal, convinced they were now the Khmers' prisoners.

Duncan tried to bring Kleat into it. "You said they went missing on June twenty-third. This means that a day later they were still trying to find their way."

"But to where?" she asked.

"Not here," said Kleat. "That's certain. They were under deadline."

"How do you know that?" asked Duncan.

"Because six days later the U.S. forces pulled out of

Cambodia. Nixon was under siege at home. The traitors at Kent State had started a firestorm."

She had wondered how he might get back at them.

"Those were American children who got shot there," Duncan said.

"Pawns," Kleat said.

"It's old history," she said. "You keep going backward."

"I'm dissecting an event. Establishing connections. And deceptions," said Kleat. "History is our clue. Kent State is the reason the Eleventh Cavalry men died here. While our troops were getting slaughtered in these jungles, the college spawn in their bell-bottoms and tie-dyed T-shirts were tying the hands of our president."

Duncan didn't rise to it. He let Kleat vent.

"Invading Cambodia was a masterstroke," Kleat said. "Then Kent State blew up and we had to give the hiding places and sanctuaries back to our enemy. June twenty-nine was the fallback date. That was the day the last American troops pulled out of Cambodia. All except for these men."

"I thought the motto was 'Never leave a man behind,' " Molly ventured.

"Within reason," Kleat said. "But the clock was ticking. This whole borderland was about to return to enemy control. These guys had two options. Keep driving around the countryside. Or hole up and pray. Their commanding officer chose to hole up. He made the choice. Whoever the bastard was, he as good as pulled the trigger on them."

23.

It was high noon, as best as she could tell inside the green bell jar of the canopy, when the expedition split into three teams. Kleat still seethed over the loss of his gun, but the Heng brothers treated Molly like a champion.

"Rambo," they said, still awed that a woman could hit like a man. For her reward, they paired her with Samnang and allowed her to keep her camera. Duncan was sent with the middle brother, So. Kleat went up the stairs watched over by Doc and Vin.

Doc made clear that their first priority was to locate the terra-cotta guardians at the back gate. But if they happened to find American bones along the way, that was fine, too. There was no more strike talk. For now, the issue of leaving was moot, and a few extra dollars paled beside the prospect of priceless relics.

Carrying burlap sacks and Molly's emptied-out mule bag, and even bunches of little blue plastic bags like the kind in a deli, the searchers climbed toward the city. Molly and Samnang were quickly left behind. They had the most freedom, she realized. The brothers expected little or nothing from an old man with one leg.

Every so often, she sat down "to enjoy the view" or "rest my knees."

Samnang was not fooled. "You're a dangerous woman," he teased her. "You make us believe we're stronger than we are."

"I'm serious," she said. "Climbing that tree wiped me out."

"Yes, and I have two good legs," he said, smiling.

From halfway up the stairs, their camp looked borrowed from the forest. The green hut was already surrounded by the tiptoe of grass. Their fire lay banked under gray ashes.

They heard Kleat arguing, high above them. One of the brothers, probably Doc, snapped back at him. The argument died away.

"Have I done the wrong thing?" she wondered out loud. Samnang knew what she meant. By disarming Kleat, she had made them defenseless. They were at the mercy of the brothers and the typhoon and fate now.

"You took the fangs from a serpent, and left him alive. It is up to him now, what he does with his poison. As for the others, their hearts are still uncertain."

"The brothers treat you badly."

"They blame me for their miseries," Samnang said. "That is natural. I survived, you see. Their parents did not. They have poison in them, too. We must wait for them to decide what they will do with it."

It was the closest he'd ever come to discussing the Pol Pot years with her. Molly waited for him to volunteer more, but Samnang added nothing. She could have asked him, but told herself it didn't matter who he had been, only who he had become, this gentle old pilgrim.

They reached the top of the stairs and found that the others were long gone. They started in among the ruins, strolling slowly, and it reminded her of their mornings, before the dawn, at the crash site. She thought of the pilot, and then of the Blackhorse soldiers.

"They could have gone anywhere," she said.

Samnang glanced at the ground. "Mr. O'Brian went this way with the middle boy," he said. "Mr. Kleat went through there with the other children." Children, he called them.

"The missing soldiers, I meant. Thirty years have passed."

"We have a saying, 'Don't despair on the winding river,'" Samnang said. "Patience. They will reveal themselves to us."

They went straight, following a once orderly avenue between the spires and temples and palaces. The tiles were split apart by roots and subterranean forces. The forest blocked their view. Rounding the flanks of monstrous banyan trees, they saw more trees, more buildings. Eliminate the trees, restore the order, and the city would still have been as complicated as a perfume. The canals and side streets and winding avenue formed a puzzle. If the architects had not designed it as a labyrinth, the city had accumulated a labyrinth within it. As they worked deeper into the ruins, Samnang began braiding grass into knots and bending saplings into Os to mark their path. That made her feel less stupid. She was not the only one feeling overwhelmed in here.

It was a kingdom of eyes, the enormous heads beholding their trespass. Molly tried to imagine the Blackhorse soldiers drifting through the ruins with her same hushed wonder, their rifles at the ready. There were a thousand hiding places in here, and she realized that the soldiers would not have left their bones in plain view. They were jungle fighters. They would have squirreled themselves away into the most unknowable spots, burying themselves wherever the enemy might overlook them. What chance did an untrained civilian have of finding them a generation later?

They came to a quadrangle in the center of the city. She and Samnang decided it had to be the center. Four avenues met here at a broad square, or park, mobbed with grass and trees.

In the middle of it all, dominating the city, stood a tower. It was a strange hybrid of a structure, both round and square. It had a dozen angular sides and as many levels, though they were really only one level ascending in a single, steady, candy-cane spiral. A staircase corkscrewed around the exterior, and doorways led off that. The tower rose into the trees. Parrots sailed back and forth to its upper doors.

Like in the canyon she and Duncan had found yesterday, its walls were carved with bas-relief. The tower was a giant storybook. Samnang recognized some of the images, here and there pausing to press his palms together and bend his head. He explained what he could, the scenes from the Bhagavad Gita and the stages—like the Stations of the Cross—of the Buddha's enlightenment.

"This goes back to the beginning of my people,"

he said. "But so much of it escapes me. The kings, the alphabet, the battles, I should know them. I'm Khmer. I do know them. Here." He touched his heart. "But not here." His head. "This comes from before the Angkor, long before."

"Duncan thinks it could be two thousand years old," she said.

"Yes, Duncan," Samnang said. "He has made this his *spécialité.*"

"He said it might have been the model for Angkor Wat."

Samnang looked at her. "Angkor and this place, or the Sistine Chapel or Notre-Dame, they are expressions of an idea. Like the statues of Buddha, or Michelangelo's God with a white beard, magnificent attempts to imagine a face for what has no face."

"Have you been to the Sistine Chapel?" she asked, hoping he might offer more of his past.

"In another lifetime," he said.

She dropped it.

The green light kept dimming. Somewhere above their hemisphere of leaves and limbs, storm clouds were eclipsing a sun they could not see. Thunder rolled like a subway train.

There was a crack of rifle fire. One of the search parties had discovered the gate and the terra-cotta statues. The others would join them. "Should we go to them?" she asked.

"Are the statues something you want?"

"No. You saw the head. Those eyes. They're terrible."

"Then let us not suffer for their desire," Samnang said. "We can stay here, deaf to the world. Anyway, we will see their treasures in camp tonight."

They went on circling the base of the tower and came across a name. Carved in deep, square letters among the bas-relief it said C. K. WATTS. Underneath was a date: 8/20/70.

Molly looked up at the tower. The logic slid together. "From up there you could see the whole city," she said to Samnang. "I think that's where they went."

"Among the birds," said Samnang. "Certainly."

She ran her fingers over the incisions. According to the ACAV map, the lost souls of the Eleventh Cavalry had pulled into the fortress on or around June 24. If the graffiti's date was right, the soldiers had languished here, alive, another seven weeks or more.

The idea moved her. They hadn't just burrowed into lairs to fight it out. They'd made their home here, and found time to roam among the ruins. One of them, at least, had passed beside the stories inscribed on this wall.

She looked to see if there was a special context for the name, and it was carved beneath a monstrous warrior, one of Duncan's wrathful deities, with a tiger circling his legs. He wore a necklace of severed heads.

She snapped a picture of the name and the demon slayer. She doubted C. K. Watts ever knew this was a ritual slayer of ignorance. But what irony, an American kid with a gun and a knife, off course and vulnerable, unconsciously appealing for wisdom. More likely he'd been taken with the image's ferocity.

"That makes four of them," she said. "Him, plus the three dog tags."

The tower reached into the middle canopy. The stairs stretched up and around, offering access to scores of gaping doorways. There would be a hundred and four of them, she remembered. Maybe she was getting the hang of the place after all.

"I think this will be of interest to Mr. O'Brian and Mr. Kleat," Samnang said. "They will want to be here."

She promised to wait at the base of the tower while Samnang went to find the others. He disappeared into a thicket of spires and trees in the direction of the rifle shot.

Her watch read 10 A.M. yesterday. The second hand crept. She tried to restrain herself. With her macro lens, she stalked a small white gecko with red spots.

But as the everlasting seconds dragged by, she chafed. The stairs lay right here before her. And the brothers might have shanghaied Samnang to carry down their plunder. Even if they released Kleat and Duncan to explore the tower, another hour or two could pass before they arrived. The afternoon was marching on. The tower might go unexplored until tomorrow. And tomorrow was a toss of the dice. It was senseless to wait.

24.

She took the winding staircase slowly.

The tower held answers, she was certain of it. Once it would have commanded a view of the entire city, maybe even of the far plains to the west, a man-made mountain on top of a mountain. Even with the encroaching forest, the tower was still the ultimate high ground. It would have given the soldiers a vertical fortress, with a honeycomb of doorways to watch for their enemies.

The deep, wide steps spiraled in a clockwise direction. When she was a kid, her stepparents had taken her to Washington, D.C., and she still remembered the marble steps eroded by millions of feet passing up and down. Add to that twenty centuries of rainfall and you had these stairs. The inner half of the steps had melted into a single sluice for running water. It forced her to walk along the outer edge where the steps wobbled under her weight, and a slip could be deadly. But she felt only a growing sense of authority.

On her left, always her left, the city unwound its

maze, a great crossroads with the tower at its center. She spied more canals and lanes and corridors veining off without landmarks that she could see. Even from this height, satellite pyramids looked identical. The place seemed built to be lost in.

On her right, the doorways yawned like ornate caves. She glimpsed statues and carvings inside, and it was entirely possible the rooms held more Eleventh Cavalry relics and graffiti. Their discovery would have to wait for another day. She wanted to see what lay at the top.

Thunder rolled through the heavens. Vines hung like slow-motion rain. She came to a summit deck, and it held a crowning structure. Molly hesitated outside the entrance, a final door.

The statue of a female lay in rubble to one side. Her twin, a half-naked Amazon with breasts as round as bowling balls, guarded the other side of the entrance with a stone sword, its point resting between her feet. Standing head and shoulders above Molly, the sentinel was voluptuous and beautiful, a change from the bestial glare of the warrior statues. She passed on the photo for now. It needed Duncan or Samnang for human scale. Not Kleat. When it came time to write the account, she didn't want to have to explain him.

From this height, the faces carved on distant spires seemed to be lowering their eyes before the tower. She peered down from the edge for the others. She could hear their voices in the forest; they were speaking her name. But the plaza was empty. Her gain, she reckoned. For a few minutes more, the tower room belonged to her.

She stepped across the stone doorsill, and the room

was richly lighted inside. The roof had a rectangular opening so large she thought it must have been built as an observatory. There were no sun or stars to see now, only the green jacket of the canopy. Leaves formed a thick, moldering carpet from one wall to the other. It smelled, not unpleasantly, like a compost pile.

Buddhas lined the far wall, or what was left of them. Side by side, each sat tucked within his own niche. She counted them: thirteen. The skylight had been built to illuminate them. At one time, the display must have been awesome.

The centuries had not been kind, however. The far end of the statue wall had collapsed into rubble. The faces were chewed down to raw stone. At least their lower bodies had been spared the ravages of time. Their long, elegant fingers twisted in ritual shapes, like gang members' hand signals. She imagined princes and monks meditating here, issuing prayers up through the aperture, to the heavens. Long ago, this must have been a transit station to the sacred.

After a minute, she pulled her eyes from the Buddhas, and remnants of the Eleventh Cavalry lay all around her in the shadows to the sides and rear. She turned in place, discovering a tangle of green web gear with worn grommets, and a rotting boot, and a snaking length of unspent machine-gun bullets. Mounds and heaps of things lined the wall. The soldiers—some of them, anyway—had retreated to this room.

She treated it like a crime scene, touching nothing, documenting everything with her camera, memorizing the line of her motions. She planted her feet as meticulously as a tai chi artist.

Using her telephoto, she reached across the leaves to a heap of emptied metal ammunition boxes with hinged lids. Two lay on their sides, one stood upright, half filled with old water. A black-and-white dragonfly hovered there, and that was a photo.

She found—but did not touch—a toothbrush with the bristles mashed wide from overuse. Some boy's mother had taught him well. Dental hygiene right up to cause of death.

Stacked boxes had rotted and collapsed, avalanching their contents out from the walls. There was a flashlight with a red lens, like something out of *Dick Tracy*. A flak jacket was propped up and empty. A broken M-16 rifle lay to one side. A tendril had grown up the barrel and out through the jammed chamber. A small white flower hung like a shell in mid-ejection.

It was as if the soldiers had shed themselves here.

As her eyes adjusted to the light, the room became more defined. The Buddhas had been defaced, not by the elements, but by gunfire. The collapsed section had been dynamited or hit by a rocket.

Bullets—hundreds of them—scarred the statue wall in long, slashing bursts. She tried to piece together their desperate firefight. Had the enemy dropped down through the roof? Or had they come running through the door and sprayed the Americans crouching beneath the Buddhas?

The place should have been heaped with bones. But there were none that she could see. Had they been scattered by animals, or had the victors carted them out and pitched them off the tower? Had she passed bits and pieces of them on her ascent without knowing it? Part of her didn't want to find them. She fastened on the idea of them rising up through the hole in the roof, body and spirit, rescued on their Judgment Day.

She passed over the hands twice before recognizing them.

There were two of them beneath a scorch mark in one corner, the bones gloved in dried black skin.

She pulled the image closer with her telephoto, not willing to cross over to them. To the side, were those more bones? Sticks, she saw, charred firewood. A cremation? But the pyre was too small. This was no bigger than Samnang's cool fire.

The hands had mummified over the years. Or been smoked by the fire. Someone had lopped them off at the wrists.

It came to her.

Cannibalism.

Trapped, battered by fear, out of food, they must have taken to eating their comrades.

A laugh—a yap—cracked through the room. It fell upon her, Luke's animal laugh. But it wasn't Luke up there. Molly looked, and there were three of them this time, like the one she'd seen in the ACAV turret. While she prowled through the room, the gibbons had stolen up and perched along the skylight rim. They had black masks and gray arms. Her pulse slowed. She took a picture of them, just to regain control.

"Hey," she said. "Just looking."

One leaned forward. He opened his mouth. He bared his teeth. Were they going to attack? But his eyes stayed fixed on hers, and he seemed to be trying out her language. That made her more afraid than the bared teeth.

They were studying her, and she was alone.

Careful not to turn her back to them, Molly began retreating from the center of the room. Something gave a muffled crunch beneath the carpet of leaves. Nut shells within the mast? She moved her foot and whatever it was shifted under there. Bones, she thought. What did anthropologists call it? The midden. She was walking across the cannibals' scattered garbage.

The monkeys suddenly bolted away.

"What are you doing here, Molly?" It was Kleat's voice at the doorway. "Sam said you'd wait."

She exhaled softly. "I knew you were coming. I heard your voices."

"Our voices? I don't think so. The old cripple had us running to save you. We were too busy catching our breath to talk."

Then she'd heard birdsong, or trees creaking. Or monkeys discussing. No matter.

"We located another gateway," Kleat said. "With clay warriors, and rooms with pottery and jars. And a tunnel blocked with barbed wire. That makes three entrances, including the one Samnang said you found."

He stood in the doorway. Something about the room troubled him. It disrupted his bravado. He wouldn't come in.

"Where's Duncan?" she asked.

"Halfway up the stairs. Crawling. I've never seen such a fear of heights." Kleat would not cross the threshold. "You shouldn't have come here alone. You could have destroyed evidence."

Duncan appeared, and there was indeed dirt on his knees. The two men stood there, blocking the light. Did they need an invitation?

"They were here," she said.

Samnang arrived last. Edging between the two Americans, he caught sight of the ruined Buddhas, and his palms clapped together like magnets. He bowed his head solemnly.

Samnang's entrance seemed to break the spell. The other two stepped inside. Molly imagined Kleat would set upon the room like a wolf, but he moved tentatively, scarcely nibbling at the relics.

She watched what drew them. Kleat went for the rifle with the broken stock. Samnang gravitated to the wall holding the statues. Duncan vacillated. He moved along the edges. He lifted the web gear and dropped it, and ran his fingers along the foot of one damaged Buddha, and shook his head sadly. Then he found the husk of a radio set propped against one wall, and that occupied him.

Molly remained near the center, surrounded by their motion, shooting them making their discoveries, waiting.

The radio was partially disassembled. Duncan flipped switches on and off and the thing was dead, of course.

"There are two hands," she said, pointing at the fire ring.

"Hands?" said Kleat. He took the pieces of rifle with him to the corner. He nudged aside the sticks of firewood and laid one of the dried hands along his outstretched palm. It was small. Too small, she realized.

"Monkeys," Kleat said.

"Monkeys?"

"The men ran out of food."

Kleat glanced from the hand to her. "Did you think they were human? Don't tell me. Ghouls in camouflage."

"No."

Duncan returned to his tinkering. "Huh," he said and pulled out a transistor tube. He held it up to the light. "Look at that."

Duncan brought it over to Molly, and Kleat joined them. He heard the crunching sound underfoot. "What's that?" He pressed at the leaves with his boot.

Duncan held out his find. "It's a condom," he said. "And there's something inside."

It was in fact a condom stretched long over a short tube and knotted at the end. He tore off the knot and peeled down the sheath, baring a roll of papers torn from a pocket-size notebook. The pages were brittle, and he didn't try to force them open.

"It must have been a journal. Or a will." He studied the outside of the roll. "But the rain got in. The ink's run. It's spoiled."

"There are still some words," said Molly. "Maybe with better light—"

"What *is* this?" Kleat said again, rocking his weight over the leaves.

Bones breaking, she thought. Monkey or squirrel or parrot bones, whatever hungry men might take from the forest. Kleat worked his fingers under the carpet of leaves.

He lifted a long fragment to expose the red stone of the floor. They weren't bones, but cartridge shells.

Duncan pocketed the papers, and Molly helped clear more of the floor. Brass shells littered the floor.

"Now we know where the side guns on the ACAV went," Kleat said. "These are shells from an M-60. They must have pulled the big guns out of the tracks and brought them up here. Look at it all, like Armageddon in here."

Molly picked one of the cartridges from the floor, and a beetle crawled out. She dropped it.

"There's something more here," Duncan said. He ran his fingers along a wide black stripe.

The three of them rolled back more of the thick mat. A big serpentine line emerged, painted onto the floor with engine grease. To its side, another line appeared.

"It's an SOS," Duncan said. They didn't need to unpeel the whole thing. Stretching thirty feet from end to end, it lay directly beneath the skylight. They looked up at the forest ceiling.

"They must have chopped a hole in the canopy, or burned it open with fuel," Kleat said. "They were trying to signal for help."

"But who would see it?" said Molly.

"A passing helicopter. Spotter planes. Our pilot."

Like a child's prayer, Molly thought. The soldiers had died making wishes to the sky.

"It's coming together," said Kleat. "They made their last stand in the tower. You couldn't ask for a better field of fire. The enemy would have had to come up the stairs one at a time. But how long could nine men hold out? It must have been hand-to-hand combat in the end."

"I thought of that, too," said Duncan. "But then there should be bones all over the place."

"This is quite odd," Samnang said behind them. He had moved from the Buddhas to the doorway and was running his hands along the back wall. He walked over to them.

He stirred the shells with a stick, and a whole colony of beetles began scuttling around their feet.

"All of these come from American guns," Samnang said. "M-60, here, M-16, this one, and this."

Molly felt Kleat's eyes on her, and knew what he was thinking: KR. The old guerrilla was exposing himself.

"This is detonation cord for plastic explosive." Samnang held up a coil. "That explains the damage at the far end. C4 *plastique*. And these I dug from the wall."

Samnang opened his hand to show a half dozen lead slugs. "All from American guns. Also, you would think their fire would be directed at the door, yes? But the walls are smooth and untouched, you see. Only the wall of statues is scarred. They alone were targeted."

"What are you getting at?" Kleat said.

"I have looked," said Samnang, "and there is no sign of an enemy."

Kleat's voice dropped to a growl. "They were fighting for their lives."

"Perhaps," said Samnang. "But against whom?"

"Okay." Kleat mocked him. "Whom?"

Samnang let the mashed slugs fall from his palm. *"Âme damnée,"* he said. His French sounded like a song.

Kleat jerked. "What?" His voice thinned to a whisper. His hard-boiled expression crumpled. He stepped back as if the slugs were poisoned. Molly saw he was retreating from Samnang. Eyes round behind his thick lenses, he looked stricken.

Not certain what to make of Kleat's sudden affliction, Molly said, "Damned men?"

"Fallen from grace," Samnang said. He acted oblivious to Kleat's recoil. "It is only my conjecture. But what if the men turned against one another?"

"Bullshit," Kleat said. Molly wasn't sure what he was denouncing though, the guesswork or its author. Or something else. He was staring at Samnang.

"How then to interpret the knife?" Samnang asked.

Kleat blinked. "What knife?"

They followed Samnang to the wall of Buddhas. Molly had not spied it through her telephoto. You had to see it from the side, jammed to the hilt in a seam between the stone blocks, the handle protruding.

Samnang let them consider the knife. Up close, the Buddhas looked eaten by disease. The knife's presence was deliberate, like a judgment rendered, or a desecration.

"A K-Bar knife," Kleat said, his certainty returning. "That's how I interpret it."

"But why would anyone stab it into a stone wall?" said Molly. "Here of all places, this wall."

"How would I know?"

"It looks so angry. Like adding insult to injury."

"We're talking about a piece of stone," said Kleat. "A dead city."

"Molly's right," Duncan said. "It does look . . . excessive."

"Excessive," Kleat scoffed. "They were fighting for their lives."

"Samnang's got a point, though. The only damaged wall is this one. And see how the faces of the Buddhas were targeted? This knife didn't end up here by accident. Someone found a joint in the stone and hammered it in with all his strength. This looks less like a battle than a signature."

"What does it matter?" Kleat said. "A bunch of old statues."

He grabbed at the handle. He was arming himself, Molly realized. Let him have it. The knife would be a rusty old thing.

He pulled, but the wall held on. He braced his other hand against the stone to pull again. Just then a clap of thunder exploded directly above the canopy.

It was so close, Molly's knees buckled. She smelled ozone, a whiff of the upper stratosphere. The men's eyes went wide and white. They looked at each other.

The seconds passed, her ears ringing. More thunder rippled in the far distance. The sense of nature returned.

The knife and the sky had nothing to do with each other. It had been thundering since morning. Just the same, Kleat released the stubborn handle with disgust.

In the silence that followed, another sound descended to them, the hushing sound leaves make when they tremble. But it wasn't the leaves.

After a minute, water began dripping through the canopy.

The rain had finally come.

25.

They fled the tower slowly. Rain fell in rivulets from the canopy. Water raced down the furrow in the winding staircase, forcing them to the edge. Molly had the advantage with her climber's balance and her youth. Twice she caught Kleat when he slipped. For a few minutes, the dangers unified them.

The forest grew darker by ounces. The rain diminished. Samnang guided them through the city to the stairs that led to camp.

The brothers had already returned from the gate. The thatch hut and campfire waited below like a lighthouse in a deep harbor. By the time they reached ground level, Molly's cold sweat had returned.

It couldn't be malaria, she thought. She was on proquanil. Then again, she was on proquanil because the Cambodian strain of malaria had grown resistant to chloroquine. Maybe the bug had morphed again.

The brothers, by the fire, were in high spirits, their gold teeth flickering like sparks in the darkness, their tattoos glistening from the canopy's slow drip. Molly arrived at the hut to find two dry green ponchos spread as a floor. Vin bustled over with a cup of steaming black tea loaded with so much sugar it made her teeth ache. She thanked him.

Kleat arrived, his bronze skull as slick as a muscle car. He was wearing the flak jacket from the tower room. Now he could pretend to be bulletproof like the brothers. The superstitions were layering over them. He didn't bother to remove his boots. Molly scooted deeper into the hut to make room for him.

He thumped her knee. "We're saved," he said.

Molly tried to evade his good cheer. But it was hard not to feel some camaraderie. Two nights ago they'd been licking their wounds in a restaurant, banished and irrelevant. All that was changed. Fame and wealth and great dreams were almost within their grasp. It did feel like salvation. She had her camera in her lap. The display screen flickered with images of the strange, beautiful city.

Duncan came in from the darkness. "Have you looked in the truck? There must be ten heads in there. You've got to get a photo of it," he said to Molly. "It's like they've decapitated the city. The heads are always the first things to be plundered. They're portable. Collectors go wild for them. They move like lightning on the art market."

Samnang entered from the night, wordless, and crossed his legs. Raindrops clung to his white burr cut. Cutting a glance at him, Kleat looked confused and at the same time annoyed, like a man who has misplaced his keys.

"They must not do this," Samnang said. "Taking the heads like barbarians."

"It's a small price to pay," said Kleat. "Play it through with them. You'll get what you want. We all will."

"You don't understand?" Samnang asked Kleat.

Kleat tsk-tsked. Dumb question. End of discussion. The fire snapped in their silence.

The Americans and Samnang dried off under the thatch roof, all except Molly, who could not quit sweating. Suddenly ravenous, she pulled the box of MREs toward her. "Spaghetti and meatballs," she said.

She offered the MREs to Vin and his brothers, out by the fire, but they waved off her hospitality, too intent on toting up their riches with a hand calculator. She would have to think up some other way to mother them. It was imperative that they not forsake the Americans.

The canopy leaked in episodes, dripping like a metronome, then spilling in vertical columns that released here, then there. It was all cause and effect, no mystery. A leaf brimming with rainwater would flip over, creating a chain reaction among lower leaves. Every few minutes another gush of water splashed in the darkness. It would go on until the canopy had lightened its load.

One of the miniature waterfalls scored a direct hit on their fire. White steam billowed up and the hut went dark. The brothers jumped to their feet. "Ho," they shouted, laughing. Then the flames jumped high again.

The brothers settled back along the edge of the fire. The dirt and embers at one end of the pit seemed to twitch on their own, like someone struggling to break free from below. Molly passed it off as shadows.

Vin was dispatched to offer the Americans a bottle of clear liquid, which he poured into their empty tea cups. Kleat took a sip. "God, you could clean paint off with that," he said.

"Not good," Samnang murmured after Vin left.

"As long as they're happy."

"The happy part won't last," Duncan said. The brothers looked over, and he smiled and raised a toast to them. "I've seen men go at each other with hatchets on this stuff."

"And us without a gun," Kleat said. He toasted Molly and took another sip of the hooch and adjusted his flak jacket.

Molly wished she'd thought of the flak jacket, not for the armoring, but the warmth. Was she the only one who felt the cold? If only they would build the fire a little higher.

Back in Kampong Cham, they had pledged to turn around at the first sign of rain. There was no question about staying through the night, though. It would be absurd to try to retrace the oxcart trail at night, and the river would not recede until morning. Neither Samnang nor Duncan could predict tomorrow's weather. Without a radio or even a view of the sky, they were reduced to speculation. The mountain would act as a natural magnet for the first precipitation, and maybe this little shower was all the sky contained for now.

They came up with every excuse to stay. They pretended the decision was theirs to make, that they were in full command of themselves. They pretended emotion had nothing to do with wanting to stay, that the very fact they were discussing caution meant caution still ruled. But the ruins were inciting them. Everyone had something to gain here. The nearness of the bones had Kleat in high gear, and the marvels of the city excited Duncan, and the plunder wound up the brothers. Even old Samnang had desires. Molly saw him lay out a row of incense sticks and knew he meant to return to the tower. They were all obsessed, herself included.

It was agreed that the rain signified the beginning of the wet monsoon and had nothing to do with the typhoon. The typhoon might have died in the South China Sea, or it might still strike them.

The bigger uncertainty was the brothers. Duncan guessed the truck held a half million dollars' worth of relics now. They could simply drive away in the morning and leave the Americans. It was all a matter of their whim. Samnang said they meant to stay. They wanted more.

The fire stirred again. Something was under there. Molly saw it again, like an invisible hand moving its fingers within the red coals. A root, she decided. The heat was drying its sap, making the root contract and twist.

Kleat spread the pieces of the broken M-16 on the poncho. The rifle clip was empty. "Once his ammunition ran out, he clubbed the rifle. How many of the little bastards did he take with him?"

"I saw that movie," said Molly. "John Wayne. *The Alamo.*"

"Explain this then." Kleat held up the shattered rifle.

"We've been there," she said. "If there was a battle, there should be other signs. Not just in the tower, but down in the city. Bullets in trees or in the sandstone."

"Laterite," Duncan corrected her. "Technically

speaking. It's a soft stone when it's first quarried. Perfect for carving before it hardens."

"Other signs," she continued. "Rocket scars on the walls. Things blown up."

"You'll see. The bones will tell."

"They could have left or been taken prisoner."

"Explain the dog tags then."

"Explain Luke," said Duncan.

Circles within circles. The sweat stung her eyes.

Night was a frame of mind. The ACAV flickered in the heights like a box-shaped moon. There were even stars, the fireflies and sparks. And constellations of animal eyes glittering red and yellow in the trees.

Like a museum curator, Duncan began delicately appraising the pages from inside the radio set. They might have been the Dead Sea Scrolls, the four curled pages of lined notepaper. Minuscule termites had wormed their way across the pages, etching in their own account of time. Ink foxed the paper in blotches. Duncan teased the pages apart and held them to the firelight, trying to candle out any legible words. When that didn't work, he gently pressed them flat, and the pages crumbled like dead leaves.

Kleat seemed gratified. "They wouldn't have told us anything anyway."

Duncan pieced the fragments together as best he could, side by side, and pored over them with Kleat's big krypton flashlight. There was precious little to decipher: " '... can't not stay anymore, where else ... darkest before dawn, oh, God, your false promise ... in the life of the stone ...' "

"No atheists in the foxholes," Kleat said. "The boy was stoked on the Bible."

"Here's part of an inventory: 'morphine, 7 amps, .50 cal, 3. . . .' " Duncan leaned down and ran out of words.

"That's all?" said Kleat.

It took another five minutes to turn the fragments onto their flip side. Duncan found a little more. " '. . . he was right, but we were wrong to listen . . . let him go like Cain, but west from Eden on foot. Maybe we should have' . . . And this, 'another visit last night. They come every night now. I know I shouldn't speak to them, but we spoke . . .' "

"What's that all about?" Molly said.

"Regrets," Kleat said. "The 'he' must have been their commanding officer. And it sounds like one of them got out of Dodge before it was too late. Obviously, they wished they'd never listened to their commander. And they wished they'd followed the man who left."

"But who are his visitors at night, the ones he shouldn't speak to? Maybe tribal people coming in?"

"Here we go, a bit more in pencil, along the margin." Duncan read several lines of a poem, something about wild cats growling, wind howling, and two riders approaching. He looked up. "They must have heard a tiger. The monsoon was coming. And they were the two riders, you know, their two ACAVs approaching the city walls."

"Useless," Kleat said. He seemed, Molly thought, glad to be done with it.

But Samnang bent closer. "Bob Dylan," he said.

They looked at him.

"Yes, those are the final words of a famous song." Samnang was excited by his discovery. 'All Along the

Watchtower.' One of my students wrote an essay on its true meaning."

"What true meaning?" said Kleat. "It's plain. They were trapped. They were dying. They wanted out of here."

"And yet the soldier chose this song," said Samnang. "A song about revolution. Why?"

"Forget the watchtower crap," Kleat said. "Forget last wills and testaments. What we need is positive identification."

"Let me take a turn," Molly interrupted.

"You have better eyes?"

She held up her camera. "Let's see what it sees."

She knelt above the fragments and took a picture of the front side of each page. Duncan began patiently turning them over.

Out by the fire, Doc snapped a command. Hands planted on his folded legs, elbows out, he looked almost like one of the kings she'd seen carved in the stone. His voice was too loud. He was drunk.

Vin hopped to do his bidding, shoveling at the coals with his machete. After a minute, he levered up the edge of a helmet. At least that's what Molly thought it was, the helmet that Kleat had found. They were using it to cook their dinner. She was wrong, though. It was a turtle.

They must have trapped it from the *baray* swamps and buried it under the coals to roast. Molly lifted her camera and zoomed in. She'd never seen a turtle eaten. Steam vented from the leg holes. The camera autofocused in the witchy light, blurring, centering, blurring. She thumbed the focus to manual and stabilized the image.

It was still alive.

Molly kept the camera between her and it. Through its glass and mirrors, she could stand almost anything.

The turtle filled her frame. There was no mistake. Its legs paddled at the air. Its neck stretched and moved. That explained the embers stirring.

The middle brother snatched the machete from Vin. He gave a light, expert chop across the belly plate. The turtle opened like magic.

The firelight pulsed. The stewpot of organs pulsed separately from the light. Alive, still alive. They used sticks and knives to spear pieces. Doc saw her shooting and, with exaggerated hospitality, held up a slippery organ to her. She shook her head no, and they laughed. Kleat laughed, too.

"There," announced Duncan, unaware of the little incident. His puzzle of fragments was ready for her. She leaned over and snapped pictures of the reverse sides. A drop of her sweat fell on one page, staining it as black as blood.

Samnang was frowning at her. He'd noticed her sweat. She rested against the box.

"Whoever the man was," Duncan said, "he rolled the pages up, closed them in a layer of condoms, and hid them inside a radio that was dead. A message in a bottle."

"No name, no date." Kleat shrugged.

"Did Samnang show you the name at the base of the tower?" Molly asked. She referenced it on her camera display. " 'C. K. Watts. August 20.' It gives us some context. And the monkey remains," she added, keeping her eyes away from the turtle, "more context. We're not without clues."

"It's a dead end, I'm telling you," Kleat said. He fished a cigar butt from his shirt pocket and whistled at Vin, who brought a lighted twig.

Molly frowned. Kleat was acting so oddly, so detached, even hostile to the possibilities. But, to borrow Samnang's French, this was her *spécialité*. She was a journalist, a detective. "We know the approximate date of their arrival. We know they left at least one of their vehicles here. They took gear and weapons and barbed wire, and some or all of them climbed into the city and apparently made a decision to hide here."

"A bad decision." With the stogie and the flak jacket, Kleat made a poor General Patton.

"Once the decision was made," she went on, "they were stuck with it. They tried to radio for help, but the radio was dead. They tried to signal passing aircraft, but no one saw them."

"A lot of nothing." It was as if he were trying to sabotage her.

"Seven weeks later," she said, "at least one of them was still left to carve his name on the tower. We know they were hungry, and despairing. There's that fragment about darkest before dawn and God's false promise. The boy sounds so desolate, like there's no hope on earth."

"The only relevant question is where they died," said Kleat. "I need teeth, whole jaws, the entire skull if possible. Pieces of bone for DNA analysis. Wedding bands, class rings, wristwatches with initials. Words don't matter."

"Of course they matter," Molly said. "They're our best clues at this point." She continued scrolling through the images on her display, landing on the photos of the journal pages. The LCD was chewing through the batteries, stealing from the future to pay for the past, so to speak, using up power she could be saving to take more pictures. But she justified it as part of the interview process. The evidence was speaking to them.

She studied the images, goosing the light, enlarging sections, penetrating the inky ruins of the manuscript. "There's more," she said. "I can't tell what order the pages go in. And anyway, he seems to have written things wherever there was space"—she turned her camera—"even upside down. Here's more of the inventory list. And some words to fill in around the segments, and a number on this page, '7/17/70.' "

"Three weeks after they arrived," said Duncan. "A month before C. K. Watts carved his name."

She tilted the display, straining to see. " 'We can't not stay anymore,' " she read. " 'Where else could we have gone? It was finished the minute the TC took the wrong turn. Now we have to live with what we've done. The TC gets the tower for his tomb, the first of us to go. And now we know it's not true that he loved the city more than us. He was only trying to preserve us all.' "

"The TC?" she said.

"The team commander," Kleat said. "There would have been two of them, one for each ACAV. But one would have had seniority. He was the fool who brought them here."

She returned to the display. " 'There is death in the life of the stone. We see that more every day. We try not to notice, but the walls talk to us. The statues speak. The city sings. The eyes see. The rain is killing us. Every day gets worse. We hide from each other, not sure who is who now. I've never been so lonely.' "

"Out of his mind," said Kleat.

Molly scrolled to another section. " '. . . he was right, but we were more wrong to become his rebels. It was mutiny . . .' And this. 'We let him go like Cain, but west from Eden on foot. Maybe we should have killed him for it. But we let him lead us into sin. So we were part of it, and now it's done. And now we are scattered.' "

They were quiet for a minute.

"And?" said Kleat.

"They were at war all right," she said. "You want glory. You want heroes. They were scared. They were boys trying to deal with an ugly, dirty little dead end. And they had themselves a mutiny. A revolution. And then they died off like animals."

"Journalists," Kleat snorted.

"Something happened here," she said.

"How about this?" Kleat said. "Their commander fucked up. They believed in him, and he betrayed them with his stupidity. They could have killed him, but they spared him and drove him out like Cain. The man who led them wrong. He's lucky they didn't put a bullet through his head."

"There are other ways to read this," said Molly. "This says the commander got the tower for his tomb."

"Whatever that means."

"Part of this was written three weeks into their confinement. The rest of it sounds like it was written later, maybe over the coming weeks or months. But one thing is clear, they were at odds with one another. He talks about rebels, *his* rebels. There was a troublemaker. Tensions must have been running high. Nine men found themselves caught in a cage. Think about it. They were bound to start laying blame for their troubles. And somehow their commander died. Whoever wrote this sounds guilty. He talks about sin."

"He also talks about talking statues and a singing city," said Kleat.

Molly stopped. "Which is it, Kleat? Either the writer was insane and none of it mattered, or his words are fact, but muddled by time. You can't have it both ways."

Kleat released a cloud of smoke. His steel rims glittered. "None of it matters."

The brothers had finished the turtle. They were passing the shell back and forth, sipping the gray broth.

Molly flipped the off switch. The camera display went black. "I'm going to bed," she said.

She fit her camera into the bag, got her shoes and flashlight, and climbed down from the hut. Duncan started to follow. "Please don't," she said. She didn't want to talk anymore.

He lagged back. "Don't give up on us, Molly," he said. "You're right. I don't know what, but something happened here."

26.

She woke suddenly, in the middle of the night. Samnang's fire cast a glimmer on her tent wall. Hours had passed. Her clothes had dried. Some second sense told her not to move.

It was raining again. Water grazed the outer skin of the forest with a muffled hiss. A rain to sleep by, she thought, drifting off.

Then she saw the shapes. The fire animated them. Their silhouettes trickled across the panels of her dome tent, bent low and ranging their rifles back and forth. *The brothers.* They'd come for her.

Crouched like cats, they stole along the terrace edge. She held her breath, looking for Vin's thin figure. Maybe he could stop his brothers. Then she saw that there were more than three out there. That made no sense.

Just then, gunfire crackled up from the depths of the camp. Molly huddled behind her screen of nylon and fiberglass poles, thinking these stalking men must be the target. She braced for the explosions they would unleash in turn.

But none of the silhouette men returned fire. Instead they grew more misshapen, even their rifles, twisted and melting. Their arms trailed tendrils and became vines. The metamorphosis left her wondering what she'd seen in the first place. Pieces of the forest, nothing more.

The gunfire rattled again in the distance. That much was real. Her knees drew up against her chest. Her eyes squeezed shut.

The tent wall rustled. One of them was trying the door.

She willed herself invisible.

"Molly," the man whispered.

He was the dark apparition of Oklahoma. She couldn't help herself. *Be a good girl.* Fear squeezed the air from her lungs.

"Molly."

Quiet, she instructed herself. Stand aside. Don't be part of it. Return when all is safe again.

More gunfire.

"Molly." Louder this time.

The door unzipped. She saw herself backed as far as possible into the corner. She saw herself with her eyes squeezed shut.

"It's me," he whispered.

She saw herself open her eyes. In the scant, cold light, Duncan hunkered at the doorway. His hair hung in long, wet strands.

The rifles crackled, on full automatic. She glanced at the tent wall. The images had fled. He was alone.

"Don't be afraid," he whispered.

She began to return to herself.

"I thought you might be afraid."

She was shaking with fever fits. Her jaw unlocked. "Duncan."

"Keep your voice down. They're drunk. It will pass."

She was convulsing. He couldn't see it from out there.

"I just wanted to make sure you're okay."

She wasn't. She had demons.

"Lie low," he said. "Keep your light off. The bullets fall back to earth, but the canopy will protect us. You're safe."

He started to raise her door to seal her inside with herself again. "Don't," she said.

He paused.

"Don't leave."

"If you need me, I'm here." He started to zip the door shut again, still outside.

"What are you doing?" she said.

"I'm here, I promise." His chivalry bewildered her. He meant to sit in the rain like some warrior monk? She needed more.

"Come in." It was so cold.

Backing inside, he zipped the door closed and sat beside her with his legs crossed.

Her teeth chattered. It finally occurred to him. His palm covered her forehead. "You're sick."

"I'm cold."

"I can't take you to the fire," he said. "Not with them like this."

"Hold me."

It surprised him. She read his surprise. The halting

way he opened his arm for her to lay her head on was like a remembered act. He had forgotten human touch.

She pressed her back to him. He was warm. They didn't talk. Eventually the gunfire tapered off. She quit shaking and fell asleep in his arms.

27.

The birds woke her.

The rain had stopped. The city waited. She opened her eyes.

Duncan startled her. She startled herself.

During the night, she had twisted. In her sleep, she had thrown one arm across Duncan. She had one ear against his chest. She could hear his heartbeat. His ribs rose and fell in slow waves.

She never woke this way with a man, holding him and being held. It did not happen, even with lovers she trusted. And while he wasn't a stranger, he wasn't a lover either. She barely knew him. And yet her sleeping self had folded against him.

Molly lay very still, trying to sort out this new development. He was warm, and she'd been afraid. She remembered the gunfire, and those silhouettes. But they weren't enough to explain her trust.

He looked almost boyish sleeping in the blue-green light. There was a powerful scent of flowers. Her eyes traveled to his shirt pocket. He'd collected an orchid yesterday.

Part of her wanted to shake him and climb back into the city. They knew their way into the ruins. She had dreamed about them last night, dreamed madly. The city was starting to inhabit her.

But she lingered, reluctant to shatter this remarkable contact. Twice men had proposed marriage to her—seriously proposed—thinking they could overcome her nightmares. As gently as possible, she'd spared them their gallantry. They couldn't save her. The rape had burned her. Molly had resigned herself to her clenching scars.

What could explain this? She was a serial disbeliever. She required truth, good, bad, or ugly. Offer her a wound for proof and she would plunge her fingers right in. Which had made the search for the bones so fitting. The missing soldiers were an unhealed wound, like a handhold, both a story and, deeper, an appeal to her missionary instinct. So how did Duncan fit into that?

It wasn't that he could protect her from the perils. The plotting brothers and the typhoon and Kleat's paranoia endangered him as much as her. Was it that she seemed to occupy him the way the ruins occupied her? He had been her welcome to Cambodia. When she was at her weakest, he had shielded her from the sun with his scarf. When the guns started going off last night, his first thought had been for her safekeeping. He'd crawled out into the rain to guard her.

He looked twenty-something this morning. The soft light smoothed his crow's-feet and softened the hawk profile, but it was something more. Years had melted from his face. His beard line looked . . . diminished. There was just stubble on his chin and upper lip. His throat was smooth. The jugular throbbed. It was like watching her own heart beat.

A long, welted scar ran in a line above his left ear. She'd never seen it before. Normally his long hair hid it. He'd survived some terrible violence, but had never mentioned it. She'd have to ask him about that someday.

She wondered, *What would he be like in Boulder?* With his long hair and seven-league boots, they'd take him for one more globe-trotter with an athlete's veins. Every other man and woman you met there seemed to be in training for some imaginary Olympics or Everest. She'd written an article on the legend of Boulder, average age 29.5 years, average body fat 11 percent. She'd dubbed it an orthopedist's paradise, with all the skiers' knees and climbers' shoulders you could wish for. Duncan would move among them like an aging lion. They could go to the movies on snowy afternoons, drink tea at Turley's, chart new travels. With Duncan, she might finally feel at home.

But there were the ruins to decipher. His destiny was here, and hers, too. She felt it powerfully. She had not ended up here by accident.

Her thoughts wheeled pleasantly.

Slowly she noticed the bamboo. It stood on the far side of his face, a slender, glossy green shoot poised almost like a snake. The trespass surprised her. The forest had invaded her tent.

She lifted her head from Duncan's chest. The bamboo had pierced the tent floor and pushed right through the thin sleeping pad. Its point was hard and sharp, the shaft slick and phallic. They could have been impaled in their sleep. That was too dramatic, of course. They would have woken at its first touch.

Only then did she notice her tent wall. It was deformed. Half caved in. A tree limb must have fallen across them.

A wall tent or pup tent would have collapsed altogether. Her dome tent had spread the weight through a system of poles. The rain must have torn the limb loose from the canopy and it had dropped during the night.

Duncan woke. He started to smile, then jerked his head away from the bamboo. He saw the deformed tent wall. "How could we have slept through that?" he said.

He pushed at the branch with his foot, but that only tightened its pressure. The tent creaked.

"These poles might not hold it," she said.

Despite the quiet destruction of her tent, Molly was grateful for the quick exit. It was too soon for pillow talk and holding hands. In escaping the tent, they would be escaping any awkwardness.

They couldn't sit upright. Then they saw more bamboo shoots sticking through the floor. Duncan got over her on his hands and knees, and put his back against the tree limb. She slid between his legs.

Unzipping the door dumped the dome's remaining strength. One of the long poles snapped, then another. She slid out and helped Duncan crawl from the shambles. They faced the wreckage.

It wasn't a fallen branch, but a vine. The thing had come untethered from the ledge above and was strapped across the tent. Its tip had burrowed into a joint in the stone. In the space of a few hours, it had muscled down and broken her tent. Molly looked around at the mist and its shapes. A giant god floated with his serene smile, and sank away.

"It's like a tidal wave, a green tidal wave," she said. "Do things really grow so fast here?"

"The forest must have been thirsty. The first taste of rain and it takes off like a rocket." Duncan aimed for levity, but it troubled him.

"I'll come back for it later." Who was she kidding? The tent was a write-off. She felt violated and put on notice. This place was not her friend. She jerked her camera bag from the collapsed doorway.

Duncan had to use his Swiss Army knife to free their shoes. A filament of roots had invaded a rip in the floor and corded them to the ground. He pretended it was normal. "Man versus monsoon," he intoned. "Who will win the primordial struggle?" But it bothered him, she could tell.

They walked along the ledge around little pickets of bamboo growing through the joints, and stepped across cablelike vines. His tent was collapsed as well. Lowering himself to what remained of it, Duncan cut an opening through the side and extracted his steel briefcase.

They finished descending to the terminus floor and wended their way through the mist.

Molly kept looking for the names carved into the trees. "There they are." She tugged Duncan after her, but then she got a closer look.

The letters were bleeding.

"It's tree sap," Duncan said.

"But they weren't like this before."

"The forest is having a growth spurt. The bark pulled apart. It's only sap."

Thick and crimson, it seeped down from the beloved names. She regretted waiting to take the picture. Yesterday morning, they had been radiant on the gleaming bark. Now they wept, though maybe that was the more appropriate mood for the photo.

Farther on, they heard a low roar building.

"Is that the truck running?" she asked.

They hurried, thinking the brothers were leaving.

But the roar was the sound of the fire. Kleat was there, piling logs onto a small inferno. The flames leaped taller than the hut, eating a jagged hole in the fog, throwing sparks with pistol shots of sap.

The furnace heat had him pouring sweat. He'd shed his shirt, but was wearing the flak jacket. His face and scalp were as bright as mercury. He looked insane.

"What are you doing?" asked Duncan.

Kleat loaded on another fat log and straightened on the far side of the flames. His glasses reflected the light. He had showers of red and orange sparks for eyes. Inside his fury, he looked afraid. "Up late?" he yelled at them.

Molly had been almost ready to pity him. "We heard the shooting last night," she said.

His chest hair was singed to black steel wool. She smelled the burned hair and Caucasian sweat, but also caught other smells in the smoke, potent smells, the scent of different kinds of wood, of ferns, flowers, nuts, coconut, even cinnamon. Once part of a royal garden, spices grew wild here. The fire was opening up the forest's abundance.

"You missed the hunt," Kleat said.

"Is that what they were doing, hunting?"

Kleat looked at them. "He should have known better."

The fire forced her back with its hot breath. Her chills were gone. She felt fine this morning. Molly glanced around. At the edges of dissolved mist, half-formed shapes moved between the vaporous white Land Cruiser and the larger bulk of the truck. She counted three shapes with rifles. There was only one man unaccounted for.

"Where's Samnang?" Duncan asked.

"He brought it on himself."

"Be clear," said Molly.

"He fucked up."

"What happened, Kleat?"

"He waited until they were drunk, then he got his revenge. But there was no way he was going to get away with it. Of course they found out." He toppled a decaying stump into the flames. White termites came flooding from its cavities.

"What revenge, what are you talking about?"

"He destroyed their artifacts, smashed them to pieces, the pots. Hid the rest. All the heads, they're missing. That's what they were trying to beat out of him. Don't ask me. I don't speak the language. One thing led to another."

"You saw it? They beat him?" While she slept soundly.

"I only came for the bones." Kleat glared at her. "You know that."

"But you were down here."

"I heard them arguing. I came down and they had

him. They were pushing him around, hitting him with their rifles. He's KR, I keep telling you. They hated him enough as it was. Then he pulls a stunt like this."

They'd gone hunting.

"What did they do to him, Kleat?"

"I didn't see anything." He bent for more wood.

It was obvious. "They killed him."

She cast around for bloodstains, but the rain must have flushed them into the earth. It occurred to her that they were scorching the evidence out of existence. That would explain this manic bonfire at the crack of dawn.

"They were working themselves up to it," Kleat said. "But then I came down. They weren't going to do it in front of me. So they gave him a head start. That's the last I saw of him."

"Where is he?"

"He went off into the night. He's a slippery old bastard, and they were drunk. They chased him and came back and went out again. They were afraid to leave the fire for very long. It went on for hours. You heard the gunfire, they were all over the place."

"And you just sat here?"

"I kept the fire going. That was my job. They made it clear. A big fire. That's the important thing. I kept them on our side. Someone had to make sure they wouldn't leave us. They could have driven off. They still could." He threw on more wood. "But not for a while."

"This is murder," she said. "And you did nothing."

Kleat's glasses flashed. "I stopped an execution. I came down and they set him loose. I saved his life." He had it all worked out in his head.

Samnang was dead somewhere, she could picture it, floating in the *baray* pools or slung over a root. "How did you save him? They hunted him. You said so."

"Three street kids against an old killer. Some hunt. They lost him." Kleat stood on the far side of the flames. "Or he left, like Luke, out the front gate. Or he's dead, okay? He's gone."

He shoved in another log. It struck her suddenly. "What's in the fire?" She dragged the log out. She reached for another.

Duncan took her arm. "That won't help, Molly."

"He's under there," she said. "They're burning his body. They're burning the evidence."

"Molly . . ." Duncan murmured.

"Get a grip, woman," Kleat said. "First cannibals, what next?"

"He was an old man." She turned away, tears blurring her vision.

"He was KR. They think he killed their mother and father, I got that much. You must have heard them," he said to Duncan.

"How would they know?" said Molly. "Vin would have been an infant. Doc would have been four."

"They've got it in their minds," Duncan said. "They say it's the reason they agreed to come along, to confront him and get the truth. I'm kind of surprised Samnang invited them. It's almost like he wanted to get it over with."

"They're thieves. They were beating him to find their plunder, not to ask about their parents," Molly said.

"Why can't it be both?" said Kleat. "They're thieves. And the old man was a butcher."

They were quiet for a minute. Finally Molly said, "He watched over me."

"So he went down in glory," Kleat said, "doing his holy deeds."

Duncan peered through the mist. "What are they up to over there?"

"Working up their nerve," Kleat said. "Go see for yourself."

28.

They left Kleat building his fire higher.

"Stay with me," Duncan said to her. "Keep your temper, do you hear me? Don't make it worse." He squeezed her arm.

"I heard you."

Broken shards lay scattered across the clearing. The forest floor was chopped and muddy. Pieces of pottery had been trod into the ground.

"This is strange," Duncan said. "Look at how deep some of these footprints are. It's like a herd of horses came through. But the prints are human."

"The rain must have softened the earth," Molly said.

"Not enough for this." Duncan stomped at the ground but didn't make a dent. "It's hard to believe Samnang could have done so much damage. And why only the pots and not the heads? There must have been fifteen heads. How could one man carry them off so quickly?"

"No idea, Duncan." She didn't care about pots and heads and footprints. Samnang was dead.

The brothers materialized in the mist. They were circulating back and forth, from the Land Cruiser to the enshrouded truck. Their rifles twitched at Molly and Duncan's approach.

At first she paid no attention to the vehicles. She'd never had a gun pointed at her. The bluing on the gun metal had worn through in places, like the finish on secondhand guitars. The guns had traveled many miles through many wars before ending up in these tattooed hands.

Duncan announced himself, arms wide, and they lowered the barrels. Toting his silver briefcase like an insurance adjuster, he spoke in quiet tones. Doc, with his full armor of body ink, shouted back at him and shook his rifle. Duncan went on talking, moving closer.

Molly stayed back, hating them for what they had done. It took her a minute to even look at their faces. She expected hangover scowls or bully glares, but their eyes were filled with voodoo fear. Their panic caught her off guard.

Then she noticed the Land Cruiser, and the truck, and was frightened, too. Tilted at ridiculous angles, gripped by vines, the vehicles were trapped. The forest was car-jacking them.

A fast-growing tree root had hoisted the rear of the Land Cruiser a foot off the ground. The back tires dangled. She went with Duncan to it.

Creepers had infiltrated a crack in the windshield. She peered inside. Vines wrapped the plastic steering wheel and were rooting into the underside of the dash panel.

The old Mercedes truck was being overrun, too.

Vines roped its hood and doors, but it was being sucked backward into the earth. The rear wheels had sunk to the hub, tilting up the front end like a bull struggling from quicksand.

In a different setting, in a museum of modern art, it would have been sardonic, nature's revenge. Here, this morning, it scared her. Her mind careered through explanations. The rain had created a mire under the truck. In the darkness, the first night, they'd inadvertently parked on top of a tree trunk. The vines were genetically programmed to raid. Mother Nature was tripping on speed. Nothing human was to blame. There was some consolation in that. They were all victims. They were in this together now.

The brothers were in a state. Vin had the machete they'd used on the turtle last night. His brother So carried an ax. She glanced at the tools, looking for blood. There was none, and her hopes rose, foolishly, she knew.

Duncan opened his briefcase and gave Doc a pack of Camels still wrapped in cellophane. What else did he harbor in there? A sketch pad, she knew, though he was too shy to show her his sketches. Maps, surely, his obsession. A day journal, perhaps, and photos of some long-lost loved one. Had he kept the stub of his air ticket from the States as a memento?

The pack of cigarettes went around the circle, and Duncan accepted one. The Heng boys skirted their smashed plunder, gawking at their precious vehicles, afraid to touch anything.

"How could they sleep through this?" she said. It was a silly question. The same way she had slept through the destruction of her tent.

"I'm not sure any of them did sleep," said Duncan. "They were drunk. And busy." Hunting in the forest.

"What do we do now?"

"We need to work with them, Molly."

"Work with them, after what they did?"

"They have the wheels."

"We should just go," she whispered to him. "This very minute, Duncan." They could fade into the mist and find the causeway, and cross between the *barays,* and slide through the gateway. There was still more forest to negotiate beyond the fortress walls, but once they reached the sun, or at least the sky, they could navigate their way back down the mountain. Villagers would feed them. Loggers would pick them up.

"Without Kleat?"

"He'd leave us and you know it."

Duncan shook his head. "We're in this together."

"That's very high-minded. But look around. You can't make this better."

"No." He had his mind made up. "The best thing is to try and help them. We'll be okay."

He joined the brothers again, moving with them, taking stock of the damage. He laid his hands on the metal and glass, and that simple act did more than anything else to break their terror. At least Doc quit shouting.

The brothers' tight faces loosened. Duncan made a suggestion, and Vin handed him the machete without hesitation.

With the care of a surgeon, meticulous so as not to scratch the white paint, he slipped the blade under a creeper binding one door and sliced it free. He cut away more vines and, opening the door, made a show of returning their machete.

Little by little, he showed them how to regain control. He got So to begin unraveling the vines from the wiring. He called Molly over, and four of them manhandled a rock into place under one of the Land Cruiser's wheels. "We'll get this straightened out," he said. He put Molly to work with a shovel.

After fifteen minutes or so, he came from the Land Cruiser carrying a burlap sack stuffed with other sacks. Vin trailed behind him with his machete and rifle. "All right, let's get Kleat," he said. He propped her shovel against the truck.

"What are we doing?" She didn't mean for her voice to be shrill.

"Everything's going to be okay."

Kleat was dragging another log from the brush. Sweat ringed his flak jacket at the neck and armpits. "We've got a deal," Duncan said. "We're all leaving today, before the rains return. But first we have a job to do."

Kleat guessed from the sacks. "They want us to mule down more loot for them."

"A little salvage work." Duncan spoke to Kleat in the same soothing tone he'd used with Doc. "They need to be made whole, that's how they see it. They'll keep digging while we go up into the ruins. Vin's going with us."

The kid had found a pebble and was playing soccer with it, batting it between his toes, waiting, with the AK-47 on his back.

Kleat had a dark thought. "You know he's taking us off to shoot us."

"No he's not. They want their share of the city, that's all."

"Then they'll do it down here," Kleat said. "Later, when they're done with us."

"Show some faith, John. We scratch their backs, they scratch ours. Everything will be fine."

"They're not on our side," Kleat said. "They could do anything to us in here. Look what happened to Samnang."

"I talked to them about that. They said he ran away. They were only searching for him. They wanted to bring him back to the camp."

"They were trying to save him?" Kleat snorted. "They had a gun at his head."

"They know that was wrong. But they say what he did was wrong, too. They only wanted to know where he hid the rest of their possessions."

"They were hunting him like an animal."

"They say it was the other way around."

"The old man was hunting them?"

"No." Duncan grew quiet. "The *prêt*. They say."

Vin heard the word and stopped his little soccer game.

"The what?" said Molly.

"They're a forest legend, like what the Romans called their nightwalkers, *lemures,* or *larva,* the Latin for spirits still forming. If you die violently—"

Kleat's face screwed up. "Not this again." He upended the log and let it fall into the fire. Sparks belched. The wet skin of the limb sizzled.

"They claim the forest is full of them," Duncan said.

"And you believe that?"

Duncan hesitated. "Of course not. But they do. Strip away the layers of Buddhism and Hinduism and you have an animistic religion dedicated to neutralizing the dead and pushing their spirits as far away and as quickly as possible. They were drunk. It was dark. We're looking for American remains. I'd be surprised if they hadn't seen things out there."

"Then add one more *prêt* to the collection," Kleat said. "The old man won't make it far on a plastic leg."

Molly still wanted to run for the causeway and find their own way back to civilization. "What if it's a trick?" she said. "He could be leading us up so they can desert us."

"They would never leave their own brother. Don't you see? He's our greatest assurance."

"That's the part I can't believe," Kleat said. "They're giving us a hostage."

"That's not the right attitude, John."

The fire glinted on Kleat's glasses. "I'll bear that in mind," he said.

29.

It should have been straightforward. They had all visited one or the other of the gates and its statues at least once, but the city was more alien than ever. The mist was like quicksand. Within minutes they were lost.

Molly had begun to memorize her way into and out of the heart of the ruins, but overnight the rapid forest had undone what little was familiar. Samnang had tied knots in the grass, but new grass had sprung up, higher and more lush, taking over the ruins. The saplings he'd bent into careful circles had sprung loose in the rain and grown beyond recognition. It was like entering a different city.

Vin kept sweeping his rifle back and forth at shapes materializing among the trees and temples. With the machete scabbard strapped to his back and its handle standing above his head like an exclamation point, the boy looked overloaded and self-conscious. The American soldiers with RE-1 had taught him how to moonwalk and chew Red Man. Molly and Duncan had treated him like a man, asking about his warrior *sak*. She could tell it was awkward for him to be using them as pack animals. Vin spoke softly to Duncan. The only word Molly understood was "please."

"Basically, he's asking for our cooperation," Duncan said. "The sooner we find the gate and the statues, the sooner we can leave."

"He wants to be friends?" Kleat said. He had his eye on the boy's rifle.

"Does anybody recognize anything?"

"If we could just find the tower," Molly said.

She longed to return to the room of the Buddhas. The yearning filled her. It overrode her fear of what was happening to them, their disintegration and the creeping violence. As a landmark, the tower might help orient them, but that was only an excuse. It was the room on that man-made summit that drew her. It held . . . something.

But this morning, with visibility cut to twenty feet, the tower seemed to have dismantled itself. As they penetrated the waist-high grass, nothing was the same. The avenue and side lanes and bridges and canals were all reconfigured. The massive faces projecting from lesser towers and the crests of flattened pyramids were no help. Their serene smiles only added to the sense of entanglement and maddening circles. Molly found herself resenting the tranquil stone expressions.

They chose a canal and followed its trickle of water uphill, reasoning that vertical gain was a direction of sorts. At least, Duncan said, they would not be going in circles. The same trickle of water could not round back on itself.

As they marched higher through the ruins, Vin kept Kleat in the front of the line, where he could watch him. The boy might be naive, but his brothers had instructed him well. As Samnang had put it, with or without his fangs, Kleat was still toxic.

As if hearing her thoughts, Kleat flashed Molly a look, then another one. She was following behind Vin, which put her within easy reach of the machete riding between his shoulder blades, practically a gift to them. She understood Kleat perfectly. He wanted her to kill the boy.

She tried to convince herself that Vin was her mortal enemy, and even that didn't work. She wondered, if things came to it, if she could even kill an animal to eat. Kleat glared at her. Her thoughts returned to the tower.

After a half hour, they found themselves back at the bridge on the canal where they'd begun. Impossibly, the downhill trickle of water had circled back on itself. "That can't be," Kleat objected.

Vin didn't question it. To him, the perpetual circling of water was just another arcane loop in a city of riddles. He and Duncan had a discussion using the lines on Duncan's palm as a map.

After a minute, Duncan said, "Okay, a slight revision. We're going to split into pairs and spread out the search. It should be simple. All we have to do is find one section of the wall, then we can follow it to one of the gates and get what we need."

Vin chose the teams, himself with Duncan, and Molly with Kleat. Kleat frightened him, and Molly frightened him, too, though differently. His puppy love was obvious, and out of decorum and modesty he did not choose her. It was almost cute.

"What are we supposed to do if we find something, whistle?" Kleat said.

"Stay within earshot," Duncan said. "Let's not lose each other."

They separated into pairs. As Molly wove through the piles of temples and narrow corridors, Kleat railed at her. "The machete was right in front of you. They want heads? We'll give them a head."

"He's a kid. He's not going to hurt us," she said.

"He's one of them. And we're going to need his rifle and machete. Think."

"Leave him alone, Kleat."

Kleat put his face close to hers. "Do you want to live or not?"

She had witnessed paranoia in her career. She'd photographed it in prisons and asylums and at a treatment center for foreign torture victims. She'd even argued with it, her own fears, in therapy and alone. But Kleat's was a species all its own.

She stood her ground, or tried to. "What kind of question is that?" she snapped.

"Don't think I'm going to die caged in like this," Kleat said. "Now's no time for bleeding hearts. When the time comes, just stand out of my way."

He bulled on, and Molly slowed. The sound of his crashing through the brush dimmed. Thunder grumbled far away. It seemed early. Without thinking, Molly glanced at her useless watch. The mist was thinning. The morning was getting on.

She strayed alongside a panel of more bas-reliefs,

and, like yesterday, they were dense with stories both alien and familiar. The carvings seemed to whisper to her. She imagined herself written in the stone, the lone bird-woman living in a tree, the queen—or goddess—watching over the city, or that infant being held up to the sky by her mother.

Then her eye chanced up, and she was being watched again. This time there was a small troop of the ghostly gray monkeys, perched in the branches and sitting on ancient masonry and terraces. They unsettled her, like in the tower room that afternoon.

It wasn't that she thought they might attack. They were cute and fuzzy, with a few infants at the long nipples and some wide-eyed youngsters. But they were wild, and there were no bars separating her from them. And they were watching her, not eating or playing, just watching, like the huge, inescapable god heads. Even the infants were staring at her.

They'd been fighting. Slowly she detected the blood. It was mostly on the larger males, whose red penises jutted out from the furred hoods between their legs. The rain must have washed much of it away, but there had been a lot of blood and it stained them in patches.

They had something up there on the ledge with them, and it occurred to her that they had taken a piece of an animal. These adorable vegetarians were feeding on some kind of meat. She started to back away. Let them feed.

One stood on the shelf and she couldn't help but look when it lifted the thing. It was a pink human leg, smeared with blood. Her mind shunted the possibility away. Then she recognized the blue high-top sneaker wired at the ankle. It was Samnang's prosthesis.

She froze. *What have you done to him?*

The monkey pounded the leg on the ledge, foot down. The sneaker didn't make a sound. But the message was clear. She was trespassing.

Stand or run, she couldn't decide. In the Rockies, you made yourself larger. You put your hands over your head to appear taller and lowered your eyes. If a bear attacked, you played dead. If it was a mountain lion, you fought. This wasn't the Rockies.

Before she had time to decide, the canopy stirred. It was the softest of breezes, just a whisper. The monkeys shifted. They looked around them, at the trees, down the corridor of ruins. The whisper was approaching. Molly remembered the gust of wind that had crashed on her and Duncan their first day up here, and this had the same rising force to it. Molly glanced up to see where it was coming from and how it would strike her.

The monkeys fled.

It was that simple. They bolted into the branches and were gone. The gust of wind rushed overhead. It missed her, and plunged on with a howl.

She was left alone. White and orange flower petals drifted down onto her head and shoulders. It was so quiet she could almost hear them land.

"Kleat," she shouted. "Kleat. Duncan." She waited. No one answered.

After a minute, bracing herself for the carnage, she climbed up onto the ledge. It was both worse and better than she was ready for. Samnang's leg lay where the monkey had dropped it, and clearly it had been clawed and wrenched from his body in a great struggle. But the object of their feast was not his body. One of the monkeys had been killed, perhaps in the fight with Samnang. They had been eating one of their own.

30.

"Samnang?" she called out.

From the ledge, she could see a thicket of towering bamboo. It swayed gently. The canopy stirred again. The breeze was starting up. Somewhere the forest was letting it in. This time she could smell the coming rain on it.

The bamboo shivered. The feathery tops soared to various heights. The stalks clattered, lines and shadows luring her. Samnang might have escaped into there, she decided.

It was like entering a giant wind chime as she sidled among the green and yellow rods. They were a grass, not a tree, she knew that much, but some of the stems were as thick around as small kegs.

"Samnang," she called again.

The stand was many generations old. On the outskirts, youngsters stood no taller than her thigh, their stems as thin as pencils. Deeper in, the stand was older and taller and denser. Dried, gray, dead monsters—thirty, fifty, a hundred years old—had pierced the canopy.

The breeze stirred their long wings of leaves, sending tremors down the stems. The shafts quivered under her open palms. They pressed against her, then pulled away. They jostled her with long, arcing nudges. Samnang slipped from her mind. She was barely aware that her attention was shifting from him to the forest.

How did you capture this in a photo? It rose in her like a desire, the urge to hold the green light and the moment. There was no controlling the sensation with her lens. *Surrender,* she thought. It came to her in a whisper.

Yesterday they had been in a race against the rain. Today she felt in synch with it. In a strange way, the rain gave them an advantage over their captors, if that's what Vin and his brothers truly were. Unless the Khmers made a quick exit, the river would trap them and the forest would devour their vehicles. By contrast, the only thing the Americans stood to lose was a season stranded, and probably some weight.

Surrender. The idea grew. She and Duncan could melt off into the forest and outwait the others and inherit the ruins. If it was in the stars—in this starless place—they might become lovers. They would survive. The city—the forest—would provide.

The quaking leaves reminded her of aspen. Their shape was different, like minnows, not coins, but they shuddered and flipped with the same playful motion, and their colors ranged from blood red to green to yellow veined with gold.

The stand tightened around her. Her senses took on new intensity. Every stem had its own pulse. She could practically taste the light.

Molly went slowly, trying to balance her progress with the bamboo's rhythm. At first she looked for a simple left-to-right or back-and-forth pattern, but it was more complicated than that. You had to feel for it, yielding and then invading, stealing through its openings. Resist, push back, and it only wore you out.

It became—absurdly—erotic. The forest was dancing with her, bending her, carrying her. Like yesterday while climbing the tree, she felt pieced away from the greed and confusion and dangers of the expedition. But it was more powerful than that. She felt embraced. She felt desired.

The stand grew thicker. She found herself snaking between the stems in brief surges. The way a boatman rests among the waves, gauging the sea and hoarding his strength, Molly paused. She stopped. It took a minute to register that she was, in a way, trapped.

One green rod pressed between her thighs, another lined up against her spine, more a saddle than a scissors. There was nothing awkward or alarming about it. She would simply have to wait for the bamboo to shift and release her.

The bamboo chattered all around her. The fat stem running between her legs vibrated. *Absurd,* she thought again. *But nice.*

The stalks had tangled their leaves high above. *Patience, a moment more,* she thought to herself. *A wicked moment more.*

It happened again. The stem pulsed from the top down, a velvet jolt traveling from the sky into the forest floor. She struggled, though not for long. *Surrender.* Another tremor, and she felt lifted off the earth.

It was unspeakable, literally . . . getting humped by a tree. Not another person in the world could ever know. She couldn't even speak it to herself. But really, what was her alternative? To fight? To cry out for help? In a moment, the leaves would untangle. The bamboo would part. She would get back control of herself.

The wood throbbed again. It was like the devil down there between her legs. It took her breath.

She pushed with her back. The bamboo bowed with her. She bent sideways, but her camera strap tangled. *Surrender.* How was this different from a sunset or a flower's perfume or the meat of a fruit? It pleased her. And where was the decency in nature anyway? The soft earth gave her feet stirrups. Bamboo appeared between her fists. She hung on.

The high leaves shivered. She let her hips tilt and would have gone through with it, would have let the bamboo finish her. But as her head settled back along the one stem, she saw the soldier.

The skeleton wore a uniform of rags. The pieces of him lay in a patch so dense it formed a forest within the forest. The bamboo shafts opened and closed like seaweed in a crosscurrent.

Molly straightened. She pushed against the bamboo, really pushed, and this time the forest released her. She freed her legs and stumbled upright.

The thicket had her penned in now, unable to move forward, unable to retreat. The breeze was blowing stronger. The bamboo quickened its jangle, changing from wind music to the clatter of teeth. There was a skull in there, its eyes covered by the helmet.

"Kleat," she shouted. "Duncan."

The rattle rose to a clashing of wood against hollow wood. She shouted again.

Thunder fell against the top of the canopy.

She yelled herself hoarse.

It was an American uniform. He had a rifle.

The breeze became a wind. The wind became a gale.

At last she saw a distant figure approaching from the outside, chopping with machinelike double strokes, a forehand from the right, a backhand from the left. A second man appeared behind him.

"Here," she shouted.

Duncan was in front with the machete. "Are you hurt?" he called. "Can you get to us?"

"Just come," she shouted. She didn't tell them more. They had to see for themselves.

The closer Duncan got, the farther away he sounded. The *toc-toc* of the machete blade paled in the mounting racket.

Vin was not with them. She feared Kleat had done something to him. But she didn't see the boy's rifle, and Kleat would have taken that.

The rain began. It wasn't like yesterday's slow leak. Driven by the wind, the drops had real velocity. They stung her face. While the men worked closer, she tried once more to move nearer the skeleton. But the bamboo held her out like iron bars.

Finally, Duncan cut through to her. He laid one hand on her shoulder, as if to take her back from the forest.

"Where's Vin?" She had to shout over the crash of bamboo and thunder.

"We sent him down for help. We thought you must

have broken a leg. Or that a tiger was at you. He gave us his machete just in case."

"Not his rifle, though," Kleat shouted. He looked almost disappointed that she was in one piece. "What are you doing in here?"

"Samnang's leg," she said. "You didn't see it?"

"See what?"

"His leg. The monkeys must have stolen it again."

"Samnang's in here?"

"I came to find him. And look."

She pointed. The bones were all but invisible through the thrashing bamboo. It took them a minute to see.

"How did you know he was in here?" Kleat shouted.

"I didn't." And yet she'd come almost directly to the skeleton. Molly tried to remember the phases of her entry, her reasoning for this detour. The monkeys had gotten her attention, and there had been the music of the bamboo, and the light, and the dance. Now, with the bamboo smashing together and the rain whipping them, it seemed off the wall.

"We can't stay in here," Duncan said. "The wind is getting worse."

"Give me that." Kleat grabbed the machete from his hand.

Molly and Duncan stood back while Kleat attacked the bamboo. He threw his raw emotions at the barrier, grunting and cursing. The blade caught each time the stalks bent in the wind, pulling the handle from his grip.

In the movies, a single swipe would have opened a small highway. Here the bamboo fought them, knocking them sideways and backward. Caught at their tops, each severed stalk bucked and stabbed in wild directions, their bottoms like tubular knives. Each stem had to be yanked loose from the canopy and laid flat before the machete could be used again.

"This is no good," Duncan shouted.

Kleat gave up. He'd gotten them closer. But the bamboo still kept them out. They could clearly see the soldier, wearing a tanker's helmet with padded ears. His rifle was trussed to his ribs by vines, barrel up, the way it had fallen from his hands. The skeleton was amazingly whole. Green shoots had grown up between the long bones. Creepers held the ribs and spine in place. Like the city, the bones were both raided and preserved by the forest.

"He shot himself," Duncan said. "Look at the back of his helmet, the hole. And see the way his rifle's lying?"

"What?" The rain glanced off Kleat's head.

"He ate his gun," Duncan yelled. "Look. The recoil tore out his teeth."

"What was he doing out here?" Molly said.

"It's an old jungle fighter's trick," Kleat said. "E and E. Escape and evasion. Bamboo makes the perfect hiding place. It guards you in your sleep. The minute anything approaches, the bamboo wakes you up."

Duncan scanned their sky of furious leaves and cane. It sounded like the clash of spears and the scream of men. His hair whipped like a mare's tail. "The storm's growing," he said. "Listen."

Molly listened. Deep beneath the clatter of bamboo, some monstrous entity was grinding its stone teeth together. The earth vibrated with it.

"It's the wind," he shouted. "There's a sail effect on the canopy. The canopy rocks the trees. The trees rock the ruins. The wind is moving the whole city. We have to return to camp."

"But this is my proof," Kleat said. "I only need one of them. I need him." His knuckles were white on the handle.

"It could take another hour to get in there." Duncan pointed at the sky. "This is the big one."

Mekkhala, Molly thought. The angel of thunder was here. But it would pass. The city could be theirs. This was their chance to be rid of Kleat.

"Let me try," she said.

Duncan ignored her. "The bones aren't going anywhere," he said. "We can come back for them."

"A typhoon could bring the whole forest down," Kleat said.

She gave her camera bag to Duncan.

Kleat had brought them to within ten feet of the remains. She pressed her palms against the wall of bamboo, feeling for its tempo. Two towering stalks parted and clashed together. When they opened again, she was ready, slipping through with a skip. The stalks clapped shut. She waited again.

Her body swayed with the stand. She waited and stepped again, and waited. Like that, she insinuated herself all the way to the bones.

31.

She stood astride the skeleton, not sure what to do next. Here was this mortal thing in her keeping. The bamboo raged around her. The rain was coming down harder now.

The uniform was just threads held together with tendrils. Moss grew in the spaces of his remaining teeth. The barrel's recoil had ripped most of his front teeth outward. Three stuck up at odd angles.

Bullied by the stand, she bent and unfastened the dog tag. They would need more, she knew. Teeth. The mandible. The whole skull.

Fastened together, the straps of the helmet would make a handle for the bucket. But when she tried to lift it, the helmet rolled away, exposing the upper face.

His jade eyes stared at her.

Molly barked and straightened bolt upright. The bamboo promptly clubbed her to her knees.

Someone had pressed the jade balls into his eye sockets years ago. Pale green, they bulged from the bones of his face. A skein of rootlets had grown across the skull and stone eyes, a mask of vegetation.

"Moll-lee." They were calling her, though it came to her as a whisper.

The J school *W*s crashed through her mind: who, what, when, where, why. The bamboo shoved at her. She couldn't think. The typhoon was coming.

The helmet had preserved his blond hair. The skull, she told herself. It was wet. His hair was coarse.

She worked her fingers under the bone to get a purchase, and the back of his head was a ragged cave. Her hand slipped, and the whole carpet of his scalp came away.

She was almost sick. "God," she yelped. The skull was fused to the earth.

"Moll-lee."

A branch of leaves whipped her face. Leave the skull. The forensics people would have to make do with pieces. She plucked the three loosened teeth from their sockets and folded them, with the dog tag, in the pouch of the scalp, and shoved the bundle into one pocket of her pants. She stood, half bent, and began her exit.

The bamboo punched her ribs. It creaked and banged. The rhythm eluded her. She went too fast, then too slow. The stand struck at her. It caught her hand. She fell, then got to her feet.

Then Duncan was pulling her through. Without a word, he gripped her arms and propelled her along their narrow path through the bamboo. Kleat was already out of sight.

She cast a last glance back at the skeleton, knowing the skull would be wearing its death grin. What she didn't expect was its knowing authority. It seemed to be nodding to her. The remains floated on sea swells of vegetation, the arms and legs spreading and rising and beckoning her back, or waving good-bye, the eyes staring.

They emerged from the bamboo, and Duncan did not stop. The clash of bamboo faded, and now she heard that deep-ocean scraping of stone on stone. Dazed by her beating in the stand, Molly looked to see if walls were shifting or spires bending. Surely the city was tearing to pieces. But it stood intact. It was nestling. The ruins were rearranging themselves deep in their foundation, settling a fraction more into the forest.

In the rain and green gloom, they could have been on a giant ark of stone. The floods were coming. Molly smelled wet fur, and it was monkeys—dozens of them now—huddled on the temples' edges and on top of giant faces, watching them, passing them from one pair of eyes to the next.

Kleat was waiting for them in the mouth of a building, out of the rain. The bamboo had knocked one lens from his steel-rimmed glasses. The remaining lens was misted over. He seemed fractured and only half present.

His one visible eye looked a hundred years old, bloodshot and milky. For all his ugliness over the past weeks, Molly felt pity for him, even a kind of respect. At an age when many men were retiring to the links or cursing the financial pages, Kleat was getting broiled by the sun and horsewhipped by bamboo, faithful to his brother.

He had the machete. Slow water bled from the metal. With the scar along his throat, he might have just returned from battle. "What did you get?" he said.

"Sit," Duncan said to her. She was shivering.

Molly brought out the bundled pelt. The soldier's hair was three or four inches long. It had grown during his exile among the ruins. She unfolded the scalp, and there were dark veins along the inside of the leather. The teeth lay on top, yellow with coffee and the decades. The dog tag was so tarnished it appeared to be blank.

"Good," said Kleat. "Very good."

She felt ghoulish crouching over the bits and pieces of a man. She set the artifacts on a stone and wiped her hands on the wall, trying to clean away the feel of his hair. Kleat could carry the thing from here on. She'd done her duty.

"There's something else," she said. "He had jade eyes."

"What are you talking about?" Kleat said.

"They were hidden by the helmet. I moved the helmet and someone had put stones in his eye sockets. It was almost like he could see."

"Who would do that?" said Kleat.

"Maybe it's a funeral rite," Duncan said. "But I've never heard of any of the mountain tribes doing a thing like that. And the only people inside the city were the soldiers."

"Get out of here," Kleat said.

"Who knows?" said Duncan. "After a few months in here, the survivors might have been losing their grip on things. Going native. Going wild. Making things up. Maybe they buried him that way, modern warriors copying ancient warriors."

"But he wasn't buried," said Molly. "He was lying in the open. He shot himself where no one could find him."

Duncan fell silent.

"This fucking city," Kleat said. He took off his glasses and cleaned his fogged lens and fit what was left of it onto his face. "At least we'll know who he was."

He held the tag up in the light. Molly watched his expression. He blinked. The muscles twitched in his cheeks. "Ridiculous," he said. His lens clouded over again. He said it a second time, in a whisper.

Duncan took the tag from him and tilted it to read the embossing. His face drew into itself. "I don't understand," he said.

Molly pulled the tag from his fingers.

" 'Yale,' " she read aloud. " 'Lucas M.' "

32.

"He's playing with us," Kleat shouted over his shoulder. He was angry.

"It's tattooed on his arm," said Duncan. "We all saw it. Lucas Yale."

They were on the move again, heading for the stairs. *Nagas* reared up along the rim. Water shot from their cobra mouths into the depths of the terminus. Channels hidden within the terraces sped it toward the waiting reservoirs. Duncan had said the history of Cambodia lay in its hydraulics. She was beginning to see this empire built on shaping the shapeless, capturing the rain with its ancient geometry.

The wind was picking up. It struck the canopy in bursts, creating huge green pinwheels that moved overhead. Maelstroms in the sky. Molly thought of Van Gogh's *The Starry Night,* and that panicked her because night was not far enough away. They needed all the day that was left for their escape.

She tried to see their camp in the abyss, but the rain drove at her eyes. Roots and fallen leaves skated underfoot. The rain was as warm as blood. She put it out of her mind. She was putting a lot of things out of her mind.

"He had free run of the place. He found the bones," said Kleat. "He saw the dog tag. He got the tattoo. Or he had this made and planted it there. Who do you think put the stones in his eyes?"

"But why do that?" Molly wondered out loud.

Kleat whirled on her. "Defiling the dead, that's what he's done," he shouted. "He's a lunatic."

His outrage was out of proportion to the event. Kleat was possibly right. Luke had somehow written himself into the last days of the Blackhorse missing. There would be some reasonable explanation. But the remains of the soldier had not been desecrated so much as adorned. Luke hadn't moved a bone. At most, he'd decorated them.

What disturbed her was Kleat. With his cockeyed steel rims and the missing lens, and that machete, he looked unraveled. His furious rationalizing was irrational. The soldier's real identity wasn't lost, only temporarily lifted. They had flesh, hair, and bone to present to the forensics lab. The soldier would get his name back. Luke's act baffled her. Identity theft was one thing, but in the middle of a jungle? What did he gain? Nothing added up.

"You're saying a madman went to the trouble of forging something so common, a dog tag?" Molly said. "And then hid it where we would probably never find it? All so we *could* find it?"

"He brought us here, didn't he? He lured us with the tags."

"I'm not so sure anymore. We brought ourselves. With our needs."

"The gypsy kid walked right up to our table in the restaurant. He'd watched us for a month and selected us out of all the others. It's so plain in hindsight."

"It's not plain at all. What does he get out of it? Why us?"

"Maybe he needed to get resupplied. Look at all the food and gear we brought with us. Plus two vehicles, with pirates to drive his riches out of here." He added, "And a woman."

"You said he'd gone. Halfway to China, you said."

"Maybe I was wrong."

Kleat was talking nonsense. He wanted things to make sense. He wanted them to connect even if they made no sense.

He strode ahead, arms swinging, that machete like a pendulum. The blade sparked against a wall. She wanted to get it away from him. Regardless of whether they escaped today or in a week or in six months, they were going to need the machete to build camps and cut wood and butcher game and keep them sustained. In Kleat's hand, it was only a weapon.

"What if he's one of them?" Duncan asked from the back. He had been quiet ever since leaving their shelter.

"One of who?" Kleat's voice was cautionary. He'd had a bellyful of ghost talk.

"One of the Blackhorse men."

"Christ." Kleat quickened the pace, leaving the thought behind.

Molly pondered it. "One of the original soldiers?"

"We know they were here. What if not all of them died?"

"A living MIA?"

She felt boosted. Amped up. Here was the ultimate survivor tale. A Robinson Crusoe in fatigues, subsisting in a lost city for thirty years, dodging enemies, and eluding the $2.6 million reward for his capture. In Luke, not the city, lay her story. If it was true.

But it couldn't be. That quickly, she dismissed it. "He's just a boy. Twenty years old." Except for his eyes, the thousand-year-old eyes.

"I thought of that, too," said Duncan, undeterred. "But what if he's a different kind of MIA? What if he's Luke's son? Or the son of one of them?"

She stopped. Kleat came back to them.

"You're saying Luke came looking for his father?" she asked. Then she remembered his young face. The war was thirty years ago, and the boy was twenty, not thirty. Once you've crossed the thirty mark, you know the difference. "He's still too young."

"Not if his father did survive."

"I don't get it."

"They were trapped. Some of them died. Maybe only one was left. He didn't dare descend. One war after another raged out there. Maybe he went mad. Maybe he was injured and suffering from amnesia. What if he went off into the mountains and some tribe took him in? And twenty years ago, he had a son. A son who could watch over the remains."

A son dressed in peasant pants and Vietcong sandals. *All borrowed together.*

"A half-breed guardian angel?" said Kleat.

"I'm only saying what if," said Duncan.

"Okay, what if he is the sentinel and this is like his own tomb of the unknowns. That doesn't explain why he went down and chose us and gave away his secret."

"Maybe that was his job. To find someone to take them home."

"That's crazy," said Kleat. "The kid's a Westerner. Blue eyes, blond hair, white skin. And where did he learn his English?"

"That's a problem," Duncan admitted.

"Not just his English, his American," said Molly. "You can't fake an accent like that. I heard it. He's from West Texas, not the Cambodian highlands."

"You're right," said Duncan. "I was just trying to come up with something other than ghosts."

33.

A surprise awaited them partway down the staircase. From there they could see into the clearing, and the brothers had not left. The Land Cruiser stood ready to go, its engine running. Molly could smell its exhaust through the rain.

"By God," Kleat said.

Her relief took over. She wanted to collapse. She didn't have to hold it all together anymore. Everything was going to be fine. They were going to drive out of here.

"Hello," Kleat shouted down. He waved the machete in the air. A tiny figure appeared on the far side of the truck and waved up at them.

"There's luck for you," Duncan said.

They passed the ledges, and Molly saw the splintered poles and shredded fabric of their tents among the relentless vegetation. Across the way, Kleat's immense bonfire was nothing but mud and charred logs. The thatch hut looked as desolate as the ACAV stranded in the tree above.

The next time she came, the forest would have consumed it all, the hut, the fire pit, and the leftovers of their tents. It would be as if they'd never been here. She felt a twinge of regret. Above and behind her, the waterways were coursing and gurgling. She wanted to see the city the way the people had seen it twenty centuries ago, with the water animating its canals and gargoyles. The city would never belong to her again the way it did at this moment. *Surrender.* Now was her opportunity.

At the base of the staircase, Kleat paused. "All right, listen up. We're going to have to work as a team on this."

"We are a team," Molly assured him. She heard the havoc in his voice. And now he had the machete.

Raindrops spattered off his scalp. The veins were rising. He took out a bundle of dollars. "We're coming down empty-handed. But we still have cash. Don't offer anything at first," he said to Duncan. "Let's see where we stand with them."

"Good idea, John," Duncan said.

"You stay to the right. I'll go in from the left." He fastened the flak jacket shut.

"That won't be necessary, John."

"Stay separated."

"It's going to work out," Molly said.

"We've got what we came for," Kleat said. He patted the pocket along his thigh. It bulged with the scalp and teeth and dog tag.

"Don't do anything," she said.

Kleat looked at her with his one fogged lens and that aged eye. He started across the clearing.

"He's going to kill them," she whispered to Duncan. "Or get us killed. Warn them."

"They'd shoot us for sure."

"But we're not with him."

"We're Americans, Molly. Do you think they see a difference?"

"We should go back up the stairs."

"How far do you think we'd make it?"

"Stop him then."

They hurried to catch up with Kleat. In their absence, Doc and So had shimmed wood and stones under the wheels of the Land Cruiser and rolled it down to safety. The engine was idling.

The truck was another matter. Its front end pitched up like the stem of a sinking ship, deeper than ever. It was a goner, but the brothers weren't giving up. With axes and shovels, they had spent the morning chewing down to the wheels and axle. Their hole looked more like a grave than true hope. A rusty cable fed from the front hitch, ready to attach to the Land Cruiser for a heroic tow.

As the three Americans approached, Doc climbed from the muddy pit, ax in hand. Molly's stomach knotted. Their rifles were probably on the front seat of the truck, out of the rain. She looked for Vin, a friendly face.

So poked his head up from the pit. Plastered with black mud, the two Khmers looked the way God's Adam must have looked like in his first moments, mud with two eyes. Molly did not reach for her camera.

Duncan greeted them. Doc spoke. "He wants to know, where's their cargo."

"Start bargaining," Kleat said, moving to flank the pit.

It was beginning. Molly wanted to freeze them all, make them as still as carvings.

Doc wasn't fooled.

"He wants to know how you got Vin's machete," Duncan said. "He wants to know where their brother is."

So pulled himself from the pit. The mud made sucking noises. He was armed with a shovel.

"Tell them." Kleat was smiling, all innocence. "We sent him to get help."

So barked at them.

"They say he never came down."

"Then he must have gotten lost. He's on his way." Kleat held up his money. Water sluiced off the bright steel blade.

Duncan frowned. He spoke with the brothers.

"I told them we should start searching for him. The ruins are moving around. A stone might have fallen on him. There are animals, too. And the typhoon will get much worse, I think. We don't want to be inside here tonight."

"Good," Kleat said, smiling. "We're on their side. Keep talking."

Duncan knelt to draw in the mud with a twig. Maps, always maps with him. Doc sat on his heels to add his own lines to the diagram. So looked over their shoulders. Molly stepped closer.

No one noticed Kleat until the door slammed shut up ahead. He gunned the engine, and with a wild glance back through his broken glasses, he took off. The Land Cruiser shot a rooster tail of leaves into the air and bucked forward over roots and tipped paving stones.

He was leaving them.

Molly was surprised by her surprise. Of course he was leaving them. He was Kleat.

The brothers gave a shout. Duncan, too. A waste of breath.

Molly watched it unfold. Duncan waved his arms in the air. The two Khmers raced around to the truck and grabbed their rifles. Duncan yelled at them not to fire. They cut loose anyway and gave chase.

34.

From behind, Molly couldn't tell one mud figure from the other. One let off a long burst that emptied his banana clip, and he changed to a fresh one without missing a step. She ran after them.

Picking up speed, Kleat reached the green mineral causeway that ran between the ancient reservoirs. He veered to miss the remains of a *naga,* putting more distance between them. There was going to be no stopping him.

The brothers ran on. The faster one sprinted ahead, not bothering to shoot, maybe gambling that Kleat would clip a statue or that one of his brother's bullets might puncture a tire. Molly continued after them. She didn't want to see Kleat punished, but she didn't want him to escape either. She just wanted to see.

She had reached halfway across the long causeway. The mouth of the gateway appeared in front of them, like the eye of a needle. Through there it would be blue sky, or almost.

One brother fired. The other chased.

The Land Cruiser suddenly lifted up on an orange blossom.

That was the first antitank mine detonating the fuel tank.

A heavy boom echoed across the water. From Molly's distance, the Land Cruiser seemed to be launching into space. It spiraled forward through the plume of fuel and smoke.

The truck started to land on one side, then jumped again, thrown by the second mine. It flipped onto its roof, still moving, and the screech of metal rippled back to her in stereo along the tops of both ponds.

Flames shot up. Smoke spilled like ink.

The reserve fuel tank went off. The fireball created a temporary sun in the rainfall. It even cast an artificial rainbow.

An arm appeared from one window. Somehow Kleat had survived the explosions. He was trying to drag himself from the burning car.

The sight of him struggling to escape renewed the brothers' fury. Molly thought of the turtle in their fire last night. They would have no mercy.

She was sure the wreck had quit sliding. But then it moved again. From her distance, it looked like translucent animals rushing up from the water and bunching around the fiery vehicle. It was the rain in her eyes, she thought.

The Land Cruiser shifted. It hit a third mine. What was left of it flipped off the road.

The water was deeper than she'd guessed. The flaming ball of metal didn't float and go under in a lather of bubbles. It vanished. The man-made lake swallowed the man-made sun in a single bite.

Molly came to a standstill.

Kleat was gone.

Plastered in mud, the two brothers howled and fired their rifles into the water, cheated of their enemy.

She wasn't sure what obligation she had to Kleat. He had left them to die. Let the prehistoric fishes have him. But someone needed to witness what was left. Someone had to say a few words over the water.

Grimly, she started forward.

In the space of an instant, she felt a hand wrap around her left ankle, rooting her foot in place. She felt its fingers squeeze.

Even as she glanced down, the image of a fist disappeared. There was the echo of a sensation, a physical resonance. Then it was as if it had never been.

She lifted her foot. A piece of green waterweed led over the road's rim, limp and flat. Her imagination was in overdrive. She had invented the hand to halt herself.

She peered over the edge to see if a wave had flung up the weed. The wreck might have caused a ripple or runoff from the city. But the water was flat and dimpled by rain. And occupied.

Something was in there. Molly moved her head to one side.

It was the other ACAV. It had sunk to the bottom and was lodged in mud. Weeds floated up from the machine-gun barrels. A goldfish the size of a carp swam from one hatch. Another peered up at her from the depths of the second hatch. She leaned out over the water, angling for a better view. Their eyes weren't spaced like the eyes of a fish. They were almost human.

"Molly!"

She pulled back from the water. Duncan was standing at the forest's edge. The machete hung from one hand. The pacifist had armed himself.

"Come back," he said.

"Kleat's gone," she announced. She heard her unnatural calm. "And I found something in the water."

"Molly, before they start back. Their blood will be up. We have to hide."

She glanced down the road at the brothers. They were prowling from side to side, searching for any trace of their vehicle or Kleat. "But we didn't do anything. Kleat betrayed us all, you and me, too."

"They'll figure that out eventually. But it will be better if we're not around when they return. Come back. We'll take some food and spend the night in the ruins. We'll go find Vin. That will satisfy them. It will all work out."

That sounded sensible. Good old Duncan. She turned.

There was a fourth detonation out on the road.

Molly looked in time to see a man flying from the road, like a puppet getting jerked from the stage. There was no ceremony to it, barely a bang.

Abruptly he stopped, in midair.

She thought that it was an illusion, that time had stopped. The arc of his flight would continue in the next moment, it had to.

Then she saw the tree branch quivering. He'd been impaled on its tip. There he hung, like an ornament. Less than that, like a bit of trash caught in the trees.

Fifty yards ahead of Molly, the remaining man froze in place. The brothers were children of the mine fields.

They knew them with the same dread and familiarity the Dark Ages had known hell. One step more, forward, backward, or to the side, and the man knew he might be maimed or killed. He stood there as if his very soul was at risk. And for him, it was. Samnang had told her that to die away from home, away from burial rites and family, meant wandering for eternity.

For a full minute, the young man didn't move. Covered in mud, anonymous to her, he was like a tar baby with a rifle stuck in his hand. Next to him, rising higher than his head, a *naga* bared its stone fangs.

The man groaned. It wasn't a word, just a noise escaping his lungs, the start of grief.

"Stay where you are, Molly."

Duncan started out to her slowly with a stick in his hand, touching gravel and leaves as if reading braille, scanning all around his feet for trip wires or metal buds or any evidence of mines.

He took hours, it seemed. Molly didn't move. The lone brother didn't move. She kept her eyes away from the man hanging in the tree.

Molly felt heavy, and yet light, magnificently light. Released. Anointed, in a way. She had been spared, but more important, she had seen. That was the crux of it.

As a photographer and a journalist, she had made a living from catching the meta-moments. In an article on a day in the life of an emergency room, she'd captured birth, suffering, and the still toes of a traffic fatality, and thought she'd seen it all, and in a sense she had, through her glass lens. No glass this time. No mirrors.

She stood obediently. Duncan was coming for her. He was almost here.

Once again, as in the bamboo thicket and when she had descended from the tree, Duncan laid claim to her. He was taking her back from the jaws of this place.

Beyond his shoulder, one of those giant god heads was smiling across the water, eyes closed but aware, deep in his dream of them. That was probably all she needed to know. They were figments of a stone imagination. And yet she wondered at it all. There was Samnang's cosmic stream, but then there were the day-to-day riddles, like land mines where there had been none before.

"How could this happen?" she asked.

"The soldiers," said Duncan. "Thirty years ago. They must have laid them."

"But we drove in this way. And now look."

"Chance," he said. "The robots of destiny. Like they say, mines are infinite war."

"No. Someone placed them here for us." She was utterly certain about that.

Duncan corrected her. "For someone like us. The soldiers were guarding themselves."

"It's like we're not being allowed to leave," she said.

"Don't say that," said Duncan.

"They were laid to keep us here."

"Not so loud," he said.

That frightened her. He wasn't disagreeing. It came to her. "Luke?" she said.

"Not now, Molly. One thing at a time."

"What about him?" The tar baby.

"I'll go for him next."

35.

It all might have worked as Duncan said. He would have led Molly to the forest and returned for the final brother. But an animal began to cry. It started as a tiny, thin keening, and Molly was sure it was some macabre birdsong.

Then she realized it was coming from the corpse skewered on the tree. The mine had lopped away his lower legs. His arms were broken at the elbows. But even with the spike of the branch punched through his chest, what remained of him was not yet dead. There he hung, above the water.

The cry rose an octave. It was awful. He didn't seem to take a breath. Like some inelegant jungle bird up there, he rustled his wings weakly, whistling a one-note song. The rain spoiled her make-believe. The mud was being washed away. She could see the red meat underneath.

The man on the road appealed to his brother. He reached up. They were only twenty feet apart, separated by the span of air and water. The dying brother gave no sign of recognition. His cry went on.

Thunder shook the pond. It came up through the mineral vein carved into the shape of the road.

The wind howled and skipped across the canopy's surface, and the branch moved. The impaled man rocked in space. His brother laid down his rifle and knelt before the carcass in the tree, hands pressed together.

Molly could barely breathe. The man shuffled forward on his knees, unnerved by the death song, drawn to it.

"He'll never last," Duncan said. Did he mean that living corpse or his brother?

"Don't move," he said to her. "Do you hear me?"

Stay with me, she thought. But he was Duncan, the savior. "Yes," she said.

Off he went, twig in hand, calling to the young man. The brother had entered a trance. He took no notice of Duncan scolding and commanding him. Duncan advanced by inches, touching the road, testing the fabric.

The part of a man continued singing from the tree, a grotesque siren drawing his brother to wreck himself, too.

Duncan refused to hurry. He tested each fallen leaf on the road, turning them with the tip of his stick. He skirted a patch of dirt and stepped over random pebbles.

There didn't seem to be any possible place to hide a mine out there. The road was all of a single piece, carved flat from a volcanic extrusion. Olivine, she guessed, keying on the color of the word. *What a photo.* Like the devil whispering in her ear.

Duncan reached the rifle and stooped to take it.

They would need that, she thought. The summer stretched before them, her forest idyll after all. They would subsist on fruit and nuts, and meat brought down from the trees.

The brother was almost to the water's edge. There his knee touched the mine.

There was nothing flashy or pyrotechnic about the explosion, a sharp blast smaller than the heavy booming that had thrown the truck. Mostly it was a matter of dust. As the air cleared, Molly saw that the brother was gone. He had been pitched into the devouring water, though she hadn't actually seen that.

Duncan was standing in place, looking off across the pond. He turned to her, and his chest seemed to be smoking, though that could have been the rain driving against him. The rifle was missing from his hands, and his twig was only a few inches long now. He started back to her, more quickly on the return, his path memorized.

Molly saw the wound gradually.

Her T-shirt with the mountain-bike wheels was bleeding.

Oh, Molly, she thought. Amazed, she plucked at the wet cloth and found a small hole through the spokes of one wheel. She lifted her shirt, and the hole went through her bra. She pried it open and looked inside at the top of her white, freckled flesh, and blood welled up where the shrapnel had entered her. The wicked thing was in there somewhere. But suddenly she didn't want to know more. She let the shirt drop down again. Later.

"Molly?" She heard the anguish in his voice.

She managed to ask him first. "Are you all right?"

Miraculously, the shrapnel had missed him. The gods were protecting one of them anyway. "You need to lie down," he said.

"No," she said. "While I'm still on my feet, take me home." To camp, she meant to say. Suddenly her legs quit on her. She sank to sitting. The red blood blanched to Barbie pink as it fanned lower across her wet shirt. There was no pain, really. She just had a need to sit.

She looked out over the green water. Lily pads the size of doormats floated on the surface. Raindrops pattered the glass. That horrible birdsong had stopped. Thank God.

Duncan materialized behind her. She felt his big hands on her shoulders.

"It's only a splinter," she said.

"I need to take a look."

It wasn't how she wanted him to see them the first time, clinically, with her on her back in the rain, filling with fear. They were nice breasts, really, one of her best features. She would have liked to make him aware that a woman can blind a man with her body.

He didn't waste time with the bra hooks. She saw the clasp knife. The elastic released. She watched his eyes. He blinked. At her beauty? At her ruin?

He lifted her breast with the fingertips of both hands, careful beyond need, though she appreciated the tenderness. Now she could feel the splinter of steel. It was lodged deep in the tissue, a metal tumor. "Can you feel it?" she pleaded. She suddenly, intensely, wanted it out of her.

He glanced up with frightened eyes. "I'm trying." He spider-walked his fingertips across the rest of her body, probing here and there. "Tell me if this hurts," he kept saying.

"No," she said. "No."

He ran his hands down each leg. Nothing broken. Only the splinter.

"Can you sit?" He lowered her shirt and fashioned a sling with his red and white *kroma*. The scarves were a whole magazine article unto themselves. Someday.

Then she saw over his shoulder. "Oh God," she whispered.

Monkeys were flocking to the body in the tree. They were playing with it, pulling at the clothes, flopping the head. Looting him the way he had looted their city.

Duncan moved to block her view. "Stick with me, kid," he said.

They were massing at the body, fighting over it. She'd never seen such a thing. He raised her to her feet. "I can carry you," he said. "But it will be better if you can follow me. Can you do that?"

"We'll be fine," she said.

36.

The wind mounted, but could not penetrate the canopy. It shrieked and beat at the forest, and great whirlpools appeared among the leaves. But the membrane held, and for now they were spared the full brunt of the typhoon.

Her bleeding slowed.

Here in camp, with the terminus walls at their back, Molly felt almost sheltered. The rain didn't drive so hard. It spilled from the canopy in long, thick, silver shafts, and funneled through the barrel of the ACAV's machine gun like a cherub peeing. Night seemed near, but she was learning that this was a constant in the permanent twilight of day.

She lay propped on her side in the thatch hut in front of the fire that Duncan had revived with gasoline and a car flare. He was reviving it all, the whole camp, and their appearance of settling in. In fact, the fire and camp were his illusion. He intended for them to escape once darkness fell.

There were two possibilities. Either Luke had rigged

the mines on his way out, trapping them inside his shell, or he was still nearby, armed with a Vietnam-vintage arsenal, playing cat and mouse with them.

"He thinks he's God," Duncan said to her. "Whether he's watching or not, he thinks the walls contain us now. We're like animals in his zoo. But even zookeepers sleep."

But God does not, she thought to herself. From the hut, she could see the half-closed Buddha eyes looming in the forest, and they seemed menacing with their wakeful dreams.

Duncan stayed as busy as a beaver. She watched through the flames and the plumes of rain steam as he came and went, stripping the truck like a castaway. The brothers' pit, dug to free the truck, brimmed with water now. The prow tipped higher as the truck slid backward into the earth in slow motion. With the machete, Duncan knifed open the canvas covering the truck bed, looting it from the side, lifting out whatever remained.

He brought whatever he could carry, waxy boxes full of MREs, jerry cans of fuel, shovels, axes, burlap sacks, pieces of plastic and canvas, a screen for sifting relics from dirt, even a pair of sunglasses and a set of keys from the ignition. He stockpiled it at one end of the hut or cut big leathery wild banana leaves to cover it, more stuff than two people could use in a month, much less what was left of the afternoon. She drifted in and out of sleep.

The wires of the truck spilled from one open door like colorful entrails, tangled by creeper vines tugging at them. The forest had disemboweled the beast.

"You should fix the wires," she told him. "You can make it run."

He bent to look at her eyes. She was cold again. Shock this time, or her fever? He wrapped a strip of canvas around her shoulders. It was hard and rough and reeked of fuel.

"The truck's gone," he said. "We don't want it anyway. The road's a mantrap. Our only way out is through the ruins and over the wall."

Up the hundred and four stairs, through the labyrinth at night? "Are you sure?" she said.

"Up and over the mountain. While the storm's still raging. He'll never expect that."

She wished he would just take her in his arms. She remembered that morning. It seemed so long ago.

He made a steeple of wood above the fire so the wet branches would dry and burn. Kleat would have been proud. Another few hours and they would have themselves an Aggie-size bonfire. He brought her a tin cup filled with hot water sprinkled with ashes. He stirred in instant coffee from an MRE.

"Rest," he said. "Eat. Drink. Gather your strength. If I could just find the med kit. And a rifle. Just in case."

"I know where there's a gun." She gave him a secret smile.

He glanced at her doubtfully. "Is that so?"

"Go to the tree," she said. "Pull the rope to the side, toward the tree. Pull it hard."

He wagged a finger at her, delighted by the trick. "Kleat's gun? You said you left it in the ACAV."

"I did. But it should slide down to you. Unless the monkeys took it." The wicked monkeys.

"After dark," he decided, "in case he's watching. For now, keep up the charade. I'll keep salvaging and gathering firewood. And you . . . you keep bleeding. I want him to think we're on our last legs."

He went back into the rain. The truck had sunk to the windshield. Duncan balanced on the hood and hit the glass with a pry bar. The windshield crazed and pouched in, and he hooked it out like a carcass. Then he lowered himself inside.

She didn't like his disappearing into the earth this way. Minutes passed. At last some packages heaved into sight. She recognized his steel briefcase, and then came more boxes of gear and food.

He emerged through the windshield muddy and with his face beaming. He held aloft the med kit like it was the greatest treasure.

Her wound became the first order of business. He untied the sling and opened the med kit, and it even had a pair of latex gloves for him.

It was different this time. Out on the bridge, they had both been frightened. Here the moment was more considered. She watched him trying to confront her breast, and it amused her. He blinked diligently. He cleared his throat.

Part of his dismay was the forbidden fruit itself. Her areola was wide and brown, and though she was thirty-something there was still no southern drift, no stretch marks, no erosion of her supremacy.

But also he was perplexed, and she was, too. A broken bone you straightened. A cut you stitched, a burn you bandaged. But a soft breast with a tiny wound? He clenched his gloved hands.

The shrapnel seemed to have migrated deeper. Again she felt panic and loathing, and again she made herself remote from it. "It's in there," she said. "It's hard to describe. I can feel the sense of it."

He tore open a Betadine swab and painted the area orange. She feared he would make himself brusque and surgical and go digging into her flesh. Instead, he confessed.

"I don't know what to do," he said. "It will get infected if we leave it in there, but I'd probably infect you trying to get it out."

In the end, he simply placed a Band-Aid over the hole and lowered her shirt and retied the sling. He rummaged through the med kit, picking up vials and packets and reading their contents. "I haven't heard of half this stuff."

"Let me look," she said. She found a bottle of Cipro. It wasn't penicillin, but she figured something was better than nothing. She downed a capsule with some coffee and pocketed the bottle.

"We'll get you to a doctor," he declared. He covered her with the canvas again and built the fire higher. The flames licked close enough to curl the edges of the green thatch. But she couldn't seem to get warm.

"Eat," he urged. "We have a long night ahead of us."

"Tomorrow morning," she bargained. "I'll be better then."

"You'll only stiffen up," he said. "Besides, we need the storm. It will give us wings."

He went back into the clearing to haul gear and further their illusion of staying. He positioned jerry cans of gas and diesel along the walls inside the hut, which worried her. With the fire so close, they seemed like bombs waiting to go off. But she trusted his judgment.

When everything that could be pulled from the vehicles had been collected, he started making rounds of the clearing, pulling up rotten stumps and hauling more firewood. His ruse even fooled her. Coming in from one of his forays, he dumped an armful of wood on the pile, and slipped the gun to her.

"You are so clever," he said. That cheered her.

The hurricane roar rotated in Dolby surround sound from one side to the other. Logs fell into the fire, setting off explosions of sparks. The rain hissed and vaporized in bursts of haze.

"How can I help?" she asked.

"We're going to need your camera bag, but without the camera. It's got to stay. I'm sorry. My stuff stays, too. We can't afford the weight, and we have no backpacks. I'll need your bag to carry food and meds. We have a long trek ahead of us."

She wanted to argue. But they were running for their lives.

"Don't make a big show of it," he said. "Just take the camera and lenses out. Line them up. Polish the glass. Remember, he could be watching."

37.

Duncan left again, carrying on with his charade of inhabiting this island. It was getting dark beyond the flames. Molly wondered when he meant for them to make their move.

She emptied the camera bag, polishing the lenses, drying the camera, and setting the lenses in a neat row. Ten grand in glass and mirrors. Let the forest and the monkeys have them. The real treasures were her images. Those she could still keep.

It took a few minutes to transfer the last of her images to her digital wallet. Little bigger than a hand calculator, it held close to a thousand of her best shots. Wrapped in a plastic bag, it would fit into her pants pocket. Duncan would never know. If she couldn't manage to carry the extra few ounces, she wasn't going to make it anyway.

While she was at it, she decided to surprise Duncan with some of his own treasures. Just because he was sacrificing his briefcase didn't mean losing everything in it. Once they reached Phnom Penh and their escape was just a memory, she would present him with a few of his most precious mementos.

She reached for the briefcase. From the first day she'd met him, Molly had wondered what it held. The stainless steel was dented and raked with scratch marks. The hinges on the bottom and the lock combination were rusted. She'd never once seen him clean the mud or dust from it. In a way, his neglect made the contents that much more mysterious, because the case was nothing to him, only a shell.

She raised the lid and the smell of mildew poured out. Inside lay a clutter of papers, photos, news clippings, postcards, and letters mixed with rotted rubber bands and rusty paper clips. At first she only registered the strata of his accumulating. There were decades of stuff in here. The bottom layers were mottled with fungus and yellowed with time. On top, his most recent acquisitions were still unspoiled by the tropics.

Only then did she see what his newest artifacts actually were, the memorabilia he'd stolen from RE-1.

Duncan was their camp thief.

Here was the stolen *Hustler* the two marines had fought over. Here were the snapshots and mail that men had reported missing.

She was dumbfounded.

Here was a page of the *Wall Street Journal* dated six years earlier, and on it the bygone dot.coms and their stock earnings that he'd talked about with such freshness and authority.

Here was a monograph on Cambodian flora and fauna written in French in 1903.

Here was his sketchbook, and it was filled from end to end with mindless squiggles and scrawl.

Here was a chapter torn from a British text on pre-Angkor archaeology, word for word the lectures he'd given them.

Here was an article from the *New York Times,* "Giant Trees Hold Ancient Temples in a Deadly Embrace," complete with *spong* and its scientific name, *Tetrameles nudiflora.*

Here was the kitchen he had built by hand, the zebrawood cabinets, the butcher-block table, and the panel of green and brown and blue bottle bottoms leaded together like a stained-glass window. Only it wasn't his kitchen, it was a magazine ad.

Here was the red setter with the bandit's neckerchief that he'd grown up with, except the setter and the neckerchief belonged to three children in a snapshot with a digitized date, two months ago.

Here was Kent State in all its bloody details—in a paperback history of the war.

Here was Duncan, the scraps of him gathered like stolen homework.

He had dissected each thing. He had underlined sections, circled faces in snapshots, written marginalia, and then dropped it in here to be layered over with more of the same. He had memorized a life.

Who was he?

She looked out into the night. Logs detonated, splitting open with loud snaps and bangs, offering their white meat to be burned, renewing the fuel. The rain evaporated in a cloud above the fire. Eventually one would win out, the rain or the inferno. For now they were in perfect balance.

Duncan came in from the darkness. "Feeling better?" He began weaving shut the hut like a giant cocoon, braiding strips of bark into a front wall. "Once we close the front door," he said, "we'll escape through the back door."

"There is no back door, Duncan." Samnang had woven solid walls to the rear and sides.

"That's what Luke will be thinking, too." He went on knitting the raw strips into a screen.

She mopped the sweat from her face. Chills shook her. The hut seemed to be spinning. If only her body would make up its mind, hot or cold.

He was either her murderer or her savior. Maybe he was both, like a Jekyll and Hyde. Was he the one who had mined the road that he was so desperately trying to lead them away from? Could this explain his reluctance to follow Luke here, the knowledge that his other self, his forest self, was waiting to stalk him? But then, who was Luke? The son of a soldier who had lost his mind in the Cambodian wilderness? Had Duncan told her everything already?

Molly struggled to piece it together. Sweat poisoned her vision. The smoke was hard to breathe. While she was still able to aim the gun, she had to judge this man. Should she confront his fiction or let herself raft along on it and hope for the best? Would he confess his mimicry or stick to his innocence? Or was he so insane that he was incapable of guilt anymore? And what about her? If it came down to it, could she pull the trigger?

He didn't look like a monster sitting there, weaving strips of green bark. But he was Oklahoma all over again, sharing some food and talk while they waited for the night to pass and the highway to carry them on. This very morning she had lain in his arms and spun a romance in her head. She had trusted him.

She gripped the gun. This had to be done. "Who are you?" she asked.

He looked up with his farm-boy smile. "Me?"

She kept the gun along her leg, out of sight.

"I looked in your briefcase," she said.

He looked at the briefcase and back at her. He was confused. "Yes?"

"I know who you're not," she said. "I want to know who you are."

"Molly?"

She had made a mistake. She didn't have the strength for this. He was too practiced at his masquerade, or too far over the edge. But she had started it now. "I'm trying to understand," she said.

"What is it?" He was earnest. He pulled the briefcase onto his lap and opened it. He lifted up papers, his sketchbook of nonsense, someone's plastic booklet of snapshots from MotoPhoto, a decomposing British passport, a plastic badge that said UNTAC. He saw what she had seen, and none of the musty pile seemed out of order to him. Was he more harmless out of his mind than in it?

"Where did you get those things, Duncan?"

He frowned, trying to grasp her point. "My documents?" He spoke without a hint of self-defense.

"Are these your children?"

"My children?"

"In that photo of the setter."

He studied it. A frown appeared. He had not seen the children before. Then his eyes clarified. "You mean my brother and sisters," he said. "With Bandit. He was a dog's dog. There's his scarf I told you about." He showed her.

"But you're not in the photo," she said.

He looked at it again. He thought. "Dad was teaching me how to use the camera."

"How old were you?"

"Gee, probably eight. I liked Cheerios." There was a box of Cheerios in another photo.

"Duncan." She didn't know what else to call him. "Look at the date."

He couldn't see it. He opened one hand helplessly.

"The digital numbers along the side," she said. "It was taken two months ago."

His lips moved. He held the photo closer and rubbed at the date with his thumb. Then he flinched.

His face aged. It was the firelight shifting, she thought. The laugh lines turned into deep creases. His forehead blossomed with worry.

"What's this?" he muttered.

"I thought you could tell me."

He was trying to think. The date confounded him. Plainly, he'd never seen the children before. He'd plagiarized the photo for a dog, nothing more. Where was the harm in that?

He pawed through more of his documents. The *Hustler* spilled open, all tits and labia. Postcards, photos, yellow news clippings.

"How long have you been doing this?" she asked.

"How long, what?" He was disoriented.

She chose her words carefully. No harsh accusations. He looked so frail suddenly. "Borrowing," she said. "Stitching together a masquerade."

"Molly?" He spoke her name as if it were a lifeline.

She wanted to believe in him. Amnesia would pardon him. It would make him a virgin almost, an understudy to everyone he'd ever stolen from. That would make sense of the skin mag and its nudes and all the rest. He was simply trying to catch up with the world.

She kept hold of the gun. Someone had planted those mines on the bridge. Someone had trapped them in here.

The light twisted again, and his face drew into itself. It didn't collapse exactly, but some aspect of him seemed hollowed out. The shadows were invading. The furnace blast of light dimmed.

The rain, she despaired, not taking her eyes from him. *It was winning.* She'd made a mistake. Wounded and ill, she'd chosen the middle of a storm at the beginning of night to unlock this man's asylum.

"The fire," she said to him. If she could keep the light strong, if she could keep Duncan occupied, if she could wear him down, if she could make it to dawn, some opening would present itself.

He peered at her. His eyes had a glaze to them, a cataract glaze. *Old,* she thought again. "Sorry?" he said.

"The fire needs more wood."

"Yes, I'll do that." He spoke softly. He sounded broken inside.

It took willpower not to reach across and pat his

arm. He had saved her time and again. She didn't want to have to pronounce sentence on him. What difference was there between an angel and the devil except for a fall from grace? Was it his fault that he had stumbled among the ruins?

He closed his briefcase and laid aside the plaited strips of bark. He brushed his legs clean. His big hands looked thinned. The fingers trembled.

He had never seemed frail to her. Her heart was racing. Had she broken his mind? Or was he only pretending . . . again?

He started to scoot out through the doorway, then stopped. Something stopped him.

Molly tightened her grip, praying he wouldn't turn to her. But he kept staring ahead. She darted a glance through the doorway.

Luke was out there, waiting for them on the far side of the fire.

38.

Duncan's steeple of logs collapsed. Sparks and steam erupted. Molly turned her face away from the fiery heat, and when she looked again, the flames were strong and Luke was still there.

He stood so close to the fire his rags of clothing were smoking. His shirt had torn open, exposing one very white shoulder, his mortality on display. The rain poured off the planes of his face as if over ceramic. His hair was gone. He'd shaved himself bald.

He was the trickster, all along. Who else? Their captor. The devil.

Duncan was frozen. He couldn't move. It occurred to her that he was Duncan's monster. Or his master. Which was it?

As a photographer, she'd learned to shoot first, ask later. But that was with photos. And what if she was wrong? She kept Kleat's Glock hidden behind her thigh.

"Where have you been, Luke?" she said. "We missed you."

Luke didn't answer. He was staring at Duncan. Into Duncan.

"You had us worried," she said. "We called for you. We thought you'd left."

"Our wandering brother." Luke spoke to Duncan. Brother, not father. And Duncan had left, she understood. But now was back.

She tried bravado. "What the hell do you want?"

She brought the gun up from its hiding place. It held Kleat's bidding in it, like a spirit resident. How else could she explain pointing it at another human being? This was her hand, but it couldn't possibly be her willpower. The gun found its perch in the space between them.

"Did you lay those mines?" she said.

Luke turned to look at her. She remembered his eyes in the restaurant, cornflower blue. Now they were rolled up into his head, only the whites of them showing. She'd known a prisoner who did that. Every time she started to snap his picture, he would roll his eyes into his skull, a one-man Black Sabbath.

"You have a job to do," he said to her. Just as she'd feared, they weren't being allowed to leave.

"Duncan," she pleaded. She didn't know what to demand with this weapon. A declaration of guilt? A promise of aid? Surrender? An end to the war? *Say something,* she thought to Duncan. But he was connected to Luke, or Luke to him.

"We saw what you did to the bones," she said.

"There's more," he promised. More carnage? Or bones?

A movement caught her eye. The darkness shifted

over Luke's shoulder. She squinted through the flames. Animal eyes flickered in and out of view. A shape climbed down from the trees, then another. The monkeys were descending, she thought. Becoming jackals.

"What do you want?" Duncan's voice broke. He was afraid.

"It's time," Luke said.

Duncan didn't move. "You don't make sense." His neck was stooped.

"We said we'd follow you to hell and back," Luke said. "We did. Only it took this long." *Out of his mind,* she thought, *him and us. Possessed by the remains of war.*

Why hadn't she listened to Kleat? He'd warned them in the restaurant. He'd said the man was a predator. And yet Kleat hadn't believed his own warning. It was he who had pushed the hardest to follow Luke into this limbo of trees with bleeding names and the labyrinth and the hiding bones.

"Leave her out of it," Duncan said. He sounded tentative. His brow tensed. He was trying to navigate. Searching for safe harbor.

"Out of what, Duncan?" she whispered.

"I don't know," he pleaded.

"It's almost over," Luke said.

"It was you," said Molly. "You mined the road."

The fire sank under the downpour. For a second, Luke's empty sockets stared at her. It was the darkness. Then the flames leaped up. His eyes returned.

"I told you to tell him," Luke said. "He lost his place with us. Now Johnny's not ever going to leave."

"Johnny," Duncan repeated, trying to remember.

"Leave him alone," Molly said. She reminded herself that she was the one with the gun.

"Molly," Luke whispered. But his jaw didn't move. It wasn't his voice. *Us.* They whispered from behind him.

The monkeys gained in size. They straightened. She was wrong. These weren't monkeys, what she could see of them. Some were naked among them. Others wore rags. Some had skin. Not all of them.

She tore her eyes from the shadow shapes. They weren't real. It was her fever.

The gun took on weight. It wavered. She slipped her arm from the sling to steady her aim.

"What do you want with him?" she said.

"Him?" Luke said.

They wanted her.

"What do you want?" She could barely hear herself.

"We've been waiting long enough, don't you think?" said Luke.

The words came back to her, Duncan's refrain at the dig.

Luke smiled at her, and she recognized them, the ruins of his teeth green with moss. Only now three more were gone, the three she'd plucked from his skull that morning. He hadn't shaved his hair off. It was gone. She'd carried his scalp off in her pocket. Lucas Yale was no forgery. He was dead.

Molly pulled the trigger.

He had not made a move. He'd done nothing but smile. No witness on earth would have called it self-defense. And yet she fired. She killed his impossibility.

There was a cry, and the sound of a body pitching into the fire. Torches of wood catapulted from the flames.

The rain hissed. Steam and smoke pumped upward, sucked by the wind. The light nearly died.

"Duncan," she shouted.

He looked at her, at the gun, at the body smoldering on the logs. He finished getting out of the hut. The shadow men—the monkeys—had fled.

Molly crawled from the hut with the gun in one hand. The rain whipped at her like cold stones. Her wound seemed distant, no longer clutched in the crook of her arm and held close to her face. It was, for now, beneath her attention.

Together, she and Duncan rounded the fire to the body. His clothes were too wet to combust quite yet. But there was that smell again, the stink of burning hair. *What hair?* And when had this rifle appeared across his back?

Duncan dragged the body, hair flaming, from the fire. They turned him faceup, and it wasn't Luke staring at them with jade eyes, not with the crude tattoos along his arms and the gold teeth sparkling between his burned lips. She had just killed Vin.

Molly let the gun drop from her hand. In her fever state, she had mistaken the missing boy for a phantom. Or the rain had infected her. It was dark. The night was diseased with shadows.

Duncan picked up the gun.

She was too horrified to care.

He aimed the gun. She saw it through a foggy lens. Her mind was shutting down. The bang of shots rang in her ears. He was firing point-blank into the hut.

She had forgotten the jerry cans stacked inside. The smell of fuel reminded her. It was leaking downhill, toward the fire.

Before her eyes, he'd built a bomb.

"Run," Duncan said.

She tried, and fell.

He caught her, and she thought he would carry her up the stairs. They would fly into the night, the typhoon for their wings.

But he was too weak. After a few steps, Duncan groaned, "I can't."

Her superhero lowered her back to the ground. He seemed frail, or injured. As they set off with her arm draped over his thin shoulder, Molly couldn't be sure who was carrying whom.

39.

The clearing lit like a chalice of light. Like Lot's wife, Molly could not resist glancing back at the destruction. Jerry cans pinwheeled out of the hut walls, whipping tails of flame. The hut was just fire squared on the edges, an idea of civilization. The ACAV glinted among the branches.

She looked for her phantom ape-men, but the light had banished them. All that remained was the body. She had imagined Luke, a dead man, even spoken to him, and then pulled the trigger. But in killing off a hallucination, she had murdered a poor lost boy. Blinded with stones. Or had she imagined his eyes, too?

She wanted to blame her fever, but feared the worst. Madness was built into her genes. Her birth mother had finally come home to roost.

"Climb," Duncan said.

Another jerry can ignited. The faces of stone giants throbbed among the trees. Shadows fled and reassembled.

"We need to go back," she said. "I need to bury him."

Who were they running from except themselves? Luke was imaginary and she had killed a child and panicked this fragile hermit into detonating the fuel. It occurred to her that she might have imagined that, too, that she was the one who had emptied the gun into the jerry cans and destroyed their final hopes for survival. It was in keeping with the family tradition, slow suicide, only by jungle, not by snow.

"Climb," Duncan whispered. "They'll be coming for us."

She forced him to stop, a matter of leaning on his shoulder. Where had all his strength gone?

"You saw them?" She spelled out her delusion. "Those others in the shadows?"

"I don't know." But his urgency was certain. "We need to keep moving."

They were being hunted. Duncan didn't speak it out loud. Maybe he thought she would stop functioning.

By midway up the stairs, the rain had drowned the scattered fires and the hut and their bonfire. The darkness gave her hope. Maybe Luke and his death squad would be reduced to hers and Duncan's same blind groping.

They climbed the stairs, resting more often than they wanted. Duncan's exhaustion mirrored hers. He seemed every bit as weak and confused as she was. She faltered, he faltered. She had wounded him with her doubt. It had to be more than that, of course. She remembered the smoke coming from his chest that afternoon, and feared he'd caught some of the shrapnel after all. Had she been so preoccupied with her own wound that she had missed his?

Near the top they huddled like invalids. Resting her head on his back, she could feel his ribs against her cheekbone. In her mind, his grip was big and meaty, but now his hand felt narrow. She blamed herself. He had shielded her so often that she'd built him into more than he was, a man, a tired man at the end of a long, terrible day.

They finished the stairs at last.

The city was alive tonight. She remembered Duncan's embrace that morning, and his marvelous heartbeat and the swelling of his lungs, and the city was like that. It pulsed with water. Its clockwork was in motion. The rain had resurrected it.

The rain had stopped, even the wind. But the city was activated. Runoff coursed through its veins.

Molly thought the storm was over. The raindrops quit biting at her eyes. The great sea roar above the canopy was silent. But Duncan wanted the calm to be just the eye of the typhoon. He wanted more tempest and fury to cover their escape. "It's our only hope," he said.

Moonlight trickled through the leaves, not in straight pencils of light, but reflecting, from one leaf to the next. It allotted a silver murk to the ruins, enough to give her sight.

To their right and left, all along the rim, water poured from the cobra mouths of *naga* gargoyles. Monuments and spires formed silhouettes with flame and flower profiles along their edges. Massive heads drifted like asteroids bearing human features.

They crept deeper into the ruins.

The city was a hydraulic monument, a celebration

of the water that had once powered an empire. Even terrified and hurting, Molly was astonished by the intellect within the ruins. Two thousand years ago, architects had designed the buildings to make music with the water.

Stealing among the moon shadows, she could hear the notes. Water overflowed from one huge bowl to another, cascading harmoniously. It streamed through stone flutes, forcing air through whistling pipes. It beat rhythms against panels lining the canals.

Each structure seemed to have a song built into its vent holes and gutters. The trenches and pipes were more than simple veins to drain away the water. They were throats designed to sing.

The Blackhorse men had heard it, the journal fragments said so. Had they felt her marvel? Had they listened to the music? It called to her from side paths and stairways, even from underfoot, beneath the paving stones. She wanted to linger and search the city, listening to its parts.

"Listen," she said. It mesmerized her. The music overruled their pursuers. It seemed more powerful than any danger. It drew her. She couldn't explain it.

Duncan kept himself immune to the temptation. "Keep going," he whispered.

They came to the tower, and she would have been happy to rest in its summit. From up there they could scout for Luke and his shadows, and Duncan could warm her in his arms. They could forget with the city's song rising up to them.

Duncan forged on. Each time she lagged, he said, "The gates."

"But the gates are closed," she said. "They're choked with wire and vines."

"One or the other will go," he told her. "I know." He stated it as an article of faith.

"I'm tired, Duncan."

"A little more."

"We can rest in the tower."

"They'd find us."

He pulled her by the hand, hustling her across a bridge. The architecture began to diminish in size. The high, dark snake back of the fortress wall appeared. The interior moat was bellowing with runoff. How many enemies had been sucked to their deaths trying to leap across that monster?

Duncan grew more wary, moving them from one pool of shadows to the next. The light began failing. The storm was returning. Clouds rushed the unseen moon. The intervals of silver gloom shortened, swallowed by darkness. The wind was finding its lungs again. The patter of leaves gave way to branches thudding like giant footsteps. Duncan was going to get the other half of his typhoon.

"There it is," whispered Duncan.

The multiheaded gate tower straddled the wall. Another bank of clouds shuttered out the moon. But they had their bearings.

"I'll go in front," Duncan said.

He was afraid of mines, she thought. Luke had sealed one entrance, why not the others? That was the mischief they had to test. And if anyone could unravel the knot of wire and vegetation, it was Duncan. They had desperation on their side, and their hunters had a whole city to search.

They edged through the darkness, connected by her fingertips on his shoulder. The noise rose as the wind hit and the sail effect began to grind the city's foundation.

Even blind, Molly could sense the gate's nearness. That vague, familiar claustrophobia began to press at her. With each step, it grew, an undertow of disease and despair. What were they thinking? The barrier was impenetrable. A curse upon trespassers. The thought drove at her.

In the next instant, she heard a sudden dull crack. Duncan gave a startled cry and collapsed backward, against her. They both fell, and she thought, *Now we are dead.*

40.

He struggled for air. His feet scraped against the slippery stone. She was certain he'd been shot.

"What is it?" she whispered. He was pushing, she realized, to get back from the gate.

She stood and dragged him by his shirt, away from the gate. It surprised her. He weighed little more than a child.

Duncan coughed in animal bursts and sucked for air. Above the canopy, the clouds parted for a brief minute. The swamp glow lit them.

Black oil—blood—spread from his broken nose and mouth and a gash across one eye.

"What?" she moaned. She had to be strong. It was her turn to play savior.

He couldn't form words, only noises, strangled and nasal, through the blood and the damage. His jaw was crooked. Had they shot him in the face? She rested beside him, searching for their attackers.

A small forest of ceramic warriors stood before the tunnel. Their heads had been returned. Their jade eyes surged with menace.

Molly tried to take it in. They had risen up. Shoulder to shoulder, they no longer lay toppled or sunk into the earth. Someone—Luke, or Samnang, or others—had dug them from the ground and propped them upright to block the exit. They were ranked in columns, more than she could quickly count.

The tumble of light made them seem alive. They were nothing but hollow shells. But with their incandescent eyes, it was almost as if they were the ones who had maimed Duncan. She searched for Luke hiding among the statues. But all was still among the legs and jade armor.

The moon died again. Darkness swamped them. She held Duncan on her lap.

He kept reaching for his face. She could feel him touching it, probing his own wounds, and that made her more afraid. They were like deep-sea creatures reduced to learning the world with feelers.

Terrified of hurting him more, Molly made herself touch his face. She deciphered blood and the bony protrusion at his jaw, and that scar above his ear. She ran one hand through his wet hair, and it pulled away in long strands. It was weeds or moss, she told herself. But it felt like hair as she untangled it from her fingers.

The stones grated under her knees. He groaned.

"I'm sorry," she whispered.

He patted her hand reassuringly.

She felt him grip his jawbone, and knew what he meant to do. He got his thumbs underneath and clutched the sides, and tugged at the bone. The bones gave a gristly pop and he groaned. But the jaw would not go back into joint. She was almost sick.

The moon returned. Duncan leaned forward to let the blood run from his nose and mouth. She got to her knees and unknotted her sling, his checkered *kroma,* and wrapped it around the gash on his forehead. What now?

The statues scared her. Luke had posed them as a warning, obviously. What other tricks had he arranged in the tunnel?

She got Duncan to his feet. He was so thin. "Put your arm over my shoulder."

Holding him gave her strength. *The endorphins were kicking in,* she thought. He seemed almost light enough to carry in her arms.

Clouds gobbled up the moon again. The gate was out of the question, and it would be foolhardy to try for the tower at the center of the city. By now their pursuers would be hounding the ruins.

She led Duncan along the moat path, following it by ear. She planted each foot with care. One slip and they would both be swept away. They shuffled higher, alongside the wall.

The wind began to scream, clamoring to tear the canopy open.

Thunder fell upon the mountain. She heard the bamboo chattering at her, and vines lashing like bullwhips. The ruins grated like the bowels of a glacier.

She felt helpless. They were the walking wounded. Even if there were a breach in the wall, how far could they hope to get? What lay out there in the night?

While she still had strength, Molly turned Duncan toward the city.

There were no more holes in the darkness, no more

moon. The storm sprang at them. Molly found her way by the songs of the ancient buildings.

She listened for hollowness and found a doorway. That got them out of the rain, but the floor was half flooded. She felt her way up a short staircase to a ledge.

By touch, quivering with fever, she tucked Duncan along the back wall and foraged moss and leaves to pile over him. When he was well covered, she burrowed under to hold him. The rain would wash away their tracks and scent and any last evidence of them. In the morning, they could start over.

41.

She woke holding an armful of leaves on a ledge, an ancient veranda that faced out upon the ruins. Maybe lovers had once cooled themselves here and shared this secret view of the street below. The light was blue turning green, and the mist was sinking in the street below. It was dawn in the city.

She lay unmoving above the ghost river. A dragonfly appeared, a jewel with wings. Gods—their wandering faces—invited her back into the great dream.

The typhoon had passed. The stones no longer grated. The water songs had dried to a faint trickle.

Duncan was gone.

She looked at her empty hand sticking through the leaves. He had gone to draw them away from her. That was Duncan.

Whispers threaded up from the mist. "Molly," she heard. They knew she was here somewhere. They were backtracking for her, which could only mean they'd run Duncan to earth. His footprints or scent, whatever they were following, led this way.

Her hand drew into the leaves. Eyes wide, she watched them from above.

They surfaced in the street mist, phantom hints of them, a bare shoulder, a hunched back, a wisp of black hair, khaki-green rags. It was a parade of apparitions, of fragments of apparitions, even of relics. Held by no one she could see, a rifle barrel, beaded with dew, swiveled from side to side.

They were mere pieces in the mist, silent except for their hiss of words. They might have been a giant serpent gliding through the labyrinth, its skin whispering against the walls.

Molly waited, hating the adrenaline that woke her body. The shrapnel wound burned with infection. She could feel the tickle of insects on her legs, the gentle suckling of leeches.

At last her hunters faded away.

She forced herself to wait, counting time in her head, devising plans. The gods smiled at her foolishness. The fortress walls stood whole. There was no exit.

She crawled out from the decay. Her vision swam in broken autofocus, soft to sharp, near to far. Glossy black leeches clung to her arms. The forest was stealing her. It took all her strength to stand, and when she glanced down, her bed looked like an animal lair.

Her thighs trembled as she descended to the street. She went the opposite way from her pursuers, both to avoid them and to find the origin of their tracking. That was where they would have left Duncan.

As the mist cleared, the spires grew taller. All around, buildings leaked their lungs of fog. It ushered out of blank doors and cascaded down stairs. It exhaled from the mouths of giant heads. Between the flags of it, she saw parrots and smaller birds wheeling in the morning air. Monkeys sprinted overhead like spies. Invisible deer barked at her progress.

They were giving her away. But her presence was already known. She accepted that.

Here and there weapons and rusted C-ration cans fanned across the road, tossed from doorways like garbage. Had the soldiers become so careless, even discarding their rifles? It was the animals, she knew. Over the years, they had rooted through the fragments and pulled them outside. Her mother had been scattered over a mile of mountainside.

It was all she could do to stay on her feet.

She peered inside a room, and it was like a lunatic's cage. Hand-sketched maps were plastered to the walls like wet leaves. Their ink had bled, but it was still possible to see the attempts to map the ruins. Each map bore a date in one corner, July, then August, and one made in late September . . . three months after their arrival. Each was scratched out, drawn over, crumpled, and smoothed. The mapmakers never had gotten the hang of this place. The ruins had defied them to the end.

When she stepped from the room, Molly saw the black bead of a gun barrel aimed straight at her. The sniper's nest was practically invisible among the leaves, but her eye went straight to it. She could not explain her gift for finding them.

The sniper sat in a fork, tied to the tree. His rifle was rooted in place, stitched to his shoulder by vines. His skull leaned against the stock, taking infinite aim with round stone eyes. Like Luke, he had been fitted with the vision of jade. It was as if the city watched itself through their eyes.

Nothing remained of his uniform, though he still wore web gear and a towel around his neck vertebrae, and the skull sported a do-rag. His leg bones and boots had long ago fallen to the ground, but his upper half still maintained a bull's-eye on the street.

Duty was one thing, this was something else. Besides tying himself to the tree, the man had cooped himself up inside a cocoon of barbed wire. His last act—hauling up the wire and constructing a shapeless ball of it—bewildered her. What had he hoped the wire would protect him against? Starvation, despair, madness? Had he caged himself to prevent his own wandering?

She recalled the monkeys plundering the body yesterday. Had he chosen the tree for his tomb and wired shut his mortal remains against the animals? Who else could he have feared among his dead and dying comrades?

Molly stumbled on, passing beneath his aim. One of the soldiers—or perhaps some of Duncan's seventeenth-century Dutchmen trekking through Indochina—had carved a cross into the wall. A red and white painted Confederate flag graced one sheltered wall, and beside it a black-and-white peace symbol. They had scratched the names of wives and girlfriends among dancing, round-breasted *aspara* nymphs.

She passed through the canyon of story panels that she and Duncan had shared, and the carvings had altered. Now the train of prisoners lay beheaded. The dragon had retreated back into the sea. The monkey-gods had defeated the humans. The crocodiles had caught the peacock and were dragging it feet first into the carved waters. She got it, she got it all, the death of the captives, the passing of the typhoon, the triumph of the monkeys, and their bodies and spirits being pulled into the underworld.

She came to a little cemetery. They had buried their dead, or at least, while they still had their strength and sanity, their early dead. But thirty years of animals had undone their labor. White bones lay strewn across the hillside by the hundreds.

The bones and relics were so obvious to her this morning. It was as if the Blackhorse soldiers were coming out of hiding. She thought the storm must have thinned the canopy to allow more light, or that the fever made her senses more acute. The bones practically greeted her.

She had no idea how many men the cemetery had held. Duncan or Kleat could have judged by the bones; they had trained themselves to puzzle together the remains. But they were gone. She was the last one left. That was her first conscious admission of the fact.

She was dying.

If Luke didn't find her, the fever would take her, or the infection. It was only a matter of time. But then who would take the soldiers home?

A rifle stood, jammed barrel down in the black earth with a helmet on top, a classic shot. She framed the picture in her mind, the rifle, the white bones, the black earth. Molly blinked. She recognized this dirt. It was the same rich black soil they had shed on their white tablecloth in the restaurant. This was where Luke had grabbed his fistfuls of mud and dog tags. Here was where her journey had started. The circle was tightening. She was getting to its center.

42.

She found the tower by looking not up, but down. Overnight, the rain had filled a long, rectangular reflecting pool that extended beneath the trees. This was a new approach, different from her other forays into the city's center. The image of the tower hovered at its far end, upside down in the mirror. There between the branches, a hundred yards ahead, stood the root of the tower. *Lost no more,* she thought. There was her destination.

As she skirted the pool, a ripple spanked the stone. She paused and the water went still. The lily pads lay motionless. She waited and, like yesterday at the reservoir, something shifted in the depths. The surface seemed to open.

Tangled with weeds, a big machine gun rested on the bottom. Coils of belted ammunition were turning green, like old pennies. The gun was not mounted on a tripod or neatly positioned. It had the look of a thing thrown away without care.

Then the surface sealed over. It became a mirror

again, and she found herself facing the gunner, or his reflected image. She lifted her eyes. What remained of his skeleton—the limp spine and his skull and a few ribs—dangled from a noose. The rope twisted. The skull turned, and he had jade eyes, also.

First Luke, then the sniper in his coil of wire, now this man. Despair had swept them like a virus. She felt it, too, trapped at the center of the earth, chased by uncertain dangers. Languishing. That was the worst part, the wheel of time turning without measure, the obsessive maps filled with circles. Even that made sense to her. Even suicide made sense.

But why had they separated from one another? When they most needed each other's company, these men had made themselves desolate and estranged. They had retreated to distant lonely hideouts, the sniper to his perch, Luke to his bamboo lair, this gunner to a noose.

There was no evidence of an enemy finding them here. Had the men taken to hunting one another, then? Or imagined themselves being hunted? Why not? The monkey meat could have passed on a brain fever. Had they been killed by their own ghosts?

She looked up, into the ever present smile of God. Where was the joke? In their suffering and confusion? No matter where you turned, the city seemed to mock you. She tucked her head down, containing her anger. Every which way, the place made you mad.

The tower seemed to drift toward her. Duncan would have led them there. It was more wish than calculation. She had no time for the rest of the labyrinth.

She came to the bas-relief crowding the base of the

tower. She looked again and the carvings really were in motion. One of the stone children—a little girl—turned and looked right at her. Molly cupped one hand against her eyes and hurried past, to the stairs.

Duncan had come this way. His red and white scarf lay in a heap on the stairs. The rain must have washed it clean. For all his blood last night, there wasn't a drop on the scarf. She draped it around her neck and gathered her courage, step by step.

Higher and higher she wound. She battled her dizziness as she kept to the precarious outer edges. The doorways whispered to her, tempting her to come in and stay awhile. She resisted their havens. She forced herself to climb on.

As she neared the top, a motion in the grass far below made her melt against the stairs.

There was no mist to hide them this time, and the green light was as good as it got. And yet they still evaded a complete inspection. They appeared in pieces from the mouth of one of the great avenues.

A man's shoulder and arm surfaced, then sank into the grass. A head appeared, scouting right and left before ducking behind a pillar. A man's hunched back appeared. Some were bearded and naked. Others wore rotted fatigues stolen from the graveyard. Some went barefoot. Rifles and rucksacks parted the grass. They were a procession of weapons and gear. Their skin and bones were little more than vehicles for the war relics.

All carried the jungle on them. She thought the vines and weeds must be part of their camouflage. But then she spotted the small animals moving on them, lizards, and a snake, and even a monkey riding majestically on one's shoulder. The forest inhabited them. They had lost their souls to this place.

They were not ghosts.

Molly refused to call them that. She clung to her powers of reason. Call them supernatural and she would lose all control over her rational world. It was not that she rejected the idea of ghosts. Her mother was a ghost. But you possessed them, not the other way around. Ghosts were data. They were pieces of your past. They allowed you a dialogue with yourself, and they had no reality except the reality you granted them.

She granted them nothing. She had conjured up none of these hide-and-seek scavengers creeping through the grass below. As eerie as he was, Luke had appeared well before she had any inkling of him, or them. There could be no Blackhorse ghosts because Blackhorse did not belong to her past. She had no connection with the Eleventh Cavalry.

And so, while these men might haunt the ruins and mimic the dead, they were real in some way. If only she could focus her mind. There had been no way to directly confront their whispering and silhouettes on her tent and their slouching through the mist, but she could dispute their unreality. They were hunting her. She was hiding from them, whoever they were. And Duncan had probably sacrificed himself to shield her. All for nothing. They were bound to find her.

The real contest was not with them anyway, but with herself. She had no hope of defeating them. There were too many of them, and this was their territory, and she was fading fast. She couldn't beat them, but she could make sure they didn't beat her. Just holding on to her sanity would be a triumph.

The line of men—looters, lunatics, or manhunters caught in a Vietnam loop—worked diagonally across the overgrown square. They moved like a patrol, spaced in a line, taking their time. They had nearly reached the far trees when the ambush caught them.

At first, Molly couldn't understand what was going on. It looked more like a squall striking the grasses than an attack. Some havoc burst from the trees. Limbs bent, leaves parted. Birds sprang from their perches and filled the air with their colors and cries. From three sides, furrows sliced through the green surface of grass.

Peeking down from the edge of the tower, Molly saw shapes, degraded shapes, pieces of creatures that were even less than these pieces of men. They were human in theory. Human in outline. But in fact she couldn't be sure she was seeing anything at all.

They seemed to be part animal, part glass—or water—as they streamed out from the trees. They cast shadows like the shadows of fish, amorphous and distorted, muscling in the green light. She saw their weapons better than she did them, not bits and pieces of the Blackhorse arsenal, but ancient things, swords and axes scything through the grass, and they appeared to almost move of their own will, racing for the kill. The forest shapes converged on the patrol.

The battle had no real form. It was over in seconds. The grass thrashed in a furious centrifuge of shapes. It bent and whipped and pressed flat. She heard a howl crowded with men shouting. Then the whole aspect of the violence lifted. It was as if the wind had touched down and gone on. The men, the suggestions of them, vanished.

She didn't move for another minute. Something had happened down there, something elemental, a microburst or a dervish. The grass lay torn and flattened in a whorl, and that howl echoed another few seconds from the forest as if a battle of spirits was swirling within the fortress walls. Then the shadows went still again. The birds returned to the trees.

She could have descended at that point. Her pursuers were gone, or seemed to be. But where would she go? Her legs were going on her. Even if she made it back to the terminus, there was nothing left but ashes.

On her hands and knees, Molly resumed her climb. She was terrified of losing the last of her strength out here in the open. She wanted enclosure. She wanted sanctuary. A fairy-tale tower where the bad men could not find her.

She had to whisper her way to the top: "A little more." She had never before felt burdened by her flesh like this.

She reached the summit deck and peered over. The city wheeled in circles down there, a mandala of ruins and emerald grass.

Even as she looked, her hunters reappeared. The patrol emerged from the mouth of one of the great avenues. A man's shoulder and arm surfaced, then sank into the grass. A head appeared, scouting right and left before ducking behind a pillar. A man's hunched back appeared.

They were repeating themselves. Endlessly recycling. Ghosts, she thought, after all.

43.

The infection had spread into her wing muscles. The walls of her chest and shoulder and back were burning with strep. And yet she managed to stand and face the door.

The blood rushed from her head. She was patient. The spinning stopped.

The stone Amazon that had toppled from her niche was now restored to her place. Molly couldn't even tell which of the twins had been broken. Even the doorway looked restored. The sagging lintel stood level. The red columns seemed brighter, the moss scrubbed away.

"Duncan?" she whispered into the room. Not a whisper back.

She stepped inside. The statue women let her pass, and the room was just as she had left it. Where she and Duncan and Kleat had peeled back the carpet of leaves, the floor still broadcast its black SOS. Brass shells littered the stones. The aperture in the roof was pouring green light onto the far wall. She was alone with the remains of the Buddhas.

Their desecration didn't shock her this morning.
She understood now. The soldiers had seen through the
cosmic smiles. The city's tranquility was a lie. Beneath
its facade, the fortress sanctuary was a deadly trap. In
chewing off the Buddha faces with their gunfire, the
men had been erasing a terrible deceit.

"Duncan?" Sweat seeped down her spine. It was cold.

Her grip slipped on the doorway. She caught her
balance. She asserted it. Once down, there would be no
getting up.

She scanned the room for a friendly patch of
ground. The monkey hands reached out from the fire
pit. The gutted radio set stood along one wall. War junk
and dank shadows crowded the corners. Animal dung
plastered the boxes and cans.

This was important stuff, the choice of her bed. It
was her Kodak moment: Someday, a hundred years
from now, another expedition would ascend this
tower. And while they weren't going to find any Sleeping Beauty, she could at least compose her mortal
remains without monkey hands and garbage for her
backdrop.

Her eyes went to the chopped, riddled Buddhas. In
and out of focus, they seemed to float in the green
light, luminous and detached from the world, separate
from one another, even separate from the wall. For all
the savagery that had been heaped upon them, for all
the bloodshed they had presided over in this spirit city,
they still promised peace. Now if only some of their
karma would rub off, maybe she could come back as a
complete human being next go-round.

She set off across the hall, shuffling through the bullet shells and beetles. The Buddhas retreated into their niches. Ravaged by bullets, they looked more like lepers than deities, like victims, not masters of the universe.

Molly glanced up at the canopy. No sun, not even a single beam? It would have been so sweet to curl up on a spot of heated stone.

She arrived at the knife in the wall.

The knife was all wrong, a spiteful thing. Would they think she had stabbed the Buddhas? Kleat had grappled with it, and she knew the blade was jammed, but she gripped the handle anyway.

The blade slid free.

The wind must have moved the canopy, which had moved the trees, which had moved the stones. The joints had opened. The knife practically fell from the seam. The weight of it, all eight ounces, yanked her arm down. It dropped from her fingers.

She stared dumbly at the thing lying at her feet. The blade was scratched and mottled, a name engraved above the blood gutter. With the next storm, the stones would have shifted again and bound the knife. She'd happened along at the right moment, that was all.

A string of saliva dangled from her mouth. Lovely. In a stupor, she lifted her eyes.

"God," she whispered, and lurched backward.

The statues were changing.

Their pox of bullet holes was smoothing over. The Buddhas were regaining their stone flesh.

It had to be a trick of the light. Clouds were crossing above the canopy. Whales passing through the deep.

She closed her eyes and staggered, fetching up against the wall. Now was not the time to be seeing things. Her mother had died from hallucinations. And yet she could feel the wall against her palms and cheek, and the cool, gutted surface really was mending itself.

She pushed away from the wall.

Molly had spent a lifetime learning the rules. They allowed for yetis and unicorns, so long as you winked. They allowed for lost cities to float out like dust bunnies. You could hold heaven as a hope. But the rules did not allow for this.

The wall—the entire length of stone and statues—was healing. The bullet tracks dissolved. Thirteen smiles glimmered into being, so many Cheshire cats paying a visit. Faces formed around the smiles.

A vine tripped her. She might have blacked out. She smiled up at the fever dream. The metamorphosis streamed on.

At the far end of the wall, where the facade had been blasted, rubble began to reassemble. Lying there, Molly could not find words to describe it. Pieces of stone did not fly through the air and into place. Somehow the wall drew the destruction back into time.

She went with it, a pleasant delirium. As fissures sealed and lead slugs pattered to the floor like hailstones and the leprous figures became beautiful again, she forgot her pain and exhaustion. She all but vanished from her own mind.

Consciousness came and went.

Perhaps the wall had never been destroyed. Perhaps she had imagined it. Or again, that wondrous thought, maybe the ruins had imagined her. If the stones could command a people to shape them into a city, if the city were nothing more than an instrument for monsoon songs, why couldn't she be that little girl carved among all the other stories? What else was humankind—all life—but a figment of a stone spinning through time?

Her eyes opened. The wall was whole again. The war was gone. It had never been. How righteous, she thought. How stoned-out cosmic cool.

She rolled onto her back, a change of view. Parrots flickered overhead like bits of flame. A gecko eased in along the skylight. A few monkeys perched along the rim. Like this, in unconditional surrender, her mother must have watched the snow descend.

44.

The afternoon thunder arrived. It came up from the earth, not down from the sky. It was still too far away to hear. The vibrations buzzed against her skull. She remembered sitting in a restaurant along a river long ago and how the sunset had trembled. *Let it rain,* she thought. *Come what may.* She was finding her happy zone.

But then she saw the soldier. He was sitting at the far end of the wall where the rubble had cleared itself away. Thirty years ago someone had buried him violently, with plastic explosives. Now he was bared to the world.

His legs and boots were crushed flat. The rest of his skeleton rested precariously upright. It must have been hot the day he died. He had no shirt. But like Kleat, expecting trouble, he wore a flak jacket.

She knew him, or at least of him, not his name or his face, but his legend. The fragments of the journal had spoken of him. He was their commander. Here was the man who had gotten them lost and found them sanctuary, and doomed them by preserving them among the ruins. This was the tower of his tomb.

She dragged herself closer, a creature of her curiosity.

Their discoverers would link them, a man and a woman, a soldier and a civilian, two Americans caught in a faraway land. Never mind that she was as old as he was dead. Details. The story was too good. They were as good as married, a Romeo and Juliet for the ages.

The rubble had flattened his left hand in his lap. It looked like some complicated fossil. He wore a wedding band.

His skull leaned on his chest as if he were in mid-siesta. His sole wound, it seemed, was a crease along the temporal bone. The bullet had not pierced his skull. It might only have stunned him, in which case he'd been buried alive.

Molly touched nothing. The skeleton looked like a house of cards ready to fall. She lay beside him, resting her head, hunting for clues.

This was not another of their suicides. For one thing, there were more certain ways to put a bullet into yourself, and the bone was not scorched or powder burned. Also there was no weapon lying close at hand. And again, the bullet did not seem to have been a killing shot. Someone had shot him, and then buried him. Her eyes wandered higher. All in front of the Buddhas.

How had it gone?

He had caught them in the act of savaging the statues and gotten between their weapons and the wall. The journal fragments whispered to her. *It's not true that he loved the city more than us. He was only trying to preserve us all.* They had looted the city, or part of it, planting that terra-cotta head on their exhaust pipe. Had he tried to protect the Buddhas? Had someone kept on firing?

There was just one wound that she could see. She couldn't find any bullet holes or bloodstains on the flattened fatigues or the flak jacket. Just the single shot along his head. Just one shooter.

Had it been an accident or an execution? Had they tried to revive him, or panicked and given him up for dead? No matter. They had blasted this section of the wall and hidden their deed under a ton of debris. That much was no accident. Someone had deliberately tried to conceal the evidence. The body, living or dead, damned them. And so they had shut it from sight.

The journal spoke of one man whipping up the mutiny. But once the commander was killed, the rebels had realized their fall from grace. At least the journal writer had expressed repentance.

The story took shape, a murder. The soldiers had driven the shooter from their midst . . . like Cain, the killer of his brother. He was the same man who had led them in mutiny. Molly knew it. The murder had shocked the rebels from their rebellion. They had scattered after the killing. The mutiny had dispersed.

The shooter had set off on foot, *west of Eden.* Did that mean he'd fled toward Phnom Penh or gone out the western entry, or was it simply the writer carrying through his biblical strand? No matter. Somewhere out there the killer had met his end. The rest of the Blackhorse men had stayed in the city, languishing, divided, hungry and diseased, drifting into madness, and, like her, too weak to leave, dying in animal niches among the ruins.

End of story. Everyone, it seemed, had paid for the sin. In a way, the commander was lucky. Of all the bones she'd seen in the city, his had come the closest to a permanent burial.

But the knife still bothered her. It could have been their way of marking the grave, but why mark a grave you wanted no one to find? No, she thought. Someone had added it to the wall as a finishing touch, after the shooting, after the killing, probably after the blast, a final piece of rage.

It was the shooter's knife. Molly knew it instinctively. He had stabbed the wall.

Thunder rippled far away. A breeze stirred the canopy.

She clutched her cold, fiery self.

"Now what?" she whispered to the bones.

It didn't seem right. They'd brought her here. *Her.* Luke had said so. But all this way for what? This was just another dead soldier from a dead war. Vietnam had nothing to do with her. She had a life. For a little while longer.

The trees moved. The floor shivered, or she did. It was like a dock that seems to move because the water is moving. The big river was waiting.

"Not yet," she said. *Where's my circle?* She deserved that much. A bit more beta. Some raw connect. Her missing link.

The tremors upset the careful construct of his bones. With the clatter of sticks and empty spools, the soldier spilled to pieces. The skull landed facing her, mouth parted, his jaw still wired in place with tendons. Weighted with vertebrae and ribs, the flak jacket tumbled into her hands. It was a simple matter to pluck the dog tag from inside.

The name was perfectly legible.

She should have known.

" 'O'Brian,' " she read aloud to him, " 'Duncan A.' "

The jaw stayed frozen, half open, caught in the act.

There was his date of birth. She made the calculation. He'd been shot on his birthday, or shortly after, twenty-one years old. She'd fallen for a younger man.

Molly cocked her head to see the skull.

His features emerged clearly now. It was almost like lying with him in her tent, watching his young face while he slept. There was his thick brow and his thin cheekbones, and the white teeth he'd brushed so religiously. She purged from her mind the poor creature dwindling in the rain last night, losing his long hair in her fingers, that phantom crumbling beneath her doubts. She closed her eyes and saw Duncan at dawn in the blue-green light.

Had he suspected his flesh encased a ghost? She recalled his briefcase full of tidbits and his confusion when she'd confronted him. And his odd reluctance to follow Luke to these ruins.

It wasn't that he'd tried to fool anyone. Duncan had been as truthful as he could remember, in fragments, with an Ace comb in his pocket, just a spirit borrowing himself together, the same as Luke and all the rest.

When had he escaped from the ruins? Obviously, Luke had been sent to fetch his restless brother back to the source, back to the underworld. But why bring her?

She had daydreamed about taking Duncan home with her. Over these last few days, that seemed to be what she was meant to do, to usher him back into America. But he'd turned the tables on her, not knowing himself. He'd brought her home with him.

More chills, more salty sweat. Her eyes rolled back in her head. Darkness threatened. Molly fought back to consciousness.

What were the laws of this place? The rain would purify them. Her bones would mingle with his. But then?

"Duncan?" she called to his spirit. Had he joined that never-ending patrol around the tower? Or flung himself up into the canopy? "Where are you?"

Suddenly she was afraid. She wanted reassurance. She had no answers, only more questions. Would she go out into the world with him now, or would they stay to wander through the ruins? How did it work? Would they take on disguises? Enter cities? Cross the oceans? Haunt the future? They could live a thousand lives. But in giving birth to themselves, would they forget their anchoring bones? Would they come to forget each other?

They had voices. Where was his voice? "Duncan?"

The flak jacket had fallen open. There was something in the pocket, an edge of plastic. She tugged and it was a sandwich bag containing a snapshot.

The photo was dog-eared and harshly faded. Even without the "Dec. '69" penned on the back, Molly knew the era by its chemicals and paper. She could have guessed the basic image. It was straight out of a war movie, the girlfriend picture.

Wife, she amended, glancing at Duncan's wedding band. The young woman had one, too. She was flashing it proudly, with bravura, grinning at their in-joke. Six or seven months pregnant, she was dressed— barely—in a polka-dot bikini. She'd snagged her man in the nick of time.

Molly laid her head on the flak jacket and studied the photo, sliding into its story. Duncan had taken it. They were on a beach. It was Hawaii, in the middle of his deployment to Vietnam. She wore a flower lei. Molly liked her. She was audacious, ripe to bursting, and wildly in love with the photographer. A real firecracker.

She did the math. Duncan had been twenty. A few months later, he had become a dad. A few months after that, he had faced his killer in this city of the dead.

Her face eluded Molly. The girl's hair cast a shadow, and that bulging tummy drew the eye. But that wasn't the difficulty. The face made no sense to her.

The girl had a hundred-watt smile and a sloe-eyed green gaze. A pair of rose-colored sunglasses perched on top of her bushy black hair. The humidity had blown her pixie cut to chaos. Molly could relate. Atomic hair, she called it. That's why she'd chopped hers short with surgical scissors. Black Irish did not go well with the tropics.

Molly stopped. The air leaked from her.

She was looking at herself.

She refused it. She had to be projecting. The fever was scrambling her mind. The ruins were stealing into her the way she had stolen into them, in darkness and fog. One step deeper, it seemed, and she might disintegrate.

The picture blurred, then sharpened. She struggled against it, then with it, finding her way into the impossible image. How could something so familiar feel so alien? The eyes, their shape, the nose, the smile, the hair . . . there was no denying it. That was her face in the photo.

Molly glanced at Duncan's silent bones, trying to fathom it. What did it mean? Had she died and wandered and finally been led to her lover? Could she be her own orphan?

A drop of rain fell from the trees. Not yet, she commanded the sky. There were facts. She recalled them, an obituary in the *Denver Post* dated 1971, a coroner's report, a grave marker among the wildflowers.

She fumbled at the belt holding her passport wallet and ripped open the Velcro and drew out her relic, a driver's license issued in 1967 in Bay City, Texas, to one Jane Drake, age eighteen. The black hair was long and ironed straight, Cher style. The eyes were green and full of blue sky, as if all her life lay ahead of her. It was the same face Molly saw in her mirror, though younger and sweeter and smooth. But it was also the face in a photo buried next to the heart of a dead soldier. How could that be?

Rain began leaking from the canopy. A drop splashed across the photo. Molly raced on.

Once upon a time, she tried desperately. Once upon a time, a war bride lost her one true love. When he went missing, she went missing, too. She wandered off into madness, into the midst of mountain gypsies, and finally, into the mouth of a blizzard. That much was true. Jane Drake had died in a roofless miner's shack in a blizzard on Boreas Pass.

Had she returned from the dead then, one ghost hunting another?

She searched her memory for Hawaii and young Duncan and the diamond on that finger, and the miner's cabin and the blizzard. She tried to feel them as memories of her own, but none of it came to her.

The raindrops splattered across the photo. The image was melting before her eyes.

Hurry, she thought. Today was for keeps. Darkness was her last call. The forest would render her to bones. She would join the wandering spirits and never know more than her name.

Molly blinked away the rain. Put away the ghosts. She was too full of ghosts. *Trust your eyes.* What was she missing?

She brought the snapshot closer. She looked at the tipped skull.

Here stood a young woman in her glory.

Here lay the bones that had broken her heart.

And—it was suddenly so obvious—in that womb slept their daughter, Molly.

The muscles in her face relaxed. The labyrinth unraveled around her. No longer a stranger to herself, she let the city take her over. Its canals became her arteries. Its stone told her story. Her tangled threads were simply paths among the ruins.

Had her mother sent her, Molly wondered, or had

her father drawn her? Did it matter? They had never
meant to lose her. They'd done the best they could, but
the world had taken them away, the soldier in war, his
bride in sorrow. She only needed to forgive them for
their love. She leaned the photo among the bones. The
rain ran from her eyes.

45.

Molly took turns. She traded bodies with the gecko clinging to the wall, and prowled a Buddha's palm. She hitchhiked on a parrot perching in the branches. She became a butterfly hiding from the rain. She spied on herself down there.

She looked like one of *Macbeth*'s witches haunting the edges of a battlefield, knife in hand. Her bloodshot eyes burned too bright in that mask of ash and smoke.

The thunder was majestic. She'd crawled to the knife. It looked like an Iron Age thing in her fist.

She knew the Blackhorse missing now. Even the bones still hidden in the forest had recited their names to her. They were all present and accounted for, even their ninth man, the rebel leader who had shot her father. His name was on the blade, "John Kleat."

There was no telling where Kleat had traveled after they'd banished him from the city. She understood his hatred of the Khmer Rouge better than he did now. His bones remembered what he did not, the enemy who had slit his throat. Maybe someday he would rise up from the black water in the *barays,* and escape these walls, and resume the search for his own remains. Maybe someday he would find the nonexistent brother who was himself buried in the hills or in a paddy or thrown down a well. More likely he would forget and join the creatures in the mud.

They were driven by urges, these unburied dead. Where memory began and ended, she couldn't say. They clung to their names, that much was certain, speaking them over and over. Also, no matter what they had become, they could not escape who they had been. She had been right to believe in Duncan's goodness. Wherever he was.

"Duncan," she called out.

She drifted in and out of delirium. The rain fell in slow strings. Now she was the gecko, now a butterfly, now a woman.

"Molly," she heard. *Let me sleep.*

They kept calling her name from the forest, the birds and monkeys and ghost warriors, enunciating all the varieties she might answer to, Molly, Maw-li, Moll-lee. They were helping her remember her name in the next life. That was her hope, that they would be kind and welcoming. On the other hand, they had summoned her to carry home her father and them, and she had failed. There was no reason to believe in their mercy.

She caught herself whispering a Hail Mary to the Buddhas.

"Molly." The voice was just outside the door, and it wasn't Duncan's.

She lay still. Her heart galloped. If only Duncan would come.

The doorway darkened. He was an emaciated thing made of rags. Part man, part bone, he entered.

She closed her eyes. The tip of bone ticked closer.

"Molly," he commanded.

He'd come for her eyes, not to take, but to give. She belonged to the city now. Would he use a spoon? What shade of green would her jade eyes be?

Please, she thought.

He heard her whisper, or maybe smelled it. "You're alive," he said.

She opened her eyes. His leg was a stick, not bone, lashed to his thigh with vines.

She thrust with the knife. It was a feeble act, and he stepped on her wrist and took the knife away. She knew better than to fight. Lie still. Let him do it.

"Lie still," the ghost said.

He stood overhead like a butcher sizing up meat. She searched for his eyes to connect with, but the rain smeared her vision.

She wanted to let go, to cast herself into the animals and scamper and fly and slither away. But suddenly she was anchored in her flesh. She couldn't leave her body. She struggled, a small motion, a whimper.

He tugged at a pouch. A dozen or more round jade balls spilled onto the floor. The eyes rolled against her cheek, and she moaned and looked away. The city was preparing her, last rites, its funeral mask. But she was still alive, or had she passed to the other side? How to tell?

"Don't fight," he said. "You're having a dream. Can you hear me?"

He lifted her shirt and looked underneath. She

squeezed her eyes shut and the rain wept down her face. Would the eyes hurt as much going in as coming out? How loud would she scream? Where were her gecko and butterfly?

"Drink." He held a leaf to her mouth as a funnel. The rain trickled onto her tongue. A kindness before the maiming.

"You're leaving," said the voice. "Take the others with you. They no longer belong. Do you understand?"

"No." They were dead. How could they not belong? Limbo had borders?

"They were lost and the city took them in." The voice chased like water through her mind. "It gave them shelter from the storm. Why them, barbarians? Compassion, perhaps, or God's curiosity, I can't say. The city took them in as children. It gave them sight. It showed them the path. But they refused to see. Do you know how many great warriors came and laid aside their armor here? Not these men. All except Duncan. He saw something, I think."

"They were only boys," she whispered to the rain.

"Blind they came"—the words were strict—"now blind they go. I've gone to each of them and taken back the dream."

On one knee, he worked Kleat's knife. She felt the steel blade worm along her breastbone. With a tug, he split the shirt and peeled it away like skin. One leg at a time, he sawed away her pants.

She was so afraid. But, oh, the rain felt glorious. It bathed her burning flesh. It warmed her like a blanket. Her lips opened to the water.

His hands began moving over her, working away.

She didn't dare look. For all she knew, he had opened her and was squatting to one side devouring her organs. Were the monkeys gathering for their share?

He pried open her eyelids and rain crashed into her brain. *My eyes,* she thought. The windows of her soul. "Please don't," she said.

"A little while longer," the ghost soothed her, plucking away leeches. "Everything will be clear."

Then he propped twigs under a large leaf to make a lean-to over her face and draped big banana leaves over her body and limbs. She was sinking.

"You're free. You freed them." He held up one of the jade balls. "But these stay. Take nothing but the bones. Forget the city. Remember the dream."

Blackness rose up.

She returned to consciousness just as he was leaving. The stick leg sounded like a clock walking away. Then she smelled the rich fragrance. Under another leaf, he had planted a handful of incense sticks. Slow smoke leaked up to the Buddhas. Only then did she recognize him.

"Samnang?" she whispered.

But he was gone, into the ruins.

46.

When she woke again, the rain was clattering on her shield of leaves and the incense sticks were ash. Her bloodstained clothes lay in a heap. She was naked and encased in black mud. Night was falling.

They were shouting her name again. They were everywhere out there. Their voices were climbing the stairs. *Duncan,* she prayed. *Save me.*

A light flashed in the doorway. Dark forms clustered behind it. More lights appeared. They wore sheets like Halloween ghosts. Ponchos, she realized.

"Molly?" The voice boomed through the room.

She watched from under her chrysalis of leaves, perfectly invisible to them.

"She's not up here," one said.

"But he told us a tower."

"It's empty. We got the wrong tower."

"We should have gotten him to draw a map of the place."

"Too late now. It's a miracle he lasted as long as he did. You saw what he looked like when they brought him in. Gut shot, bleeding out. The fuckers even took his leg."

"What the hell did she get mixed up with?"

"Bad company, man."

One had a cough. Others were winded. Their voices thundered, as if her last few days had passed in whispers.

The room lit green with distant lightning, then went dark. The sky rumbled.

"We don't belong here," a voice complained. "The captain gave us two hours. Night's coming. You could get lost in this place."

"Sam said she'd be here. Here's the city. Here's the tower."

"That was yesterday. She could have gone anywhere since then. We'll try again in the morning. It will look different in the morning."

It was like swimming up from a deep recess. Sam? The captain? She knew these voices. RE-1 had come for her.

And now they were leaving. Molly tried to speak. But her tongue had turned to leather. There wasn't enough breath in her lungs for even one word.

Their lights twitched away. It was over. She would never last the night.

But then the bones sighed beside her. "Boys," they whispered. *Duncan.* His wisp of a spirit.

Somehow they heard through the thunder. It caught them. Their lights swung around. One splashed on the skull.

"Christ, there's another one. And a flak jacket, look."

They came across the room in a siege of boots and

the *whip-whip* of wet plastic and the one man coughing. One stumbled against her leg.

"There's something here."

They converged in a circle and stripped away the leaves, staring down at her from the caverns of their ponchos, faceless, awed. Even in the rain, she could smell them. That struck her, too, the smell of living men.

"Is she still alive?"

"What did she do to herself?"

One bent to her. "Molly? Can you hear me? It's us."

"What's she staring at?"

"We've got you now, Molly."

Voices like thunder. They filled the room. "Get a litter. Bring ropes. Tell the captain."

Shedding their ponchos to hold as a roof over her, they took on familiar faces, the hunters of the dead. As they pulled off their shirts, they made themselves half naked to warm her.

They couldn't seem to hear the hymn of the city. She looked into the rain, listening as it faded. It was harder and harder to hear for the clatter of gear and the thud of feet and the creaking of pack straps. Men were shouting down from the tower's ledge, calling out the good news.

So faithful, she thought, these warriors sent to harrow the underworld and unshackle every last American soldier's soul. Year after year they hunted the bones, even as the fragments drifted deeper, towed under by insects, roots, and the shifting earth. In the end their quest would falter. The worm would win.

But for the moment it was like a great battle had

been fought, and they had carried the day. In finding one alive, even if she did not belong to them, the soldiers could put death aside. They could dream of themselves tonight, free to believe they were more than a dream of the ruins.

ACKNOWLEDGMENTS

The Reckoning takes history for its haunted house. In order to construct and inhabit it credibly, I sought out men and women who have lived various aspects of that history. They will be the first to notice my poetic license with procedures, details, and events. Any and all inaccuracies are mine alone.

I wish to thank army lieutenant colonel Gerald O'Hara, army chief warrant officer Tom Monroe, and retired marine master sergeant Joe Patterson of Joint POW/MIA Accounting Command (JPAC). They patiently detailed the grueling search and recovery process that seeks a full accounting of American soldiers who went missing in foreign wars, particularly in Vietnam, Laos, and Cambodia. Because my story takes place in 2000, three years before JPAC was formed, I refer to its two earlier sister entities, Joint Task Force-Full Accounting (JTF-FA) and the Central Identification Lab in Hawaii (CILHI).

I am indebted to Earl Swift, a staff writer for *The Virginian-Pilot*. Though he was writing his own book about the military's forensic quest (*Where They Lay,* a superb nonfiction account), this generous man did not hesitate to give me several hours of civilian perspective drawn from his trips with JPAC.

Many thanks to retired army colonel Charles L. Schmidt for enduring my questions and offering his advice about the 11th Armored Cavalry in Vietnam. Thanks as well to Geof Childs, whom I peppered with spontaneous phone calls about the military and Vietnam.

I am especially grateful to Sophea Chum Satterwhite for helping guide me through Cambodian customs, language, and history. My other guide through Cambodia was Melissa Ward, the bravest person I know, who led me through the devastation and recovery during her assignment with UNTAC in 1993. Wherever in the world you are, Tiger Lady, thank you. And keep your head down.

I owe deep thanks to my editors Emily Bestler and Mitchell Ivers, who refused to leave me lost among my ruins. And with humble appreciation, my thanks to Sloan Harris, my agent and literary sensei.

Finally, Barbara and Helena, you are the blessings I count each day.

ATRIA BOOKS
PROUDLY PRESENTS

THE FALL

Jeff Long

Available in hardcover January 2006
From Atria Books

Turn this page for a preview of

The Fall . . .

When God throws angels down, it starts like this.

A breeze stirs. It carries the slightest distraction, a scent of trees perhaps, or a hint of evening chill, or a song on a radio in a car passing almost four thousand feet below. In some form, temptation always whispers.

High above the earth, toes smeared against the stone, fingers crimped on microholds, the woman turns her head. Not even that: she turns her mind, for an instant, for even less. That's all it takes.

The stone evicts her.

The wall tilts. The sky bends. Her holds . . . don't hold.

She falls.

By now, eight days high, her body is burning adrenaline like common blood sugar, one more fuel in her system. So in the beginning of her fall, she doesn't even register fear. She is calm, even curious.

Every climber knows this rupture. One moment

you have contact, the next it's outer space. That's what rope is for. She waits.

Her mind catches up with her body. A first thought forms, a natural. *My hands.*

All our lives, from the cradle to the grave, our hands are our most constant companions. *Like the back of my hand.* They give. They take. They roam and shape the world around us. But hers have turned to stone. Or time has stopped.

Each finger is frozen just so, still hooking on holds that no longer exist. Her high arm is still stretched high, her low arm still bent low. One leg is cocked, the other is straight to the tiptoe of her climbing slipper. She could be a statue of a dancer tipped from its pedestal.

Her paralysis does not alarm her. Hollywood shows victims swimming through air, limbs splayed and paddling. In reality, when a climber is climbing—really climbing, not fretting the fall, but totally engaged—and the holds blow and you peel, what happens is like a motor locking. "Rigor" is the formal term, as in rigor mortis. Your muscles stiffen. Body memory freezes, at least for a moment. It doesn't matter what your mind knows. Your body stubbornly believes it is still attached to the world.

What surprises her is the length of the moment. Time stretches like a rubber band. The moment is more than a moment. More than two. *Patience,* she tells herself.

There will be a tug at her waist when the rope takes over. Then there will be an elastic aftershock. She knows how it will go. She's no virgin.

Her synapses are firing furiously now. She overrides her Zen focus on what civilians call pulling up, and what climbers call pulling down. The rock has let go of her. Now she forces her body to let go of the rock. Her fingers move. She starts to inhabit her fall.

For the last day, they have been struggling to break through a transition band between two species of granite, one light, one dark. In this borderland, the rock is manky and loose. Their protection has been increasingly tenuous and their holds delicate as sand castles.

And so she was—necessarily—way too high above her last piece of protection, climbing on crystals of translucent quartz, almost within reach of a big crack. She had the summit in sight. Maybe that was her downfall. It was right there for the taking, and maybe she grabbed for the vision too soon.

From the ground up, the beast has begrudged them every inch. They have done everything in their power to pretend it was a contest, not a war, nothing personal. Now suddenly it bears in on her, the territorial imperative of a piece of rock. El Cap is fighting back.

Part of her brain tries to catalog the risks of this fall. Much depends on the nature of the rope, the weight of the falling object, all 108 pounds of her, and the length of the drop. Any point in the system could fail, the runner slings, the carabiners, her placements, their anchor, the rope. The weakest link in that chain of mechanisms is the human body.

On her back now, helpless, she glances past her fingers. The rope is making loose, pink snake shapes in the air above her. She's riding big air now.

A dark shape flashes past. It is last night's bivy camp,

gone in a blink of the eye. *Do they even know I'm falling?* At this speed, the camp is the last of her landmarks. The wall is a blur. Her braids with the rainbow beads whip her eyes.

Except for the grinding of her teeth, she falls in silence. No chatter of gear. No whistle of wind. Oh, there's a whiff of music, a spark in the brain. Bruce, the Boss. "Streets of Philadelphia." Faithless kiss.

She's fallen many times. At her level of the game, no climber has not given in to gravity. You build it into the budget. It comes to her that she's counting heartbeats, six, seven, eight. . . .

Her freefall starts to ease. Finally.

The serpent loops straighten. A line—hot pink—begins to form in the dead center of her sky. The seat harness squeezes around her pelvic bones.

Abruptly the line snaps taut with a bowstring *twang*.

The rope claims her. She gains weight, a carload of it, a solid ton of shock load.

The catch—or its commencement—is brute-ugly. Her arms and legs jack down like puppet jumble. Her spine creaks. Head back, medusa coils flying, throat bared to the summit, she comes eye to eye with the abyss behind and below her.

It's totally still in the valley. Autumn is in high gear. The leaves are blazing red and orange. But there's hunger in the beauty. Pandemonium. You could get swallowed alive down there. She jerks her head from the hypnotic sight. She tunes it out. Turns it off.

The rope. She grabs for it.

The summit. She centers herself.

Eyes up, she takes a breath, her first since coming

off, a deep, ragged drag of air. Like breaking to the surface again, she gasps.

Her fists lock on the rope. Sunshine is painting the rim. She curses, full of fighting spirit. They were so close, just hours shy. The fall will cost them.

She blames herself for rushing. They were banking on making land by night. They had gorged on all but the last gallon of their water, and eaten all but some scraps. They'd even high-fived their victory. Dumb. Jinxy. The wall moves with a tempo all its own. Full of wishes, too ready for flat land, she'd pushed too fast.

She yo-yos on the rope.

The recoil dangles her up and down in the depths. Eleven-millimeter kernmantle is built for shock. A fifty-meter section—the standard for climbing—has a break strength of five thousand pounds. Cavers shun "dynamic" climbing rope: it's too bouncy for them in dark, bottomless shafts. But for a climber, elasticity is the very hand of the lord and savior.

Her mind brims with next thoughts. She doesn't offer thanks. Fate is action, that's her mantra.

The rope's still quivering, and already she's doing damage control. The fall could have been bad. She could have hit the wall or blown her harness. The line could have tangled in a limb or wrapped in a noose and snapped her neck. If not for years of yoga practiced everywhere, in gyms, dorm rooms, friends' apartments, and campgrounds, her vertebrae would be scrambled eggs. But she's whole, unwounded, not even a rope burn. The soreness will come, but not, by God, before she gets back on the horse.

Twisting in midair, she gathers herself together. The

woods are darkening below. The sun band is creeping higher up the headwall, ebbing away. No way they'll beat night today.

Knowing it will never work, she tries pulling herself up the taut, thin line and gains not an inch. It's too thin, too taut, like a wire. She quits to save her strength. She settles into her harness, waiting. She needs a pair of jumar clamps and stirrups so that she can ascend the rope. One of her partners will lower the necessary gear, they'll know.

She is impatient to return to the headwall above their hollow and finish what she started. It's more than stubbornness, more than getting back in the saddle. She's raving on endorphins, wild with energy. Her memory of the moves is crisp. She knows the holds. She's cracked the code.

Come on, girls. "Yoo-hoo," she calls. And waits.

As the moments go by, she rehearses the sequence of moves: left toe here, pinch the white quartz crystal, reach right, stack her fingers on a seam hidden in a splash of sunlight.

In her mind, she makes it all the way to the big crack running straight to the skyline. The crack was so close, just a move away, and then she would have owned the stone. Now she's forfeited the day. They'll have to wait until tomorrow night for their seafood and wine at the Mountain Room Restaurant.

At last a voice seeps down from their camp in the vertical hollow. It is a single syllable, her name. But also it is a warning. Pain, she hears, and desperation.

Something is wrong up there. Her fall has wreaked some kind of havoc in the camp, there can be no other explanation. Clutching the rope, still as a fawn, she peers up in time to see the pink sheath blow.

For all its strength, a rope is a fragile thing. A grain of sand infiltrating the sheath, a spot of acidic urine, even the rays of sunlight can destroy the core's integrity. In this case, the rope fails at the threshold of their sanctuary. The hollow's rim is not a knife edge, but it's an edge just the same.

A hundred feet overhead, right where it bends from sight, the rope bursts into flower. It happens in a small, white explosion of nylon fibers. It looks like a magician's trick, like a bouquet springing from a wand. *Chrysanthemums, how pretty*. But she knows the truth of it.

Quick as a bird, she steals a sip of air. *Faith*. She grips the rope with all her might and wills the world to freeze, the rope to weave itself together, her body to be light as a feather. Abruptly she is weightless.

It breaks her heart. She whispers, "No."

It was not supposed to end this way. You climb hard, get high, tango with the sun. When you fall, you fall with grace and the rope takes over. You heal, if necessary, and reach into your heart. Chalk up, tighten the knots, and get on with the climb. That's the way of it. Ascent abides. Always.

The physics of the breaking rope flips her sideways, and then facedown. Like that she goes, chest first into a hurricane of her own making.

She could close her eyes. She wants to. But of course she can't. This is the rest of her life.

The air cools instantly. The light changes. It goes from that golden honey to starved blue steeples. She has dropped into the shadow zone. *Already?*

This is a different kind of falling. This one is full of forbidden thoughts. She has never not known hope. That's the greatest shock. She is staring at the end of time. There is not one thing she can do to improve her situation. And yet she hopes. She can't help herself.

Her mind goes on grasping. Command, of a sort, comes second nature to her breed. Even as she plunges, she calculates madly. In the back of her mind, *Like a cat, land like a cat. On your hands and feet. Light as a cat.*

Climbers have a natural fascination with falling. Its discussion, usually held by a campfire or on long road trips, draws heavily on legend, anecdote, and personal experience and includes falls one has survived and falls one has witnessed and even falls one has merely dreamed about but forgotten they were dreams. You learn from the fuckups. The accident reports almost always come with names, if not of the victims, then most certainly of their routes, and dates, and the type of gear and precise condition of the rock, ice, or snow involved. Often they list the temperature. Anything to make the unknown seem known.

For many climbers, "terminal velocity" refers to a death drop, also known as "cratering." In fact, the term specifies that point when a falling object reaches zero acceleration. Air resistance from below becomes equal to the mass of the object times the force of gravity. You don't slow down, but for what it's worth, you quit falling any faster.

All of this occurs to her in an instant. A million synapses are firing now. Images, words, forgotten smells, and emotions all spring loose in a flood. She remembers sparks from a campfire, the exact scent of cedar smoke, that taste of his lips, his finger. *Butterflies, the seashore, Mom, a singsong alphabet*. More and more.

The terminal velocity of a human averages 120 miles per hour, or roughly 165 feet—the length of a fifty-meter rope—per second. But it takes time to reach that state of zero acceleration.

In her first second, she falls just sixteen feet. By the end of her third second, she has covered 148 feet; by the end of the sixth second, some five hundred feet. That leaves roughly a half mile to go, and she is just reaching terminal velocity. What it comes down to is this. She has eighteen more seconds to live.

The wind robs her lungs. It just sucks her empty. It makes her deaf, that or the blood roaring in her head.

She commands herself to see. She keeps her eyes bared. This is for keeps.

The ground does not rush up at her. If anything, it opens wide, growing deeper and broader. She is a pebble tossed into still water, except the ripples precede her in great concentric expanses of earth.

Swallows make way for her.

The forest becomes trees.

Out beyond the road, the river runs black through the white autumn meadow.

Such beauty. It fills her. It's like seeing for the first time.

She knows the blood chemicals must be taking her away. How else to explain this sense of being chosen? Of being received. Of being freed. She's never felt such rapture. It's glorious. *I'm going right through the skin of the world*.

And yet she fights paradise. The glory is too glorious, the abyss too welcoming. It means to kill her. That quickly she despairs.

If only she could catch her breath. There is no in between. Fear, ecstasy, anguish: each extreme, all amok. *Death*. She keeps that word at bay. She tries.

And yet here is the sum total of every climb and every ambition and every desire she's ever felt. Stack them end to end and they reach to the moon, and for what? It strikes her. She has wrecked her life. Her barren life. *A fool's trade*. All for nothing.

It is then that she spies her savior.

The trees part and there he is, a tiny, lone figure moving along the valley floor. He is approaching El Cap. But also, impossibly, and yet absolutely, he is making a beeline for her.

Everything changes. Her fear dissipates. Her wolves lie still. A great calm pacifies the storm.

I'm not alone.

It's so simple. Whoever he is, he's coming for her. Nothing else explains it. Random chance does not exist for a woman with no chances left.

From high above, settling through the air, she watches him labor between the trees, bent beneath his loaded pack. He's a climber, plainly, and well off the main trail. In forging his own path, he is marrying hers. It's deliberate. It's destined. There is not the slightest doubt in her mind. Whoever he is, he's traveled the earth and followed his dreams and timed his days exactly to receive her.

If only he would lift his head. She wants his face. His eyes.

Above the trees, she opens her arms. She arranges

herself like some beatific creature. The air sings through her fingers. The feathers of her wings.

And still he is unaware of her. She wants him to look up and see her. She wants him to open his arms and embrace her. With all the love in her, she loves this man. Every memory she contains, all her being, lies in his hands now.

Her heart swells, her giant heart. Oh, she loves this life. There was so much more to do. Even one more sunset. And children, God.

She pierces the forest, thinking, *Forgive me.*

Not sure what to read next?

Visit Pocket Books online at
www.SimonSays.com

**Reading suggestions for
you and your reading group**
New release news
Author appearances
Online chats with your favorite writers
Special offers
And much, much more!

How would he make love to her?

Her simple touch froze him.

They both looked at their hands, resting on the plate.

"Is this weird?" she whispered.

"A little bit." He rested his other hand at the small of her back and turned to face her. "The question is, do we care?"

She smiled. "No, I guess I don't care."

"We're adults and we can do whatever makes us happy." Kissing her would make him happy, but he didn't want to push her. He wanted her to be the one to initiate the intimacy their arrangement required.

"You have to, like, track when it's most likely to happen, right?"

"I have been, for a while. And, ironically, my most fertile time should be right now. The next couple of nights are the best time."

Brady's train of thought came to such an abrupt stop, he was surprised he didn't hear the squeal of the brakes in his head.

The next couple of nights are the best time.

Their gazes locked and he gave her a slow smile. "There's no time like the present, right?"

Dear Reader,

Welcome back to Blackberry Bay, New Hampshire! I love Christmas romances, both as a reader and as a writer, and there's something extra charming about small towns during the holiday season. Wreaths and hot cocoa and Christmas parades. It's my favorite time of the year!

In *Their Christmas Baby Contract*, a woman who has the worst luck when it comes to men asks a man who's known for having maybe too much luck with women to father her child, but they're not *supposed* to fall in love. Setting Reyna and Brady's journey to happily-ever-after against the backdrop of a Blackberry Bay Christmas was so much fun, and I hope their story brings you holiday joy.

You can find out what I'm up to and keep up with any Blackberry Bay news on my website, www.shannonstacey.com, where you'll find current news as well as a link to sign up for my newsletter. And you can also reach me by emailing shannon@shannonstacey.com or look me up on Facebook at Facebook.com/shannonstacey.authorpage.

I hope you enjoy *Their Christmas Baby Contract* and that you'll visit Blackberry Bay again in February for another story of love, life and laughter in a small town.

Happy reading!

Shannon

www.ShannonStacey.com

Their Christmas
Baby Contract

———

SHANNON STACEY

HARLEQUIN
SPECIAL
EDITION

SPECIAL EDITION™

Recycling programs
for this product may
not exist in your area.

ISBN-13: 978-1-335-89493-9

Their Christmas Baby Contract

Copyright © 2020 by Shannon Stacey

This edition published by arrangement with Harlequin Books S.A.

For questions and comments about the quality of this book,
please contact us at CustomerService@Harlequin.com.

Harlequin Enterprises ULC
22 Adelaide St. West, 40th Floor
Toronto, Ontario M5H 4E3, Canada
www.Harlequin.com

Printed in U.S.A.

A *New York Times* and *USA TODAY* bestselling author of over forty romances, **Shannon Stacey** grew up military and lived many places before landing in a small New Hampshire town, where she has resided with her husband and two sons for over twenty years. Her favorite activities are reading and writing with her dogs at her side. She also loves coffee, Boston sports and watching too much TV. You can learn more about her books at www.shannonstacey.com.

Books by Shannon Stacey

Harlequin Special Edition

Blackberry Bay

More than Neighbors

Carina Press

Boston Fire

Heat Exchange
Controlled Burn
Fully Ignited
Hot Response
Under Control
Flare Up

The Kowalski Series

Exclusively Yours
Undeniably Yours
Yours to Keep

Visit the Author Profile page
at Harlequin.com for more titles.

For my mom. Thank you for the years of happy Christmas memories and traditions that live in my heart not just during the holidays, but all year long.

Chapter One

"Nice day for a hockey game."

Reyna Bishop would know that smooth, deep voice anywhere and, after tucking her debit card into her back pocket and accepting two steamed hot dogs from the vendor, she turned to face Brady Nash.

A ball cap with the minor league hockey team's logo was covering his thick, dark hair, but the brim didn't hide the blue eyes Reyna wished she didn't find so attractive. They'd probably been in middle school when she discovered she had a thing for blue eyes and a hint of dimples, thanks to him. "Hi, Brady. I didn't know you'd be here."

"No reason you would," he responded, a not-so-subtle reference to the fact they hadn't spoken beyond polite greetings in a few years, despite having been friends since childhood.

"But half the town's here, at least, so I probably could have guessed."

The game tickets had been sold as a fundraiser by the eighth-grade class, which was hoping to take a trip to Washington, DC, in the spring, so she'd seen quite a few residents of Blackberry Bay in the stands. It was a long drive, but everybody loved a school fundraiser.

"A soft pretzel and a lemonade, please," Brady told the vendor, and Reyna was about to take the opportunity to make her escape, but he looked at her again. "Who did you come with?"

Her face warmed, which was ridiculous since nothing she did was any of his business. "Lucas. My boyfriend."

"Right. The guy you brought to the Fourth of July fireworks?"

"Yeah." That had been their first date, but Brady probably knew that since they had a lot of mutual acquaintances. It was hard not to when you'd gone to school with a guy since kindergarten.

"He looked…stable."

She leveled him a *seriously?* look because she knew that was his way of saying Lucas looked boring. Maybe Lucas didn't ooze charm and sex appeal, but she was looking for a life partner, not a fling. "I'm surprised you'd recognize stability, since it's not something you're familiar with when it comes to dating."

He chuckled and put his hand over his heart as if she'd wounded him, but before he could say anything else, she turned and walked away. Lucas was waiting for her, and their hot dogs were getting cold for a conversation that was only going to keep going south.

It was always awkward when she ran into Brady, but she wasn't sure how to fix it. About four years ago—a year before Reyna's dad passed away from cancer—she'd run into him at a bar. She'd been out with friends, and so had he. Years of chemistry and flirtation had escalated pretty quickly, and they'd both ditched their companions and left together.

Falling into bed with him had been an utter disaster and they'd avoided each other whenever possible since. Blackberry Bay, New Hampshire, was too small a town to allow for much of that, though, and somehow they'd gone from awkward avoidance to straight up not speaking to each other unless they had to.

She couldn't really do anything to fix it since she wasn't sure she even understood it. So he'd been too quick on the draw, she'd been unsatisfied and they'd both been embarrassed. So what? They'd known each other their entire lives and it should have been the sort of thing they could laugh off and move past. Unless he couldn't stand the fact she knew he wasn't the ladies' man everybody in town believed him to be.

"No mustard?" Lucas asked when she reached the empty seat next to him and handed him his hot dog.

"Sorry, I got distracted." She didn't really want to tell him what—or rather, *who*—had made her forget condiments, so she changed the subject. "Anything interesting happen while I was gone?"

"Some raffles and then some sort of competition for little kids." She wasn't sure if it was her imagination, but she thought she heard a hint of irritation in his voice and she wondered again why he'd bothered coming with her to an event that clearly wasn't his thing. "I was beginning to wonder if you were coming back."

If he was that worried about how long it took to get his hot dog or not getting his mustard, he could go with her next time, instead of letting her go alone. "The line was long."

"The game's starting again," he said with about as much enthusiasm as he'd announce he was making an appointment for a dental cleaning.

Reyna and Lucas had been dating for several months, so when he'd heard about the hockey fundraiser, he'd assumed they'd go together. That had surprised her, since he didn't care about sports, but maybe he was trying to support *her* interests, which was nice. She'd originally planned to take her friend's daughter, Sophie, to her first hockey game, but she'd caved and invited her boyfriend instead.

Boyfriend. She was still having some trouble wrapping her head around the word, though she supposed that's exactly what Lucas was. She'd met his sister and she was supposed to go with him to see his parents for Thanksgiving. It was a lot for so early in their relationship, but she'd had a run of bad luck with men before she met him, so she was going with it.

He lived twenty minutes away, which worked for her. They could get together easily, but not so easily she felt suffocated by him. He was a tax accountant she'd met through a recommendation when she and her mom needed advice after her dad passed away, and he dressed nicely. His sandy-blond hair was always perfectly cut, and he had great manners. He was stable and nice and would probably be a solid family man.

That made him a strong contender for being Mr. Right. That stability that Brady mocked was one of the things she found most attractive about him because that's what she was looking for in the father of the children she was more than ready to have. He'd be patient and help with homework—especially the math. He was the kind of man who'd make pancakes on the weekend and show up to parent-teacher conferences. He'd be the rock of their family, and when it came to men, that was a priority for her.

He was pretty much the opposite of Brady Nash, she thought as she took the last bite of her hot dog, and then she was annoyed she'd allowed him to creep into her thoughts again.

"Having fun?" she asked Lucas, wanting to distract herself.

"I always have fun when I'm with you," he said, giving her a smile that lasted only a few seconds because the crowd was standing to cheer as a couple's fiftieth anniversary was announced on the big screen. "It's very loud, though."

"That's part of the fun."

Everybody was clapping and cheering for the couple, so Reyna did the same. Lucas was rubbing his hands together, as if he was nervous, instead of clapping, but she didn't think anything of it. He was probably trying to decide how long he had to stay before he could suggest they sneak out, since sports weren't exactly his thing.

She was pondering whether she wanted popcorn or nachos next—because the junk food really was the best part of any sporting event—when she heard her name echoing around the arena and realized it had come from the PA system. Looking up, she was horrified to see her face on the giant screens suspended from the ceiling.

Yes, that was definitely her. Long red hair in a ponytail pulled through a Boston Bruins ball cap because she didn't have a hat for the team she was watching. Her blue eyes wide and practically unblinking. And that was definitely her Bishop's Auto Care sweatshirt.

And she was even more horrified when Lucas grinned at the camera before getting down on one knee next to her, which wasn't easy considering how tight the seating was. Cheers from the crowd rose to a deafening level as he tugged on her hand, urging her to look at him instead of the screen.

Oh no.

"Please don't do this," she whispered, but he seemed intent on ignoring her. Or maybe he couldn't hear her, but he should have been able to read the plea on her lips.

"Reyna Bishop, I love you. Will you marry me?" he asked as he opened a box and showed her one of the most gorgeous rings she'd ever seen.

In her peripheral vision, she saw the words flashing on the Jumbotron. *Reyna, will you marry me?*

"We've only been dating three and a half months," she said, trying to make sense of it.

"And I knew from our very first date that you were the one for me."

Their first date had been watching the town's Fourth of July fireworks display, where he'd bought them each a caramel apple. It had been an odd and unsexy food choice for a first date, but he'd seemed nice, so she'd seen him again. And he'd kept on seeming nice, so she'd kept on seeing him.

She didn't want to marry him.

Well, she did. But not *yet*. She was ready to settle down and start a family, but not so ready she'd rush into marriage before she *really* got to know him. She didn't even know what color his toothbrush was yet.

"*Please* don't do this," she said again, louder this time, even though it was already done.

"Reyna?" Maybe if he'd sounded heartbroken or humiliated, she would have accepted the ring for the benefit of his pride and the crowd that was growing quieter by the second, and then figured it out later, when they were alone. But he was scowling, and the impatience and anger in his tone rubbed her the wrong way.

He'd been the one who'd sprung a very public marriage proposal on a woman who hadn't even invited him home to her mother's for Sunday dinner yet.

"No, Lucas. I'm sorry, but I'm not ready to marry you," she said, and because the noise in the arena was ringing in her ears, she said it a lot louder than she'd intended to.

The crowd fell silent for a few seconds before the boos started. Not many, but enough to spread hot flames of embarrassment over Reyna's pale skin.

"I can't believe you did this," Lucas said as he closed the ring box with a snap and shoved it into his pocket.

"I can't believe *you* did this," she shot back.

He turned and walked away from her, shoving past the people in their row, who scrambled to get out of his way. When he got to the end, he turned back.

Music started blaring through the rink as he spoke, but she had no problem reading his lips. "We're done."

Damn right they were done.

She looked up at the Jumbotron again, and she was relieved to see there were birthday wishes scrolling down the screen and her moment in the spotlight was over.

"That's our Reyna. She's hell on men, that one."

She couldn't place the voice. The noise level was high and whoever said it was probably several rows behind her and was yelling to be heard by her friends. One of the older women from Blackberry Bay, no doubt. It was a phrase she was familiar with, having heard it countless times since her teenage years.

She's hell on men, that one.

No, she wasn't. She just wasn't very good at picking the right one. And forgive a girl—even a teenage one—for having standards.

She'd broken a few hearts in high school. But it was high school. They were all immature and none of the relationships, such as they were, lasted very long. Honestly, the adults in the town probably wouldn't even have noticed if she hadn't broken up with the baseball team's best hitter and been blamed for the slump that dogged him for the rest of the season. That was the first time she heard it.

And once she was an adult, those standards just got higher and when a man wasn't going to work out long term—whether it was antiquated gender role expectations or not clicking with her family or any other reason—she didn't waste any more of their time. For the past few years, those standards had come to include a man's willingness and ability to be as good a father as she'd had, and they'd all fallen short.

She'd thought Lucas was going to be the one. She'd been wrong. Again.

She didn't want to listen to any more of it. She didn't want to hear any clucking tongues or see the sympathetic looks. Or even worse, the looks that clearly said she was crazy for turning down such a grand and romantic gesture.

Stepping carefully over feet and half-empty containers of nachos, she made her way free of her row.

But as she scanned for the red Exit sign, a face in the crowd caught her attention and she felt that hot flush across her cheeks again.

Brady Nash.

Great. Just in case her very public humiliation hadn't been bad enough, of course he had to have witnessed the entire thing. He looked concerned for her and it looked like he might even push his way to her, but before he could, she made a beeline for the exit.

Being proposed to and broken up with on the Jumbotron had been bad enough. The last thing she needed tonight was another run-in with Brady.

Brady Nash was a glutton for punishment. It wasn't something he would have guessed about himself, but it was the only way he could explain why he left his seat and followed Reyna as she exited the rink.

There were a lot of people from Blackberry Bay here tonight. There was no reason to think she wouldn't ask for a ride back to town from any one of them. But he also knew she was as proud as she was private and there was a chance she'd just start walking instead.

He wasn't wrong. She was leaving the parking lot to walk who knew where when he finally caught up to her. "Reyna!"

"Leave me alone," she yelled without stopping.

"Where are you going?"

"Home."

"It's a long walk back to Blackberry Bay, you know."

She stopped then, whirling to face him. Her face was red and he could see her anger in the rise and fall of her chest, but at least she wasn't crying. "Then I'll get an Uber or something."

"Even if you could find one willing to make the drive, can you imagine how much it would cost? Just get in my truck and I'll drive you home."

She didn't want to and he knew it, but he could see her accepting that he was right, especially about the cost. "Why?"

"Okay, so we don't talk much anymore." Or at all, really. Not since that night. "But we've known each other our whole lives—we used to be friends—and you can't believe I'd just leave you here like this. Let me drive you home. You don't even have to talk. You can turn the radio up and pretend I'm an Uber driver, except you don't have to tip me."

"I'm picking the radio station," she said.

She was pretty bossy for a woman with so few options, but that was Reyna. "Fine, you can pick the station."

Once they were in his truck and the arena was disappearing in the rearview mirror, she started to relax. A classic rock song she'd landed on filled the cab and she hummed along, closing her eyes as she rested her head against the headrest.

Brady glanced over at her occasionally, but she didn't open her eyes. He had expected some angry venting or maybe even tears—though Reyna didn't cry easily—but he would have thought she'd fallen asleep if not for the way her jaw kept flexing and the furrow between her brows. She might not be airing her emotions, but they were clear in the lines of her face and the fact her hands were balled into fists on her lap.

He drummed his fingers on the steering wheel as he drove, overcome by a rush of anger toward Lucas whatever-his-name-was. Not only had he hurt Reyna and humiliated her in front of a crowd that included a whole lot of people she knew, but what kind of idiot let a woman like her get away?

If he hadn't blown the one shot he'd had with her and had been lucky enough to call her his girlfriend, he would have done anything to keep her. And he definitely wouldn't have made a public spectacle out of their relationship. He knew Reyna, and what had happened tonight had been more about Lucas's ego and very little about the woman he claimed to love.

Miles passed before she sat up straight and turned the radio down. "I know I'm not acting like it, but I do appreciate the ride."

"I didn't expect you to chat about the weather or

anything, so don't worry about it. I meant it when I said you didn't have to talk if you don't want to. I just want to make sure you get home and that's all."

"There were probably dozens of people who could have given me a ride home if I'd stayed at the game," she pointed out.

"Did you really want to stay, though? Or be trapped in a back seat with a bunch of kids? Or listen to a play-by-play of what happened?"

"No, this is definitely better."

She pulled out her phone, and he assumed she was going to send a text to her mother or her friend Meredith, but after a couple of minutes, he heard her sharp intake of breath, and then she muttered a curse word not quite under her breath.

"Everything okay?"

"There's video. And it's already everywhere and not just on Facebook. Hashtag *she said no*, apparently. What's it been? Twenty minutes, if that?"

"Oh damn, I'm sorry. Stuff spreads fast on the internet. But something else will happen and go viral, and this will be forgotten just as quickly."

"People I *know* are sharing it, Brady. Why would they do that?"

He shook his head, tapping his thumb on the wheel. "You know how Blackberry Bay is. The town is boring and they have nothing better to do, so people have to amuse themselves somehow."

"Sally Barnard added the hashtag *hell on men* when she shared it." Reyna clicked her screen off with a snort of disgust. "She's friends with my mom, but whatever."

He wasn't sure about other guys, but she'd been hell on *him*. But it wasn't her fault he'd been in love with her since first grade and never had the guts to tell her.

She made a low growling sound in her throat. "Why would a guy propose to a woman he's been dating for three and a half months? Why?"

"I don't know anything about proposing. It's me, the official town ladies' man, remember? Just running around dating women without ever settling down with just one." He grinned to hide how much he hated when people said that because it was far from the truth.

But when Reyna snorted and looked out the window, the grin faded because he knew why she made that sound and it still cut him. He'd had one shot with her—they'd crossed paths at a bar and had a few drinks—and he'd been so caught up in finally having Reyna naked in his arms that his performance had been subpar. *Very* subpar. It hadn't been much of a performance at all, and the awkwardness since that night had grown and settled into outright avoiding speaking to each other whenever possible.

Now she probably thought he dated around because he couldn't satisfy a woman enough to keep her.

"Everybody in town thought he was finally the one for you," he said after a few minutes, just to get images of that night out of his head. "He must have jumped to the same conclusion."

"Yeah, a little prematurely," she replied, and he winced at her word choice.

When she made a sound that sounded a lot like a strangled laugh, he glanced over to find her trying to compose her face into a look of innocence and knew she'd seen him wince.

He decided to ignore her amusement at his expense. "If he was really the one, he would have known a spectacle in front of a crowd, with the Jumbotron and everything, would be the last kind of proposal you'd want. It's not really your kind of thing."

"No, it's not." She looked at him and he could see her face illuminated by the dash lights in his peripheral vision. "How come he didn't know that?"

He shrugged. "Guess he wasn't the one."

But he knew that about her and he didn't seem to be *the one* either, so he decided to keep his relationship advice to himself for the rest of the ride.

Most people in Blackberry Bay knew Reyna was a private person who preferred keeping to herself, so it didn't make him special to know she wouldn't want *will you marry me* flashed on a giant screen at a hockey game. There might even have been a time in his life when he daydreamed about proposing to her and there hadn't been a single Jumbotron involved. Or even a fancy restaurant. A picnic maybe. Or sitting on a hay bale—one of the more private ones behind the town gazebo—drinking hot cocoa after the Christmas parade.

But he'd had his shot with her and blown it so badly, he hadn't even been able to face her for weeks afterward. And it was still awkward years later.

"Thanks again for the ride," she said when he pulled up in front of her building. She had an apartment over Bishop's Auto Care & Bakery, since her father had owned the building and now, presumably, Mrs. Bishop did.

"No problem. I'm sorry for what happened tonight."

She got out of the truck and stood next to the open door. "I don't know if I'm all that sorry Lucas and I are done, to be honest. But I really hate that he made us Blackberry Bay's latest viral sensation. Like I need more bad press."

He chuckled. "Well, you *are* hell on men."

"Whatever. Good night, ladies' man." She laughed and closed his door before walking away.

He waited until she'd let herself in and the door closed before putting his truck in gear. And he chuckled to himself as he drove away.

Damn, he'd missed her.

Chapter Two

"It's been almost two weeks, Mom. Almost two weeks and people are still talking about this?"

Jenelle Bishop dusted maple sugar over the top of the cupcakes she'd just finished frosting and then set the tray in the display case. "It's a boring time of year, you know. The foliage is past peak and the leaf-peepers are gone, but the ski area isn't open. People have nothing to do between tourist seasons, honey."

"I feel like you could have taken a more sympathetic direction than that," Reyna said, using her finger to scoop a small remnant of buttercream frosting out of the empty mixing bowl.

"I gave you sympathy for days. I also told you to stay off of social media, and you refuse to listen. You ignoring my advice and my lack of sympathy at this point are not unrelated."

"I can't just stay off the internet, Mom."

"Why?"

"Because." She was sure there was a good reason, though she couldn't come up with one at the moment. Sure, she had to be online for her side business nobody in this stupid town knew about, but she didn't have to scroll through her Facebook feed or go on Twitter or, even worse, the YouTube channel with a bunch of subscribers that had picked up the video. *#shesaidno* and *#hellonmen* were not her favorite hashtags.

"Turn the sign to Open and then you go get to work," her mother said. "Sally called me twice to see when her transmission would be done."

"Oh, Sally Barnard? How come she hadn't called me since I'm the one actually fixing her transmission? Because she knows I'll tell her *hashtag, it sucks to be you*, that's why."

Jenelle laughed. "You need to let that go. She got caught up in the moment and she's very sorry she added to your pain."

"She wasn't sorry until she blew her transmission," Reyna pointed out, and then yelped when her mom snapped a towel and hit her in the butt.

"I love you. Go to work."

After turning the bakery sign over to welcome customers, Reyna went down the hallway that connected the two businesses and entered the Bishop's Auto Care office. It had been her dad's and she'd grown up in the garage, often choosing his company over being home with her mom. When he'd gotten cancer, she'd left her job as a restaurant hostess, dropped the community college business classes she was taking and moved home from the city to help him out. After he passed away, she'd stayed to get her mother on her feet and help her open the cupcake shop, and then she'd never left. Now she couldn't imagine doing anything else.

It was warm enough to have the big garage door open to the parking lot behind the building, and it wouldn't be warm enough for much longer, so she raised it up and got to work. It didn't take her long to finish with Sally's transmission—she might have been dragging her feet just a little out of spite—and she'd just washed her hands when a truck pulling a trailer pulled into the lot.

It wasn't until she saw *Nash Electric* on the door that she realized the truck was Brady's, since Blackberry Bay didn't suffer from a shortage of black, late-model Chevrolets, and the little tingle of excitement totally took her by surprise.

That was weird. Been there. Done that. Didn't particularly enjoy the very short ride.

But the 1970 Chevelle on the trailer got her to step outside. It was rough—like one-wheel-in-the-vehicular-graveyard-level rough—but it was arguably one of the greatest cars Chevrolet ever made and if her bones were still good...

"Hey, Reyna."

"Where did you get this?" she asked, skipping right over the niceties. She was too busy fighting the itch to climb up on the trailer and start looking her over.

"A friend of mine's dad was clearing some land he bought and found her abandoned in some scrub brush at the back of the property. They did the paperwork to make it legal, but didn't want to keep it, so I picked her up for next to nothing."

Reyna laughed. "You? What are you going to do with it? You can't even change your own oil."

"I can change my oil," he said, giving her a look. "I just choose not to."

"Sure." She stepped closer to the trailer, bending in an effort to see the car's frame.

"I was hoping you and I could talk about restoring it," he said, rubbing his palms together in a nervous gesture. "Like, maybe if it was a side project you worked on in your spare time, it wouldn't cost a million dollars."

She already had a side project, though she had no intention of telling him that. But it didn't stop the thrill she felt at the thought of this challenge. Or the pang of regret that her dad wasn't still here to take it on with her. They'd always talked about restoring an old muscle car, but they'd never gotten to it.

Maybe this Chevelle could fill the voids in her life, she thought. A void left behind by her dad. And the void that wasn't going to be filled by the baby she so desperately wanted anytime soon.

Over the last couple of weeks, she'd come to terms with the fact her reaction to Lucas breaking things off with her after she rejected his proposal hadn't been heartbreak. His disastrous proposal had humiliated her, but she hadn't been sad to lose him, which meant she probably wasn't falling in love with him anytime soon. He'd been nice and she had genuinely liked him. But mostly he'd been the sort of man she thought would make a good father and she'd hoped that would be enough.

Clearly, she was going about this all wrong. She didn't necessarily want a husband. She just wanted a child.

"Reyna?"

Startled, she turned away from the car to face Brady. She'd forgotten he was there. "She is in *really* rough shape."

"Nobody better than you to save her."

"Flattery will get you… Well, it might get me to consider it." She laughed and put her hands on her hips. "I won't know anything until I get under her and check out the frame at the very least. If you want to drop the trailer, I can look her over for a couple of days and then we can talk about what it would take for a frame-off restoration, or if it's even worth it."

"Sounds like a plan."

She stared at the car while he moved the truck and backed the trailer out of the way so he wouldn't block the lot. Then, as he unhooked the trailer, she watched him. She'd always been physically attracted to him, though she'd never told anybody that. Not even her friends in school. And even after that disastrous night they'd hooked up, she still got a thrill from watching him.

Blackberry Bay's resident ladies' man, she mused as he bent over to chock the trailer wheels. He had no interest in being a husband, as far as she could see. And he'd probably be a pretty terrible one, based on his history with women.

As far as Reyna knew, the longest Brady had dated anyone was three months at the most. She could only assume he made them no promises since all the women he'd dated had taken the inevitable breakups unusually well. There had never been any whispers about him cheating, so he seemed to be capable of monogamy, but only for the short term. Definitely not husband material.

But he sure would make pretty babies.

And he had blue eyes, like her, so they'd probably have pretty, blue-eyed babies. And that thought hit her like an unexpected ocean wave, almost knocking her off her feet. It was ridiculous. She couldn't ask Brady to father a baby for her.

She probably couldn't afford it, anyway. She'd looked up the cost once, of having a baby with donated sperm so the fact she was hell on men wouldn't be an issue, but just the estimated costs had been enough to put that dream on a *maybe someday* list. But someday never seemed to come around, and neither had Mr. Right. She wasn't getting any younger.

"You okay?" Brady was finished dropping the trailer and she hadn't even noticed. "You seem a little...distracted."

She was *very* distracted, actually. "I'm fine. So give me a couple of days with her. Maybe stop by Saturday around lunchtime and we can talk about it?"

"Yeah. We can hit up the café, if you want. Grab something to eat while we discuss the car's future?"

"Sounds good. I'll be here."

She stood outside the garage door until his truck was out of sight, and then went back inside with that single thought still echoing around in her mind. Maybe she could have a baby, after all.

Brady Nash's baby.

On Friday night, Brady drove the twenty minutes to his brother's house for their traditional end-of-the-week dinner. Chris's wife, Marcy, taught fifth grade and they always celebrated the arrival of the weekend with Chris cooking while she soaked in the hot tub with a glass of wine. When they had their first child, his brother had roped Brady into helping him out and he'd become part of the tradition, too. And with two boys—one a rambunctious three-year-old and the other just starting to walk—Chris still needed all the help he could get.

As soon as Brady walked into the cookie-cutter Colonial house that looked like every other Colonial in the two-year-old housing development, he could hear the screeching. Not a mad screech, though. More like a kid trying to sound like a fire truck siren and, sure enough, his nephew CJ turned the corner from the family room at a run. Benny followed at a fast crawl, his palms and knees slapping on the laminate floors with a sound that made Brady wince.

CJ didn't slow down as he launched himself into his uncle's arms, though he thankfully stopped making the siren sound. Brady ruffled the blond curls the boy and his brother had both inherited from their mother, and then did the same to Benny when he used Brady's pant leg to haul himself to his feet.

"Why are you so quiet all of sudden?" Brady heard Chris yell, and a few seconds later his brother stepped into the foyer with a pair of barbecue-sauce-coated tongs in one hand, with his other hand underneath to catch the drips.

"Uncle Brady's here!" CJ yelled, just in case it wasn't obvious.

"What happened to the cute little *wee-woo*?" Brady asked his brother, referring to the much quieter sound they'd taught the child that fire trucks made.

"Last week one went by us in full-siren mode when we were walking back to our car from winter coat shopping and it was not making a cute little *wee-woo* sound."

"They go like this, Uncle Brady!" Before they could stop him, CJ took off and the house echoed with an earsplitting screech Brady never would have believed could come from such a small kid.

Benny was either trying to pants him or wanted to be picked up, so Brady swung the baby up and carried him into the kitchen behind Chris.

His brother picked his phone up off the counter and chuckled. "A text from Marcy, wanting to know if that's a smoke detector going off or our son."

While he responded to her, Brady looked over the

ingredients on the massive center island and guessed Chris was making pizza for dinner, which was always fine by him. He was tempted to pop out the sliding glass door onto the deck and say hi to Marcy, but he knew from experience if Benny saw her, he would want to stay with her and Mom's Friday night hot tub time was a kid-free zone. And Benny had Brady's shirt balled in his fists, so he wasn't ready to be put down.

"What can I do to help?" he asked his brother, even though he already knew what the answer would be.

"I've got this." Chris waved a hand in the direction of the family room. "If you go hang out with the boys, I can finish this up. And you can take any leftover pizza home if you can get CJ to stop being a fire engine for five minutes."

"Challenge accepted."

All it took was the bucket of building blocks and letting the boys take turns knocking down the towers he built. For whatever reason, the blocks tumbling to the ground made them laugh. Or maybe it was the greatly exaggerated looks of horror he put on every time they did it. But it was a fun game that didn't involve sirens, so as far as Brady was concerned, it was the best game ever.

Nothing made him happier than hanging out with his nephews. He liked kids in general, but he *really* liked these two, and in a perfect world he would have one or two of his own already so the group of cousins could grow up together and be almost as tight as a sibling group.

But it wasn't going to happen. At the rate he was going in his search for a woman who took him seriously and wanted to start a family, there would be too big an age gap between his kids and Chris's for them to be really close. He'd even expanded his dating pool to include tourists and dabbled in online dating, but all of the initial sparks fizzled after a few dates.

He was starting to wonder if he'd have to move to a new town if he wanted to find the future Mrs. Brady Nash. Blackberry Bay had shoved him into a box they thought fit him, but it didn't. They called him a ladies' man, so the women who expressed interest in him were only looking for a temporary good time with no pressure. Women who were looking for husbands and picket fences didn't knock on Brady's door.

And maybe in a new location, he'd meet a woman who knocked his emotional socks off. Every time he went on a second or third date with a woman and thought maybe this time it would stick, he'd run into Reyna. It wasn't fair to ask any woman to be with a man who thought of another woman every time he closed his eyes, so he always broke it off.

Though he sometimes imagined it, he knew he'd

probably never move away from Blackberry Bay—especially since his mom lived alone—so everybody would just go on thinking they'd put Brady in the right box. That he obviously couldn't commit to one woman. But what they didn't know—what only Chris knew—was that he *could* commit to one woman. But that woman was Reyna and he'd blown the one shot he had with her.

He'd been in love with her so long that his excitement over finally having her in his arms overpowered his self-control and he'd been too quick on the trigger. She hadn't stuck around long enough to give him a chance to rally and try again. The next time they'd run into each other, it had been so awkward they'd barely spoken. The only way to put it behind them was to talk about that night and neither of them seemed to want to talk about it, so they'd just stopped speaking to each other instead.

When a very relaxed blonde woman appeared in the doorway, Brady put the last block on a tower and smiled at her as Benny knocked it over and laughed. "Hey, Marcy."

"How's the Nash Demolition Company doing?"

He laughed and pushed himself to his feet with a slight groan. He was getting too old for sitting on the floor. "The demolition is fine as long as nobody calls the F-I-R-E department."

"I hope this is a very short phase," she said, but

her eyes were warm as she looked at her older son. "Okay, boys. Pick up the blocks while Uncle Brady helps serve the pizza, okay?"

Happy to avoid the cleanup, since there were blocks everywhere, Brady went into the kitchen, where Chris was using a rotary cutter to slice two mini cheese pizzas into triangles for CJ and little bites for Benny. He'd also made two big rectangular barbecue chicken pizzas, which seemed like a lot for three adults.

Brady laughed. "You hungry tonight?"

"I might have made too much."

"I'm glad, since I get to take the leftovers home with me."

"The big ones need to cool another minute or two before I cut them." Chris pinned him with a familiar look that signaled a serious talk was coming Brady's way. "Let's talk about why you hauled an old Chevelle over to Bishop's Auto."

"Seriously?" Brady held out his hands in an *are you kidding me?* gesture. "You don't even live in Blackberry Bay anymore. How do you already know about that?"

"I ran into Finn at Home Depot yesterday. He told me he'd heard from somebody else that you dropped an old Chevelle off with Reyna, but nobody seemed to know why, and he hadn't had a chance to call you yet."

Brady and Finn Weaver had been friends for so long, neither had a clear memory of the first time they met. He assumed it was kindergarten, since their friendship was solid enough by first grade so Finn was the only person Brady told when he decided he was going to marry Reyna Bishop someday. But apparently that friendship didn't extend to him keeping his mouth shut when talking to Brady's brother.

"Since when is it news that somebody dropped a car off at a car repair shop?"

Chris's expression made it clear he'd be having none of that. "First off, what are you even doing with an old Chevelle? You've never been a car guy. And, secondly, Reyna? How many times are you going to burn yourself touching that hot stove?"

Brady's skin heated and he regretted ever confiding in his brother about that night. He hadn't even told Finn about it, and he told his best friend almost everything. "Who else would I take it to? Of course I'm going to take the car to Bishop's."

"Calling it Bishop's doesn't make it any less Reyna's. And just how much is this ridiculous gambit to get back in Reyna's good graces going to cost you?"

"It's not a gambit. It's a cool-looking car and, if it turns out I don't like driving it and I sell it, I'll make a good profit since I didn't pay much for it. Assuming getting it back on the road doesn't cost more than I'm willing to pay, in which case I'll throw it up on the internet in as-is condition. I'll get that number tomorrow."

Chris leaned against the counter and folded his arms across his chest. "So what I'm hearing under all this car nonsense is that you're meeting with Reyna tomorrow."

"Leave it alone."

"Okay, I'm sorry. I'm your brother, Brady. I worry about you and… That's it. I just worry about you."

"I know." He picked up the boys' mini pizzas and nodded toward the dining room. "Let's go eat. I'm good, I promise."

He was good as he could be, anyway, considering the fact his brother wasn't wrong. He was going to show up at Reyna's tomorrow and touch that hot stove again. And just like last time, he was going to get burned.

Chapter Three

Reyna was up before the sun on Saturday, which wasn't like her. She was an early riser because she had to be, thanks to the bakery and the garage, and not because it came naturally to her. It usually took a loud alarm and a couple of slaps at the snooze button to get her out of bed.

But she'd gone to bed with her mind racing and been restless all night, in and out of sleep before finally giving up and getting out of bed before her alarm went off. After brewing herself a cup of coffee, she opened the door to what she thought of as her craft cave and flipped on the light.

Nobody—not even her mother—had been in this room, and Reyna liked it that way. It was her sanctuary, where she went when she needed to find some peace or to unwind at the end of a long week. It had also become the room where she made what her grandmother would have called *pin money*. A little extra money that didn't have to be accounted for in the very strict budget keeping Bishop's Auto Care & Bakery—as well as their households—in the black required.

She'd discovered a knack for making beautiful things with polymer clay in a high school art class, though she didn't give it a lot of thought once the class was over. But when her father first started having health issues, before he was even diagnosed with the cancer that eventually killed him, she'd seen a display of colorful polymer clay in a craft store window and bought some on impulse.

In the beginning, her craft cave had been a battered but comfortable reading chair with a lap tray and some storage totes, but now she had an entire wall dedicated to organizing her supplies and a well-lit worktable. Over the table was a large bulletin board where she hung photos for her current projects.

For whatever reason, she had a gift for taking photos of special things—wedding cakes, especially—and making replicas in polymer clay. Usually charms or Christmas tree decorations, but sometimes little statues. And being paid to spend time with a relaxing hobby wasn't exactly a hardship.

The first time she'd replicated a photo, it had been her parents' wedding cake, which had been made by her maternal grandmother. Grandma Marie was definitely where the baking gene came from, and she'd created a stunning floral cake, but with bright wildflowers rather than traditional roses.

Her mom had cried when Reyna gave her the clay replica, but when she'd asked her where she'd gotten it, Reyna had lied. In the split second before she opened her mouth and the words came out, she decided she didn't want anybody to know about her obsession with polymer clay, and she told her mother she'd commissioned it from an Etsy store.

Now she had a well-reviewed Etsy store of her own and nobody in Blackberry Bay knew about it. She even did all of her shipping on Tuesday afternoons, driving down to Concord to mail everything because she didn't want anybody in line or behind the counter to ask her what she had to send out so regularly. She liked having a secret. And she liked having something nobody else knew about in this town where everybody seemed to know everything. She also didn't want her mother thinking the garage or helping her in the bakery was holding Reyna back from doing something else she wanted to do.

This morning she didn't bother opening any clay.

Despite being up early, she didn't really have time to immerse herself in a project—even in one of the simple cupcakes or pop culture minis she often made to have ready-to-ship items available. And she was too unsettled to lose herself in anything, even her craft.

In a few more hours, Brady Nash was going to show up looking for a quote for his car. Which meant she had only a few more hours to decide if she was going to ask him for a favor.

Setting her coffee on the table, she leaned back and scrubbed her face with her hands. It was a lot more than a favor. And even though she'd spent a lot of time running lines through her head, trying to come up with the right words, she wasn't sure she had any idea what she was going to say when the time came.

Or even if she had the courage to say anything at all.

By the time the lunch hour rolled around, she was so tense the spot between her shoulder blades was starting to ache, and she actually flinched when the bell over the door rang to let her know somebody had entered the office.

Wiping her hands on a shop rag, she took a few deep breaths—it might not even be him—and went through the door to the office.

It was him.

Brady smiled at her and her stomach knotted as he

held up something wrapped in aluminum foil. Why did he have to be so incredibly handsome? "Hey, Reyna. We can go to the café if you want, but I have some leftover barbecue chicken pizza from my brother's last night and it's really good. I wasn't sure if you'd rather just eat here so we can talk without everybody wondering why we're out to lunch together."

Reyna laughed and struck a modeling pose, running her hands down her sides as if to show off her outfit. "What, you don't want to go out to lunch with a woman in gray overalls and grease on her hands?"

"And her face," he said with a chuckle. "I'll totally take you and your gray overalls to lunch, but it's really good pizza."

Maybe this was a sign they were meant to eat in her office, where they could have a private conversation. "I like pizza. I can run into the bakery and heat it up if you want."

"Up to you. I heated them up right before I left the house, just in case, so they're still warm. I didn't bring plates, though."

"For pizza? Who needs a plate?" She sat on her stool and, when he set the packet down on the counter, she peeled open the foil. "This does look good."

There were a couple of stools on the customer side of the counter and Brady chose one. She was thinking about how unlikely this was—she and Brady sharing a lunch in her garage after years of barely speaking—as she took a bite of barbecue chicken smothered in cheese on a perfect crust.

It was so good she didn't even mind the silence as they each ate a slice. And it was so good she barely remembered that it had been only about fifteen minutes ago that she was so nervous, she wasn't sure she'd ever have an appetite again.

"Did Chris's wife make this?" she asked when her slice was gone and she'd wiped her mouth with a piece of coarse blue paper towel that was better for grease on the hands than pizza sauce on one's lips.

"Chris made it. I helped." She must have looked skeptical because he laughed. "Okay, I confess. I mostly kept my nephews occupied while Chris made the pizza."

She knew he had nephews, of course. She'd seen them around town—usually for special occasions since they'd moved out of Blackberry Bay—but she hadn't spoken to Chris for a while.

"How old are they now?"

"CJ's three and Benny just turned eleven months. He's starting to walk, but he still crawls a lot because, damn, that kid crawls fast. And he's usually trying to keep up with CJ."

He talked more about them—Benny's impending birthday and what CJ was up to—and she didn't listen very well, but it wasn't because she didn't care. Rather, she was distracted by the way his face lit up when he talked about the boys and the way her pulse quickened as the nerves returned.

Obviously, he adored his brother's kids, and she wasn't sure if that went into the pro or the con column in her head. He was more likely to want to father a child if he actually liked kids, but for her plan to work, he couldn't actually want to raise one of his own.

"I guess it's time for the bad news," he said, snapping her out of her thoughts. "How much did I screw up when I spur-of-the-moment handed over three grand for that Chevelle?"

"Three thousand? I don't think you screwed up, even though it's not the SS model. You got it cheap enough so you could probably sell it as is and not make a big profit, but you won't *lose* money." She hopped off the stool and grabbed the paper with his name at the top from a pile. "Let's go outside so I can show you a couple of things."

She walked him through a few of the key points. The frame looked good and the body was still solid under the extremely rough paint that was left. Either it hadn't been sitting in the field as long as they'd estimated, or they'd just gotten very lucky. But she couldn't start it without draining the fluids, cleaning the carb and giving it new plugs and wires at the very least, and she wasn't doing that work for free.

"That's fair," he said.

"Okay, back to the actual estimate. First, the numbers reflect this being a side project for me with no deadline, so it doesn't interfere with the garage's regular business. And I do some minor touchup work on older vehicles for my regular customers, but I don't have a paint booth or the supplies and skill to do body and paint work that'll do that car justice. You basically have three options. You can have me do all the mechanical work and get her running like a dream, and then take her to somebody who can make her pretty from the frame up. You might want to rob a bank first. The second option is to have me not only do all the mechanical, but do as much of the cosmetic restoration as I can, and then have the actual paint and chrome handled by a guy I know. The third option is to hook up to your trailer and drive away. No hard feelings."

When she was finished laying it out, she handed him the sheet of paper, which had two estimates on it. One was the number for mechanical only and one was a really rough ballpark number for labor for the second option, not counting parts. His eyes widened as he scanned the breakdowns for each.

"As it says in the fine print, those numbers are ballpark, not binding. Restoring a car this old means hunting for parts, and figuring out whether repair or replacement is the way to go. You'll be consulted on a *lot*, so you'll have some control over the pricing.

And also, just so you know, those amounts are for a car that'll turn heads. But a 1970 Chevelle that'll win blue ribbons at car shows is out of my league."

He was still staring at the paper. "Ouch."

He was a smart guy, so he'd probably done some research and knew her estimate was extremely reasonable. Of course, he'd try to knock it down a little, so she'd padded in some wiggle room, but she was very good at what she did and she wasn't giving her time away for anybody.

"I'm sure you can find somebody who'll do it for less money. But just know up front that when you have a restored Chevelle that runs like crap because you took it to somebody else to save a few bucks, that I'm not going to fix it."

"Do I get some kind of discount because we've known each other since kindergarten?"

"Discount? More like a surcharge." She laughed at his expression and after a few seconds, he joined in.

"I get it. It's the same for me, you know. If you're building a new house, I can tell you how much it will cost to wire it. If you want me to rewire an old house, I can ballpark it, but I don't know what I'll find when I start getting in the walls and the old service, so it becomes a matter of time and material."

"It makes it a lot easier that you understand that."

He looked over the sheet again and then gave a sharp nod. "Let's get her running. Rebuild the engine, replace or repair what's gone and get her on the road. Then we'll revisit the cosmetics, once I know how much the mechanical cost me. At that point, if I want to tap out, she's worth more running, so still not a loss."

"You've never been a car guy. I have a hard time picturing you keeping it, to be honest."

"I was thinking it might be fun to cruise around when the boys are older, even though it's not a convertible. Old muscle cars are cool."

"Until CJ has his license and wants to take it for a spin around the lake," she said, and then she laughed at his look of horror. She should get his name on the dotted line before he changed his mind entirely. "If you come inside, you can sign the estimate and make it official."

"Oh, sure. I just thought I'd sign it when I stop by with the deposit."

"I…" Her stomach knotted and she had to pause and breathe for a few seconds. She was really going to do this. "I have something else I want to talk to you about, and I want this on the books, so to speak, before I do."

"Sounds ominous," he joked, but the nerves had returned in full force and all she managed was a tight smile.

Once they'd done the paperwork and come up with a plan for moving the Chevelle to the old garage at her mom's house, which had been the original home of Bishop's Auto Care, she fussed with the papers and the pen until Brady cleared his throat.

"So what's up, Reyna?"

There was no way she should be doing this. She was out of her mind.

"Come on," he urged when she didn't speak. "Spill it."

This could be her only chance. "I want to be a mom. I have for a long time, actually."

"You'll be a great mom," he said.

"Thanks. But what I'm not great at, I guess, is finding the right man to start a family with—to have kids with. And I'm tired of waiting, Brady. My dad got sick and I had to focus on him and the garage. Then helping my mom after and now... I thought maybe Lucas was going to work out and I'd only have to wait a little while longer to start a family. Obviously, you and half the town, as well as a bunch of strangers on the internet, saw how wrong I was about that."

"That's on him," Brady said firmly. "The fact he didn't know that was totally the wrong way to propose to you proves he was totally wrong *for* you."

"I know that, but it still means starting all over again. Trying to find a guy to date. Getting to know each other. I don't want to keep waiting until it's too late."

"Single women have babies all the time, though. You can even pick hair color and whether you care more about height or IQ and all that."

"I can't afford that," she admitted as heat crept up her neck and into her face. "That process is time-consuming and I'd have to travel to appointments and it's just too much. Too much time and definitely too much money. I need a man who'll father my child without wanting to be fully involved or asking me to put my heart out there again or expecting me to wait two or three years."

He didn't say anything when she paused, but she couldn't blame him. What was he supposed to say? But with him looking at her with compassion in those blue eyes, she knew she had to get it out fast before she lost what little courage she had left.

"The people in this town won't even bat an eye-lash at the news you're going to be a father. They're probably surprised you're not already."

His brow furrowed for a few seconds before his expression changed from confusion to outright in-credulity. "Jesus, Reyna. What are you asking me?"

"I'm asking you to have a baby with me."

Reyna Bishop wants to have my baby.
Never had Brady imagined putting those seven words together into one short, mind-blowing sentence, but here they were.

A baby. With Reyna.

It would be a dream come true on an epic scale if the rest of the words she'd said weren't slowly sinking into his brain. *Without wanting to be fully involved* and *people in this town won't even bat an eyelash at the news you're going to be a father.* She didn't want *him* to be her child's father. She wanted the version of him that everybody assumed to be the truth.

He should say something. She was watching him with wide eyes and flushed cheeks, and he knew he needed to respond. The right answer was that he was flattered, but they should focus on finding a way for her to afford leaving it to the professionals.

But an image of Benny scooting across the floor flashed through Brady's mind. If he had a baby soon, his kid and Chris's younger son would be close enough in age to play together. That thought made it difficult to focus on the fact this was probably a bad idea. And he should start with trying to make her believe he wasn't the reckless serial dater everybody made him out to be. Not by choice, anyway.

"You don't even like me" was what actually came out of his mouth.

"That's not true."

"You haven't talked to me since…" He let the sentence die away because he didn't really want to say the words out loud. It was bad enough that night was burned forever into his brain. He didn't need to vocalize it.

Judging by the way her cheeks flushed, he didn't *have* to say the words aloud. She obviously hadn't forgotten that night, either. It had been memorable, for the worst possible reasons.

"I admit it was awkward after that night," she said, "and then we started avoiding each other, and I guess we just got stuck in that awkwardness. But I've never disliked you."

"Good to know." There were so many thoughts fighting to be the focus in his head, but they were drowned out by the memory of CJ's and Benny's laughter as they knocked down his towers of blocks. How ironic that just last night he'd been thinking about how much he wanted a child of his own, and now that it was a possibility, he couldn't even think straight. "Why me?"

"I've known you my whole life. You're a good guy. And I like your family a lot." She smiled. "It doesn't hurt that your brother's kids are absolutely adorable, of course."

"You know they probably get that from their mother, right? Also, I should bring CJ by the garage and let him entertain you with his fire truck siren impression for a few hours."

She winced. "That sounds fun."

"Especially when Benny's in the mood to mimic

his big brother." He fiddled with the aluminum foil that was balled up on the counter. "I feel like knowing my family aren't jerks and thinking my nephews are cute isn't enough reason to choose me to be the father of your child, though."

Saying the words out loud—*the father of your child*—still blew his mind, but his pulse was slowing and he was hopeful he'd be able to think logically about all of this very soon.

"Who else could I ask?"

That stung, and he hoped it didn't show on his face. "You sure do know how to flatter a guy."

"I didn't mean it that way. It's not like you're the last man on earth or anything. You're not even the last guy in Blackberry Bay. But I don't think there's anybody else that not only fits what I'm looking for, which is a man I know from a family I know, but who doesn't have attachments or commitments in his life that could be a problem. You don't answer to anybody and don't seem to care about your reputation."

She was wrong about that. He hated that his fellow citizens of Blackberry Bay thought he was happy to play around and never settle down. But he couldn't really prove them wrong unless he *did* settle down, and he hadn't found a woman who affected him as strongly as Reyna did yet.

"Also, I trust you," she continued. "This would be the lead story at every tea party in town for a long time, so I have to trust you not to run your mouth about it, no matter what you decide."

It made him feel a little better that she had that faith in him. "I wouldn't do that to you."

"I know." She gave him a weak smile. "I wouldn't have asked you if I didn't truly believe you're a good guy. And the blue eyes don't hurt."

He tried not to think about little blue-eyed kids with Reyna's hair and his dimples running around his house, but he couldn't help it. That was the future he wanted. He just needed to remember that wasn't the future she was offering.

"How do you see this working, exactly?" He couldn't believe he was actually considering this. Not only becoming a father, but the father of Reyna Bishop's baby.

"Well, sometimes two adults—"

"You're funny." But he did chuckle before clearing his throat. "I mean the part about you and me sharing a child together. Forever. I need to know what your expectations are, because if one of those expectations is that I'll just do my part and then walk away and pretend it never happened, that's not going to work for me."

"Of course not. I hardly think everybody in town pegging you as a deadbeat dad is exactly the angle we're looking for."

"I don't give a damn about everybody in town,"

he said, though it wasn't true. "The fact I won't be that kind of father has nothing to do with what anybody might say, and everything to do with the fact I *want* to be a father and I also wouldn't let you bear the financial burden alone. Period."

Her eyebrows drew together as she inhaled deeply. "You *want* to be a father?"

"I wouldn't say it's been at the top of my to-do list, but I've thought about the fact it would be cool to have a kid close enough to Benny's age so they could hang out." He was watching her face, so he saw the way her mouth twisted at the corner for a second. "You know, for a woman asking me to be the father of her baby, you don't look too thrilled about me wanting to be a father."

"I just don't want..." She stopped talking and looked at him for a long moment before trying again. "I want a baby. I don't want the whole family thing. I don't want a man."

Ouch. "Okay."

"I'll be totally honest with you, Brady. Ideally, I'd be artificially inseminated and not deal with a father at all. But it would be a long time before I could afford that and I'm tired of putting off what I want. So I guess we would be like any *real* couple who broke up and shared a child. But I would have primary custody."

"And I'll have fair visitation rights."

She nodded slowly. "It would be good for the baby to have cousins. And, like you said, to be close enough in age to play with Benny. My mom and I don't have any family but each other, so I guess that's in the plus column."

"Okay, next question. What would we tell our mothers? Because that has the potential to be really messy."

"That's an understatement." She sighed. "I've been thinking a lot about this, and I don't want to outright lie to my mom."

"I don't, either. And I don't want my mom to think the baby is an accident or a mistake."

"Same. But on the other hand, I also don't want the entire town talking about how Reyna Bishop hit up Brady Nash for his sperm because she couldn't keep a man."

"This has the potential to be messy."

"It *is messy,*" she said. "But I think it's worth navigating the tough parts."

"I'd rather, when the time comes, just tell our families that we both wanted a baby but neither of us were going to be walking down the aisle anytime soon, so we decided to go for it." He shrugged one shoulder. "I mean, the worst-case scenario is everybody in town finding out that's the truth. That's not so bad."

"No, it's not, I guess." She sighed, then gave him

a sheepish smile. "I was hoping for a more…typical situation, if that makes sense. Something that won't follow the child around as he or she grows up because it's too boring for the gossips."

"So we pretend we're dating and then you get pregnant and eventually we break up," he said, even though he knew that was easier said than done. Dating Reyna and having to pretend he was pretending to like her would probably be harder than being a father.

"Do you think we could pull that off?"

"I don't see why not. We hit a bump a few years back, I know, but we were friends before that. There's no reason we can't hang out."

As Reyna considered what he'd said, Brady concentrated on keeping his expression as neutral as possible. It wasn't easy considering the possibility of "hanging out" with Reyna was within reach.

"Does this mean you're on board?" she asked quietly.

He needed to focus less on the hanging-out part and more on the major—and permanent—life change they were considering. "Do I get to think about it?"

She laughed, and he could hear the underlying anxiety, but he still loved the sound. "Of course. It's not the kind of decision you should make spur-of-the-moment."

The phone hanging on the wall, with a coiled cord

and everything, rang with a jangling sound that made them both jump.

"Come over for dinner tomorrow night," he said as they both slid off the stools. "Six o'clock? We'll talk more."

She hesitated, but then gave a sharp nod. "Sounds good. I'll be there at six."

He heard her answering the phone as he closed the door to the office behind him, so he thought it was safe to sit in his truck and process what had just happened for a few seconds before putting it in gear. And he chuckled to himself as he passed by the Chevelle because he'd forgotten all about the car.

There was a good possibility he was going to have a baby with Reyna Bishop.

Chapter Four

A little over twenty-four hours later, Reyna locked her door and set off toward Brady's house on foot. It was about a mile, but it wasn't too cold and she could use the walking time to clear her head. Or try to. She felt as if she hadn't had a truly clear head since the idea of asking Brady to father her child had first popped into her mind.

On some level she'd known Brady wasn't the kind of guy to just father a child and then walk away, even if it was something he'd agreed to up front. Unless one of them moved, they would always cross paths and he wouldn't be able to ignore his own kid. She appreciated that he'd been honest about his unwill-ingness to be hands-off yesterday.

And when he'd talked about wanting a son or daughter close to Benny's age, something had clicked inside her. Cousins. When she'd thought about being a mom, she'd pictured her and a baby. And her mother, of course.

She hadn't imagined Brady actually *in* the pic-ture with them.

But this way the baby would also have his or her father. And cousins, an aunt and uncle, and another grandmother. And as far as Reyna was concerned, the more people who loved her baby, the better.

When she reached his street, she realized there was an added bonus to walking because her car wouldn't be seen sitting in Brady's driveway. If all went well, it wouldn't matter if the gossips talked about her visiting him at home. But if tonight ended in disappointment, she didn't want that added sprin-kle of salt in the wound. They were probably still talking about her turning down Lucas's marriage proposal, so until there was good news for them to spread around, she'd rather give them nothing at all.

Once she reached Brady's house, she stood on the sidewalk with her hands shoved deep into her coat pockets.

When she'd talked herself into believing Brady Nash was the perfect man to father her child, she hadn't stopped to consider where he lived. He'd bought the place about six months after their disastrous interlude, which had taken place in the apartment he'd been renting over the credit union.

The two-story brick Colonial looked like a freaking postcard with an electric candle glowing in each window and the light dusting of the season's first snow blanketing the roof. Because it was situated on a quiet back road she and her mother used as a shortcut when they walked to the lakefront park, she knew that the large front and backyards were bordered by colorful perennial garden beds in the summer.

It was a perfect home for a family. Too bad they weren't actually going to be one.

The door opened, and the light inside the house silhouetted him in the doorway. "You trying to decide whether you're coming in or turning around and going home?"

She didn't want him to think she had any doubts about what she was asking him to do, so she shrugged and started up the walk toward him. "I was admiring the electric candles in the window. Trying to get a jump start on decorating?"

He laughed and stepped back to welcome her into the foyer. "I leave those up year-round because I like the way they look. But I might have already put in my wreath order with the ag class at the high school."

"I've seen it with the wreaths and all the lights.

When it's done up for Christmas, it's one of the prettiest houses in Blackberry Bay."

"Thanks." He closed the door and took her coat. "Still working on the final touches inside. The previous owners struggled with the upkeep and focused most of their time and money on the exterior."

Reyna watched him hanging her coat in the closet, trying not to notice the way faded jeans and an old blue Henley shirt hugged his body, and failing miserably. She'd always found him physically attractive, which was why she'd been all the more disappointed the night she'd given in to his charm, despite knowing he wasn't the kind of guy who stuck around.

"I'm almost done with the remodeling, though," he continued as he closed the closet door.

"Did you do it yourself?" The interior was very simple in an elegant way, with warm cream walls and what looked like original woodwork, but meticulously refinished. The floors were hardwood, but she didn't think they were original. The new boards were a good match for the trim, though.

"Most of it. After work if I had nothing going on and a lot of weekends. A *lot* of my weekends." He chuckled as he led her down the hall into the kitchen. "I tried to stay true to the original design, but I did knock out a wall to open up the kitchen and dining area."

"It's beautiful." Remodeling this house while running his own electrical business must not have left him a lot of free time. "Now that you're almost done with the house, you decided to restore an old car?"

His laugh echoed because the house might be beautiful, but it had the bare minimum of furniture. "My mom always seems to have a project going, so I must have inherited that from her."

"Dinner smells amazing, by the way." There was a large island in the kitchen, with a smooth gray top, and she took a seat on one of the four stools set around it.

"I made a lasagna because, of course, I'd accidentally choose to make a dish with a red sauce on a night you're wearing a cream sweater. I've had it on warm for a while, so it should be ready to eat as soon as the bread's heated."

She appreciated his easy humor as he moved around the kitchen, but all she could think about now that she was here was the conversation that lay ahead of them. It wasn't clear to her if they were going to talk about her proposition before they ate or after, and she was too nervous to bring it up herself. She wasn't sure she'd be able to enjoy the lasagna with the knot in her stomach, though, so maybe she should work up the courage to broach the subject.

After he'd taken the lasagna out and set it on top of the stove, he popped a foil-wrapped loaf in the oven and then turned to the island. He fiddled with the jar of garlic powder for a few seconds before rubbing his hands together while inhaling deeply through his nose. At least he was as nervous as she was.

"So," he said, shoving his hands into his pockets. "I think you and I would make a great kid together."

"I can't really tell if there's a *but* coming or not." She smiled, keeping her hands clenched in her lap so she wouldn't be tempted to fiddle like he had been. And maybe to hide the fact her hands were shaking. Maybe even her entire body, actually, though she hoped he couldn't see it.

Were they having a baby together or not?

Having Reyna sitting in his kitchen, looking gorgeous with her red hair spilling loose over her cream sweater, was something Brady had allowed himself to imagine a time or two while remodeling the room. It was a house made for a family, and it was hard to picture a woman in the house without seeing Reyna's face.

"There's definitely no *but* when it comes to knowing you and I would make a great kid," he said. "*But*... I do have a question."

She chuckled. "Just one?"

"No, I probably have a lot of questions, but most of them are the typical questions two parents who are splitting up would have to answer. There's one big one that's unique to our situation that stuck in my head last night, and that is how long you see us trying."

"How long…" He watched the real question he was asking sink in and realized she didn't have an answer. "Oh."

Underneath his very real desire to have a child, there was another layer for Brady. He wanted redemption. He wanted to take this woman to his bed and show her that he *did* care about her and her satisfaction. Would it be easy? No, because he still wanted her as badly as he had that awful night, and for years before that. But he'd do algebra equations or run through box scores in his head, or whatever he had to do to make sure she left his bed with a smile on her face.

But he also knew it wouldn't be healthy for him to let it go on too long. This arrangement called for him to walk away from Reyna at some point, and the longer they pretended to be a couple—and the longer she was in his bed—the harder it was going to be.

"Obviously we're talking months here," he said. "The pretending to date part. The actual conception, which isn't even in our control. And then the continuing to date until we go our separate ways. That all adds up, but there has to come a point when we've tried, but maybe it wasn't meant to be. I just need to know if you have an expectation of how long we'll try."

"Maybe we try for three months? I know it might not happen because a lot of people try longer than that, but you can't put your life on hold forever. Even if we only try for three months, that's at least six months you'll be wrapped up in this." She frowned, catching her bottom lip between her teeth for a second. "That sounds like a long time."

"Not in the grand scheme of things," he replied, trying to put her mind at ease. "Six months from now, we'll probably be doing the same stuff in life we are now, except in shorts and T-shirts. Except, maybe this time when six months from now rolls around, we'll be expecting a baby."

Her face practically glowed when he said that, and the warmth in her eyes melted him inside. "So you want to do this?"

He nodded. "I want to do this."

Her entire body shuddered as tears filled her eyes, and she laughed as she swiped at them. "Sorry. I'm just… I've wanted to be a mom for a long time and just to actually have a chance means a lot to me."

"Me, too." He wasn't sure what to do next, so he went to the oven and pulled out the wrapped loaf of garlic bread. "Now we can eat and we'll figure out the rest as we go, I guess."

They managed small talk while he cut and served

the lasagna, and some of the tension had eased out of his body by the time they were sitting across from each other at his small dining room table. But when she slid the first bite of lasagna between her lips and made a low sound of appreciation that was almost a moan, his muscles began tightening again.

He was going to make love to this woman. At her request. It was like a very early Christmas present—though he wasn't sure if wanting a second chance to take a woman to bed meant he'd been very good or very naughty—and this time he was going to take his time enjoying her, and he would do anything she asked of him.

"You made this yourself?" she asked, one eyebrow raised as she gave him a challenging look across the table.

"I'm a man with many skills," he replied, but he regretted the quip when her mouth twitched from her effort not to show how amused she was by that statement.

Reyna had cause to doubt his skills in the bedroom, but that was going to change soon. He'd make sure of it. The next time she made that sound of pleasure, he wanted it to be in his bed.

When they'd had their fill of lasagna and garlic bread, Reyna insisted on helping him clean up. He would have left it to deal with later, but there was something calming about performing a simple domestic chore with her at his side. Their relationship had been something of a roller coaster—from good friends to a night of bad sex to several years of avoiding each other to deciding to have a baby—and the quiet task made him feel as if his feet were firmly under him.

Then she reached for a plate at the same time he did and her hand landed on his. They both froze and, just like that, he was on the roller coaster again. He expected her to pull away, but she didn't move. Instead, they both looked at their hands, resting on the edge of the plate.

"Is this weird?" she whispered.

"I think it's a little bit weird." He rested his other hand at the small of her back and turned his body to face her slightly. "The question is, do we care?"

"That it's weird?" She tilted her head, smiling at him. "No, I guess I don't care."

"We're adults and we can do whatever makes us happy." Kissing her would make him happy right about now, but he didn't want to push her. He wanted her to be the one to initiate the intimacy their arrangement was going to require because it was the only way he could be sure she was totally comfortable with it.

He didn't want to initiate the kiss, but he also didn't want to move away, so he decided to talk instead. "We'll have to, like, track when it's most likely to happen and all that, right?"

"I have been, for a while. Since before I started seeing Lucas, actually, because I knew at some point, having a baby alone might be my best option. Of course, I didn't know then how much it costs." Pink colored her cheeks as she chuckled. "I just got in the habit of keeping everything in a journal and, ironically, my most fertile time should be right now. The next couple of nights are the best time, so we'll just have to figure out when we want to start and count from there."

Brady's train of thought came to such an abrupt stop, he was surprised he didn't hear the squeal of the brakes in his head.

The next couple of nights are the best time.

Their gazes locked and he gave her a slow smile. "There's no time like the present, right?"

Reyna's breath caught as Brady's lips curved into a naughty grin, and she couldn't seem to make herself stop staring at his mouth.

There's no time like the present, right?

Why was she tingling in all the best places? Her head knew not to get her hopes up because they'd been there, done that, and it hadn't been all that. But her body seemed to have forgotten that she'd surrendered to the promise in those blue eyes before and been disappointed.

But she was keenly aware of the warmth and weight of his hand on her back, and all she had to do was lean in and kiss him.

And she should. Wasn't that the point? They were going to have to get naked in order to make a baby, so this jolt of desire currently scrambling her thoughts was actually a good thing.

"That must be quite an argument you're having with yourself," he said in a low voice that made her shiver, and then his hand fell away.

She took a step back, trying to get a hold of herself. The last thing she wanted was for him to think she wasn't into him. The fact they'd been avoiding each other for several years was proof enough that he was as aware as she was that the sex hadn't been good between them.

"I just…" She just what? She couldn't tell him she was struggling with how much she wanted him to kiss her. That didn't even make sense. "Getting pregnant means unprotected sex and there are other ramifications of that."

"Oh," he said when he got what she was trying to say. "I get tested for everything when I get my yearly physical and I haven't been with anybody since my last one, which I passed with flying colors. I can probably find the results recap if I go rummage around in my filing cabinet."

"I believe you." Brady would never lie to her about something that important. She wouldn't be having this conversation with him at all if she thought he was capable of that. "I don't know if I have results on paper lying around because, unless they're work orders, I'm bad with paper. I write on the back or throw them out or spill coffee on them, but I'm the same."

"And I believe you. No need to dig through stacks of crumpled, coffee-stained papers."

When he put his hands on her waist, sliding them just under the hem of her sweater so his thumbs brushed her bare skin, she sucked in a breath.

"I guess the only thing now," he said in a husky voice that made her shiver, "is making sure you absolutely want to do this."

"I absolutely do."

"I'm not taking about *having* a baby." He kissed the side of her neck. "I'm talking about you and me *making* a baby."

She knew what he was doing. He was testing her—being just forward enough to make her uncomfortable if she wasn't ready for the next step. And maybe testing his comfort level, too, although he didn't seem very shy about sliding his hands down to cup the curve of her bottom.

"I know what you're talking about," she said,

sliding her hands up his back and pulling him even closer. "And I absolutely want to do this."

"Let me know if you change your mind at any point," he told her right before he backed her up against the island and kissed her so fiercely her fingers clenched the fabric of his shirt and balled it in her fists.

As his mouth claimed hers, his hands slid under her sweater again, and she savored the feeling of his work-hardened skin against the soft flesh of her back.

She tried to dampen the hot, aching need building inside of her. It wasn't the first time she'd felt Brady's hands on her, and she'd left still aching that night. But when his fingertips skimmed over her ribs, she couldn't hold back a small moan against his lips.

"Should we take this upstairs?" he whispered against her mouth, and she reluctantly broke off the kiss only because there was the promise of something better.

"Definitely," she said, and he took her hand to lead her up the stairs.

She had a glimpse of the same simple color scheme and sparse furnishings on the way to his bed, but she cared less about the decor and more about the fact they started shedding clothing as soon as they crossed the threshold from the hall.

Unlike their first time together, though, there was no rushed fumbling. He kissed her between every item of clothing they removed, his hands exploring each new inch of revealed skin.

When she was naked, he stretched her out on the bed and kissed every part of her body. He talked to her, too, telling her how sexy she was and how hot she made him. She ran her hands over his shoulders, her short nails digging into his muscles as he licked his way down her stomach, and then she tangled her fingers in his hair when he reached her thighs.

It wasn't until she stopped shaking from her first orgasm that he kissed his way back up her body, stopping to lavish attention on her breasts while she scraped her fingernails up his back to encourage him to keep moving.

His grin when he looked down at her was wicked and maybe even a little smug as he settled between her thighs. And then he was inside her, moving with slow and measured strokes, and she sighed at the sensation.

His hand cupped her face and he stared into her eyes. Beneath the sizzle was a tenderness that took her breath away. He stroked her cheek with his thumb, all the while moving deep within her, and then lowered his mouth to kiss her.

She moaned against his mouth as he thrust deeper into her, and the strokes quickened in response. When she buried her hand in his hair and whispered his name, he groaned and bit gently at her bottom lip.

When he reached down and stroked her with his thumb, it was too much and she cried out when the orgasm hit. She dug her fingers into his upper arms as her back arched off the bed, and he groaned as her body clenched around him.

He quickened his pace, thrusting deeper and faster until his orgasm shook him. And then he gently lowered himself on top of her, kissing first her mouth, and then her breast and finally her neck as he settled onto her body.

She ran her hands over the slick muscles of his back, trying to catch her breath and enjoying the feel of his heart beating against her chest.

They lay like that for a few minutes, until he kissed her neck again and carefully rolled off of her. But he didn't roll away. He rested one arm across her, his fingers toying with her hair, and captured one of her legs under his.

Reyna was more than content beside him, until she felt sleep creeping up on her. And she could tell by the way Brady's breathing slowed and grew more even that he wasn't far from it.

"I should go," she whispered.

"Are you done already?" he whispered back.

She laughed, slapping his arm. "Are *you* done?"

He was not done, and he spent the next twenty minutes or so proving it to her. It wasn't until she was draped over the bed, totally out of breath and with muscles that felt liquid, that he allowed himself a second orgasm, and he gave a ragged chuckle as he collapsed next to her.

"Okay, now I'm done."

She came even closer to falling asleep that time, not only because her body was in a state of blissful exhaustion, but because it was probably past her bedtime.

"Now I really have to go," she murmured, nudging him because it sounded like he was starting to fall asleep.

"Just stay. We don't even have to turn around and put our heads on the pillow. We can just stay like this."

"I can't stay here all night. And you don't have to move because walking home is no big deal."

"First, there's no way you're walking home alone at this time of night, no matter how small this town is. If you want to go home, I'll drive you. But secondly, why *can't* you stay the night? I get up early, so I can get you home in time to get ready for work."

She didn't know how to explain that sleeping and waking up with him seemed too intimate, considering what they'd just done, and that maybe that was a boundary line for this relationship. And the silence was starting to feel loud in the room.

"Hey." He kissed her shoulder before he sat up. "I'll drive you home. And don't tell me again how you can just walk. That's not happening."

She slid out of bed and started pulling on her clothes, while he did the same. "Are you trying to be the boss of me, Brady Nash?"

"Never." He chuckled. "Okay, so you can walk home. But I'm going to follow you in my truck the entire way and we'll just look ridiculous."

She let him drive her home, and she tried not to dwell on how sweet it was that he sat in his idling truck until she was upstairs and had closed her door behind her. The fact he was *not* bad in bed was enough to process. She didn't need him turning on the charm, too.

Chapter Five

It never failed. As soon as Brady was at the top of his ladder, with his arms stretched over his head to reach some task—in this case, changing out a ceiling fan and light fixture combo—his phone would start buzzing silently in his pocket.

He almost dropped the frosted dome he was about to fit over the center bulb, not because it startled him, but because it might be Reyna. He'd spent the morning with most of his mind on his work, but she'd been occupying enough space in his head so he was thankful he had easy and fairly mindless jobs scheduled today.

They hadn't really established a protocol for what happened next, and that had been distracting him since the moment he opened his eyes this morning. Was he supposed to call her? Were they already doing the dating-in-public thing? Or were they waiting to see if they could actually make a baby together first? There were a lot of questions he didn't have answers to, but it was too late to go back and make himself wait. To hold off until they'd figured *every-thing* out, even if it meant waiting another month.

By the time he finished and was able to climb down the ladder, he was practically vibrating with anticipation, but Mrs. Yeung was eager to see her new fan and light in action, so he forced himself to leave his phone in his pocket. After showing her how to use the speed controls and the dimmer on the wall, he carried his tools to his truck and accepted a check and a plastic bag of freshly baked cookies from her.

Being an electrician in a small town definitely had benefits.

Only when he was in his truck and ready to go did he pull the phone out of his pocket.

The missed call was from his mother, and he forced back the wave of disappointment at not seeing Reyna's name on the screen. He was going to have to control his emotional reactions better if he was going to be able to pull this off. She didn't want *him*, he reminded himself for the umpteenth time. Just a baby.

There was no voice mail message. Since they'd all gone to cell phones, Christy Nash rarely left messages for either of her sons. She knew they'd see the missed call and call her back when they got a chance. Brady wasn't a fan of the habit since he had no way of knowing what he was in for. Knowing if there was an errand to run or a problem to fix versus her just being bored and wanting to talk would be nice.

But it didn't matter. If she needed dog food, he'd pick it up for her. If she wanted company, he'd go visit. She was his mom, and since Chris lived farther away and he and Marcy had their hands full juggling their careers and two kids, Brady was often on deck.

It was technically the hour he left open for lunch, so rather than call her back, he munched on the cookies as he drove to his mother's house. The turn onto her driveway was only five minutes out of town, but it took another five minutes on a good day to navigate her dirt driveway. It twisted through the woods and in places had a decent incline—which was fun in January and February when it had a tendency to ice over—before it opened into the clearing where the house and a variety of small outbuildings sat.

He managed to get out of the truck and have his feet firmly planted on the ground before the dogs went into full greeting mode. The two yellow Labs tried to behave, as a rule, but their enthusiasm for company and the mutual adoration between Brady and the dogs meant a lot of bumping against his legs and jumping up to compete for affection and head rubs.

Taffy and Bean had been six months old when his mom rescued the sisters from the shelter, and at four years old, they didn't have any less energy than they had as pups. It was a good thing they lived out in the woods, he thought as they ran off to let Mom know he'd arrived. She was probably out back in her greenhouse, making sure everything was ready for winter, and though she would have heard the truck pull up and the dogs' ecstatic barking, it would take her a few minutes to finish what she was doing and wash her hands.

Brady took the time to look over the front of the house, looking for anything he and Chris might have to address before winter hit. It was a small house. Only one story with a large open living space in the front and a loft bedroom over a small bedroom and bathroom along the back. He'd shared that loft with Chris and there hadn't been a lot of privacy, but they'd managed. It had been a good home and piece of land for two boys to grow up on.

And it was in good repair, thanks to Christy having raised two adult sons without a man around to help. If something needed doing, they figured out a way to do it. If they didn't know how, they went to the library and learned. The only stumbling block in their younger years had been money—Christy had worked what jobs she could get during school hours—but they'd made do. And now he and Chris both did well for themselves and made sure she had everything she needed.

"Brady!" His mom walked around the corner of the house, the dogs on either side of her, and her face lit up in a smile when she saw him. "I was only calling to tell you the dogs are down to about a week's worth of food and I swear they think they must be bears because they're determined to pack on some winter weight."

She could have told him that via voice mail or a text, but then he might not have stopped by. It was one of the subtle ways she had of making sure she saw her sons on a regular basis. And he didn't mind. When she wrapped her arms around him, he kissed her cheek and hugged her back. "You look clean today. Not working in the greenhouse?"

She laughed and shook her head. "Nope. I know you're practically impervious to the cold, but we've already had a hard frost and first snow. Not much to do out there, so I'm working on a project. Come inside."

"An inside project? I'm intrigued."

The inside hadn't changed much since he was a

kid. A lot of sturdy wood and rugged fabrics. It might have felt dark, but the house had a lot of windows and plants, so it was more welcoming than oppressive.

"What do you think?" she asked, gesturing at what looked like a cross between a couch and a small bed. It had a wooden frame she'd clearly refinished herself with her usual attention and skill. "It's a trundle, so CJ can sleep on the couch part and Benny on the pull-out. It'll be a while yet before they can climb the ladder to the loft, but I want them to be able to stay over."

Brady chuckled because he and Chris had been up and down that ladder pretty much as soon as they learned what it was for, but times changed. Marcy wasn't exactly a helicopter mom, but she wasn't going to be okay with her two little ones up in that loft.

"I think it's perfect, Mom. And it'll be fun for them to run around here during the summer. Or when Chris and Marcy need a break. Did you find our fishing poles yet?"

"Of course. I cleaned them up and they'll work just fine for the boys." She put her hands on her hips and smiled at the homemade trundle bed. "And by the time you have kids who are ready to stay with Nana, CJ and Benny should be able to sleep up in the loft. It'll be perfect."

Brady pressed his lips together, afraid he'd say

something he shouldn't. Not yet, anyway. Not only because he didn't want to get his mother's hopes up, because he wasn't ready to talk about the possibility he might be giving her a third grandchild a lot sooner than she expected.

"Of course, you having kids will require you to settle down," she added, giving him an affectionate *mom look* that made him blush. "You don't seem like you're in a hurry to do that anytime soon. Sometimes I wonder if it's your father's genes, I swear."

It wasn't the first time he'd heard it, so he only shrugged. His mom didn't hold any animosity or resentment toward the man she'd once been married to, so it wasn't an accusation. It was just a fact that, when it came to settling down with one woman, Brady might take after a man he couldn't remember. And he was content to let her think that.

Their father had run off a long time ago. Chris had vague memories of him, but Brady didn't. It had always been him, his brother and their mom. And dogs. There were always dogs.

According to their mother, Chip Nash had been passing through Blackberry Bay on his motorcycle and stopped for a soft serve at the ice cream stand where Christy had been working. Love at first sight, she always said. He'd moved into the tiny house in the woods that had become hers when her parents left for warmer climates and they'd had two babies together. But small-town life wasn't for Chip and he'd hit the open road while Brady was still in diapers. A dump truck on the wrong side of a yellow line had put an end to Chip's roaming a few years later and, as far as Brady knew, his mother hadn't had a serious relationship since.

"Maybe I don't mind being alone," he said. "Which I guess I'd get from *you*."

"I'm done trying," she said, and then she chuckled and rolled her eyes at him.

"You only tried once, though."

Because he was looking directly at her, he saw the shadow of something cloud her expression before she smiled and shrugged. "Once was enough. Besides, Taffy, Bean and I take up the whole bed and there's not much chance I'm going to find a man willing to sleep up in the loft."

As tempting as it was to poke at her a little more—to find out why that glimpse of sadness had been there—it must be a sore spot, so he left it alone.

"Speaking of the dogs," he said. "You know they're going to want to sleep with CJ and Benny on that trundle bed, and Benny's small. There's a good chance he'll get pushed onto the floor."

She laughed. "It's only a couple of inches off the ground. They'll figure it out."

Brady could picture it so clearly in his mind. The boys and the dogs playing together. Sleeping together. But in his mind, there were three kids. Maybe three boys or maybe two boys and a little girl with red hair like her mama's. He could imagine him and Chris sitting on the riverbank that was the property's west boundary, teaching Benny and his little one to fish. CJ, being a little older, would know how and be bossy about it.

His heart ached in his chest, just thinking about it. He wanted that. And now there was a possibility that dream was going to come true in an unexpected way.

The truth that had been lurking in the shadows of his mind since Reyna left his bed last night didn't want to be denied anymore. It wasn't going to be enough. He wanted a baby. He wanted his life filled with the ups and downs and love and laughter of making memories with a child.

But he wanted Reyna, too.

And that was the problem. The dream he was chasing didn't feel complete without Reyna in the picture. He wanted to experience the ups and downs of raising a child *with* her. He wanted to not only make memories with a child, but share those memories with the child's mother.

During the years he and Reyna hadn't been speaking, he'd thought about her a lot. Definitely more often than he should have been, considering he'd been looking for some other woman to settle down with since he couldn't have her. But those thoughts had been mostly replays of that one night and all the ways it could have gone better. Or trying to come up with ways to initiate a conversation and smooth over the rift between them.

The last few days had brought the *real* Reyna back into his life—the Reyna he'd been friends with since childhood—and now that he had her, he wanted more of her. Several times during the day, he'd thought about them eating and cleaning up in his kitchen, and how sharing those moments with her had made the old house feel more like a home than any amount of decorating could.

Two separate dreams. One of being a father and one of Reyna being his. But this plan to have a child together blended the line between the two and his heart had jumbled them into one big dream. And now he wasn't sure if he could be truly happy with just half of that dream coming true.

An oil change and rotating tires shouldn't have taken so long, Reyna thought as she hit the button to lower the lift. She'd been doing those basic tasks for so long she didn't even have to think about them.

Which was good, since her mind was squarely on Brady Nash today.

She should be in a *much* better mood.

After all, she'd done it. Maybe not *all* of it, since it was highly unlikely she had conceived on their first try. But she hadn't second-guessed herself into inaction. She hadn't put it off until her life was more settled. Until the bakery and the garage were making more money. Until she had a home that wasn't over the garage. Until she had a husband and a white picket fence. For once in her life, she boldly went after what *she* wanted. She'd just taken the leap...

Right into Brady's bed, where she'd had unexpectedly wonderful sex.

And that was probably why she'd awoken this morning feeling unsettled and out of sorts. It wasn't supposed to be wonderful. It was supposed to be a means to an end. Probably mediocre and over quickly, like the first time she'd slept with Brady.

Instead, her muscles were still languid from a night of pleasure she wasn't going to forget anytime soon. If ever. And she didn't know what to do with that. It made their decision to try for a baby a lot easier, of course. But she couldn't get the image of Brady's face out of her head. The way he'd looked at her—it hadn't been the look of a man who was spending the night with a reasonably attractive woman because they were on a mission. The heat in his eyes hadn't been only sexual. There had been an underlying warmth that made her feel as if there was no other woman he'd rather be with in that moment.

She'd liked it. She liked that feeling and she was afraid if she got used to it, she'd end up wanting more of it. Before long there were going to be a lot of feelings wrapped up in their arrangement, and that would be messy.

By the time she could close the garage and take a shower, her stomach was so tied up in knots, she almost dropped her phone when it buzzed in her hand. And the message was from Brady.

Are you coming over tonight?

She didn't want to sound too eager. Sure.

I'll be here, so whenever.

She drove over, even though it was a mild night, because she didn't want a repeat of last night. When she was ready to leave, she wanted to be able to leave on her own. And she parked in his driveway because it really didn't matter who noticed. That was kind of the point of the plan.

But the closer she got to Brady's front door, the tighter the knot in the pit of her stomach felt. Tonight felt even harder than last night, which was ridiculous. Last night the biggest decision of her life had been up in the air and out of her hands, and tonight she knew what to expect.

Except tonight she knew there was a risk of falling for him if she wasn't careful. And falling for him would be a disaster, since she'd made it pretty clear she didn't want him. Just the baby. She'd even said it outright—*I don't want a man*—so there was no room for interpretation. The agreement they'd made together called for pretense and it wouldn't be fair to him to change the rules after the fact. A genuine emotional connection to him would just lead to heartache and the kind of co-parenting mess she was trying to avoid.

As soon as he opened the door, she could tell something had changed for him, too. He smiled, but it didn't reach his eyes. And something about his energy felt off, too. Quieter. Calmer. Or maybe nerves.

"Hey, come on in."

She went in, but she didn't take off her coat or her shoes. Something told her she wouldn't be staying long.

"Did you eat yet? I didn't make anything, but I have some leftovers if you're hungry."

"I'm not hungry."

He shoved his hand through his hair, looking as if he wasn't sure what to say next. Whatever had made things easy between them was gone. "Do you want me to take your coat?"

"I'm not sure I'm staying."

His brow furrowed, though he didn't look surprised by her statement. "Why not?"

"Because something's wrong. What's going

through your head right now?" When he inhaled deeply and looked down at his feet, her stomach dropped. "You changed your mind."

"Reyna, I…" When she turned away, he put his hand on her arm. "Let me explain."

She inhaled deeply and held the breath for a moment before slowly letting it out. "You don't have to explain, Brady. Having a baby is a very big deal and I should have made you take more time to think about it. And we absolutely should never have gone from talking about it to your bed so fast. It's okay."

"There's more to it than that," he said, but she shook her head.

"It's okay," she said more firmly. Maybe if she sounded like she meant it, he wouldn't guess she didn't. "We both want to be parents, but this probably wasn't the right way to do it. Let's just forget this ever happened."

"I am *not* going to forget last night."

Neither was she, which was why she forced a smile onto her face as she put her hand on the doorknob. "Orgasms aren't bad, as consolation prizes go."

And then she was through the door. He reached for her, but he wasn't fast enough. And he called her name, but she didn't turn around because she didn't want him to see the tears in her eyes.

"See you around, Nash," she called, and then she was safely in her car.

She drove carefully back through town, and she hesitated at the intersection where she could choose to go home or choose to head to her mother's house. She really could have used a hug.

But she wouldn't get the hug without having to explain the tears, so she drove home and crawled into bed, where she cried herself to sleep.

Chapter Six

For two and a half weeks, Reyna did the jobs she was scheduled to do. She helped her mom in the bakery whenever Jenelle needed an extra set of hands. She spent her spare time in her room, crafting trinkets to celebrate other people's dreams coming true, and trying not to think about how close she'd come to realizing a dream of her own.

But life went on and she had plenty to keep herself busy, especially as everybody turned the corner toward the holiday season. The bakery saw a sharp increase in advance orders, and there was a flurry of automotive work people wanted out of the way before they started Christmas shopping.

It was a relief to get an invitation for her and her mom to join Meredith and her family for Thanksgiving. They were instructed not to bring a single thing, but that would be the day Jenelle Bishop showed up for a dinner without a dessert. Because Meredith had already made pies, they showed up at her door with a peach cobbler that might not have been traditional for the occasion, but which Reyna had been thinking about all day, and a special cupcake for Meredith's daughter, Sophie.

But as soon as she stepped through their front door and the formerly beloved aroma of Thanksgiving cooking washed over her, Reyna's stomach did a slow roll. She stopped in her tracks and closed her eyes, willing the wave of nausea to recede.

It was probably the transition from the hot car to the frigid outside air, and back into heat. Whether it was from the oven or thermostat setting, Meredith's house was very warm.

"Hey, Reyna." Meredith's fiancé, Cam, appeared to take the baking dish out of her hand. "You feeling okay? You look a little pale."

"I'm good." She thought she was, anyway. "It's a little warm in here after being outside."

He looked over her shoulder. "Yeah, that's a long twenty feet from the car to the house."

"You're a funny guy. Now I see why Meredith agreed to marry you." She took off her coat—which didn't help settle her stomach much, despite being instantly cooler—and then held the cupcake so her mom could do the same.

"Reyna!" Sophie, who had recently turned seven, dumped a handful of silverware on the table and ran to get a hug.

She squeezed the little girl and then introduced her mother. "Sophie, do you remember my mom? Mrs. Bishop?"

"Hi," she said shyly before running back to finish her task.

The beautiful lakefront home was very open concept, so Meredith was able to wave to them from the stove. "Happy Thanksgiving! Mrs. Bishop, that isn't a dessert I see in Cam's hands, is it?"

Reyna took advantage of everybody's distraction as they fussed over the food and Cam stowed their coats to take a few deep breaths. She hoped she wasn't coming down with anything, though she couldn't remember being around anybody who was sick. But a lot of people came through the bakery and the garage's office, so there were probably germs everywhere. What a miserable time to not feel well, though.

She loved everything about Thanksgiving dinner. The turkey, mashed potatoes and stuffing drenched in pan gravy. Cranberry sauce. The green beans with French fried onions on top. Sweet potatoes with marshmallow topping. And pumpkin pie with double the whipped topping. It was a day when nobody questioned seconds and calories didn't count.

It was when she looked at Sophie, who was showing off the turkey made from tracing around her hand that she'd made at school, that another reason for her unwelcome and inexplicable aversion to her favorite smells struck her.

Her hand went to her stomach and as soon as she realized it, she yanked it away. Nobody seemed to have noticed, since Sophie still had the spotlight, and Reyna slipped into the guest bathroom because she definitely needed a minute.

Her period was late. Not by a lot. Maybe a week, she thought as she stared at her pale reflection in the mirror. Closing her eyes, she tried to visualize the small journal she kept for tracking such things. Usually she was more on top of the dates, but she hadn't looked at that page since the day she and Brady decided they weren't having a baby after all. She had known she'd go back to it sooner or later, but it had hurt too much to think about her cycle after that.

Forcing herself to open her eyes, she reminded herself she didn't know anything for a fact yet. It could still be a stomach bug. Or maybe it was the combination of heat and smells in Meredith's house. Feeling a little queasy didn't mean she was having a baby.

Right now she just needed to get through Thanksgiving dinner without the two women who asked the most questions about her life thinking there was a reason to ask her any questions. After splashing a little cold water on her face, she dried it a little more enthusiastically than necessary with the guest towel to give her cheeks some color and rejoined the festivities.

Thankfully the nausea abated and she was able to get through the meal without anybody suspecting something might be up with her. She didn't go back for seconds of the marshmallow-topped yams as she usually did; she didn't want to push it before dessert. It was going to take more than a little nausea to keep her away from that peach cobbler.

Cam and Meredith, who'd hit it off when he spent the summer in the cottage next door because he hoped to find out more about his biological family, were wonderful hosts. Actually, they hadn't hit it off right away. The sparks that originally flew hadn't been of the fun variety, but that had changed over the summer. And the relationship between Cam and Sophie, who would officially become his stepdaughter in a few months, was a joy to watch.

"I heard you're restoring an old car for somebody," Cam said during dessert, and Reyna almost choked on her cobbler. "A Chevelle?"

"For Brady Nash," Meredith added, giving her a knowing look.

She didn't know the half of it. "Yeah, he got it cheap because it was abandoned in a field or something. It's going to be a side project for me, so it'll probably take quite a while."

"I didn't realize you did restoration work," Cam said.

"I don't. I mean, I can do a little bit. Mostly I'll be doing the mechanical work to get her running like a dream again, and helping him run down some of the stuff it'll need cosmetically."

"That'll keep you both busy," Meredith said. "Together."

If she wasn't afraid she'd miss and hit Sophie, Reyna would have kicked her friend under the table. "It'll keep me busy for sure. Hey, Sophie, how's school going?"

Judging by the look she gave her, Meredith recognized the diversionary tactic for what it was, but Reyna didn't care. Sophie's chatter about her teacher and her friends and the school library dominated the rest of dessert and by the time she took a breath, everybody seemed to have forgotten about Brady and his Chevelle.

Reyna couldn't forget about him, though. When she was finally home, she took out her journal and sure enough, her period was a week late. That still didn't mean anything, she told herself. There were a lot of reasons for a cycle to go awry. And she knew that sometimes a woman's wishful thinking could be so powerful, her body would react. But she was going to have to find out for sure. Very soon.

The next five days were a jumble of occasional but mild nausea combined with a heap of contradictory feelings. On the one hand, she wanted to have a baby so being pregnant would definitely be a cause for celebration. But on the other hand, Brady had made it clear he'd changed his mind, which was going to escalate their situation from awkward to possibly painful.

She needed to know, one way or the other, but the last thing she wanted to do was walk into a Blackberry Bay store and buy a pregnancy test. There were a few places in town she knew she could buy one, and she knew the employees at all of them. Some well enough so they'd comment on the purchase, and it wasn't something she was ready to answer questions about. And some just well enough so they wouldn't say anything to her, but would definitely enjoy using that story to revive the *hell on men* hashtag. So she'd decided to wait until her regular trip to the city.

Tuesday afternoon, she went to the post office first to ship a few things from her Etsy shop, as usual. Then, before she lost her courage, she drove directly to a drugstore and bought two home pregnancy tests. After stowing them in her glove box, she took a deep breath and made her way to the big warehouse store to stock up on supplies for the bakery.

By the time she got home and helped her mother put everything away, Reyna was practically vibrating with anticipation. She wasn't sure if it was a good anticipation or more like dread, but all she could think about were the tests in her car.

"Are you okay?" her mom asked when they'd turned off the lights and Reyna was walking her to her car. "You've seemed a little, I don't know…off? For a while now."

"I'm fine." She didn't like fibbing, but she also wouldn't like her mother dragging her upstairs and standing outside the bathroom door while she peed on a plastic stick. Not that her mom would be upset—she'd probably be thrilled—but she would definitely want to know the results, and sooner rather than later.

"Are you still upset about Lucas?"

Clearly her mom didn't believe her. "I'm not upset about Lucas, Mom. I'm not upset at all. I promise."

"Okay." She kissed Reyna's cheek and got into her car. But she had to give one last shot as she closed the door. "When you're ready to talk, you know where to find me."

She waited until her mom's car was out of sight before she retrieved the tests from her glove box, and then she went up the stairs to her apartment. After setting the drugstore bag on the bathroom vanity, she went out and made herself a grilled cheese sandwich and heated up a can of tomato soup. Not only was she starving, but she also wasn't sure if being cold could affect the test, so she wanted it to warm up to room temperature before she used it.

Or maybe she was just afraid, she admitted to herself as she bounced from app to app on her phone, none of them able to hold her attention long enough to be a distraction.

But once bedtime rolled around, she knew there was no sense in putting it off any longer. It wasn't going to be easy to go to sleep after getting the results, no matter what the test said, but she wasn't going to sleep anyway. Not until she knew for sure.

Reyna went into the bathroom, and a few minutes later she took a deep breath and picked up the plastic stick. In the little plastic window was an unmistakable plus sign.

She was having a baby.

There had been many feelings in his life Brady would have described as *nervous* but as he stood wiping his palms on his hips and waiting for Reyna to hit the button to open her door, he was afraid his knees would give out and he'd topple down the exterior staircase and land in a heap in the parking lot behind the building. His stomach was in a knot and breathing regularly seemed to be something he suddenly had to focus on.

Can you come over? The door at the top of the stairs behind the building.

When he'd read her text, his first thought was that it had something to do with the Chevelle. But on the way over, it had occurred to him that didn't make any sense. If she had a question about the car, she would have just asked it. Or called him. And she probably would have invited him to stop by the shop during regular business hours.

Instead she'd invited him, after hours, to her apartment. She wanted privacy for whatever she wanted to talk to him about and that could only mean one thing. She wanted to talk about the baby.

And there was a certainty deep down in his gut that she wasn't looking to plead her case again and get him to change his mind. He was good at math.

He was considering making a run for it before he vomited his nerves all over whatever was under the stairs when Reyna opened the door. When her gaze met his, he felt the familiar punch of desire. He could barely remember a time those blue eyes hadn't had that effect on him.

Then he noticed how pale her skin looked and the way her lips pinched even as she smiled. "Hi."

"Come in," she said, stepping away so he could enter.

Brady looked around as he reached back to close the door behind him. He'd always wondered what her place looked like because she was very private and it was hard to imagine what her tastes were. Apparently they were plain, with beige leather and old but sturdy wood furnishings filling up the small space. The walls were beige, and the blue carpet was the only real pop of color.

He noticed the doors. "This is a two-bedroom?"

"Yes. It's small, but it's big enough for me. And not only is the price right, but you can't beat the commute."

He chuckled at her joke and resisted craning his neck to get a better view through the open door to her bedroom. All he could see was a slatted footboard that looked like maple, and a blue floral armchair with clothes flung on it.

"The bathroom's the door in the middle," she told him, and he could tell by the way she said it, she'd noticed he was staring at her bedroom.

"What's in there?" he asked, assuming she'd tell him it was storage or something like that.

"It's not part of the tour."

That was mysterious. "But now I'm curious."

"Don't be. You've seen what you need to. You know where the fridge and the bathroom are. What else does a guy need to know?"

"If I try to guess what's behind that door, will you tell me if I guess right?"

"Nope. Do you want a water or…?" She paused as she pulled open the fridge. "Or a water, I guess."

"I'll take a water." If nothing else, holding it would give him something to do with hands.

She must have had the same thought because she cracked the seal on her bottle, but then just twisted the cap back and forth without taking a drink. She was also looking anywhere but directly at him, so when she took a seat at her small table, he moved the only other chair to the spot directly across the table before sitting down, so at least he'd be in her natural line of sight.

She was still twisting her cap, but then she set the bottle down, exhaled sharply and looked at him. "So, I have news."

"Is it good news or bad news?"

The anxiety in her eyes almost broke his heart, as did the slight tremor in her voice when she spoke. "I…don't know. I think it's good news. I'm not sure if you'll think so."

"I need you to say it."

"I'm pregnant."

It was as though fireworks went off in Brady's

brain—his entire body, actually. Huge and terrifying and exciting and bright and thrilling. He knew he should say something, but he honestly felt as if he'd forgotten what words even were and there was no way he would string any together in a coherent way.

But her shoulders relaxed and her mouth curved into a genuine smile that made her teary eyes crinkle. "You look like it's good news."

He nodded because he still wasn't sure about words. And then he got up and walked around the table because, no matter how their relationship stood, he was going to hug the woman who'd just told him she was carrying his child.

She got to her feet as he reached her and stepped into his embrace. With his arms wrapped around her, he rested his cheek against her hair and closed his eyes.

"We're having a baby," he whispered.

"Yes, we are," she whispered back.

He held her until he was fairly confident he had his emotions under control, and she was smiling when he pulled away. After going back to his seat, he took a long swig of the water and she did the same. Then he took a deep breath because they had a lot to talk about.

"It worked the first time," he said, putting off the harder stuff. "How does that even happen?"

"We had health class together, so I know for a fact

you heard Mrs. Wells say 'It only takes once, ladies and gentlemen' about three times per class."

"I thought she was just trying to scare us into abstinence."

"Apparently it's actual science."

"Huh." He twisted the water bottle in his hands. "Do you feel okay?"

"Yes. I've had a little queasiness around strong food smells, which took a little fun out of Thanksgiving dinner, but I feel fine."

"Good. That's the most important thing. Do you need anything? Do you..." He let the question trail off because now was not the time to trigger Reyna's pride.

"I'm good. I have insurance, and I do well for myself with the garage."

He almost asked her what her plan was for a maternity leave with a one-woman shop, but he bit his tongue. None of that was for tonight. "I'm here for you. Anything you need."

"I need sleep," she said with a low chuckle. "It's been a rough couple of days, and I'm exhausted."

He stood up. "I'll get out of here, then. There's plenty of time to figure out the rest."

Reyna followed him to the door and watched him put on his coat. "About that. I know we have a lot to talk about, but are we... I don't know. Reverting to the original plan?"

"I think that's for the best. And obviously, we should start being seen together as soon as possible." He was about to suggest meeting at the café for dinner, but then he had a better idea. "The town Christmas festival is Saturday. If we go together, everybody in town will know we're dating by the time they light the tree."

"Good point. And a good plan."

"I'll come over before the parade, then. And now you should get some sleep." He had his hand on the doorknob, but he turned back to her. "It *is* good news, Reyna. As Christmas gifts go, I don't see anything ever topping this one."

That made her smile. "So it's a gift, then? Not a lump of coal?"

"Definitely a gift. The best gift ever, actually." He grinned back at her. "We must have been really good this year."

"I wasn't sure if you'd be happy about it. I know you said you wanted a baby, but then you changed your mind, so…"

"I didn't change my mind about wanting a baby. It wasn't so much being a father as the…*us* part that didn't feel right."

She flinched. Just slightly, but he saw it and realized she'd misunderstood because she didn't have all the information. But, before he could figure out if or how to explain, it was gone. She smiled and shrugged one shoulder. "Yeah, the you-and-me part wasn't going to work out."

It was his turn to flinch, but hopefully it didn't show on the outside. He already knew she felt that way, but the casual way she said it made his chest ache. He'd meant sleeping with her while hiding his true feelings, but that was a hard thing to say out loud. And now he wasn't going to try to explain it. It would easier to accept that he and Reyna weren't meant to be.

"So I'll see you Saturday?" she asked as he pulled open the door.

"I'll be here," he promised.

As he walked to his truck, he tried not to think about how accepting that he and Reyna weren't meant to be was going to be made a lot harder by spending the next few months pretending they were.

Chapter Seven

Reyna was afraid Brady wasn't going to show up right up to the moment he knocked on her door. While he'd seemed happy about the fact he was going to be a dad, they'd already figured out they had some issues as a couple. All they had to do was fake it for everybody they knew, she thought. They could do that. Probably.

She hesitated before responding to his knock, giving herself a second to calm herself so he wouldn't be able to see what a wreck she'd been since the last time she saw him.

But when she opened the door and he smiled at

her, she felt the somewhat expected and wholly unwelcome pang of attraction.

"You ready to get your holiday spirit on?"

She grabbed her coat off the hook and wasn't surprised when he took it so she could slide her arms
into the sleeves. "I'm definitely ready for Christmas cookies."

Reyna lived within walking distance of the town
square and it wasn't too cold, so they left their vehicles in the parking lot. They hadn't gone very far
before they saw the first person they knew and, after
saying hello and moving on, Brady brushed his hand
against hers before interlacing their fingers.

Her pulse quickened, but she only smiled and kept
walking. The point of showing up together to one
of the largest events of the year was to convince everybody they were dating. It made sense that he'd
hold her hand.

They certainly turned a lot of heads as they wandered down the main street. She saw the raised eyebrows. The sideways looks as they whispered. But
what she hadn't given a lot of thought to was running into Meredith and her family.

"Auntie Reyna!" Sophie yelled and Reyna turned
in time to witness Meredith's reaction to seeing her
holding Brady's hand. She was definitely surprised.
And confused.

"Hey, Sophie." She had to let go of Brady's hand

to give the little girl a hug, but he rested his hand on the small of her back as Meredith and Cam approached.

"Hi," Meredith said, and how she managed to pack so much curiosity into one word was beyond her, but Reyna heard the question.

"Hi, Meredith," Brady said. "Cam. Nice day for a Christmas party."

"I want hot chocolate," Sophie said, grabbing Cam's hand and trying to tug him forward.

"Cam, why don't you take Sophie to the hot chocolate booth. And take Brady with you. You two should get to know each other better."

Every one of them knew exactly what she was doing, but there was no way for any of them to call her on it without making the situation more awkward than it already was.

"I love hot chocolate," Brady said, smiling at Sophie. "And cookies. I'm a big fan of cookies."

"Only one for her," Meredith warned as they started to walk away.

"That was not very subtle," Reyna said when they were alone, more or less. It was impossible to actually be alone, but they did manage to slide into a fairly private spot between two buildings.

"I might have done better if I wasn't too busy being super confused because you said—or at least strongly implied—that Brady was disappointing between the sheets. So if you're looking for a fling, it's not likely you'd choose him. And if you're looking for until-death-do-you-part, that's a very long time to be disappointed."

Reyna had known Meredith might remember their conversation about why things were awkward between her and Brady, but she still squirmed at the way her friend drilled right down to the heart of the matter.

"It's complicated," she said, even though she knew that wasn't going to satisfy Meredith.

"Not really. A few months ago you two were barely speaking and you were not at all impressed with the night—or part of a night—you had spent together, but now you're here holding hands? There's a story there, Reyna."

"A complicated story," she insisted, because that's exactly what it was. But her friend just crossed her arms and tilted her head, waiting. "When he brought that car over, we started talking again and one thing led to another and… That one night before was a fluke because I was *not* disappointed this time."

That was an understatement, she thought, trying not to show her amusement. She'd not only been utterly satisfied between the sheets, but they'd managed to conceive a child on the first try. Brady was a man who knew how to make up for a prior shortcoming.

Meredith's eyes narrowed. "It just feels weird to me."

"It feels weird to me, too." She shrugged. "Who would have guessed Brady and I would end up dating?"

"I know I teased you at Thanksgiving about all the time you'd be spending together, but only because it was such a ridiculous idea we both knew you'd never actually hook up with him again."

"Not so ridiculous, I guess," Reyna said.

"Does your mom know?"

"She's here somewhere—I think helping do the photos with Santa—so I'm sure she does by now."

She sighed. "Reyna, I just… It feels weird."

Leave it to her to have an overly perceptive best friend. "He's single. I'm single. We're just enjoying each other's company for a while. There's not really anything weird about that."

"But it's Brady. You know how he is."

"I know how other people say he is. I'll see how he *actually* is for myself." She grabbed Meredith's shoulders and smiled. "Lighten up. It's really not that big of a deal."

"Okay, fine. I hope you know what you're doing. Let's go find my daughter before those two fill her full of sugar cookies."

"They better leave some for us."

They found the guys and Sophie in front of a booth selling gingerbread cookies to raise money for the school's art club. They had little tubes of decorative icing and if you bought the cookie, you could decorate it yourself.

"Oh, Cam," Meredith said when she saw Sophie's gingerbread cookie was wearing a red suit from neck to toes. "You don't have any past experience with red food coloring, do you?"

"No," he said, looking down at the front of his shirt where Sophie must have smeared the icing because it looked as if he needed to go to the emergency room. "But I do now."

"Brady used red, too," Sophie said.

Brady held up his gingerbread cookie, on which he'd painted a lot of curly red hair. "Look, it's Reyna."

"You're not done, silly," Sophie chided. "She doesn't have any clothes on."

Luckily the child was too young to know why everybody laughed—especially Cam and Meredith—and steered her away from the gingerbread booth with the promise of finding Santa so she could have her photo taken with him.

"We're going to wander," Reyna said, because they were still getting used to this pretend-dating thing and figuring it out in front of her best friend was a little too much stress on day one. "I'm sure we'll run into you again."

They decided, since it wasn't too crowded, they'd sit for a minute in the gazebo. It was at the center of the park and had started out life as a bandstand.

Though they still occasionally hosted live music in the park, most of the citizens under sixty or so just called it the gazebo. It was white, built in the typical round bandstand fashion, and it was liberally outlined in Christmas lights that wouldn't be turned on until they lit the tree a little later in the festivities. But it was lined with benches inside and, even with other people in and out of it, it was one of Reyna's favorite places to sit.

"Wait," she said, looking at Brady's hands. "Did you eat that cookie?"

"Yes. It was good, too. Did you want a bite?"

"It's too late now. Plus, since you made it look like me, that would have been weird."

"I thought so, too, which is why I ate it while you were talking to Lisa about her tires."

"I would apologize for the work talk, but we also got sidetracked by that guy asking you about an outlet for a wine fridge for his wife, so I guess you know how it is."

"Do you ever want to go up to…let's say the market's owner and ask her to list everything that's on sale next week so you can make your grocery list?"

She laughed. "Sydney's a good friend, so she'd probably tell me."

"Bad example, but you know what I was getting at."

"I do. But I tell myself that it's basically marketing. We're their friendly neighborhood mechanic and electrician, I guess."

He had his arm draped over her shoulder and Reyna noticed more than a few of their neighbors doing double takes. Usually that would make her squirm, but she forced herself to look relaxed.

"I haven't seen your mom yet," Brady said after a few minutes. "That seems unusual."

"She and some friends made some special mini Christmas tree cookies for the tree lighting ceremony. I haven't heard from her for a while, but I feel like I should be helping her, too."

"Then go," he said. "I'll roam around and then we can meet back up when it's time for them to light up the tree."

"Are you sure? I hate to leave you alone, especially since we're…you know."

"I think word about us is getting around just fine. And I don't mind at all. I can come help if you want."

"No, you stay. We haven't seen the Weavers yet and they have to be here somewhere. I know you'll want to see them. I won't be long, since the tree lighting starts soon."

"I'll be near the tree somewhere."

When she started to get up, he stopped her by putting his hand on her thigh. Then he leaned close and gave her a quick kiss on the mouth. Her eyes widened, but he only smiled as she stood.

"Just want to give them something to talk about," he said.

* * *

Brady finally managed to run into the Weaver family when it was almost time for the tree lighting ceremony. He'd been looking for Reyna, actually, and was about to text her and see if she was still at the bakery when he spotted them.

Joel and Alice had been like second parents to him when he was growing up, and Joel was probably the closest thing he'd had to a father figure in his life. He hugged them each, but they were on their way to meet friends for a quick bite to eat while everybody else was watching the tree lights because the restaurants would be packed afterward.

"Finn's right behind us somewhere," Alice called over her shoulder. "He was talking to your brother a few minutes ago."

Brady winced because, even though he felt guilty about it, he'd been hoping not to run into Chris and his family tonight. If he did, he'd handle it, but he'd rather not answer the inevitable questions Chris would have while Reyna was around.

Luckily they must have moved to a different spot in the park because when Brady spotted his friend, he was alone and walking toward him.

Finn lived on the coast, a little over an hour away, where he owned a financial management company with another guy. The Portsmouth area was home to a lot of money and wasn't far from Boston, which was why Finn had gravitated there after college. But he was close with his parents and his grandmother, so he wasn't a stranger around town.

"You made it," he said, shaking Finn's hand.

He nodded. "I never miss this if I can help it. It doesn't feel like Christmas without the Blackberry Bay Christmas festival, you know?"

"Yeah. Though I heard you were also here not too long ago since you ran into my brother at Home Depot and told him about me taking a Chevelle to Reyna's about five minutes after it happened."

Finn snorted. "It was more than five minutes. It was at least an hour. And you have to admit, there was a lot to talk about. You with an old, beat-up muscle car? You going to Reyna's place of business? So many questions."

And Brady didn't feel like answering any of them. "If you had an issue with a vehicle while in this town, where would you take it?"

"Bishop's."

"Okay, then."

"But I didn't—"

"Don't." He did *not* want his longtime crush on Reyna rehashed while standing out in the cold surrounded by people. If he could go back in time, he'd set the machine to first grade and take back ever telling Finn anything about his feelings.

"Speaking of Reyna, I've heard some buzz you two are here together, but I don't see her."

"She went to check on her mom. They baked a bunch of mini cookies just for the tree lighting ceremony and Mrs. Bishop had some friends helping her pack them up, so she wanted to make sure it was going okay. She should be back any second, actually."

"Wait. So you *are* here together?" Finn blinked. "I thought it was just the grapevine playing its regular game of telephone. Like, you two pass each other on the sidewalk and say hello and by the time it makes the gossip circuit, you're engaged and having a kid."

Brady was thankful he wasn't drinking anything because he would have done a spit take all over his friend. "Not quite."

They definitely weren't engaged.

Over Finn's shoulder, he saw Reyna approaching and he must have looked happy to see her because Finn arched an eyebrow before turning to see what he was looking at.

"Hey, beautiful," Brady said when she reached them, dropping his arm around her shoulders. She blushed slightly and gave him a little jab with her elbow.

"I saved you a cookie," she told Brady. "But then I ate it because sharing cookies is apparently a thing we don't do."

"I bet your mom will give me one," he said, but the saucy grin she gave him let him know that Jenelle had probably been briefed on the gingerbread cookie situation and that he would not, in fact, be getting a free cookie from her.

"What are you doing here with this guy?" Finn asked, and she laughed.

"What can I say? I'm a sucker for a guy who drives a Chevelle."

"Yeah, I saw his Chevelle and it's going to be a long time before he can drive that."

Brady smiled when Reyna's chin lifted and her eyes narrowed. "Are you insulting my abilities?"

It was Brady's turn to laugh out loud when his friend turned red and started stammering.

"Relax, Finn. I'm kidding." She gave him a friendly slap on the shoulder. "And yeah, it's going to be a while. It's in pretty rough shape."

When they heard the high school chorus start singing "Oh Christmas Tree," they all turned to face the large Christmas tree that stood off to one side of the park. It was a little out of place, surrounded by maples and smaller trees, but it had been planted before any of them had been born and carefully tended over the years by the town.

As the last notes of the song died away, there was a drumroll—probably an audio file saved on somebody's phone—and the hundreds of multicolored lights wrapped around the tree lit up. A few seconds later, the lights on the gazebo came on and everybody clapped and cheered.

"Merry Christmas, I guess," Finn said, still looking at the tree.

But Brady was watching Reyna's face, and when she turned to him he smiled and said, "Merry Christmas."

"Merry Christmas to us," she said, and then she smiled a secret smile that warmed his heart and definitely kicked his holiday spirit into high gear.

A baby, he thought. They'd made a baby for Christmas.

Chapter Eight

"You haven't missed one of Abe's holiday parties since the year you turned twenty-one," Sydney said. "You can't start now."

It would be so much easier if she could just tell her friend she was pregnant and Abe's holiday parties were a lot less fun if you were the only sober person there. His annual parties, held the second Saturday in December, were legendary and open to all of the locals of Blackberry Bay. Needless to say, a lot of people didn't attend, but enough did so it was a big deal.

"I don't know." She looked at the total on the cash register, since Sydney was too distracted by the possibility of Reyna missing out on the party to tell her the total. "Are you guys going?"

"Absolutely. We got a sitter and I intend to have fun, even though we can only go for a little while." Sydney watched her swipe her debit card and then handed her the PIN pad so she could punch in her number. "I guess I assumed you and Brady would be going together."

Reyna felt the tips of her ears get warm and cursed being so damn fair that she blushed over nothing. "Maybe. It's kind of casual."

"I had my hands full with two kids jacked up on sugar, but I did see him kissing you in the gazebo."

"I heard your mom refused to give him a cookie at the tree lighting ceremony," the woman behind Reyna in line said in a hushed tone that was meant to carry. She hadn't realized that was possible until she became aware of how gossip spread when she was a teen. "Maybe she's not happy about you two dating."

She could have corrected the woman—told her it was payback for Brady not sharing *his* cookie— but she didn't bother. Let them think whatever they wanted. She picked up her bags and rolled her eyes at Sydney. "If I go, I'll see you there."

"Text me," Sydney called after her.

As she walked home with her groceries—just a few things to hold her over until she went into Concord again—she pondered the problem of Abe's party. She wasn't great at walking and texting at the same time, so she hit the button to call Brady before she could change her mind.

Just the sound of his voice saying hello made her smile. "Are you busy?"

"Nope."

"Okay, because I'd hate to call you if you have your hands stuck in a live electrical panel or something."

"I try to kill the power before I stick my hands in anybody's panel, but I can assure you if you ever call while I *do* have my hands stuck in a live panel, I won't answer the phone."

"Good to know." She sighed. "I was just at the market and Sydney asked me if I'm going to Abe's party. And she seemed to assume I'd be going with you."

"I always go. You always go. And we were kissing in the gazebo, so going together would make sense."

"We weren't exactly kissing in the gazebo," she said, earning her a sideways look from a man in a suit going the other way. "It was a quick kiss goodbye."

"My lips were on your lips. In the gazebo." There was a sound in the background, like somebody talking. "Yes, Mrs. Jensen, it's a personal call and no, I'm not charging you for the time I'm on the phone."

Reyna laughed as she reached her building and

started climbing her stairs. "I guess it's a good thing our relationship is the opposite of a secret."

"Probably. I think she's actually writing down the time I answered the phone on a sticky note, so I should probably get back to work. Just text me what time I should pick you up and we'll go over."

"Just a quick appearance, though. I don't want to stay long."

Though she did text him that six o'clock would be good, Brady ended up on an emergency call and it was almost seven before he pulled into the parking lot. Reyna was ready and waiting in the office so he wouldn't have to climb the stairs, but he still got out of the truck to open her door for her.

"Sorry I'm late. Electric heat not working and twin toddlers. I couldn't say no."

"I assume you got it working for her?"

"As much as I would have hated to cancel on you, I wouldn't be here if I hadn't."

Walking into Abe's house, as big of an old farmhouse as it was, was like walking into a wall of heat and noise, and Reyna immediately regretted showing up for it. With so many people there, nobody would have noticed.

After about forty-five minutes, she'd already had enough. She'd lost Brady at some point, when he got pulled away for a sports conversation she had no interest in. She talked to Sydney and her husband for a little bit, then other friends. The crowd was always in motion.

By the time Brady finally appeared at her side again, she was so glad to see him, she reached out and took his hand. "Maybe I felt differently when I was six, but can I just tell you how awful fruit punch and sherbet is when it's not mixed with a whole lot of alcohol?"

"You must be pretty sneaky because I just did like ten circuits of the entire room and didn't hear a single whisper about how Reyna Bishop isn't drinking and, *ohmigosh*, you must know what *that* means."

His impression of any number of Blackberry Bay busybodies made her laugh. "I happened to be in the kitchen when Abe was getting ready to mix up another batch and—thanks to the fact I think he's been testing the batches all day—I was able to sneak some straight-up punch and plop some sherbet into it. I've been nursing it and let me tell you, it doesn't age well."

"Why didn't you just tell people you're on a medication you can't mix with alcohol?"

She snorted and poked his side with her elbow. "Can you imagine the possibilities people would come up with? It's a lot easier to pretend I'm drinking Abe's punch."

"Good point."

She let go of his hand so she could wipe her forehead. "Is it always this hot in here?"

His entire demeanor changed so fast, she almost took a step back. He straightened and leaned toward her, his brows drawn together in a look of concern. "Are you okay? Do you need to sit down? Everybody's had so much punch, I shouldn't have any trouble tipping one of them off a chair."

She laughed and put her hand on his arm. "I'm fine, Brady. Please don't start dumping drunk people on the floor. It's just a little warm."

"It is warm, but it's not overly hot. I've heard Abe shuts his heat off at noon the day of the party so it's not overheated once everybody gets here." He was grinning, though his eyes were still intensely searching her face for signs of distress. "One year, he forgot to turn it back on and by the time he woke up with a hangover, he could see his breath in his bedroom."

"I'm surprised there wasn't enough residual body heat to keep the place warm for a week." Somebody walked past her wearing a perfume that made her stomach roll and she shifted closer to Brady. "I'm ready to call it a night."

"I'll get our coats."

It wasn't the kind of party that required a goodbye tour—people just kind of showed up and left at random—so she was at the door by the time he'd found the coats, and she draped hers over her arm. Walking into the wall of cold waiting on the other side of the door refreshed her, though she put the coat on before climbing into his truck. Since he'd been nursing one beer all evening and had tossed half of it, she let him drive and relaxed against the heated lumbar support, which wasn't a perk her car offered.

"Better?" he asked as he maneuvered through the crowd of vehicles parked around Abe's property. A hardpacked field might offer space, but it didn't come with parking lines or volunteers with glowing orange parking beacons.

"Much. As soon as I walked out the door, I felt better. Being hot was one thing, but there was a perfume in the mix that was too much."

When he parked the truck on the side road next to the garage because the space was closer to the stairs than the back lot, she turned to face him. "It's still on the early side. You want to come up and watch a movie or something?"

He turned the ignition off. "Sounds great."

"Perfect. It'll be good to have your truck seen here after dark, if you know what I mean."

Usually she tried to avoid being the topic of conversation in town, though she often failed at that through no fault of her own, but right now she needed people to know they were not only dating, but doing the kinds of things that led to showing up at the market with a baby bump.

* * *

Brady sat on Reyna's couch and watched her scroll through the Christmas movie options, but he didn't really care what they watched.

He'd chosen the end of the couch that didn't have the slightly worn and indented look indicating it was her usual spot. And after she'd made them each a decaf coffee, claiming she needed something warm and strong to drown the lingering memory of fruit punch and sherbet, she sat at her end and put a throw pillow next to her. While she was using it to rest her arm on while she channel surfed, it was also a subtle way of making sure they stayed in their corners.

He'd already gotten that message, loud and clear, when she'd invited him up and then added that it was so people would see his truck parked at her place. It was time for the *fake* dating part of their plan and there was no need to pretend they were a couple behind closed doors.

But he didn't mind. Watching a movie with Reyna beat going home and watching a movie alone.

"You pick," she said after she'd scrolled through the entire on-screen guide. "I didn't see anything that jumped out at me, but I don't really care what we watch."

"Christmas Vacation," he said, and he told her the channel number to save them from scrolling through the menu again.

"A comedy guy, huh?" She tossed the remote onto the table and took a sip of her coffee before setting back against the cushion.

"I'll watch almost anything," he said. "But I watch this one every year because it's not only funny, but it makes me think about my mom."

"*This* movie does? Really? Please tell me she doesn't make a Jell-O mold."

"Nope. When Chris and I were little, we'd decorate the trees outside of the house and we had one of those little ceramic trees with the tiny colored light bulbs. But then we got old enough to realize other people had actual Christmas trees in their houses and we started begging for one right after Halloween."

"We had one of those ceramic trees, too, but we had a real tree in the living room. My dad always took me out to one of the Christmas tree farms where you cut your own."

Her eyes got a faraway misty look, and he gave her a few seconds to savor the memory of times with her father. Everybody in town had loved Jimmy Bishop, but he and his daughter had been almost inseparable, and Reyna had to have been devastated by his loss.

When she sniffed and then looked at him questioningly, he continued the story. "It was just the two of us boys and my mom, so we went to a lot in town where they were already cut and spent close to an hour finding one we all agreed on. Looking back, I know my mom had to do a lot of steering to keep us on budget—which was small—and then Chris and I helped her tie the tree on top of her car. We had to run ropes through the windows and everything."

"I'm picturing you guys driving through Blackberry Bay like the Griswold family now," she teased.

"Kind of, but our tree was a *lot* smaller. It was also very, *very* dry." He paused, chuckling at the memory. "When we finally got home and got out of the car, there were almost no needles left."

"Oh no!" She laughed. "You had a naked Christmas tree?"

"It was not a happy-looking tree. And my mom just had this…look, you know? Like she'd tried so hard to make us happy and now we had a dead tree on the roof of the car. Even through Chris and I were young and pretty self-involved, we somehow knew that we had to step up in that moment. So we brought it inside and draped some of my mom's green yarn around it like garland. Then we cut out paper snowflakes and strung popcorn and berries, and it didn't turn out half-bad. Okay, that's not exactly true. It was a pretty motley-looking tree and there are photographs somewhere that prove it, but we loved it. And it's still one of my best Christmas memories."

"I love that." Her face was soft and the warmth in her eyes made him smile.

His mom had struggled to raise them on her own, but they'd had everything they *needed*, if not everything they wanted, and they'd been happy. It was one of the reasons he and Chris had both stayed close to home and visited all the time. She was one of the reasons he'd never seriously considered leaving Blackberry Bay. He'd just burn more gas driving back and forth from wherever he moved to.

They turned their attention back to the movie, and Reyna laughed a lot. He loved her laugh and if he had his way, they'd do nothing but sit around and watch funny movies every night.

"Do you realize you already rest your hand on your stomach?" he asked when the final credits were rolling.

"Do I?" She deliberately moved her hand away. "It's weird—in a wonderful way, of course—to think there's a little speck of a baby in there."

"I think it's cute, the way you do that already." He wanted to touch that spot, too, though there was no bump yet. And he didn't want to make it weird.

"I'm going to have to tell my mom," she said quietly. "I can't keep something like this from her, especially if I'm giving off pregnancy signals without even realizing it."

"Of course you have to tell her." He knew how close she and Jenelle were, so he knew it wasn't going to be a secret very long.

"So you should probably tell your mom, too. It wouldn't be fair not to."

"I agree." He shoved his feet into his boots and then put his coat on. "But it's still early, so maybe we could ask them to keep it quiet for a while. That'll probably be harder for your mom than mine."

She nodded. "Definitely. But she won't tell anybody else until I say it's okay. I just need for her to know."

"Tomorrow, then? I have some errands to run and I can swing by Mom's at some point. She usually bakes on Sundays, so I have a habit of randomly popping in."

"Yeah, I'll tell Mom tomorrow."

"Let me know how it goes," he said, and she nodded.

This felt like the moment where he would lean in and kiss her good-night, but they weren't doing that anymore without an audience, so he just gave her a final smile and opened the door. There was a light snow falling and, even though it wasn't accumulating yet, he hoped Reyna would realize she should start using the interior stairs and not the wooden exterior staircase. It probably got slippery when the weather was bad.

She didn't turn her outside light off until he'd started his truck and the headlights came on, and he waved when he turned around in the parking lot behind the garage, just in case she was still watching.

As much as he'd enjoyed her company tonight,

especially watching a funny movie with her because he loved hearing her laugh, his body ached from not being able to touch her. He wanted her to cuddle against him during a movie. He wanted to kiss her.

It was going to be a very long few months.

Chapter Nine

Reyna liked being in the old garage next to her mother's house. It was where her dad had started Bishop's Auto Care, and her first memories of learning what tools were and what they did were here. She'd been seven or eight when her grandmother passed away, and Jimmy's inheritance had been enough to buy the building that now housed the garage and the bakery.

Right now the space was full of old Chevelle, and Reyna had spent the better part of two hours covering the long workbench with fresh Kraft paper, which she stapled down on the ends. Then she'd opened the hood and started pulling parts and hoses.

The hoses went into one of several buckets, which sorted the junk, and the parts went on the bench.

There was something soothing about taking apart an old engine with the tools her father had taught her to use. When he'd opened the garage, he'd had one of those companies bring in massive commercial toolboxes and a shiny set of mechanics' tools, but these were old and dinged up. And the Chevelle's motor was simple, without the computers and fancy sensors that gave her a headache on a regular basis.

The task freed her mind to roam, and mostly it kept roaming in Brady's direction.

Last night had been awkward. It had felt like a date, and there were definitely parts of her body that wanted it to be a date, but she'd reminded herself over and over that it *wasn't* a date. Whether they were at the party or watching the movie, she'd been so aware of him and how much she wanted to be closer to him that she'd barely been able to think straight.

And right now, she was supposed to be figuring out how to tell her mom she was having a baby, not mooning over the baby's father.

With a sigh of frustration and resignation, Reyna wiped her hands on a shop rag and closed up the garage. There was no sense in putting it off any longer.

When she went into the mudroom off the kitchen, she peeled off the coveralls and hung them on a hook and stepped into slippers that were set on a box. Then she went inside and used her elbow to lift the water lever so she could wash her hands. After scrubbing any trace of grease away—including using a stiff nailbrush—she dried her hands with a paper towel and then used that to wipe the door handle off. Jenelle had established *very* strict rules many years ago in order to keep the grime of the garage out of her house.

"I thought I heard you come in," her mom said as she entered the kitchen. "I was vacuuming upstairs, but I need to empty the stupid canister again. I miss when they used to have bags. They held so much more and sometimes, by the time I'm done emptying this stupid plastic thing, I made more of a mess than what I cleaned up."

It was a familiar complaint, so Reyna didn't bother to remind her they could still get a vacuum that took a bag, but they were usually bigger and heavier, and she hated those, too. Her mother really just hated vacuuming.

"Do you have a few minutes, Mom?"

Jenelle finished dumping the contents of the canister into the trash can and then set it on the counter. "Oh, are we finally going to talk about it?"

Reyna froze, her eyes widening. She knew mothers' intuition was a thing, but her mom couldn't possibly have guessed she was pregnant. "Talk about what?"

"Whatever it is that you've been wanting to talk to me about but also not wanting to talk to me about, which has you going in circles and occasionally opening your mouth and then closing it again." She chuckled. "You're a pretty open book, Reyna."

"Not to most people."

"I'm not most people. I'm your mother." She leaned against the counter and folded her arms, which was familiar body language to Reyna. It was her way of saying they weren't going anywhere until she heard the whole story. "Does this have anything to do with Brady Nash?"

"It has a lot to do with him, actually." She chuckled and scrubbed her face with her hands, wondering where to even begin.

"The fact you two are seeing each other isn't exactly a secret."

"I know. We weren't trying to keep it a secret and, even if we were, we've both lived here our entire lives. We know better."

"Okay. Then what's the thing you don't know how to tell me?"

If she knew how to tell her, she could have by now, Reyna thought. But she couldn't put it off any longer, waiting to find the right words when she wasn't sure there even *were* right words. "I'm pregnant. Brady and I are having a baby."

There weren't many times in her life Jenelle

Bishop had been speechless, but Reyna watched her mother open and close her mouth three times before she gave up and just looked at her. Reyna couldn't read her expression, and she realized her statement hadn't given her mom a lot to go on as to how *she* felt about it.

"We're happy about it," she said. "If that helps."

She hadn't thought it would be easy to explain the situation to her mom, and yet when her mother's face lit with joy and she actually clapped her hands together, Reyna realized it wasn't hard at all. She was having a baby and she was happy about it. That was all that truly mattered to her mom.

"When?" Tears were spilling over her mother's eyelashes. "When am I having a grandbaby?"

"The end of July. It's still early, but I couldn't *not* tell you."

"Of course you had to tell me." She opened her arms and Reyna moved in for the hug because she really needed one. "You know you can tell me anything, but you can *definitely* tell me the happiest news I've ever heard."

Once her mother had gotten her fill of hugging her and had dried her eyes, she went to her fridge and pulled out what looked like the remains of a blueberry cobbler, which she took the plastic wrap off of and popped into the microwave. "So you're both happy about this baby? You said *we're* happy before."

"Brady is happy about the baby, too. We've both wanted to be parents for a while."

When her mom nodded, but gave her a searching look, Reyna tried not to squirm. None of that was a lie, but it was going to get messy if her mom dug too deeply. While she knew she could explain how they'd come to conceive a baby together, what she didn't want her mom worrying about was the inevitable split. That would make her sad, and Reyna wanted nothing but joy in her life right now.

"But we're not getting married," she added, just to make that clear up front.

Her mom snorted. "I should hope not. You just started dating, for goodness' sake."

The microwave beeped and her mom split the cobbler into two bowls before pulling a pint of French vanilla ice cream out of the freezer. She put a scoop into each bowl and, after putting the ice cream back, grabbed two spoons and set them on the table.

Reyna sat, even though she knew this was one of her mother's most fierce tactics for getting her to have a conversation. She didn't have the willpower to turn down any kind of cobbler—or pretty much anything else her mother baked—and her mom knew it. So if she wanted to have a hard talk with her daughter or was going to ask questions Reyna wanted to dodge, Jenelle never hesitated to break out the fruit cobbler.

But after a few bites and a few glances at her

mom, who seemed lost in happy thoughts, she realized this was simply a celebration and relaxed. The sweetness of the ice cream melted over the blueberries was exactly what Reyna needed, even if she hadn't known it before, and she savored every bite.

"I don't want to say too much because it's so early," her mom said in a quiet voice. "But I can't wait to bake cookies with my grandbaby."

"It'll be a while, yet," she replied with a chuckle. But not as long as if she hadn't worked up the courage to approach Brady with what had seemed at the time like an outrageous plan. Now it just felt like the *right* plan.

Her mom had to blink away tears again, and when she looked up for a few seconds, Reyna's eyes got blurry, too, because she knew she was thinking about Reyna's dad.

She didn't want to cry right now, so she concentrated on getting every bit of blueberry out of her bowl while her mom had a moment.

"Are you going to lick it clean?"

Looking up with a guilty grin, Reyna shrugged. "If the bowl wasn't so deep, I would and I wouldn't even feel bad about it."

Her mom reached across the table to rest her hand on Reyna's arm. "Don't ever feel bad about things that make you happy, honey."

So much for no tears, she thought as one slid over her cheek.

* * *

Taffy and Bean met Brady's truck in front of his mom's house, as they always did, but they were even more enthusiastic in their greeting than usual. It probably had to do with the few inches of fresh snow that had fallen overnight, since snow was one of their favorite things.

He played with them for a few minutes—tousling their fur and throwing snowballs for them to catch—before he brushed the snow off his pants and went inside. The house smelled like freshly baked bread and his stomach rumbled in response, but he tried to ignore it. He was hoping to make dinner for Reyna tonight, but it wouldn't be much of a meal if he'd filled up on fresh bread slathered with real butter.

"You should at least look up when somebody walks in," he teased, walking up behind her to kiss her cheek.

She pulled one hand out of the soapy dishwater to fling some bubbles at him. "Trust me, those dogs tell me it's you before you even get out of your truck. Anything special bring you by today or did you just stop to visit?"

"Maybe I could smell that bread all the way in town."

"You and your brother do share a knack for showing up right after I finish my baking."

"Actually, I did want to talk to you about something, if you have a few minutes."

Maybe she heard something in his voice, but she immediately rinsed and dried her hands and gestured for him to sit down. "Should I make some tea?"

"I'm good, but I can wait while you make one for yourself if you want." He sat at the table and looked over at her latest project. She'd finished stuffing the arms and back and upholstered those pieces, so it was starting to look like a small couch. She had a different fabric on the couch cushion and trundle mattress, so he assumed she'd be making a removable, washable cover to match the rest at some point.

"I'm already working on a cup," she said, sitting across from him. "The bed's coming along nicely, isn't it?"

"It is." He cleared his throat, trying to figure out how to even begin. "So when that trundle is out for Benny, do you think there will still be room in there for one of those portable playpen-type bed things?"

"I'm sure there will. But why?"

"Because you'll be the grandmother of three soon." When she just blinked at him, obviously trying to figure out what was happening—or maybe if Chris and Marcy were expecting again—he knew he just had to say it outright. "I'm going to be a father."

"Oh!" She sat straight in her chair with her teacup still in her hand, eyes wide, and then she smiled at him. "Well, I guess it was bound to happen eventually."

"No, Mom. I'm saying that I'm *choosing* to become a father. On purpose."

She stilled, then slowly leaned forward and set her tea on the table. It was a familiar move, meant to buy her a few seconds to think about what she wanted to say, and she must have really been struggling, based on how long it took her to set the cup down. "Didn't you just start dating the Bishop girl?"

"Yeah, I did."

"Okay." She folded her hands in her lap and then leveled him a *mom* look that he was pretty sure could see into the depths of his soul. "I guess my first question is whether or not she's the expectant mother."

"Reyna's having my baby, yes."

"And you planned this? Deliberately?" He nodded. "But why Reyna, honey? You know what they say about her."

That Reyna sure is hell on men. "I know what they say. But considering how much *they* say about me that isn't true, this general *they* doesn't have a lot of credibility with me. I'm pretty sure you also taught me to judge a person based on my relationship with them, and not what others say."

"Caught me there." She picked up the tea and he noticed her hand was trembling slightly as she took a sip. Then she held the cup between her hands instead of setting it back down. "I have so many questions, I don't even know where to start."

"I guess the biggest question is why we decided to have a baby together when we just started dating."

"That's probably the most important one, yes."

"We both want to be parents, Mom, and have for a while. But neither of us have a great track record when it comes to finding a forever partner, and we're tired of waiting."

"So you're not *really* dating? You're not getting married, are you?" She gave a nervous chuckle and set the cup down again. "Not that I don't want to see you happily settled down, but this sounds more like an arrangement than a happy family."

This is where it started getting messy—walking that fine line of what to share with their mothers and what to keep to themselves. Maybe because they'd both lost their dads, he and Reyna were both particularly close to their mothers, so they didn't want to lie. But they also didn't want the entire truth of the matter making its way around Blackberry Bay.

"We are dating, Mom. And, as you know, we're not exactly strangers. So we don't know where our relationship will go, but we do know we want to have a baby."

"And you talked it through?"

"Of course. You know me, Mom. I'm a pretty laid-back guy and sometimes I do impulsive things, but I'm never reckless. There's a difference."

"I didn't know you had such a strong urge to have a baby."

He shrugged one shoulder, looking down at his hands. "I didn't really tell anybody, but I kept thinking about how it would be nice to have a kid close to Benny's age."

She was smiling, but it was slight and she seemed to be staring at some faraway spot over his shoulder. He was usually good at reading her expressions, but he wasn't used to her looking distant. And her eyes looked almost sad, which wasn't one of the reactions he'd expect her to have to this news.

Then she blinked and focused on him with a smile so warm and genuine, he decided he must have imagined the sorrow. "When is she due?"

"At the end of July," he said, hoping she wouldn't start doing the math and asking more questions.

"I have plenty of time to knit a blanket, then."

She'd knit each of Chris's boys a soft, beautiful blanket, so he could picture himself holding a newborn wrapped in one, and his throat tightened. Before he could get too emotional, he pushed back from the table and stood. He was planning to pour himself a glass of water, but when he walked around the table, his mom stood and pulled him into a strong embrace.

"I'm so happy for you, Brady."

"Thanks, Mom. I know it's unexpected, but Reyna and I are both super excited."

"Then I'm excited, too." She backed away and rested her hand on his cheek. "I hope you'll bring her up here sometime so I can get to know her better. I know Jenelle a bit, but I only see Reyna when I need to take my car in for service."

"I'll tell her. Maybe we can go out for dinner with her and Mrs. Bishop at some point."

He gave her credit for nodding, even though she preferred to live simply and privately on her property and went into town as seldom as possible. "That would be lovely."

He hid his smile from her because he knew that was a phrase she used when she was sure something was going to be anything but lovely, but she would do it anyway.

"I should run. I have a couple of things to do on the way home, and I'm having dinner with Reyna." He hoped, anyway.

"Give her my best," she said after kissing his cheek. "And congratulations to you both."

He had to throw a few more snowballs for Taffy and Bean before they'd let him get in his truck, so he didn't reach Reyna's garage until it was almost closing time.

Now that it was colder, she usually kept the overhead doors closed, so he went into the office. She wasn't behind the counter, but the door between the office and the garage area was open so he stuck his head in.

She was standing under a car that was dangling over her head and it took every ounce of his self-control not to rush in and drag her out from under the vehicle. He knew that, technically, it wasn't dangling. It was secure on a hydraulic lift he knew that Jimmy Bishop—and Reyna after him—had been meticulous about maintaining and inspecting.

This was what she did. She'd grown up in the two Bishop garages, fetching tools for her father as soon as she could walk, no doubt. And it was not only her livelihood, but if he had to guess, he'd say it helped keep her mom's bakery afloat during the winter months. During the summer, Jenelle had all she could do keeping the tourists in fancy cupcakes, but the skiers didn't show up with quite the same numbers.

Even if seeing her underneath several thousand pounds of vehicle made his mouth dry, there was nothing he could do about it.

"How'd it go?" she asked, and he realized she'd known he was standing there, staring at her.

"Good. Did you tell your mom?" When she nodded, he leaned against the doorjamb and folded his arms. "So both of our moms know now. Mine's pretty happy about the baby."

"Less so about the baby's mother."

"I didn't say that. And neither did she."

"That Reyna Bishop is hell on men, you know," she said in an eerily good impression of his mother.

"She didn't say that, either." Not in so many words, anyway, but Reyna didn't need to know all the details. He sighed. "I'm not a great poker player and she is. Let's just say I'm glad she didn't ask me too many questions, but she's definitely thinking them."

"Our moms are both too intuitive for our own good."

He chuckled. "You've got that right. How much longer are you going to be working on that? I thought it was closing time."

"I'm a little behind." She paused and looked it over with her hands on her hips. "Maybe thirty minutes. I hope. The owner will be here in forty-five, so thirty would be good."

"Do you have dinner plans?"

"My plan was to make a turkey sandwich and heat up some leftover chicken soup."

"Would you like a *better* dinner plan?"

That piqued her interest. She turned her attention away from the exhaust system over her head and looked at him. "What are you offering?"

"Grilled pork chops, roasted potatoes and some of my mom's blue ribbon chunky cinnamon applesauce."

"She won that blue ribbon over my mom's blackberry preserves," she said, and he grinned because he had remembered that. "And I'll deny it if you ever tell anybody I said this, but that applesauce deserved that ribbon. What time should I be there?"

Chapter Ten

Reyna used a hair dryer to warm the small ball of red polymer clay in her hand—just a little to soften it, because too much and it would start to harden. There had been a learning curve when she first started working with the clay, but now she had a good feel for it.

She was making a tiny Santa hat for a Christmas version of a popular children's book character for Sophie, and it was meticulous work requiring a lot of time and concentration, but she was almost done. And she'd shipped her last special order for the holiday season yesterday during her weekly trip to Concord. She usually spent the last couple of weeks of

December and the beginning of January making little ready-to-ship figures with a Valentine's Day theme, along with a very limited number of special orders for the February holiday, but she wasn't sure if she'd be doing that this year. It would probably depend on how much time she spent with Brady.

Once she had all the pieces of the figurine assembled, she set her oven to a low temperature and spent the preheating time going over the figurine with a magnifying glass, looking for any rough spots or errors. Then she put a sheet of white paper over the ceramic tile she used for baking and set the figurine on top. Then there was nothing to do but set a timer and wait for the oven to work its magic. Tomorrow, she'd go over it with a very fine-grit sandpaper to make sure there were no fingerprints and then she'd apply the clear glaze.

She used the baking time to clean her bathroom and a few other housekeeping tasks, but one of the nice things about a small apartment was that it didn't take long to clean. And it was definitely small.

At least the baby would be able to stay in her room for at least a year, if not longer. Eventually she'd have two choices. She and the baby could move into her parents' house with her mother. Or she could lose her craft room. Neither option was ideal, but she might be able to make a craft corner in her bedroom. She'd need to dig up a tape measure and start making plans.

Her phone rang and, after glancing at the timer on the oven, she picked it up. *Nash Electric* came up on the screen and she chuckled. She should probably change that to his name in her contacts. "Hello?"

"Hey, are you busy?"

It was Wednesday night, and she hadn't seen Brady since their dinner together on Sunday, and she didn't realize until she heard him speak that she'd missed the sound of his voice. Maybe it was the hormones, she thought. But whatever it was, she needed to get a grip.

"I'm not particularly busy at the moment," she said. "What's up?"

"My mom accidentally told Chris. He stopped by and she was showing him this trundle bed thing she's making for his boys and mentioned that CJ would outgrow it by the time my kid's ready for sleepovers, and when he made a joke about his kids going off to college before I had a kid and when she didn't laugh, he figured it out."

The annoyance in his voice amused her, but his words also drove home the fact her child was going to have a family life she wasn't really a part of. It wasn't a bad thing. Liking his family was one of the reasons she'd picked him, after all. But it was weird to be thinking about co-parenting already when her pregnancy was a missed period and a plus sign on a plastic stick.

And an unfortunate aversion to the smell of Thanksgiving dinner.

"We knew it wouldn't stay a secret forever," she said, not wanting him to be annoyed with his mother.

"No, but I was hoping for a week, at least." She laughed, and didn't manage to move the phone away from her mouth first. "Okay, it's not the end of the world."

"It's not," she assured him. "At this point, it's like any other pregnancy. We told our moms and now word's going to filter through our family and friends. People outside of the family might assume we're not good at using birth control, and so what? We're having a baby."

"You're right."

"I usually am."

He laughed, and when he spoke again, the annoyance was gone. "If I agree with you, do I get to ask a huge favor?"

"I asked you to have a baby with me. I'm pretty sure your favor will be less huge than that."

"How do you feel about having dinner with Chris and Marcy and the boys on Friday?"

She cringed because, honestly, she didn't feel great about it, but she didn't want to tell him that. "This Friday? As in the day after tomorrow?"

"Yeah. I know it's short notice, but I always eat with them Friday nights, and the Friday after that is Christmas and then New Year's Day. Marcy is on break from school, obviously, so they'll do their own thing. And they have plans with her family the weekend after New Year's, so we'd be into mid-January if we don't do it this week."

She didn't see anything wrong with mid-January. The oven timer dinged, and she put the phone on speaker so she could set it on the counter and have both hands free to remove the ceramic tile. The little figurine was adorable, and Sophie was going to love it. Of course, when Meredith asked where she found it, she'd have to say an Etsy shop. She just wouldn't say *which* Etsy shop.

Or maybe she should just tell Meredith. The gift was perfect for Sophie and would mean more if she knew her Auntie Reyna made it special for her.

"Reyna?"

"Sorry. I had to take something out of the oven."

"Something good?"

He sounded hopeful and she laughed. "No. Nothing good."

"Now I'm going to spend the whole night wondering what thing that comes out of the oven could possibly be bad."

"Why do you want me to have dinner with your brother already?" she asked, because she'd rather talk about that than field more questions about what was in the oven. "And they can't give the baby any Christmas presents. It's *way* too early for gifts."

"I didn't peg you for the superstitious type, but I agree. It's too soon for gifts."

"It's probably too soon for me to have dinner with your brother, too."

"Not the same thing. Look, he and Marcy invited you and they were pretty insistent about wanting to congratulate us together and in person." He paused for a few seconds. "We're a close family and I think they want the chance to get to know you better before the baby comes so they'll be a part of it, too."

And that's how, two nights later, she ended up standing in front of a large house in one of those neighborhoods that measured the residents' lawns during the summer.

"How did I let you talk me into this?"

He gave her a playful bump with his elbow. "You've known my brother your entire life."

"Not well."

"I'm starting to think you don't know *anybody* well, Miss Introvert. But he's not a stranger. And you've met my sister-in-law several times."

"Briefly."

"You know they're watching us right now, right?"

She snorted. "This is the kind of neighborhood

where literally everybody is watching us right now. It's like a condensed version of Blackberry Bay, except with higher taxes."

"And you're stalling."

He laced his fingers through hers so when he started walking, she either had to follow him or end up in a tugging war on the sidewalk. She chose to follow, since she knew on some level that she was being silly. Chris and Marcy were nice people.

It was the questions she was dreading. Their mothers were busy basking in the joy of a new grand-baby on the way, so if anybody was going to ask tough questions, it would be Brady's older brother.

"Uncle Brady!"

They were barely inside the door before Brady had to let go of her hand to catch his nephew, who obviously trusted his uncle would catch him if he flung himself at him. Reyna watched them with amusement. Between Sophie and CJ, she was figuring out that kids liked to greet people by yelling their names as loudly as possible.

She looked up to see a smaller version of CJ toddle around the corner before falling over sideways. Before she was about to step forward—to see if he was okay or needed help—he gave a screeching laugh and started crawling toward them at a remarkable speed.

Seeing Brady with his nephews made her heart

ache with how sweet and funny he was. It was clear the boys adored him and that the feeling was entirely mutual.

Marcy appeared to rescue him after a few minutes, and she smiled at Reyna. "It's good to see you again. I'm glad you could come tonight."

"Thank you for inviting me."

"How come you're not in the hot tub?" Brady asked, and Marcy blushed slightly.

"Because we have a guest." She gestured for Reyna to follow her into the kitchen. "I teach school, so by Friday night I'm ready to soak in the hot tub and let the guys take care of the kids and make dinner."

"That sounds like a perfect Friday night. Especially if Chris cooks as well as Brady does."

"Why do you think I married him?" Marcy asked in a stage whisper her husband was meant to hear.

Chris waved from the stove. "Hi, Reyna. How have you been?"

"Good, thanks." Brady was in the fridge, holding up drink options, and she nodded when he held up a bottle of water, which he tossed to her.

"Reyna and I are going to go in the other room so you guys can do your thing." She started to walk away, but then stopped and pointed to the calendar on the fridge. "Brady, I want to double-check that you're taking your mom to her appointment on Monday, right? Chris thought so, but you know he doesn't write anything down."

"I've got her, yes."

Reyna looked over her shoulder as she followed Marcy out of the kitchen, using her expression to let Brady know she hadn't signed on for being alone with his sister-in-law for what was probably going to be an interrogation. He held up his hands as if to say he had no control over the situation, but she could see the underlying amusement.

But other than asking her how she was feeling and offering herself as available if Reyna needed any advice or recommendations, Marcy was content to make small talk about teaching and Christmas and Reyna's work. The boys were in and out, usually with Brady appearing to lure them away with the promise of playing with trucks or something else fun.

Over the course of the evening, it became very clear to her that Brady was going to be an amazing dad. He wasn't just the fun uncle—though he was certainly that—but didn't hesitate to speak to one of the boys in a soft but stern voice if they got out of hand. And even when he did have to stop being fun for a moment or two, the love between them was still obvious.

On the ride home, she must have been quiet because he reached over to nudge her. "What are you thinking about?"

"Nothing, really. Just lost in space."

"I was afraid that, after a couple hours of seeing the Nash genes in action, you were wondering what the heck you've gotten yourself into."

She laughed and shook her head. "That is definitely *not* what I was thinking. Watching you with CJ and Benny just made me even more sure I picked the right guy."

"Good." He drummed his fingers on the steering while for a mile or so. "Not that it matters, obviously, but were there other guys on the list?"

It was tempting to tease him, but she sensed the vulnerability in his question and shook her head. "No, there were no other guys on the list. You *were* the list."

He gave her a smile that took her breath away before turning his attention back to the road, and Reyna looked out her window for several miles, trying to will away the feelings he could trigger with just a look.

She was just going to keep blaming the baby hormones because she was *not* going to fall for the father of her child.

Brady had been prepared for his mother to be a little out of it when her dental surgery was over, but she was barely coherent and he had to hold on to her the entire way to his truck. After helping her climb into the passenger's seat, he went around and got in. He had to fasten her seat belt after she missed the latch three times, and he put the small bucket he'd thought to bring on her lap in case she got sick.

She was in and out on the ride back to her house, and he thought about taking her home with him instead. He could grab some food for Taffy and Bean and take all three of them to his place until she felt better.

But they'd told him the drugs might take a little time to wear off and then she'd be okay, except for some localized pain in her mouth. He decided he'd take her home and stay with her. He wouldn't fit on the trundle couch, but there were still two twin beds up in the loft if he decided she shouldn't be alone. It made more sense because his place wasn't yellow Lab–proof and he didn't feel like being dragged around by their leashes in his icy backyard.

Luckily, the dogs listened when he told them to settle down and, as if they knew somehow that his mom wasn't feeling well, they were quiet and gentle as Brady helped her into the house.

She'd worn comfortable sweatpants and a long-sleeved T-shirt with a hoodie over it to her appointment, so all he had to do was help her take the sweatshirt off and help her into bed. He put an extra pillow under her head to keep her elevated and tucked the blankets around her before kissing her forehead.

"The baby's so pretty."

The drugs were certainly taking their time wearing off. "The baby's not born yet, Mom."

"She looked just like me, you know. It was like she was a little clone of me instead of my daughter."

Brady's brain seized up and for a few seconds the only thing he was aware of was his heart pounding too fast in his chest.

He didn't *have* a sister.

Had his parents had a daughter who died before he was born? Before Chris was born? He wracked his brain, but couldn't remember ever seeing a photo of a girl he didn't know or any other kind of memento he would think a woman who'd lost a child would have in the house.

"I wonder if she still looks like me now that she's grown," his mother murmured, her words slurring slightly as she drifted toward sleep, but still unmistakable.

"Who? Mom, who looks like you?"

"My Anna. I left her."

He wanted more. He wanted to sit her up and demand to know why he was just now hearing about a daughter named Anna who looked just like her, but the drugs—either the ones still in her system or the painkillers they'd given her—won and she was out. Even if he could get her awake, she probably wouldn't be coherent for a while.

Sitting on the edge of the solid hope chest Chris had built for her in high school, he watched his mother sleep and tried to wrap his head around what was happening. The temptation to get up and tear apart the house until he found some answers was strong, but he didn't move. On the heels of that thought came the need to call Chris. There was almost no chance his brother had known about this without ever telling him, and he wasn't that much older, so he had few memories he didn't share with Brady—except for memories of their dad, of course.

But it wasn't a conversation to have over the phone, and he couldn't leave his mother alone in the condition she was in.

His phone vibrated and he worked it out of his pocket, assuming it was from Chris. Brady had called to let him know everything went okay, but that didn't mean he wouldn't be reaching out for updates.

But the text message was from Reyna. How did everything go?

The dogs were already curled up on the braided rug, though he knew they'd be up on the bed as soon as they thought he wasn't watching, so he went into the other room and brewed himself a cup of coffee. Only when it was done and he was seated at the kitchen table with it did he type out a response to Reyna.

Everything went fine. She's sleeping now and the drugs hit her pretty hard so I'll probably stay with her tonight.

I'm glad it went well. Good luck with your sleepover. If either of you need anything, let me know.

He felt numb, his mind unable to grasp the mystery of his mother's ramblings. Maybe it wasn't even *her* reality. She could have seen something on the television or have been reading a book and her drugged brain got confused. But he didn't think so. His gut told him his mother was hiding a secret.

But he forced his focus back to his phone. Reyna had not only remembered his mother was having dental work done today, but cared enough to check on her, and the swell of emotion that triggered in him broke through the numbness.

Thank you. And thank you for checking on us. It means a lot.

When she sent back a happy face emoji but no words, he assumed that was the end of the conversation and set the phone down. He could put the TV on, but he wanted to be able to hear his mother if she called out to him or tried to get out of bed. He knew a book, of which there were many to choose from around the house, wouldn't hold his attention.

So he simply stared at the dogs through the open bedroom doorway and wondered who Anna was. And why this was the first time he'd ever heard her name.

Chapter Eleven

It wasn't the most festive Christmas Eve they'd ever had, Brady thought as he sat at Chris and Marcy's table and looked at a mountain of food he had no appetite for.

When Chris married Marcy, the Nash boys' tradition of showing up at their mom's on Christmas Eve and not leaving until Christmas morning had changed. Now Chris and Marcy hosted a Christmas Eve dinner so Brady and Christy could open gifts with the boys. Marcy's family got Christmas afternoon, and Brady usually went and ate Christmas dinner with his mom and the dogs. All of the food, family and festivity without Brady having to spend the night on one of the small, ancient beds in his mother's loft.

But this year, there was a cloud hanging over the holiday and even though the boys were spilling over with Christmas spirit and Marcy did her best, the Nash family couldn't shake it off.

It had only been three days since his mom's surgery and the question of Anna still lingered unanswered. When Chris had stopped by after work, Christy had still been sleeping and after giving him an update on the dental work, Brady had filled him in.

And later, when she'd slept off the grogginess, they had asked her about it. She waved it off as some kind of delirious rambling, even offering up the television excuse that had crossed Brady's mind. They had no choice but to accept that, but deep down inside, he didn't think she was telling them the truth.

"Would you like some more mashed potatoes, Christy?" Marcy asked. "I tried to make a variety of softer foods, but you're not eating a lot."

"The pain isn't bad anymore, as long as I don't try to chew something hard on that side of my mouth. I'm just saving room for that beautiful Christmas cake."

Mention of the cake, which had come from Jenelle's bakery, made him think of Reyna. He probably wouldn't see her again until Friday, since she and her mom celebrated the end of the holiday baked goods rush by spending Christmas Eve and Christmas Day in their pajamas, doing absolutely nothing for their two days off. And because of that baked good rush, he hadn't seen Reyna since the day before his mom's surgery. He missed her.

Sometimes text messages just didn't cut it.

"*Mom*, can we do presents *now*?" CJ said from his booster seat, his voice not quite a whine, but definitely an urgent plea. Marcy always made them eat first because once presents were opened, she knew she'd never get them away from their new toys.

A solid hour of chaos ensued, with shrieks of joy and flying paper and Marcy trying to salvage instruction sheets from the rubble. Brady had been tense since Monday, but watching his nephews eased his mood and he found himself relaxing.

He also found himself imagining what his own Christmas would be like a few years from now. A little boy or a little girl of his own, tearing up paper and bringing him a toy to put together, only to forget about it when the next toy was opened.

And maybe, by the time their little one was old enough to really celebrate Christmas, if Reyna hadn't found somebody else to share her life with—because he already knew he wouldn't—she'd be a part of it, too. They could celebrate as a family.

"Where did you go off to?" Marcy asked, taking

a dump truck still in its box away from him because he'd only gotten two of the annoying twist ties off so far and Benny wasn't happy about the delay.

"Nowhere." When she gave him a skeptical look, he grinned. "I was imagining doing this for my own kid."

"Next Christmas, your kid won't have any clue what's going on, but the one after *that* Christmas will be fun. It's when they hit CJ's age that it really kicks into gear, though. I'm pretty sure three-year-olds are why spiked eggnog exists."

"How are you going to get them to calm down enough to sleep?"

"I'm not," she said, wincing when Benny protested CJ touching one of his gifts with an earsplitting screech of outrage.

Sure enough, they didn't calm down so much as crash. They still protested going to bed, but they were out of gas and Marcy told Chris to start serving up dessert while she got them to sleep.

The tension seeped back into Brady's muscles when he was seated at the table again, but this time with only his mom and Chris. Without Marcy and the boys to distract them, the elephant in the room couldn't be ignored anymore.

Brady caught Chris staring intently at him, as if willing him to say something, but he only gave his brother an arched eyebrow in return. What was he supposed to say? Not only had their mom made it pretty clear the mystery daughter was off-limits, but it was Christmas Eve.

When Christy cleared her throat, Brady looked over to find her giving him a stern look before turning and giving that same look to Chris. Then she sighed and shook her head.

Brady gave Chris a *see?* look meant to convey that now was not the time or the place to broach the subject and his brother rolled his eyes.

Christy slapped her hands down on the table so hard, the centerpiece rattled. "Boys, that's enough."

"That's not really fair, Mom," Chris said.

Brady nodded. "He's right. We respect that you don't want to talk about this, but you need to respect that you changed everything we believed about our family and we need to process that."

The silence stretched on until it grew oppressive again before she spoke. "I'm going to tell you boys what happened and then I never want to talk about it again."

Chris topped off his glass of wine and handed the bottle to Brady to do the same. They didn't bother offering it to Christy, who took a very long sip from her water glass before starting to speak.

"After I graduated, I met a guy and we fell in love and I left town with him. We just went all over the country, working odd jobs and free to do whatever we wanted. We drank wine and made love and didn't worry about anything else. And then I got pregnant." She stopped, staring at Brady's glass. "I hated being pregnant. And Anna changed everything. We weren't free anymore. I wasn't a good mother. I drank more wine and wished we could be the way we were before. I felt like a failure. And sometimes I'd think about how we'd be free again if something happened to Anna. And I hated myself, so I drank more wine."

"Mom." Chris covered her hand. "It's normal to struggle after having a baby. Marcy needed a lot of support after each of the boys, you know. Postpartum depression is serious and real."

"I do know that…now." She sniffed, dabbing at her eyes with her napkin. "But you have knowledge. And money. And you *wanted* those boys."

Brady just listened because, though he'd be a father soon, he didn't really have a lot of experience with postpartum depression other than doing what he could to help out Chris while he helped out Marcy.

"He was so good with her," his mom continued. "He was a good man and a good dad and I was hurting them both, so I left. Several years later, when I had stopped drinking and felt whole again, I reached out to him. He'd married someone else and Anna didn't remember me, of course. She thought his wife was her mother and she was happy and healthy. I knew I'd made the right choice for her and I came back to Blackberry Bay, to my parents. I met your father. I have regrets, but staying away is not one of them."

"Maybe it is," Brady said, trying to keep frustration out of his voice but not succeeding. "Since Anna's what you were talking about after your surgery, clearly your subconscious thinks you regret it."

"I think it's because you're having a baby," she said. She wrapped her hands around her water glass, though she didn't lift it. "I thought about her a lot when Marcy was pregnant with each of the boys, too. Because if they'd been girls, would they have looked like her?"

"You've never told us we have a sister, Mom," Chris said in a tone that was much more tempered than Brady's. "You can see how that's a lot for us to take in."

"There is a woman out there who has the same maternal DNA as you. She has a family who loves her, and I do *not* want to be the cause of her life blowing up and coming between her and the woman who has been her mother for her entire life. I gave her up so that she could have that chance. It was my decision then and it's my decision now, and I want both of you to promise me that you'll respect that."

"That's a lot to ask," Brady insisted.

"I know it is. But I know in my heart I did the right thing."

"Then we'll have to respect that," Chris said.

"I know with the internet and everything, it's easy to find people now, but I'm asking you not to. You know her name is Anna, but I'm not giving you any other details. Let her live her life and we'll live ours, and focus on CJ and Benny and the new baby that's coming."

Chris nodded and reached over to give her arm a comforting squeeze before looking at Brady. He wished Reyna was here right now. She'd hold his hand and probably know all the right words to help him feel better about this.

But he didn't want to tell her. She'd chosen him to be her baby's father because he was a good guy and his family were good people. Maybe she hadn't remembered that before his father died, he'd actually run off and abandoned his wife and sons. And now he knew his mother had run off and abandoned an infant daughter.

They might be good people, but they weren't good at sticking around for their children.

Except Chris. Chris would never walk away from Marcy and he couldn't be dragged away from CJ and Benny. All he could do was hope he took more after his older brother and less after his parents.

"I promise," he said in a low voice, just as Marcy came down the stairs and joined them in the kitchen.

"I am so ready for a glass of wine," she said. "And pie. Chris, you didn't serve the dessert?"

"Sorry, love. We got talking and you know how it is."

When Chris stood to help his wife—who was probably too exhausted to read the mood in the room—get some dessert, Christy reached over and rested her hand on Brady's. He stared at it for a few seconds before turning his so he captured her fingers. Then he leaned forward to kiss the back of her hand.

"I love you too, honey." When she smiled, he was able to recognize the shadows in her eyes—the emotions of a mother who'd given up her baby to save them both. "I really do."

"I love you too, Mom." That was all that really mattered now. "I really do."

"Can you reach the remote control from there?"

Reyna looked at her mom and then at the remote control that was sitting on the coffee table, obviously out of her reach. "Nope."

"I think if you stretched, you could reach it."

"I think if I hadn't just eaten half a cherry pie, I could stretch."

Her mom laughed. "You didn't eat half of it. You can't have because I'm pretty sure I ate *more* than half."

"I think we just have to watch this channel forever now."

Her mom sighed. "Or at least until I have to pee, I guess."

Christmas with her mom had become one of Reyna's favorite days, which she never would have imagined during the first holiday after her dad died. Hunkering down in their pajamas with their favorite comfort foods had been their way of hiding from the festivities and joy all around them. Instead, they'd found joy with each other and a new way of celebrating together.

She couldn't stop wishing Brady was with her, though, and that was a new twist. When she'd first come up with the idea of having a baby with him, her ideal scenario was that he'd just do his part and walk away. He'd laid that plan to rest pretty quickly, and co-parenting a child with a friend seemed like a perfect scenario. And yet here she was, with her hand rested on a baby she couldn't even feel yet—whose heartbeat she wouldn't hear for a couple more weeks—and she felt as if something was missing because Brady wasn't there.

Hormones, she told herself, even though she had no idea if that was even a valid excuse at this point in her pregnancy. Hormones and too much pie.

When her phone chimed, she frowned because it was on the coffee table next to the remote control, which meant she'd have to put her feet down and sit up because nobody sent random text messages on Christmas Day. Yesterday she'd stopped at Meredith's to do a Christmas Eve thing with her, Cam and Sophie—who had squealed so loudly when she opened Reyna's gift that the dog and cat both disappeared under a bed—and they were supposed to be arriving at Meredith's parents' house about now.

Or it could be from Brady. That was the thought that finally got her to move and, with a groan, she sat up so she could reach the remote control, which she tossed to her mom. Then she picked up her phone.

It was from Brady, and the second she saw his name on the screen, she smiled. Merry Christmas.

Merry Christmas, she sent back. And then, because it felt like there was nothing encouraging him to say anything else, she sent another message. I hope you had fun with your family last night.

The bubbles to indicate he was typing came up and then disappeared. And then returned. Disappeared. After the fourth time, a message came through. CJ and Benny are extra fun at Christmas. Are you having a good day with your mom?

She wondered what he hadn't said in all of those disappearing attempts. Yes. Too much pie, though.

You're eating for two.

Or eating for five.

There was a delay before the next message came through. I hope that's a joke about how much you've eaten today and not any kind of test results.

She laughed out loud before remembering she wasn't alone, and she turned to see her mother giving her a very interested look. "It's Brady."

"I assumed as much. You should invite him to stop by and eat some of that food."

"We're in our pajamas. It's our thing."

"I didn't say I'd get dressed. I'm sure he's seen a grown woman in flannel before. It's up to you, of course." She smiled. "But he *is* part of the family now, you know."

The guilt that stabbed Reyna made her look back at her phone. Her mom had no way of knowing that Brady was always going to be the baby's family and kind of family-adjacent to her and her mom, but that he wasn't going to be *actual* family.

Another text came through before she could decide what to do. I'm about to head to my mom's for dinner. Can I swing by for a minute or is it a mother-daughter only day?

You can stop by. My mom was just telling me to invite you to come over and eat some of this food.

I can't stay long and I definitely can't eat a lot of

food, but I have a small gift for you. See you in about ten minutes.

"He'll be here in ten minutes," she told her mom, setting the phone beside her.

"Maybe I'll be able to move by then. Next year, when we're filling the baking orders, we need to *not* make extras for ourselves."

"We said that last year."

"This year, I mean it," her mom said in a solemn voice.

"You said *that* last year, too."

When Reyna heard the truck pull into the driveway, she got up and shoved her feet into her boots to go out and meet him.

"Merry Christmas," she said when Brady reached the back step.

"Merry Christmas." He looked as if he was fighting a grin, and he lost. "That's quite a Christmas look you've got going."

Reyna looked down at the flannel pajamas covered in Christmas penguins and her feet shoved into unlaced work boots. She'd bundled her hair into a messy bun on top of her head when she woke up and hadn't touched it in the hours since.

"Thank you," she replied with a little curtsy. "Come inside. It's freezing out here and this is cute flannel not functional flannel."

"Merry Christmas, Brady," her mom said when they got inside. She'd not only gotten off the couch, but—unlike Reyna—had brushed her hair.

"Merry Christmas, Mrs. Bishop."

"You know you can call me Jenelle, right?"

"Absolutely, Mrs. Bishop."

Her mom laughed and waved a hand over the veritable buffet of baked goods spread across the counter. "Help yourself to whatever you'd like. And have seconds, and thirds. Take some to your mother. Shove some in your pockets."

He groaned. "I'm still full from Marcy's last night. And my mom's making a dinner, even though it's only the two of us."

Jenelle opened her mouth, but before she could issue what was surely going to be an invitation for his mom to join them instead, Reyna gave a sharp shake of her head. Her mom was already calling Brady part of the family. She didn't need the entire family to start acting as if they were already in-laws.

"You can at least have a slice of pie," is what she said instead. "And take something for your mom."

"Yes, ma'am."

"Good."

The three of them stood there for several seconds in awkward silence, until Reyna turned to Brady. "Want to see your car?"

"Sure. Do I get to wear one of those nifty jump-suits?"

Reyna laughed. "No. We're not going to touch anything. I promise, Mom."

She shoved her feet back into her boots, but this time she threw her coat on over her pajamas. The garage had heat, but only from a woodstove and they weren't going to be out there long enough to get a fire going.

"Wow," he said when she'd unlocked the door and turned on the overhead lights.

"Believe it or not, she's not in as bad a shape as I originally thought. A lot of stuff can be cleaned and rebuilt, rather than replaced."

He looked at the long bench covered in parts, though she noticed he was careful not to touch anything. "And you know how all these go back to-gether?"

She laughed. "Of course. That's literally my job, Brady."

"I know. It's just…a lot. I can't really make sense of it."

"Which is exactly what would happen if you gave me a bunch of wire and circuit breakers and told me to wire an electrical panel."

He dipped his head. "Good point."

She reached up to a shelf, careful not to brush her coat against anything, and took down a small, wrapped gift. And when she turned around, he was also holding a present, which would have barely fit in his pocket.

"That's not for the baby, right?" she asked as they each held out their hands. She wasn't going to accept it if it was.

"Nope. We both said no gifts for the baby yet. Marcy was pretty vocal about how unhappy that made her, by the way."

"It's too early."

"This is for you," he promised, and they exchanged gifts.

When he made no move to unwrap his, she sighed and slowly peeled the tape and paper away from the box. Inside, nestled in a bed of white tissue paper, was a small journal with the silhouette of a woman holding a baby embossed on the front.

"You said you have a journal and you tracked dates and stuff," he said, and she could hear the nerves in his voice. "That one's for journaling your pregnancy and not just dates and stuff, but like…all kinds of stuff."

It was so sweet that tears blurred her vision for a few seconds before she wiped her eyes with the back of her hand. "I love this. Thank you. Open yours now."

While she waited for him to unwrap his, she understood how nervous his voice had sounded when she'd opened hers. Gift giving always made her anxious, and his was so personal that she could only hope he liked his as much.

He lifted the Christmas tree ornament out of the tissue paper and held it up. It was a house that was clearly a simplified version of his, framed by a Christmas wreath. The bottom of the wreath had a banner with his last name and the year he bought the house painted on it.

"This is amazing. I love it." He looked at her, and she could see by his expression he really did love it. "How did you get this?"

"Online," she said. And then, because she knew the math on a custom order's dates, she changed the subject. "So CJ and Benny had a good Christmas?"

"They did. They're a fun age for it, though Benny's still not sure exactly what's happening. In a couple of years, they're going to be out of control from Thanksgiving to New Year's." He ran his thumb over the front of the ornament before tucking it back into the tissue, closing the box and tucking it into his coat pocket. "That's a perfect gift. Thank you."

"And thank you for my journal. I'm going to enjoy having a special place for baby notes."

They looked into each other's eyes so long, she shivered. She wanted him to kiss her and she knew without a doubt he wanted to kiss her, but neither of them closed the short distance.

"I should go," he said in a quiet voice. "My mom's waiting for me."

He didn't want to go. She knew if she stepped just a little bit closer and tilted her head back, he would kiss her until they forgot what day it was and what they were supposed to be doing. But that was for couples and they were only a pretend couple.

A hug between friends was perfectly acceptable, but with the tension crackling between them, even the most innocent of touches wasn't going to be innocent for long.

"If you don't go in and get some food to take with you," she said, "my mom might chase you down the street, trying to throw it into the back of your truck."

He laughed, stepping toward the door, and the moment was lost. "I'm tempted to start driving away just to watch her try."

She turned off the lights and locked the door, and they took their time walking back to the house despite the cold.

"I can't believe how much work you've done on the Chevelle," he said, his breath making white puffs in the air.

"Breaking it down is the easy part. And, since you brought it up, I don't know if I'll have her running before the baby comes. If that's an issue, it's not hard to throw the parts in a box."

"Of course it's not. I told you I was in no rush,

and I already knew that at some point, keeping up with regular customers is going to be enough on your plate. I hope you're keeping track of the time you put in, though."

She laughed. "I'm my father's daughter. I don't work for free, and if you ask me about a strange knocking sound your car is making, you better at least be paying for my coffee."

"Okay, you're in charge of teaching our child how to be self-employed," he said with a chuckle. "I'm a soft touch, unfortunately."

"I know." When he glanced sideways at her, she shrugged. "There was one time I was at the café with Sydney and you were sitting at the counter. The guy next to you asked you about a thing his motion detector light was doing and you spent like twenty minutes telling him how to fix it. And then *you* paid for *his* coffee."

"Oh yeah, that guy. If it helps, at least fifty percent of the time, those people end up calling me anyway, because they either made it worse or realized they shouldn't be messing around with wires. And they call me instead of somebody else because I'm such a great guy."

"Was that guy one of the more than fifty percent?"

"No." He opened the door for her and rolled his eyes when she walked by him, laughing.

Her mom had already packed up some pastries

and other goodies for him to take, and she'd even found a basket because a paper plate with plastic wrap wasn't going to cut it.

"My mom and I are never going to be able to eat all of this," he protested when she handed him the basket.

"Not with that attitude, you won't." She patted his arm. "I believe in you, though."

When he was ready to go, Reyna reached for her coat, but he stopped her. "Don't go through all that again just to walk me to my truck. Stay in here where it's warm, and I'll talk to you soon. Maybe when I recover from my sugar and carb crash."

They were all laughing when he went out the door, and without thought, Reyna moved to the window to watch him drive away. Maybe he'd been as certain as she was that if she'd walked him to his truck, there would have been a kiss goodbye.

A very long, hot kiss goodbye that might have changed everything.

"He could have given you a kiss goodbye, you know," her mom said, startling Reyna. If her mother started reading her mind, she was in trouble.

Then she remembered that she and Brady were the only ones who knew they weren't *really* dating. And people who were dating generally kissed each other goodbye. "Public displays of affection in front of moms is all kinds of awkward, Mom."

"I would have turned around."

"You didn't send him all of the pineapple upside-down cake, did you?"

"Reyna Marie Bishop, you must be joking right now."

"Well, I don't want it right *now*," she said. But nothing beat cake when it came to eating your feelings and Reyna had a *lot* of feelings to eat.

Chapter Twelve

By mid-March, they'd fallen into a comfortable routine that worked for both of them. They went out occasionally, but mostly they liked to stay in, and the people of Blackberry Bay were no longer interested in Brady's truck being parked at Bishop's Auto Care or Reyna's car being parked in Brady's driveway.

They cooked together. Played board games. Watched television together. They were friends, Reyna thought as she ran her hand over her small baby bump. Buddies. And if there were times—many, *many* times—she regretted that it couldn't be more than that, she reminded herself that this was best for her baby. She and Brady were friends and they'd co-parent as friends. There was nothing messy about that.

When a truck pulled into the lot a few minutes before she closed, she looked up and wasn't surprised it was Brady. And that thrill of anticipation and desire she felt no longer surprised her, either. She wanted him. She'd come to terms with that. But she wasn't letting herself have him because that *would* be messy.

"Hey, how was work today?" she asked when he stepped inside the office.

"I swear Tess Weaver is going to be the death of me. How is Finn's grandmother going to give *me* more gray hairs than she gives him?"

"Because he was smart enough to move an hour away." Reyna laughed. "I hope I'm that much of a pain in the ass when I'm… What is she? Seventy-five?"

"Early seventies, I guess? I don't know and I'm not going to be the one who asks her."

"What's she up to now?"

"She called me to tell me she was standing on a chair because the last light bulb in her ceiling fan blew, but one broke when she tried to unscrew it. She was about to use a potato cut in half to get the broken light bulb out, but then she realized potatoes are a little wet, so she just wanted to know if it mattered if the light was on or off before she stuck the potato on it. And that she couldn't tell if the light was on or off because all of the light bulbs were blown."

"So I guess changing a ceiling fan light bulb was on your job list today."

"Probably the fastest house call I've ever made. What about you?"

"Just another day. I put together an estimate for changing a catalytic converter and ruined that customer's day, and now I'm shutting everything down."

They made small talk while she did the end-of-the-day accounting and turned off her ancient computer, but something was bothering him. Brady wasn't quite himself tonight, though she couldn't put her finger on what was wrong. His eyes didn't crinkle when he smiled.

"Everything else go okay today?" she asked as she did a final walkthrough of the garage to make sure everything was off and no chemicals had been left open.

"Yeah."

"You seem like maybe something didn't go okay today, though." When he gave her a questioning look, she shrugged. "Something's bothering you."

"I don't know. I don't like secrets, I guess."

Somehow she didn't think he was talking about their situation. "Everybody has secrets. Some big. Some small."

"What are your secrets?" he asked, one corner of his mouth quirking up.

Since she was in the process of slipping out of her gray coveralls, she was able to gesture at the bump her new maternity T-shirt was showing off. "I don't think I have secrets anymore, actually."

He laughed, but then leaned against the counter. "Okay. Then where do you go every Tuesday afternoon?"

She froze, frowning at him. "I run errands."

"Mmm-hmm."

"How do you know I go *anywhere* every Tuesday afternoon?"

"Well, your hours are posted right there on the door and you close at two o'clock on Tuesdays. And I work all over the place. I've seen you leaving town several times, about a half hour after you close up shop." When she raised an eyebrow, he shrugged. "I'm not tracking your movements or anything. I've just noticed it."

"I go to Concord and buy supplies for my mom because it's a lot cheaper to buy them in bulk in the city than to buy it all at the market in town."

"Really." His expression and the way he nodded his head made it clear he didn't totally believe that. And he wasn't wrong. "Seems strange that Jenelle wouldn't go with you."

"It's faster if I take the list and go alone. You get that woman in a store and you might need a nap in the bedding section before you can get her out again."

"Now, I feel like there's more to it. And the fact you don't want to tell me just makes me think it's a big one."

She rolled her eyes, but maybe it was time to tell him. She'd already been toying with the idea of telling her mother and Meredith. It was inevitable that one of them was going to want to get into that room and turn it into a nursery. And she was surprised Brady hadn't asked about that very thing by now.

"Can you keep a secret?" she asked, her mind made up. It was time to share her secret hobby with him.

He laughed. "You're literally carrying my child because you *know* I can keep a secret."

"True. Well, that and your good genes."

"Oh, was I wearing my good jeans that day?"

She groaned. "I don't think you can make dad jokes before the baby's actually born."

"I want to be prepared."

"If you really want to know, then come upstairs." At least his sense of humor had improved since he first walked through the door, she thought as they went up to her apartment. She took off her shoes and washed her hands while he took off his coat and boots. She had a sink and a pumice cleanser in the garage, but she liked to wash them again upstairs with a kinder soap. After she dried them, she rubbed in some moisturizer she kept on the windowsill.

"I'm probably going to tell my mom and Meredith this secret soon, but for now, you will literally be the only person who knows it."

His eyes widened. "Your mom doesn't even know?"

"Nobody knows." She went to the craft room's door, but paused with her hand on the knob. "It's not nearly as exciting as you might think it is. Just so you know."

"As long as whatever's behind that door won't lead to a documentary on one of the murder channels, I'll just be happy knowing what it is."

She laughed and opened the door, and she took a deep breath as she gestured for him to enter.

He stopped just inside the room, and she watched him look at the pictures pinned to the board and the finished projects she had lined up on a shelf. There was one sitting on the craft table—a miniature replica of a wedding cake that had pushed her ability to work with tiny details to the limits—and he bent low to look at it.

"That one's cured and glazed, so you can pick it up if you want," she said. "But if you drop it, we might be the ones who end up in one of those documentaries after all."

He grinned at her before gingerly lifting the cake so he could get a better look at it. The minute flowers and ribbons had come out exceptionally well, and she felt a surge of pride when she saw the look of disbelief he turned her way.

"Reyna, this is incredible." He held the cake up near the cluster of pictures the groom had sent her so she could make a gift for his bride on their first anniversary. "You're an artist."

"I have a shop online and I do custom orders, like that cake. And I make fun little things to sell ready-to-ship. I won't get rich, but the store pays for the hobby with a little pin money left over. I made a cupcake for my mom, but I told her I bought it."

"I don't get it. Why don't you want anybody to know about this? It's so cool and fun and people would love to have you make things." He looked up from the tiny cake in his hand. "Is that why it's a secret? Are you afraid everybody will expect you to make these for them?"

"That wouldn't bother me, as long as nobody expected me to make them for free." She shrugged one shoulder. "It's kind of hard to explain, I guess."

"I wouldn't mind hearing you try. I guess that makes me nosy, but I'm just really interested in why you want to keep this gift to yourself so badly."

"I think at first, it was because I didn't want either of my parents to think I'd rather be doing this than helping them out. I don't know if I could make a living do this, but even if I could, I wouldn't want to give up the garage and I couldn't trust that they would believe that. And then... I think there's a part of me that liked having something that literally nobody else knew about me."

"I think you could make a living doing this, though." He very carefully set down the cake and then looked over the pieces on the shelf. "I really do. And if you made little Christmas ornaments that were unique to Blackberry Bay, I bet Sydney could sell those at the market for a ridiculous amount."

"See?" She shrugged when he looked at her. "That's...a lot. Is it going to be my fun, relaxing hobby once it's actual work? And I know there are people who think I still run the garage because it was my dad's and my mom and I don't want to let it go, but I actually love being a mechanic."

"And you're good at it." He put his hand on her arm. "Did you *make* my Christmas ornament?"

Her cheeks burned as she nodded. "I did, but I didn't want to tell you."

"No wonder I love it so much. I didn't put it away with the rest of the Christmas stuff, you know. I like looking at it."

"I'm glad you like it that much. And honestly, I have thought about the tourists." She gestured for him to follow her and walked out to her fridge. On the front was a magnet that she took off and handed to him.

It was a small basket of blackberries, and the clay

bow tied to the basket's handle had *Blackberry Bay* painted on one end of the ribbon and *New Hampshire* on the other.

"This is what I meant," he said, putting it back on the fridge. "You could sell a ton of those."

"I could. But making the clay basket-textured takes forever and the thought of making a lot of them turned me off. Honestly, I couldn't even bring myself to make a second one, so making enough to sell to tourists? No thank you."

"Then don't. There's nothing wrong with having a hobby." He surprised her by pulling her close and wrapping her in a strong hug. "I feel special now, because you shared it with me."

Exposing her craft room secret had been worth it to feel his arms around her again. She rested her head against his shoulder and breathed in the smell of him, and it took all of her self-control not to run her hands down his back. And she didn't have the self-control to be the one to pull away.

Instead, she stood and soaked in the contact, waiting him for step back.

Brady held Reyna in his arms, breathing in the scent of her hair. Sometimes spending the day surrounded by motor oil and exhaust fumes overwhelmed the crisp scent of her shampoo, but not tonight.

His heart was pounding in his chest, and he hoped she couldn't feel that against the side of her face. He knew he should let her go, but it had been so long since he'd held her in his arms that he couldn't bring himself to break off the contact.

When it reached the moment he either had to let her go or kiss her, though, he told himself he *had* to do the right thing and he let her go. Stepping back, he shoved his hands in his pockets.

"Are you hungry?" she asked, turning abruptly toward the kitchen. "I have some leftover meat loaf and mashed potatoes from my mom. I could heat it up for us."

"That sounds great. Thanks."

She talked while they ate, telling him she'd be having an ultrasound soon, but that she didn't want to find out the baby's gender, if they could even tell yet. He was fine with that. And the fact she invited him to go with her made him happy in a way he hadn't thought possible.

It was a good distraction from the fact he was going mad with wanting her lately. He always wanted her—he always *had*—but lately it had been escalating from a need to a hunger.

"Have you thought about names at all?" he asked, desperate to keep his mind away from imagining her naked in her bed. His bed. The couch. He didn't even care where as long as she was naked.

"A little bit, I guess." She frowned. "What if it's like a dog, though, where you really want one and you spend all kinds of time coming up with the perfect name, but then you get a dog and that name totally doesn't fit its personality?"

"I don't know a lot about babies, but I don't think you can wait until the kid's personality shines through to pick a name."

She laughed and slapped his shoulder. "I know *that*. But still. There's a big difference between names like, say, Cornelia and Bitsy, and there's no way to know which would suit a baby."

"Those..." He paused and reconsidered how to phrase the question without possibly offending her or hurting her feelings. "Are those names you're considering?"

She laughed, and he felt a rush of relief. "No. They're just examples."

"I've met our families and it's highly unlikely we're going to have a child serious and stern enough to be called *Cornelia*."

"You should have spent more time with my paternal grandfather. I'm pretty sure if he stared at a plant long enough, the leaves would start shriveling."

"I vaguely remember him, so I admit there's a slight chance you and I could have a serious and stern baby, but that's definitely a recessive gene."

He smiled at her. "There's a good chance of blue eyes, though."

"That's true. Have *you* thought about names?"

He shrugged one shoulder. "I guess I'm trying *not* to think about that, to be honest."

"How come?" When he hesitated, she nudged him with her elbow. "And keep being honest."

He wasn't sure he could explain it to her without ruining the evening, but he knew she wouldn't let it go. "You're carrying our baby and I'm going to be a part of this baby's life and I'm grateful for that. But I also know when you first asked me to be a part of this, you kind of wanted me to walk away. The baby's name is a really big deal and I don't know if you already have one picked out or if you expect or want me to be a part of that."

"This is our baby. I'll tell you up front that if it's a boy, I want his middle name to be James, for my dad."

He nodded, because he'd assumed she would want to do that. And they sure weren't naming a child after *his* dad. But thinking about his dad made him think about the day he'd had with his mom, and he didn't want to do that when he'd finally started relaxing.

"We probably need to involve a professional in this, you know," she said.

"A professional what? A professional baby namer? Is that a thing?"

"No, not for the name. But the other stuff. Like a professional…paperwork person." When he laughed at her, she rolled her eyes. "I don't know what we need. Maybe we just write something out and have a notary public witness the signatures?"

"The only notary public I know of in this town is Mrs. Jarvis, and half the town would know before the ink from her stamp was dry."

"So a lawyer, then," she said. "They're not allowed to tell anybody."

"I'll find somebody and we can go and talk about how to protect us both and the baby," he promised, because she was right. It was time to start hammering out the details.

After they'd cleaned up the dinner dishes, they sat on the couch like they usually did—each on their own end—and watched an action movie they'd both seen before. He didn't care what they watched because he couldn't shake the conversation he'd had with mom earlier.

He had a sister and he just couldn't come to terms with the fact she wouldn't talk about it.

"I wish you'd tell me what's bothering you, Brady. I could see it as soon as you walked into the office tonight."

He sighed and dropped his head back against the couch because he didn't want to talk about it. But he knew he had to—she had a right to his family details now—so he slid his hand across the cushion, palm up. When she put her hand over his, he curled his fingers through hers and swiveled his head to look at her.

"You know how liking my family is one of the reasons you thought I'd be a good father?"

"It was mostly about you, but liking your family didn't hurt."

"Remember when my mom had dental surgery right before Christmas? Well, she talked about a daughter named Anna that she left."

"What do you mean by *left*?"

"When the drugs wore off, she said she'd had a little girl and she left her with her dad because she wasn't a good mom at that time of her life and she drank too much and was worried for the baby."

Reyna squeezed his hand. "I don't know what to say, Brady."

"She got pregnant after she left town with the guy and she came back alone, so nobody here ever even knew she had a baby."

"And she hasn't contacted her since?"

"No. Anna was a baby at the time and probably knows nothing about it, so she doesn't want us looking for her. Mom wants to leave it in the past. She says that chapter of her life was closed before she met my father and she doesn't want to reopen it. But I stopped by today and she was crying, and she finally told me she thought she saw a woman on the television who liked what Anna would look like now. I asked her for the last name—for the father's name—but she refuses to tell me."

"I'm sorry. That has to be hard for you." She stroked the side of his hand with her thumb. "That was like three months ago. How come you haven't said anything before now?"

"It's not really my secret to share, you know? And it's a big one." He sighed. "And maybe because my dad took off and left me and Chris, and now I find out my mom took off and left a child. So I wasn't such a good choice, after all."

"Hey!" She yanked on his hand so hard, he fell toward her.

And when he tilted his head to look at her, she let go of his hand so she could cradle his face. "Don't ever say that again. You were the *perfect* choice."

Brady needed to get up and probably get out or he was going to be in so much trouble. But then she ran her fingertip across his bottom lip and it was too late.

He was doomed.

Chapter Thirteen

With Brady's blue eyes staring up at her, the vulnerability on his face fading and being replaced by that intense look that made her want to strip his clothes off and have her way with him, Reyna lost her will to resist him.

She shouldn't have touched his face. She *definitely* shouldn't have traced that very kissable bottom lip with the tip of her finger.

And when he captured that finger with his teeth and then sucked it into his mouth, she shouldn't have whimpered. But it was too late.

"There's no harm in it," he said in a low voice, the corners of his mouth quirked up in a slight smile.

Wasn't there? She was already struggling to maintain that line between what was real and what wasn't between them. Sex wasn't going to help make that line any clearer.

But would it really make things harder? To her mind, there was already a level of intimacy between them that had crossed that line. They ate together and washed dishes. They argued over movies. They shared the highs and lows. They'd even had the *what do you want to eat/I don't care* circular debate, which seemed to be the hallmark of every relationship.

If they'd already gone that far, what harm *could* sleeping together do? They both knew it was all temporary. They just had to keep remembering that and everything would be okay.

"If I'm out of line, tell me now because wanting you and not being able to have you might actually do me harm," he said, and his tone was only half-teasing.

"Let's go to bed," she said, and then she laughed when he almost tumbled to the floor in his rush to get up.

Even though it was her apartment and her bedroom, he took her hand and led the way without even stopping to turn off the television or any of the lights. She didn't mind. Him wanting her so badly he couldn't wait was a huge turn-on, as if she needed to be any more turned on.

He kissed her as if she was ice water after a trek across the desert, and she ran her hands over his back and down his arms. She wanted to touch him everywhere, but she also didn't want for him to stop kissing her long enough to remove the layers of clothing between them.

"I've been thinking about this since that first night," he said. But then he lifted his head and frowned. "No, since the second night. We don't think about that first night. Ever."

Laughing, she tugged his shirt up and over his head before flinging it aside. "Trust me, you have totally erased that memory from my mind. When I think about us, I only think about that second night."

He slid his hands under her shirt, lifting it as he cupped her breasts. "Do you think about us a lot?"

"Only constantly."

He grinned and lowered his head to suck her nipple through the fabric of her bra and she moaned with pleasure. Her breasts were a little more sensitive now, and the sensation made her knees weak.

By the time they'd stripped down and he had stretched out on the bed, she was practically trembling in anticipation. He made love to her slowly, teasing and tasting, but he refused to give her what they both wanted until she growled in frustration and forced him onto his back.

She rode him with his hands digging into her hips

until they both climaxed with so much intensity she cried his name. And when she collapsed onto his chest, he held her so tightly, kissing her hair, that she never wanted to move.

When she finally rolled off him because she was losing feeling in her legs, he tucked her against his side and pulled the covers over them.

"I don't know why we haven't been doing this all along," he murmured after a few minutes.

She knew why, but she didn't want to admit out loud that her feelings for Brady had gotten very messy since they got themselves into this. "You left the TV on, you know. And the lights."

"I figure you'll wear me out and I'll need a midnight snack to regain my strength. I didn't want to walk into anything."

"A snack sounds good. I have a wicked craving for pizza right now."

"That's it?" He chuckled, and she propped herself up on her elbow to scowl down at him. "I thought pregnant women craved weird things like pickles dipped in ice cream or tuna melts."

"Tuna melts aren't weird."

"Tuna melts are *very* weird." His exaggerated grimace made her laugh. "What kind of pizza are you craving? Pepperoni? Mushrooms and black olives?"

"Hawaiian."

"No."

"What do you mean *no*? You can't say no to my craving. It's literally *my* craving."

"Pineapple doesn't belong on pizza."

"One could argue barbecue chicken doesn't belong on pizza, either, but you showed up at my garage with barbecue chicken pizza."

"Barbecue chicken is a meat, and meat goes on pizza. Pineapple is a fruit and fruits don't."

"Ha!" She jabbed his chest with the tip of her finger. "Technically, tomatoes are a fruit, so by your own logic, pizza sauce doesn't belong on pizzas, either."

He shook his head. "Tomatoes are widely accepted as both a fruit *and* a vegetable nowadays, but nice try."

"So you know how on TV the man always goes out and buys the pregnant woman whatever she's craving? I think that's a real thing."

He laughed, which didn't bode well for getting what she wanted. "You do realize that there are no businesses in this town open at this hour. And there is definitely nobody out there making a Hawaiian pizza right now."

"If we lived in the city, we could not only get a pizza right now, but they would actually deliver it."

We. She realized too late that she'd said *we*, as if they would move together to a city and lie in bed and have pizzas brought to them in the middle of the night.

That actually sounded like a pretty nice life.

He ran his hand over her stomach. "Maybe you need to be distracted and you'll forget about pizza."

"I don't know. I think it would take a *lot* of distracting to make me forget about Hawaiian pizza right now."

He grinned as he cupped her breast, running his thumb over her nipple. "Challenge accepted."

Two weeks later, stepping through the door into the elegant office decorated in tones of gray did nothing to calm Brady's nerves. The seating arrangement might be casual and he might know the man who stood to greet them, but that didn't make this visit any less official.

"Reyna. Brady. It's good to see you." Preston Wheeler shook her hand first, and then Brady's. "Have a seat."

Reyna was going to sit in one of the armchairs, but Brady gestured for her to sit on the love seat and then sat next to her because he needed her moral support in this. Their legs were touching and he lifted his hand to take hers before he remembered why they were here and he dropped it back into his lap. They'd been spending nights in each other's beds often since the night he'd told her about his sister, but right now it felt as if there was a wall between them.

They were here to lay the groundwork for breaking up.

"Can I get either of you some water? Coffee?" When they both declined, Preston sat in the chair across from them and rested a legal pad on the arm. "Reyna, I want to start by repeating what I told Brady on the phone. I'm a lawyer who chose to specialize in estate planning, but I *am* still a lawyer. I should be able to handle whatever you need but, if it gets too complicated, I'll help you find somebody who specializes in family law."

"Okay." Reyna rested her hand on her stomach, as if taking comfort in the little bump. Or maybe taking courage from it. "Brady said he was pretty vague on the phone and before we go any further, I just want to… I don't know. This is a really small town. You're not allowed to talk about anything we tell you, right?"

"Everything you say to me is confidential. I know you guys both know my wife, Zoe, and she's from here, so she knows everybody. When we sit down for dinner and talk about our days, she knows she won't get details. We talk mostly about her bookstore, to be honest. She doesn't ask and I wouldn't tell her anything if she did."

"Good to know," she said.

"Not that she doesn't know her share of gossip," he continued, and they all chuckled. "Like I said, she knows literally everybody. But this office is never her source for info on anyone. So what are we looking to do?"

"We need to find out how to do some legal paperwork," Reyna said. "Like a custody agreement and stuff like that."

"Oh, I didn't realize you were breaking up. I'm sorry to hear that."

"We're not breaking up," Reyna said, and Brady felt that annoying flare of hope again. "Well, we are. But not yet."

"Maybe we should start at the beginning," Preston suggested.

"We're not...together." Brady shifted and cleared his throat. "Not like that."

"Okay." Preston looked down at his legal pad, brows drawn. "I must have misunderstood. I thought you were a couple."

"That's what we want you to think," Brady said. "We want everybody to think that."

"I couldn't afford to medically conceive a baby on my own," Reyna explained when Preston still looked confused. Not that Brady could blame him. "I've known Brady my whole life and he was unattached, so I asked him to father my child, but we'd rather other people think it was a little more traditional than that."

"Okay." He nodded and, to his credit, he didn't look uncomfortable or scandalized. He just made a few notes on his legal pad before looking back at them. "Did you have discussions about custody and co-parenting while making this decision? If you already have something of a plan, it can cut down on the questions I need to ask."

"We're basically going to have an arrangement like a divorced couple would, I guess you could say," Brady said.

"But I'll have primary custody," Reyna added.

Brady nodded because that's what he'd agreed to. "But with very Dad-friendly visitations, and we'll need to figure out a fair child support amount."

"I don't need your money."

"I know you don't need it. But you also don't need to bear all of the financial responsibility, either. That's not right."

Preston cleared his throat again. "So it's obvious there are some discussions that still need to happen. I think at this point, I should come up with a list of talking points for the two of you because there's actually a lot to agree on beyond child support. For instance, Reyna will obviously claim the baby at tax time because she'll have primary custody. But who's responsible for the child's health insurance?

Are there expectations when it comes to religion, schooling, etcetera? If I email you an overview, I think you could work on your arrangements and we could meet again in a couple of months and start solidifying a plan."

"That works for me," Brady said, and Reyna nodded.

"If at any point an issue becomes contentious, though, I want you to call and we'll meet sooner. You're having a baby together and we don't want anything to deepen into a rift between you."

It felt like a small miracle to him when, seconds after they walked out of Preston's office, Reyna slipped her hand into his. He locked their fingers together and squeezed, because he knew how she felt.

"It sounded like a lot," he said, "but most of it will be common-sense stuff that we'll figure out. And Preston will guide us through any formalities and making it legal."

"I know. It's just…hard, I guess. It's the not-fun part."

There was nothing fun about planning for their breakup, Brady thought. It was something he didn't want to think about and now he had to not only think about it, but there would be paperwork and a lawyer and it would all be very official.

"Hey." He tugged on her hand to make her stop walking and then pulled out his phone. It only took him a second to find the picture he'd added to his favorites album, and he turned the screen so she could see it. "This is the fun part."

The fuzzy black-and-white photo of their baby made her smile, as he'd hoped it would. They'd gone together to her appointment three days before and he'd held her hand while they ran the wand thing over her little baby bump. It had been strangely intimate, and the fact she'd invited him to be a part of that moment still got him choked up if he thought about it.

But right now he wanted to think about it. He wanted to think about what they were doing together and not what they would be doing apart. But the fact they'd fallen back into bed together had made it all more complicated, and he didn't want to think about that, either.

Mostly because he didn't want to stop.

"That's definitely the fun part," she said, giving him a bright smile. Her mood obviously improved. "And to continue focusing on the fun parts of life, we should have ice cream."

"A dish or a soft-serve cone?"

"Soft serve. Twist with chocolate jimmies," she decided.

By the time they'd gotten their cones and walked to the gazebo so they could eat them while looking out over the water, it felt as if they'd found their balance again. Everything would be okay, Brady thought as Reyna sighed and rested her head against his shoulder.

It had to be, for the baby whose first picture was on his phone.

Chapter Fourteen

"Taffy, you can't sit in my lap while I'm driving," Brady explained for what felt like the twentieth time since they'd left the vet's office.

Bean was content to sit in the back seat and lick the window while occasionally giving a happy *woof* when he spotted a person, but Taffy kept trying to squeeze between the two front seats and not to sit on Christy's lap.

"Sit, Taffy," she said for what was probably the twenty-first time and Brady chuckled. The dogs were pretty well behaved, but for some reason riding in the car was so exciting their exuberance overcame their admittedly basic training, which was why he usually drove the three of them to vet appointments. They often went with Christy to run short errands, but on longer drives, Brady preferred not to have to worry about Taffy taking control of the steering wheel.

"Thank you for driving," his mom said when they'd finally parked in front of her house and released the dogs into the yard. "Do you want to stay for dinner?"

"I have plans," he said, tossing her the keys and taking his own out of his pocket. "But thanks for the offer."

"I have some leftover ham if you want a quick sandwich. Or there's banana bread."

The banana bread was tempting, but he thought about the paint samples sitting in a bag on the passenger seat of his truck. He was excited to show them to Reyna and see what she thought of the colors he was considering for the room he'd chosen to be the baby's.

"Please," his mom said quietly. "Can you just stay for a few minutes?"

There was something in her voice that drew his attention away from the prospect of debating paint colors. "Are you okay?"

"Yes, but I'd like to talk to you and I don't really want to do it standing in the driveway."

Dread curled through his gut as he imagined all

the things it could be, since his mom usually chattered away wherever they were—garden, porch, shed, driveway. She was never shy about having a conversation, no matter the surroundings.

Then he took a deep breath. He'd probably know if she'd had an appointment with the doctor, so she wasn't sick. Anything else, they could figure out.

"Just sit on the porch with me for a minute," she added. "It won't take long, I promise."

"Of course," he said, feeling like a heel for hesitating in the first place.

"I know I said I never wanted to talk about Anna again," she said when they were seated, and Brady felt himself tense.

"You made that pretty clear."

"I really *don't* want to talk about it. But I have to accept that it was hard on you boys to find out about her, especially the way you did. I just need to know if we're okay."

Her voice cracked a little as she spoke, and Brady reached over to cover her hand with his. "Mom, we love you. Yeah, this has been a lot to wrap our heads around, but that doesn't mean we're not okay."

"And you're both willing to just let it be? I…" She stopped and thought for a second, tears shimmering in her eyes. "When we're together as a family, I don't want it to be like it was Christmas Eve. It was painful and I felt distant from you both."

"It was *very* fresh on Christmas Eve," he reminded her. "Is it hard to just let it go? Yes. But Chris and I have talked about it a couple of times since then, and we know that trying to find her would not only hurt you, but could potentially blow up her life. That's not something we want to do."

Breath seemed to rush out of her lungs, and the relief on her face broke his heart. He didn't want his mother ever questioning if her sons still loved her as much as they had before they found out she had a daughter they didn't know. "Thank you. I love you both so much, you know."

"We love you, too, Mom." He stood so he could kiss her upturned cheek. "You don't need to worry about us. Or about all of us being together as a family. I promise we're okay."

"Good." She wiped tears from her cheek and stood. "So you said you have plans tonight. Are you and Reyna going out?"

"I'm making dinner for her, so they're not really grand plans, but there's marinade involved, so I don't want to run too late."

"Dinner in is always nice," she said as they walked toward his truck. "Even if you have to wash your own dishes."

"I don't mind. We clean up the mess together." It was one of his favorite parts, though he didn't tell his mom that. He loved the simple things about his time with Reyna. Washing dishes. Working in the yard, cleaning up the early spring mess.

And getting her opinion about the paint colors he'd chosen, he thought, which renewed his desire to get home and get dinner started.

"Tell her I said hello," his mom said, squeezing his hand.

"I will. Love you, Mom."

"I love you, too, honey."

He looked in the rearview mirror as he drove away, watching her for a few seconds as she threw a stick for the dogs and laughed. She looked happy, and it eased some of the weight he'd felt since finding out he had a sister out there somewhere.

Now that the shock had worn off, he knew it was right to respect her decision to let Anna live her life in peace. And the Nash family would look forward. They had CJ and Benny, and a baby on the way. They would all be okay, and he also knew that decisions his parents had made had nothing to do with what kind of father he would be. His baby might be just a tiny bump right now, but he already knew there was no way he would ever leave his child. He felt incredibly peaceful as he turned up the radio and pulled onto the main road.

But an hour later, when Reyna's car pulled into his driveway and he felt the happy anticipation of seeing her he always felt—*Reyna's home*—that peaceful bubble deflated just a little.

Reyna wasn't home. Reyna was at his house for dinner. They'd eat. Hopefully look at paint samples. Make love. But no matter how much pleasure he found in those moments with her, he had to hold on to that small piece of painful truth.

This wasn't Reyna's home. And it becoming hers wasn't part of the plan.

"Something smells good," Reyna said as she dropped her wallet and keys on the table next to Brady's and made her way to the kitchen.

He'd just taken the broiler pan out of the oven and set it on the stovetop, and he didn't bother to take off the oven mitts before pulling her into his arms. She thought she glimpsed a flash of something—sadness or regret?—in his eyes, but then he kissed her hello so thoroughly she was convinced she must have imagined it.

While they ate delicious broiled steak tips and Caesar salad, he told her about his trip to the vet with his mom, Bean and Taffy. She'd had an annoying day that included a customer who didn't want to pay the price he'd signed an estimate agreeing to and being shipped the wrong part for another car, but the lingering frustration that a hot shower and a half hour in her craft cave hadn't cured faded away as they talked and laughed.

Dinner had become her favorite part of the day. She looked forward to it while she worked, knowing that once the workday was over, this man would be there to laugh with. To relax with.

She knew they should be going out. The point of fake dating was so that people would know they were seeing each other, and staying behind closed doors—whether his or hers—didn't do much for that story. But she didn't care. She'd rather be alone with Brady than out in public with him any day. This time was important to her.

Besides, as long as they were parked in front of each other's places, the story was being told.

"I had to run to the hardware store today," he said when they were finished cleaning up.

"You're at the hardware store so often, I'm surprised you don't have your own parking spot in the employee lot out back."

"That would be handy in the summer, when there's no parking. But while I was there today, I grabbed some paint samples. Want to see them?"

"Sure. What are you painting?"

"I'll show you."

Assuming it was part of the ongoing renovation of the house, she followed him up the stairs and past the master bedroom. She knew from an earlier tour of the house that he was taking her to a medium-sized bedroom on the back of the house. It had big windows that let in a lot of natural light and over-looked the backyard.

When he stepped back so she could enter, she gave him a questioning look, but he just smiled and flipped the overhead light on since the sun was already setting.

The room was still empty, but now there were paint chips taped up on the walls. The pastel colors cued her in immediately to the fact this room was for the baby, and her stomach knotted. She pressed her hand to her belly as he moved to stand beside her.

"I picked this room for the nursery," he said, and the enthusiasm in his voice just made her feel worse.

She felt like she was playing house with this man, but at the end of the day, she was going to take her doll and go home.

Except the doll was their baby and she *liked* playing house with the man in question. When they were cooking and cleaning and puttering around in his garden beds to get ready for planting, it was easy between them. Comforting, even.

But this room wasn't easy. Being in this room and hearing him call it the nursery reminded her that this wasn't her home. That their baby would live with her, in her apartment, and sleep in a crib in the corner of her bedroom. This room would be for weekends and probably longer visits during the summer, although that wouldn't really matter since they both lived in the same small school district.

How old would the child be before it realized this house was a whole lot nicer than Mom's apartment over the bakery?

"I like this really pale pastel yellow," Brady said, walking over to one of the paint chips. "I think it's cheerful and warm, and it's gender neutral. You can match any of the other pastel colors with it."

"It's pretty," she said, hoping her voice and face wouldn't give away any of the inner turmoil she was feeling.

She *wanted* Brady to be excited about the baby. She loved that he was so happy to be choosing just the right color for the room he'd picked to be the nursery. The joy and excitement were almost palpable.

But she wasn't sure he realized that she wasn't a part of what this room was going to become. This would be where the baby slept when it was *Dad's turn*.

"Are you okay?" he asked, and she looked away from the paint chips to find him frowning at her. She really wished she was better at masking her thoughts.

"I'm fine," she assured him, but she knew he'd want more than that, especially considering this was a happy thing in his mind. "Don't you think it's a little early for this?"

That explanation must have worked, because his expression cleared and he chuckled. "Again with superstition? You're like halfway through your second trimester, and all your appointments have been perfect. I think we're safe to paint the walls."

The *we* in that statement stuck out in her mind, but she was determined not to darken this moment for him. And no matter what, this would be her child's room. Even if it was for weekends with Dad, she could take joy in helping make it a perfect nursery.

"You're right," she said, giving him a genuine smile. "You're also right about that yellow. I like that it's such a subtle color, but also bright at the same time."

"Like sunshine." He picked a stack of chips up off the floor. "The trim is harder, though. I can't decide if white is too bright against it. But a contrasting color is less neutral. Know what I mean?"

"I like that soft country blue," she said. "Girls like blue, you know."

"They do look good together." He held the paint chip next to the yellow one, and stood back as far as his arm's reach allowed. "We should look at them during the day, too, when there's more natural light, but I like them together. What kind of light fixture, do you think? And do babies like ceiling fans?"

"I don't think I've ever heard a baby give an opinion on ceiling fans one way or the other."

He laughed. "True. They're nice on low speed just for circulating the air, I guess."

She listened to him talking about fans and dimmer switches and carbon monoxide detectors, letting the sound of his voice wash away her earlier worries. This was a good thing, she told herself.

They were going to have a baby who was loved and nurtured and kept safe by both of them. That was all she'd wanted.

If what she wanted had changed since the day she asked Brady to father her child, that was something she would have to live with if she wanted to protect this happiness they were sharing right now.

"Once we decide on the colors, I'll have Chris come over and help me paint," he was saying. "But what about the floor? I love the hardwood, but carpet is quieter. And softer."

"I like the hardwood, and it'll be easier to play cars and build Lego blocks on someday," she said. "But a big area rug would look nice, matching the window trim."

He nodded and after a long moment during which she could see that he was imagining what the finished room would look like, he pulled her into his arms. "I'm obsessing, aren't I?"

She laughed and wrapped her arms around his

waist. "A little bit. But it's adorable, to be honest. Seeing you so excited."

"Adorable?" He wrinkled his nose.

"Sexy?"

"That's better." He pulled her hips against his. "Want to go visit *my* room now?"

"Is that a new pickup line? Want to go back to my room and see my paint chips?"

He ran his thumb over her bottom lip and she shivered. "Hey, if it works."

"Let's be honest. You had me at broiled steak tips."

After turning off the light, he closed the nursery door behind them when they left it, and Reyna breathed a sigh of relief. That room was for the future—a future that didn't include her rocking her baby in that room or eating broiled steak tips in his kitchen.

When Brady lifted her hair to place a hot kiss on the back of her neck, Reyna put the room and that future out of her mind. Tonight, all that mattered was the *right now*.

Chapter Fifteen

When mingled female laughter filtered through Christy's screen door, Brady stopped what he was doing and moved a little closer.

He was supposed to be doing some of the small but numerous spring chores that he and Chris had fallen behind on. Right now he was on the porch, dealing with the buckets of sand that his mom had swept up over the last couple of weeks. They made sure, when winter hit, that she had several barrels of a salt-and-sand mixture—including one on the porch—so that she could treat her walkways around the property. She'd managed to fill two buckets with what she swept up now that they were hopefully past any late snowstorms.

But he couldn't help wondering what his mother and Reyna were talking about that would make them laugh like that. Hopefully his mother wasn't sharing any embarrassing stories from his youth.

"You know we can see you, right?" his mom called. "If you press your face any closer to that screen, you're going to have a mesh mark on your face."

"The way you two are laughing makes me nervous," he confessed.

Reyna appeared on the other side of the screen, hands on her hips. "We were laughing at Bean, but now I know there are things in your past you're nervous about."

"I think every guy has things from his youth he'd rather his mother not share. Moms know pretty much everything. They even know the things we don't think they know."

His mother's chuckle from the other room sounded almost sinister. "Never forget that."

He stepped back when Taffy pressed her head against the screen door, pushing it open so she and Bean could join him on the porch. Reyna followed them out and the dogs almost ran him over in their haste to go find sticks for her to throw.

This was the third time he'd brought Reyna to his mom's with him, and the two women in his life seemed to have taken to each other pretty well. He wasn't surprised. They were both practical and didn't really care a lot what other people thought of them.

Taffy and Bean loved her, of course, and the feeling was totally mutual. They'd been almost to the house the first time when he realized he wasn't sure what would happen if the dogs didn't like Reyna. Or, even worse, she didn't like dogs. Luckily, that hadn't been a problem. It was too late now, but if he'd thought of it ahead of time, not loving dogs would have been a deal breaker for him.

"I'm almost done here," he said. "But fair warning, you throw a stick once, and you'd better be prepared to throw it again and again. They're relentless and there are two of them."

"It's good exercise." When the dogs dropped their chosen sticks at her feet, she threw Taffy's and then Bean's. "I'd love to have a dog. But a tiny second-floor apartment and a parking lot for a backyard isn't ideal for a dog like these. I mean, I could have one of the little breeds that like to sleep on a pillow all day. Or just have a dog bed in the corner of the garage, but that doesn't sound fun."

She was killing him, he thought as he snapped the lid onto the five-gallon bucket between his feet.

It took every bit of self-control he could muster not to remind her he had a great backyard with lots of grass and plenty of room for a baby *and* a dog.

She wasn't moving in with him. The three of them weren't going to be one family in one house. For all that they looked and felt together, they weren't *actually* together, and it was getting harder for him to remember that every day.

Her laughter drew his attention and he watched Taffy and Bean try to bring back the same stick, each of them holding an end.

"What do I do now?" she said.

"Wait until they drop it and then try to throw it so it lands close to the other stick." He shrugged. "If that doesn't work, they'll just keep bringing it back together."

She threw the sticks until he was done with the things he'd wanted to get done that day. Before the month was up, he and Chris would have to take a Saturday and help their mom do a big cleanup around the place, especially around the garden and greenhouse, but for now he was calling it good.

"I need a nap now," she said when they were in his truck, on the way back to her place.

"I could use a nap."

She laughed and slapped his shoulder. "I mean an *actual* nap. Those dogs wore me out."

"They love you."

"I'm pretty sure Taffy and Bean love everybody." She smiled. "Maybe when the baby's older, like potty-trained and stuff, I'll get a dog. Kids should have a dog, I think."

"I think so, too," he said, though he refrained from pointing out that if she lived with him, they could get a dog whenever she wanted.

That night that he'd made the decision to have a baby with Reyna, he'd had it in his head that they'd go their separate ways well before their families were too emotionally invested in them as a couple. Not too separate of ways, of course, because of the co-parenting. But he'd never intended for it to go this far.

He wasn't sure when that moment to split should have come. Definitely before they started sleeping together again, though. Their fake relationship not only felt very real, but he'd dreamt of it for years. How was he supposed to just pull the plug on it when they felt so right together?

Maybe she'd changed her mind.

He tried to ignore that little flicker of hope, but it flared up so brightly, he wasn't sure he could douse the flame. When she'd first asked him to have a baby with her, they had barely had any relationship at all, even though they'd known each other forever. But in the months since, she'd gotten to know him—gotten to see how good they were together—and maybe he wasn't the only one who wasn't pretending anymore.

He just needed to be brave enough to ask her. Soon.

* * *

Reyna was running late, which was unusual for her. But she'd decided to walk to the café to meet Meredith and Sydney because even April felt warm after a long, cold winter. But she didn't walk as fast as she used to, thanks to the baby, so the other women were already seated when she walked in.

Rissa, the owner, met her at their table with a menu. "I put you at a table instead of a booth because I wasn't sure if the baby would fit."

"Funny," Reyna said, laughing as she took the menu. "If Abe can fit in a booth, I can fit in a booth, baby and all. And it's still barely more than a bump."

They all ordered burgers, fries and milkshakes, which was basically the same thing they'd been ordering since high school. Sydney's family had moved to Blackberry Bay their freshman year because her dad got a job at the middle school, and being the only Black student had been tough, but she and Meredith had gotten to know each other in gym class and they'd all become friends. Meredith had moved away for college and stayed in California until her husband died. When she'd come back to town, their friendships had picked up where they left off, more or less.

"Meredith has her notebook out," Reyna said once Rissa delivered the shakes. "What are we planning?"

"You're having a baby in a little over three months," Sydney said. "Since Meredith and I have both had babies, we felt it was time to tell you that you really kind of need a plan."

She groaned and sucked thick strawberry shake through a small straw. Usually she got chocolate, but the baby wanted strawberry, apparently. "A plan for what?"

Meredith paused in the act of opening the notebook to give her a look of disbelief. "Where do we even start? How about where the baby's going to sleep?"

"In a crib."

Sydney kicked her under the table, but more gently than she would have before she got pregnant. "Don't push her buttons."

"What? The baby's going to sleep in a crib in my bedroom." She tried not to think about the gorgeous yellow nursery that Brady was working on.

"Okay," Meredith said. "Your bedroom…in your apartment?"

"My apartment is where my bedroom is, yes." She shifted her legs so Sydney couldn't kick her again.

Sydney sighed. "We want to know why you haven't moved into Brady's huge, gorgeous house yet."

"We were going to be more discreet," Meredith said.

"The café closes in a few hours, so maybe less discreet and more actually making a plan."

Reyna listened to their familiar banter while she sipped her shake, hoping they'd keep at it for a while because she had no idea what she was going to say.

Why hadn't she moved into Brady's house yet? Because that was never the intention, but nobody but she and Brady knew their relationship wasn't real.

It wasn't *supposed* to be real, anyway. It looked real to everybody. More importantly, it certainly felt real. The lines between pretense and reality had gotten very blurry over the last month, since they'd bared their secrets to each other. And then bared more than that when they ended up back in bed together.

"Reyna?"

"What?" She set her shake down and looked at Meredith. "I missed the question."

"Pregnancy brain," both women said at the same time.

It was more like *Brady brain*, but she didn't bother to correct them. "What did I miss?"

"Okay, it's going to be baby shower time soon," Meredith said, and Sydney kicked Reyna's ankle when she groaned. "It's going to happen, so you may as well help us get what the baby needs. So knowing what your plans for the near future are will help us out."

"I know that there's this," Reyna said, waving her hand over her burgeoning belly, "but Brady and I have been seeing each for less than six months. Would you be asking why I don't live with him yet if I wasn't pregnant?"

"Maybe," Sydney said. "It's a really nice house."

They all laughed, and luckily neither of them noticed that Reyna's was a little forced because she was wondering if Brady was fielding the same kinds of questions. He was coming to the same realization that the people in their lives were going to start looking at their relationship and the baby on the way and wondering about some of their decisions. Or lack thereof.

Why *would* Reyna choose to stay in a tiny apartment and lug a baby in a car seat up and down a flight of stairs if she and Brady were such a happy couple? If she was Meredith or Sydney or anybody in their lives, it wouldn't make sense to her, either.

If they waited until her pregnancy was more advanced, Brady would look like a jerk. And he'd definitely look like a jerk if they waited until she had a newborn. Right now, it could still look mutual. And she could avoid having to dodge totally reasonable questions just because she didn't have answers to them.

It looked as if their "pretend to be dating, get pregnant and then break up" plan had come to the breaking-up part.

"Reyna, are you okay?"

She heard Sydney's voice and she nodded, but she was definitely not okay. How could she be when it was impossible for her to imagine what life without

Brady would look like? She'd see him, of course. There were would be years of pickups and drop-offs, and milestone occasions they'd both attend.

But *she* wouldn't have him. No more cuddling on the couch. No more sharing their days over dinner. No more cutthroat games of rummy or Scrabble. No more hand holding or kissing. No Brady in her bed. How could she possibly be okay?

"Is it the baby?"

"No." The sharp concern in Meredith's voice finally snapped her out of it, and Reyna held up her hand since they were both poised to get up and take action, even if they didn't know what action was needed. "I'm okay. Heartburn."

"Oh," they both said, and they instantly relaxed.

"Do you want to change your order?" Sydney asked, already looking for Rissa.

"No, I want that burger. Besides, they're probably almost done making them."

Sure enough, not even a minute later, Rissa delivered their lunch and Reyna's heartburn fib was forgotten as they dug in.

But the food didn't distract Meredith from her notebook. "Okay, so the registry doesn't need to include all the stuff to outfit the baby having a big room of its own. But you have that second bedroom."

"The baby's going to be in my room for the first year, probably, and I don't have room to store stuff."

As soon as the words left her mouth, she winced and hoped neither of them remembered that, other than the section that was open to the roof to accommodate the vehicle lift and her small apartment, the entire length of the garage and bakery's building was storage. "I just need basic baby stuff, really. Nothing fancy or big."

"No wedding plans, I guess," Meredith muttered, drawing a line through something on the page.

Sydney gave Reyna a preemptive kick, and Reyna tucked her ankles back as far as she could under her chair. It was a habit left over from high school, when Reyna would push Meredith's buttons and Sydney would try to stop her. But adult Sydney's shoes were pointier than the sneakers she'd worn back in the day.

"Did you sign up for birthing classes?" Meredith continued. "If so, is Brady going with you? Who's going to be in the delivery room with you?"

"I…hadn't thought about that yet." A fire alarm would have been nice right about then. Just a false alarm, of course. Smoke from the grill or something. "My mom. My mom's going to be my person."

"And Brady too, right?" Sydney asked.

In the delivery room? She and Brady hadn't discussed that at all, and she was beginning to realize how much they'd avoided talking about things that a "real" couple probably took for granted.

Like whether Brady wanted to see his child being

born. She could tell herself if it was important to him, he'd say something, but she remembered the hesitant way he'd approached the baby's name. He was trying to be careful about stepping over a line, but the line was blurry and didn't stay put.

"Reyna?" Sydney prompted.

She tried not to squirm in her seat as her friends waited for her answer. "My mom really wants to be with me."

"You can have two people in the room," Meredith said.

"He could be busy. Or get called away."

Sydney's eyebrows arched. "He's an electrician, not a trauma surgeon."

"Fine," Reyna said, her brain working in overdrive as she tried to come up with something plausible. "I just don't know about having him in there. It's not like we've been together *that* long. He hasn't clipped his toenails in front of me. I haven't shaved my legs in front of him."

Both women laughed, and the motion of Meredith's pen was an obvious check mark. "I guessed that one totally wrong. Let's see… What else?"

"Are you going to find out the gender?" Sydney asked.

"Nope." They both looked disappointed and she laughed. "Sometimes they're wrong and I hate doing returns and exchanges. There are plenty of neutral colors to choose from."

"Do you have names yet?" Sydney continued.

"Nope."

"Those questions, while totally valid, are not on the list," Meredith pointed out. "Are you going to stay with your mom for a couple weeks after the baby? Or is Brady going to stay with you? Trust me, it's nice to have somebody else in the house because a first baby is scary."

"I'll probably stay with my mom. I don't like her going up and down the stairs at my place." She was compelled to stick up for Brady, though. She didn't want her friends who didn't know the truth of the situation thinking badly of him. "Brady will probably be there most of the time, too. It'll just be easier for me and my mom if I stay with her."

"If you're staying with Jenelle, we definitely don't need to line up frozen meals, then," Meredith continued, crossing something off the list.

"How many more things are on that list?" Reyna asked, running out of patience. She needed time alone. Maybe some time in her craft room to think and try to sort through her tangled emotions when it came to Brady.

"You'll need to get us a list of people to invite to your baby shower."

"You two. My mom." When they just kept looking at her. "Oh. Probably Christy Nash. And Chris's wife, Marcy."

"You know what?" Sydney said. "We'll figure that out, too. I'm starting to remember why we threw you off the prom committee."

"Because I didn't see the point of throwing away thousands of dollars on an event space when we had a perfectly good gymnasium? Especially when the event space was just a glorified old barn."

"Maybe we'll host the baby shower in the garage, then," Meredith said.

Reyna shrugged. "Just let me know when so I can sweep it out."

Sydney laughed. "We're having the baby shower at Meredith's house. Right on the lake? Summertime? I think the theme will be lounge chairs and cocktails. Oh, and lemonade, since you're the guest of honor."

They went off on a baby shower planning tangent, and Reyna tuned them out again. Not deliberately, but she had more pressing concerns than how many chairs they could get their hands on, and whether it would be rude to ask the baby's grandmother to make the cake for the shower.

She had to figure out how to tell Brady that it was time for their fake relationship—no matter how real it felt—to come to an end. She'd promised to cut him loose, and it was time.

Even if she didn't want to.

Chapter Sixteen

Brady stood in front of the open garage bay and watched Reyna reaching for something in the engine compartment of a sedan. She stretched, but her belly—as small as it still was—got in the way and she had to readjust in order to reach whatever she was after.

Frowning, he considered the best way to approach her about her plans for the increasingly near future. Her pregnancy was going to get in the way of what she did for a living. Literally.

The reality was, she was going to be on her own. Not alone, because she had too many people who cared about her for that. Including him. But she was an independent woman who owned her own business and had chosen to have a child. It was probably scary, and it was important to him that she know that he might not be able to rebuild a carburetor, but he was going to be there for her. Always, and no matter what.

"I'd ask you to hand me a four millimeter socket, but I'm not sure you know what that is," she teased, looking over her shoulder at him.

"You're funny. Electricians have tools, you know." He went inside and grabbed the four millimeter socket out of its slot to hand to her. "And Chris and I had to learn to do the basic stuff to keep Mom's cars running before we got good jobs and could afford to have your dad do it for us."

He watched her work for a few more minutes, and then she closed the hood. After wiping her hands on a shop rag, she reached in through the open window and turned the key in the ignition. It started immediately, and he had no idea what she was listening for, but after a minute, she nodded and killed the engine.

When she went into the office, he followed her in and sat on the stool while she made a note on the repair order. Something was up with her today. Usually she would have stopped to kiss him on her way past, and it seemed to him she wasn't even really making eye contact.

Maybe a bad day, he thought. Sometimes Marcy

had been cranky and off and claimed it was just pregnancy hormones, though Brady would never dare suggest that to Reyna out loud.

"Why are you looking at me so intently?" she asked, frowning slightly.

"Sorry. I didn't realize I was." He shrugged when she arched one eyebrow. "Just a lot on my mind, I guess."

"Anything you want to talk about?"

He guessed now was as good a time as any. "I was watching you work and it looks like it'll get a lot harder as the baby gets bigger. What are you planning to do about the garage? So you can take a maternity leave, I mean."

She shrugged. "I'll figure it out."

"It's not like you can just give customers a heads-up that you're closing up for a couple days to actually give birth. What you do won't be easy after a certain point in your pregnancy. And I know that you'll have your mom around and stuff, but she can't fix a transmission or mount and balance tires."

"Actually, my mom *can* mount and balance tires. She can also do oil changes. But no, she won't be working in the garage."

Her prickly attitude about this rubbed him the wrong way and he frowned. "I get that you probably think this is none of my business—"

"Because it's not."

"But you're carrying my child, so how you take care of yourself actually *is* my business."

She stared at him with slightly narrowed eyes for so long, he was starting to think she wasn't going to respond. But then, in a flat tone that made it clear she didn't agree that it was his business, she spoke. "I've already arranged to have Joey Millson start as soon as school lets out. He's been doing the automotive program at the tech, so it's kind of an internship situation. I'll be supervising, but he'll be doing any heavy lifting. When the time comes, I'll have to close the garage temporarily, but I have savings and because we own the building, overhead expenses are minimal. I'll be fine."

"You can't be mad at me for worrying about you."

The way her eyebrow arched let him know he was wrong about that, too. "You're not worrying about my health. You're worrying about my business."

"They're kind of tied together. Pushing yourself too hard or losing sleep over the garage could affect your health, and I don't want to see you stressed out further down the road." He should apologize for bringing it up, but he wasn't sorry. "You're not alone in this, Reyna."

"But I *want* to be," she snapped, and he felt her words like a physical blow. "I told you when I asked you to father my child that I wanted a baby but I didn't want a man."

The hurt was so immediate and so strong, he could feel a trembling deep down inside.

He'd known this day would come. Because she *had* made it clear from day one that she wanted a baby and that was it. Any hopes and dreams that might have taken root in his heart since then were his. That wasn't on her.

But he knew she cared a lot more than she was allowing herself to show right now. There's no way that he'd misread the looks. The touches. The things she said and the little ways she had to show him how much she cared.

No matter what he felt, though, and no matter how much she had come to care for him, it must not be enough. If she had fallen in love with him, she would be able to tell him.

"You're right," he said when he was sure he could speak without his voice cracking or shaking. "Your business is none of my concern."

"I shouldn't have…" She closed her eyes briefly, but when she opened them there was still resignation under the contrition. "I'm sorry that came out that way."

"I'm going to go," he said, sliding off the stool. "We can talk later."

"Brady."

He shook his head. "You're right, Reyna. You did tell me you wanted a baby and not a man. We had an agreement to look to everybody else like we were going down a traditional path and it didn't work out. And that's where we are now."

"We still need to talk," she said, standing up.

They did, but he couldn't do it right now. "Later. We'll talk later."

He walked to his truck without looking back because the trembling sensation was spreading through his body, and he was not going to have an emotional breakdown in the parking lot of Bishop's Auto Care.

When he got home, he silenced his phone and stretched out on the couch so he could stare up at the ceiling and try to control the pressure cooker of feelings that was building up steam inside of him.

Reyna Bishop was the hot burner he just couldn't stop touching. And this time he'd really gotten burned.

For the first time since taking over Bishop's Auto Care, Reyna called in sick. She didn't have a boss to call, though, so she just messaged the customer who had an appointment that she'd have to reschedule and left the closed sign in the window.

She curled up on her couch and tried to cry as little as possible. She didn't really know if the crying disturbed the baby or not, and the little peanut didn't deserve to be miserable because its mother had been absolutely awful.

For twenty-four hours, she replayed her words over and over in her mind. And she couldn't close her eyes without seeing the shock and the pain in his eyes.

She'd panicked. Even though she'd known the time had come for them to either face that what they had might be real or to go their separate ways, she couldn't bring herself to confess she had fallen in love with him. She'd promised him she wouldn't— that she wouldn't ask anything of him but a baby. And she'd fallen in love with him anyway.

But she also couldn't summon the words to tell him that, if they were going to part, it had to be now. That the reality closing in grew more painful every day. So when he'd questioned how she was running the garage, she'd taken the annoyance and made it a big deal. A big enough deal to force a conversation. But in her panic, she'd hurt him, and watching him walk away had hurt so badly it still made it hard to breathe if she pictured it.

Her phone chimed and it felt as if her heart skipped when she saw Brady's name on the screen.

We have an appointment with Preston at 5:30 on Friday. I'll see you there.

Dropping the phone, she wrapped her arms around her belly as if she could shield the baby and cried.

* * *

At 5:29 on Friday afternoon, she saw Brady waiting for her outside Preston's office, and all of the things she wanted to say bottlenecked in her throat, choked off by emotion.

He looked pale and tired, and when he smiled, it was empty. His eyes were flat and when she opened her mouth—with no idea what she would say—he opened the office door and gestured for her to go ahead of him.

Brady sat in one of the armchairs, leaving Reyna to sit alone on the love seat. She listened as Preston spoke, too numb to cry or to do anything but agree to the terms she and Brady had reluctantly discussed over the last several months. When it was over, she signed where Preston told her to and nodded when he said he'd be in touch about the next step. Then she shook his hand and Brady held the door open for her again.

When they stepped out onto the sidewalk, she touched his arm and his flinch gutted her. "Can we get a coffee or something? Or go for a walk?"

"No." He sighed and didn't look her in the eye. "Not yet. We will, because we're going to get past this and be amicable for the baby's sake, but…not yet."

"Amicable," she whispered. What a horrible word to describe what they were going to be to each other.

He shook his head. "You know, we agreed from the start that you and I weren't going to work and that we were going to have to talk about where we were going with this pretty soon. But I honestly thought you cared enough about me to not be cruel."

I love you. The words were there. They were in her heart and in her head, but the idea of saying them and having them rejected scared her so badly she couldn't get them to come out of her mouth. "I'm sorry."

"You might not be hell on men, Reyna, but you're hell on me."

He spun and walked away before she could say anything else. She wasn't sure what she would have said even if he was still standing in front of her.

We agreed from the start that you and I weren't going to work.

That was it, then. They'd made a plan. They'd made a baby. And now the part of the plan that involved Brady kissing her and holding her hand and looking at her as if she was the only woman in the world he'd ever wanted was over.

She realized she was still standing in the middle of the sidewalk, staring at the corner Brady had disappeared around, and probably looking like a woman whose world had just come crashing down around her.

Straightening her shoulders, Reyna smoothed her hand over her baby bump and walked to her car. No matter how broken her heart was or how much she'd hurt Brady, she had the baby to think of.

They would be okay. Just the two of them—her and her baby—just the way she *thought* she had wanted.

Chapter Seventeen

The last thing Brady wanted to do after a long day that had started with him waking up on the wrong side of the bed was do another job, but the call had come from Finn. And Finn was calling on behalf of Tess, who Brady wouldn't have been able to say no to even if Finn hadn't been one of his best friends.

It always amused him when he pulled into Tess's driveway because the house he'd grown up in probably would have fit in half of her downstairs level. It was the kind of historic home that would have been on Blackberry Bay postcards if it wasn't in need of a paint job.

The big old house had an incredible view of the

bay, but it was too big for Tess since her son was long since grown and her husband had died. It had actually been too big *before* then, Brady thought, but it had been in the family a long time or something like that.

Now it had the shabby, overgrown look of a property that took too much labor and too much money to keep up, and Tess was too proud to ask for financial help from her family. She also refused to consider selling it. Finn and his parents tried to help as much as they could, of course, but what it really needed was a complete remodeling from the inside out.

The property was worth the investment. The location was perfect. The house and the outbuildings had good, strong bones. And it was one of the older homes in Blackberry Bay, so nobody liked seeing it get run-down. But being worth the investment only mattered if she had that money to invest, and she most definitely didn't.

Finn met him at the front door, an apologetic look on his face. "I'm sorry to call you out here on short notice, but the outlets in her dining room aren't working and that's where she does her crafts, so she's got three extension cords running in there to power an LED lamp and I'm pretty sure she found those cords in a box marked '1969.'"

Brady winced. "I told her no extension cords

last year. Why didn't she call me when the outlets stopped working?"

"You know how she is. She doesn't want to bother people." Finn shrugged. "And I kind of get it. I mean, every time she has to ask my dad for help, he or my mom will bring up the fact she should sell this place because she'll get enough to buy a cute little condo somewhere with a nice nest egg left over. She's not going to sell it so she doesn't want to hear the lectures."

"But I'm not family. Calling an electrician is a pretty standard thing for a responsible and capable homeowner to do."

Finn tilted his head, giving him a *yeah, right* look. And Brady had that coming, since he wasn't family, but also wasn't just a random electrician she'd found on the internet, either. Tess wasn't stupid and she had a lot of friends in town, so she had to be aware that Nash Electric did her work for an extremely discounted rate. And he charged her the nominal amount he did only because she refused to let him work for free, even when it was a small thing outside of his regular hours.

"She's got company, so at least she won't be looking over your shoulder or trying to help," Finn said as they walked down the narrow hallway toward the back of the house, which was one of the drawbacks of the massive old houses. They tended to have very small rooms with a lot of hallways.

After passing through the doorway into the kitchen, Brady stopped as abruptly as if he'd walked into a glass wall.

Reyna was sitting at the table with Tess and Meredith, and all three women looked up when he walked in.

His chest tightened and the only reason he was sure he was still taking breaths was the fact he hadn't passed out yet. Their gazes locked and all he could do was stare into her pretty blue eyes and wish seeing her didn't hurt so much.

"Brady!" Tess pushed her chair back with a sound that tore his eyes away from Reyna, but it didn't matter if he was actually looking at her or not. All of his focus was on the fact they were both here in the same space. But he tried to force his attention to the woman hugging him. "Did Finn call you? I told him not to bother you."

"It would bother me a lot more if you burn this house down around your ears," he told her, letting a little more admonishment seep into his tone than he usually did. She needed to take his warnings about piggybacking ancient extension cords a *lot* more seriously, but he wasn't at all surprised when she made a scoffing sound and slapped his shoulder.

"Go fuss over the extension cords with my grandson, then," Tess said, shooing them toward the dining room.

Neither of the other women had spoken since he walked into the kitchen, and a glance at Meredith told him she probably had no intention of speaking to him at the moment. That was understandable, since she was Reyna's best friend and probably the first to hear they'd broken things off. There was definitely an underlying tension in the room.

But that didn't stop him from looking at Reyna again. She looked healthy, if not happy, and his gaze lingered on the swell of her stomach and the way her hand rested lightly on it. He wanted to go to her and kiss her and rest his hand on top of hers, but he couldn't do that anymore.

"Hi, Brady," she said in a fake, casual way that cut him to the quick.

"Hi, Reyna. Meredith, it's good to see you." That didn't feel mutual at all, so he gave the women an awkward wave and followed Finn into the dining room.

"I didn't know Reyna was here," Finn said in a hushed voice once they were alone. "I only beat you here by a few minutes and I saw Meredith's car, but I got distracted by a nail starting to pop up out of the floor in the hallway and hadn't been in the kitchen yet."

"It's fine." It wasn't really fine, but there was

nothing he could do about it now. "It's not like we're going to go the rest of our lives without seeing each other again. We're going to have a child together. Forever."

"Good point. Oh, and the Chevelle, too."

Brady hadn't even thought about the car. With his heart being broken and his entire world crashing down around him, the Chevelle hadn't crossed his mind. "I don't care about the car. It'll get done eventually. Now, which outlets aren't working?"

Once Finn had pointed out the problem, Brady was left alone to work, and he liked it that way. From the sounds of it, the women had moved to the front sitting room, which was good because going down into the cellar required going through the kitchen. Making multiple trips would have meant walking past Reyna more often than he thought he could stand.

All he could do was keep his head down and get his work done, and eventually the pain would fade. Maybe not completely because he couldn't foresee a day he wouldn't love Reyna, but it would dull over time into a chronic ache he could live with. He hoped it would, anyway. They were going to be seeing each other on a regular basis for the rest of their lives—or at least until their child was an adult—and if it continued to hurt as much as walking into Tess's kitchen and seeing Reyna's face had, he was doomed.

* * *

Reyna hadn't expected to see Brady today, and even though she was drinking the decaf coffee Tess had made for her and was pretending to listen to her and Meredith's conversation about the Price-Maguire bunch's plans for school vacation, her attention was fully on tracking his movements through the house.

She'd been relieved when Tess had suggested they move from the kitchen to the sitting room to get out of Brady's way. Seeing him had made her heart ache in a way she hadn't been prepared for. She missed him. She missed his face and his laugh and his touch. She missed how much pleasure he got out of cooking for her—and she missed the food, too—and the way he liked to be touching her in some casual way. Sometimes his hand over hers, or his leg pressed against her leg.

Tess's house was old and she could hear the creaking in the floorboards sometimes. Or the squeak of the cellar door hinges, followed by his footsteps on the ancient wooden stairs.

"I should go check on those boys," Tess said, getting to her feet.

"I'm sure the two grown men, one of whom is a professional, can handle it," Meredith said, but Tess just scoffed at her and kept walking. "Poor Brady."

Just hearing his name said aloud sent a fresh wave of sadness through Reyna, and this time her friend wasn't distracted by Tess, so she didn't miss it. "Do you want to leave, Reyna?"

She *did* want to leave. She also *didn't* want to, because she could hear the low murmur of Brady's voice and she'd missed it so much.

Meredith got out of her seat and walked over to join Reyna on the love seat so she could lean close. "I can see how hard it is for you to be here. We can just go before he finishes and then you won't have to see him again."

"But I want to see him," Reyna whispered. "I miss him."

"Maybe this isn't the place, though. I still don't understand exactly why you guys broke up, but I don't think having Tess in the middle of it is going to help either of you."

"I guess you're right."

"Take my keys and go wait in the car. I'll go tell Tess something came up and then we'll get out of here."

She didn't have the emotional strength to tell Tess goodbye and thank her for the coffee because that would mean talking to Brady again, so she took the keys. But sitting in the car meant having Brady's truck directly in her line of sight, and by the time Meredith slid into the driver's seat, tears were spilling over onto her cheeks.

"Where do you want to go?" Meredith asked once

they were heading back into the heart of the town. "Do you want to go somewhere and talk?"

"Can you drop me off at my mom's?"

"Sure. Isn't she at the bakery right now, though?"

"Yeah, but she'll be home soon and it'll give me some time to relax."

Of course, her relaxation was heading into the old garage. After a detour through the house to use the bathroom, she pulled on a pair of coveralls. She wasn't going to be able to zip them for very much longer, she thought as she ran her hand over the baby.

When she stepped inside and turned the overheads on, she felt a fluttering and shifting in her belly and smiled. She liked to think the baby could feel the comfort the sights and smells of this place brought to its mommy.

She ran her hand over the curve of the Chevelle's rear quarter panel as she walked around the car. When she'd first taken on the project, she'd been thinking about her dad. Jimmy Bishop would have jumped at the chance to be a part of putting her back on the road and Reyna had felt the thrill of that challenge. But now it just made her think of Brady.

Someday she'd see him cruising down the main street in this car, maybe with a car seat in the back seat. And maybe with some other woman riding shotgun.

An hour later, she watched her mom's car pull

into the drive. It was another beautiful spring day, so she'd put the overhead door up. It was a manual door, unlike the doors at the new garage, so it had been a task, but worth it to have fresh air circulating around her.

"You're home early," Reyna said, setting down the wire brush she was using to clean a part.

"It was a slow day."

"How much time between Meredith dropping me off and calling you?"

Her mom chuckled. "A few minutes because she didn't call. She stopped at the bakery so she could tell me she was worried about you *and* get a cupcake."

"She's always been a smart one. But I'm fine, Mom."

When her mom crossed the threshold and walked toward her, Reyna raised an eyebrow. Jenelle Bishop never went into the old garage. She rarely entered the new one, and only if she had to. But Reyna couldn't remember ever seeing her actually inside this one. She either yelled from the back step or stood at the doorway.

But her mom got close enough to hold Reyna's face in her hands so she couldn't look away. "You've been wiping tears off your face with greasy hands and you look like you're about to deploy on a secret military mission in the jungle. You are *not* fine."

That was all it took. The tears started again and,

when her mom's arms wrapped around her, she gave in to the grief that had been strangling her since she and Brady ended their relationship.

"I don't understand why you two split up," her mom said once the worst had passed. "Honestly, nobody does. I had hoped because Meredith and you are so close and sometimes you tell your friends things you won't tell your mother, that she'd have some insight, but everybody seems to be at a loss."

"There's nothing I would tell anybody that I wouldn't tell you, Mom. The reason everybody's at a loss is that nobody knows the whole truth."

Her mom's brow furrowed. "What whole truth?"

"You can't tell anybody else. Not even Meredith." When her mom gave her a look, she smiled. She hadn't needed to say that. "Brady and I were only pretending to date."

Jenelle actually barked out a laugh. "That was pretending?"

"I've wanted a baby so much for so long. And you know, Dad got sick and everybody in this town knows I have the worst luck with men. When Lucas and I blew up on the Jumbotron, I knew I was looking at probably years before I could be a mom. So I asked Brady to have a baby with me."

"Oh, Reyna. We could have come up with the money somehow. For artificial insemination, I mean."

"No, we really couldn't. We do okay. We don't

do *that* okay. And we know Brady. We know the Nash family."

"Okay. Why pretend to be a couple, though?"

"You know how this town is. Me having a baby was going to be gossip no matter what, but I wanted it to be the most boring gossip ever."

Jenelle laughed. "You are just like your father, I swear. You want something, you get it."

"We had always planned to break up before the baby was born." She rubbed her hand over her stomach.

"Ah." Her mom nodded, her mouth curved into a knowing smile. "Since neither of you are award-winning actors, I'm going to guess your plan went off the rails because you are both obviously in love."

"I can't even tell you when it stopped being fake because I don't even know. He's just…" She couldn't come up with words to encompass her feelings for Brady, so she just waved her hand in the air. "But that wasn't the plan. I told him I wanted a baby and I wouldn't ask anything else of him. He wanted a baby, too, though, so we'll share this little one. But as co-parents, not as a couple."

"Why now?"

"Meredith and Sydney were talking about the baby shower and the nursery or whatever, and they were surprised I wasn't planning to move into Brady's house because it's big and gorgeous and it would make sense. And I realized we'd reached the point where people would start asking questions we couldn't really answer as a couple. Then he got pushy about my plans for the garage and maternity leave and I pushed him away." She took a deep, shaky breath. "I pushed hard."

Her mom pulled her in for another hug. "Maybe it's for the best. You love him. I believe in my heart he loves you. If you're meant to be together—and you are—then you'll come to each other out of love and not because it was planned or because of this baby or any other reason. Just love for each other."

Reyna wanted to believe that. She wanted to believe there was still a chance that she and Brady could be together—that his feelings for her were as real as hers for him—but the thought of reaching out to him was so terrifying, her hands were shaking.

"For now, let's go in the house. You need to wash your face and then we're going to start making a list of things we need to get done before my grandbaby's born. We're going to focus on the joy today because that's what you and this baby need."

"We also need something salty and crunchy," Reyna said, wiping her cheeks with the coveralls' sleeve, which probably did nothing to clean her face.

"I was going to make mashed potatoes with tonight's dinner, but maybe we'll make homemade chips instead."

They pulled the overhead door down and Jenelle waited while Reyna turned off the lights and locked up. Then she tucked her arm through her daughter's as they walked across the yard.

"The important thing is that you're going to be okay," she said. "You have me and this baby and good friends who care about you."

"I know, Mom."

But she wanted Brady, too.

Chapter Eighteen

The Dock probably wasn't the most original name for a restaurant, but it made sense seeing as how it was actually a dock—built on the edge of the bay, with a large outdoor patio they kept open year-round for anybody who wanted to brave the cold, and a long dock so people could arrive by boat. It also had great wings and a bartender who did a fair pour.

Since it was only four o'clock in the afternoon, the fair pour was lost on Brady, though. He was drinking a beer—the same beer he'd been nursing for almost an hour while he picked at the late lunch he'd ordered but didn't really have an appetite for.

"Saw your truck outside," he heard Finn say from

behind him. "Stopped in thinking you were doing some electrical work and find you moping at the bar?"

"What are you doing in town?" Brady asked, kicking out the stool next to him as an invitation to sit down.

"I'm actually passing through. I had some business in Concord and decided to take the long, scenic route back so I could mooch some of my mom's cooking. And then, like I said, I saw your truck."

"I'm not great company. Just going to say that up front."

"I didn't know she was going to be at Tess's the other day or I would have given you a heads-up. But since I *did* see you together, I have to ask. What the hell happened?"

Brady took a sip of the warm beer before shrugging one shoulder. "You know what they say. I can't be tied down and Reyna's hell on men."

"That's a load of crap on both counts. Don't forget who you're talking to here."

"It's complicated."

"No, it's not. You love her. She loves you. You're both being hardheaded and hiding how you really feel." Finn snagged one of his fries and then grimaced because they weren't exactly hot and fresh anymore. "I was really hoping for a more original story."

"You're free to go sit with somebody else, you know. Anybody else."

"I actually have to get going because I gave my mom an ETA and I think she has a to-do list for me to check off before she'll feed me." He stood, but then rested his hand on Brady's shoulder. "In all seriousness, this is it. This is the moment you have to put it all out there—*all* of it—or you're not going to get another shot. Don't let her get away, man."

When the door swung closed behind Finn, Brady took a long sip of the warm beer and grimaced. It was time to either order another or get up and go, and he didn't want another beer.

But he also had nowhere to go. He didn't want to go home to his empty house. He didn't want to drag his mom or his brother down with his mood. All he wanted was Reyna. He wanted to wake up with her in the morning, kiss her goodbye as they went off to work, and then kiss her again when the workday was over.

Don't let her get away.

But Finn didn't know everything. He didn't know that Brady had signed up for this heartache. Or rather for a baby, but he'd known this heartache would be part of the package. It was why he'd tried to walk away before it was too late. But it had already been too late, and here he was. Sitting in a bar, trying to drown heartbreak and regrets with warm beer.

There was one regret that no amount of alcohol could ever drown, though, and that was walking away without telling Reyna how he felt.

She had a right to know that he was in love with her. He needed to tell her that so she would know *why* he'd overstepped. So she would know why being reminded he didn't have any place in her life except as the father of her child had hurt him so deeply.

And he needed to know that he'd at least put it all out there. He had to take his shot.

An hour later, Brady parked in the Bishop's Auto Care lot and killed the engine. He'd arrived right at closing time, but he hadn't counted on a customer picking up a car, so he sat in his truck until the woman came out of the office and then got to the door before Reyna could lock it.

He watched the emotions play out across her face when he stepped across the threshold. Her eyes lit up when she saw him, but then there was the flash of pain. Sorrow. Maybe a little anger because he'd shown up with no warning.

"What can I do for you?" she asked in a quiet voice.

"I have some things to say to you, Reyna Bishop. Things I should have said a long time ago."

"Okay." She settled herself on the stool and waited, which flustered him. He'd rather not do this with the counter between them, but he also didn't want to move into her space without invitation.

"I'm just going to lay it all out for you," he said. "It's going to hurt like hell, but not as much as it'll hurt me to go through the rest of my life without you and wondering if telling you the truth could have made a difference."

Tears gathered in her eyes and he hadn't even started yet. "The truth about what?"

"I love you, Reyna. I've loved you in some way for as long as I can remember. You can call Finn right now and ask him about that time back when we were in first grade that I was going to marry you."

Her eyes widened, and then she shook her head. "Did it ever occur to you, at *any* time over the last almost thirty years but especially over the last few months, that you should tell *me* that?"

"I do see now how that probably would have been a better strategy than telling Finn, yes." He shoved his hands in his pockets, determined to tell her everything. "That night you came back to my place and things didn't end great—well, great for me, but not so much for you—anyway, it went down that way because I was so overwhelmed by finally getting to kiss you and touch you. I'd been waiting my entire life, so I wasn't so great at the self-control, if you know what I mean."

"Why didn't you tell me that?"

He took his hands out of his pockets and held them up in an *are you kidding me?* gesture. "Seriously? We had a few drinks and went back to my place and you think me telling you I've been in love with you since we sat next to each other during story time is a totally normal thing to do?"

She laughed, and the sound was like a balm to his soul. "Okay, I admit that would have been weird and I probably would have gone home, but you could have told me before then. There were literally *years* you could have said something."

"I guess…" He sighed and shrugged his shoulders. "I guess you can't tell me no if I don't ask you."

"I also can't say yes."

"Good point." He shouldn't ask. He knew he shouldn't, but he couldn't help himself. "At some point during those years, if I had asked, would you have said yes?"

Reyna looked into Brady's blue eyes and tried to focus on his question, but her mind was reeling from the revelation that he'd loved her for years and she'd never known, and that was making it hard to concentrate.

"I don't know," she finally said, because she could see by his face he'd already assumed she would say no. "Honestly, I don't know what I would have said.

You've always had a bit of a reputation for playing around, you know."

"So they say. The same *they* that say you're hell on men," he reminded her. "But I don't think playing around and having relationships with no promises of commitment made are the same thing. If I'd found a woman who made me feel the way you do, maybe I would have settled down."

"This is a lot," she whispered, and then she ran her hand over the curve of her belly when the baby fluttered. "Let's go upstairs. Lock the door and turn the sign over, and then hit the light switch here when you come up."

She went up the interior stairs to her apartment and wasn't surprised when she heard his footsteps on the bottom steps before she hit the top. She wasn't moving as fast as she used to, and she had to be extra careful on the older, wooden staircases.

"Do you want anything to drink?" she asked after she'd turned on the light and he'd closed the door behind them. She kicked off her shoes and wiggled her toes for a few seconds. Her feet weren't swollen, really, but they did tend to get a little puffy by the end of the day.

"I'm good. Why don't you sit down and put your feet up and I'll get *you* a drink?"

"I just drank an entire bottle of water while wrapping things up for the day downstairs." She sank on her couch, sitting sideways so she could have her legs up, and she wasn't surprised when Brady sat at the other end and pulled her feet onto his thigh to elevate them. "So, I have a question."

"You can ask me anything," he said. "And I'll be totally honest with you."

When he started rubbing her feet, putting just a little pressure with his thumbs, she closed her eyes for a few seconds. That felt really good. Then she rested her hand on her stomach and looked at him again. "Why did you agree to father this little peanut? Was it just because of your feelings for me?"

"I agreed to father that little peanut because I wanted a child and you wanted a child and neither of us had picket fences looming on the horizon, so it made sense. My feelings for you are why I changed my mind after our first night together."

"You said the *us* part didn't feel right."

"It didn't, but not because I didn't like *us*. But because it wasn't right that you thought we were two people who'd been friends—more or less—for decades who chose to have a baby together, without knowing how I actually felt about you."

"Why didn't you ever say anything? Since then, I mean? When it stopped feeling pretend."

"Because *you* said the you-and-me part was never going to work out."

"Which is basically the same thing you said," she pointed out.

"But I said it because I knew I was in love with you. You said it because, obviously, you thought the you-and-me part wouldn't work."

It would be so easy to dodge or deflect, but he'd bared his soul for her. She owed him honesty. "After that first night, I did think the you-and-me part was a mistake, but not because I didn't think we could work out as a couple. I was surprised by how much I...felt."

"I obviously redeemed myself then," he said with a wry chuckle.

She laughed. "No, not felt in that way, although yes. I was very pleasantly surprised the second time around. But the problem was that I felt the stirrings of feelings that were emotional in nature, and I had promised you that I just wanted a baby and nothing else from you."

The way he looked at her was so intense, she barely noticed he'd stopped rubbing her feet. "So this whole time, we've been pretending to be a couple who are only pretending to be a couple."

"Yes, I think we have."

He swung her feet to the floor and stood. Then he put out his hands so she could stand in front of him. "I have always loved you. I love you now. I am *always* going to love you."

"I love you, too." Tears spilled onto her cheeks, but she didn't want to let go of his hands to wipe them away. "And maybe I didn't see you clearly enough before, but I do now and I am so in love with you. And I'm going to be in love with you forever."

He let go of her hands and pulled close so he could wrap his arms around her. She tilted her head and he kissed her until she could barely breathe, though she wasn't sure if it was the kiss or how tightly he was holding her. She didn't care. She never wanted the kiss to end.

But when he broke off the kiss and tucked her head against his chest, she liked that, too.

"Will you go for a drive with me?" he whispered against her hair.

"How far are we going?"

"Not far. Probably a quarter of a mile or so."

She pulled back, giving him a confused look. "Why don't we just walk?"

He pointed at her feet. "I think you've done enough walking for today."

"Oh, that's standing on a cement floor all day. It's good for me to walk, actually, and there's a big difference between my sneakers and my work shoes."

A few minutes later, they walked hand in hand down the street. She didn't know where they were going, but didn't really care. They tossed casual greetings to the people they knew, but didn't stop to talk to anybody.

"We're probably confusing the gossips," he said.

"On the bright side, we don't have to tell all the people in our lives we came to our senses. They probably already know."

He led her to the gazebo, which was empty. It wouldn't be long before tourists took over every public space in town, but for now they could sit and look out over the still water of the bay in peace.

"This is beautiful." She sighed and leaned her head against his shoulder. "No matter how much this town gets on my last nerve, I still love it."

"I love *you*."

"I love you, too." She lifted her head so she could look at him through a sheen of tears. "It feels so good to say that out loud."

"Even more than I could imagine." He grinned. "And I think we've established that I've been imagining this for a *very* long time."

"Now we get to imagine being here with our child. Together."

"I've imagined that, too." He leaned closer, his head almost touching her. "I would get down on one knee, but there are still people around."

He nudged her hand and she looked down to see a small velvet box in his hand. When he opened it, she gasped and had to blink away a fresh sheen of tears. There were three rings in the box, and the top one was a beautiful diamond, winking at her in the fading light.

He lifted the diamond out of the box. "Reyna Bishop, will you marry me?"

She swiped at a tear on her cheek as she nodded. "Yes. Definitely yes."

He slid the ring onto her finger and she let out a sigh of relief when it fit. Her hands could be puffy sometimes, but it slid over her knuckle and she held up her hand to admire the sparkle.

"I got that ring for you because I want you to have it. Maybe you can wear it after work or for special occasions, but these are matching silicone wedding bands. I figure, since I stick my hands in electrical panels and you've got your hands in car engines, that the usual metal bands wouldn't be our thing."

Reyna looked into Brady's eyes and felt the certainty of his love for her flood through her. This man knew her. He *saw* her. And they were going to spend the rest of their lives together.

"I love you," she said again, and then she laughed through the tears. "I'm probably going to say that a lot."

"I'm never going to get tired of hearing it." He stood and helped her to her feet, tucking the box with the silicone bands back in his pocket.

If she had her way—and she would—they wouldn't be in a box long. She wasn't going to wait to marry him.

She reached up and cradled the back of his neck, pulling him down for a kiss. With his arms wrapped around her and his lips against hers, Reyna felt a sense of peace and happiness so strong she hadn't even known it was possible.

When they left the gazebo, she moved to his left side so he was holding her right hand, leaving her free to admire her ring as they walked back to the main sidewalk. There were still people milling around and she saw more than a few faces she recognized watching them.

"Hey, everybody!" she yelled. "Reyna Bishop is marrying Brady Nash!"

Brady laughed and swung her into his arms. "Hashtag *she said yes*."

"I love you," she whispered again, and then she kissed him right there on the main street.

Epilogue

"Are you sure you don't want me to carry him for a while?" Reyna peeked at her five-month-old son's sweet face. Parker James Nash was wrapped in a warm red bunting and cradled in a baby sling over his father's shoulder, sound asleep.

"Nope, we're good. You could get me another cookie, though." Her husband gave her such a sweet look, she couldn't refuse.

They'd lucked out and the first Saturday in December turned out to be almost unseasonably warm, so they'd joined in the town's Christmas festivities with their infant son. They'd watched the parade, with Brady covering Parker's ears while she held him. Then they'd wandered around the town square, visiting with people. Christy had managed to get a photo of both of her sons and their families in front of the town tree, although CJ was slightly blurry because there was a lot of sugar and excitement to be had at the holiday festival.

They wandered by the booth that was selling very limited-edition handmade Christmas ornaments—a wreath decorated with blackberries instead of the typical red berries—with all proceeds benefiting the Spurr Memorial Library. Only Brady and Jenelle, who was taking a turn manning the booth, knew that Reyna had made them, and she laughed when her husband insisted on buying one.

"That way nobody will suspect you," he'd teased.

They sat on one of the hay bales, eating cookies and sipping hot chocolate while they lit the tree, and Reyna sighed when Parker started to fuss. It was past time for him to eat, so she knew it was time to head home.

"Maybe next year we can drive the Chevelle in the parade," Brady said as he stood up. "I can get some classy magnetic signs that say Nash Electric and Bishop's Auto Care to put on the doors."

She laughed. "By the time you're done paying to make that car pretty, you're not going to want to stick *anything* to the doors, magnetically or otherwise. You'll probably want to sell it."

"That's never going to happen. That car's special to me." He leaned close so she would be the only person who could hear him. "How many guys show up at a garage to get an estimate and get offered a baby?"

Nudging him away with her elbow, she gave him a look. "You may *not* tell that story to our future grandchildren someday."

They walked home, Parker snuggled against his father's chest, and Reyna smiled when they turned up their walk. Brady had gone full out on the decorations this year, adding a ridiculous amount of lights in addition to his usual electric candles and wreaths. And because he was a dad now, he'd added a few fun inflatables to the yard. The Nash house was definitely not lacking in Christmas spirit.

Parker got fussy during the unbundling process, but he calmed when she fed and changed him. Brady had turned on the Christmas tree lights and he took Parker before settling on the couch. "Come join us. We had a big day and it's snuggle time."

"I like snuggle time, but in a minute. I have something for the tree. Well, it's for you, but it goes on the tree. Stay here."

It only took her a minute to go upstairs and retrieve the small box she'd stowed in her top drawer, but by the time she walked back into the living room, Parker was asleep on Brady's chest. Her husband had his head back against the couch cushion and his eyes were closed, but she knew he wasn't asleep.

She paused in the doorway, savoring the peaceful scene between father and son. Sometimes she'd think she was as happy and in love as it was possible to be, and then there would be a moment that the love swelled so much she could hardly breathe.

As if he could sense her watching him, Brady opened his eyes and turned his head to look at her. Whatever he saw on her face made him smile, and he patted the cushion next to him. As she sat, he slouched a little more so the baby was secure on his chest with just Dad's arm under him so he could take the box she handed him. Because he had the baby, she lifted the lid and peeled back the tissue paper.

"Oh, wow," he whispered, and then he had to clear his throat because he was a little choked up.

He lifted the polymer clay ornament out of the box by the string so it dangled in front of them. It was a tiny red Chevelle with a bare Christmas tree tied to the top. It had been the most challenging piece she'd ever made because the naked branches were so thin, but she'd persevered and the look on Brady's face made it all worth it.

"I thought it would be a good way to kick off a new tradition of family ornaments for our tree," she whispered.

"You'll have to come kiss me, because my hands are full."

She laughed softly as she swiveled to her knees so she could lean down and kiss him. "Merry Christmas, husband."

"Merry Christmas, wife. Here's to a lifetime of Nash family Christmas memories," he said, and he kissed her again.

* * * * *

WE HOPE YOU ENJOYED
THIS BOOK FROM

✦HARLEQUIN
SPECIAL
EDITION

Believe in love. Overcome obstacles. Find happiness.

Relate to finding comfort and strength in the
support of loved ones and enjoy the journey
no matter what life throws your way.

6 NEW BOOKS AVAILABLE EVERY MONTH!

HSEHALO2020

#2803 A COWBOY'S CHRISTMAS CAROL
Montana Mavericks: What Happened to Beatrix?
by Brenda Harlen

Evan Cruise is haunted by his past and refuses to celebrate the festivities around him—until he meets Daphne Taylor. But when Daphne uncovers Evan's shocking family secret, it threatens to tear them apart. Will a little Christmas magic change everything?

#2804 A TEMPORARY CHRISTMAS ARRANGEMENT
The Bravos of Valentine Bay • by Christine Rimmer

Neither Harper Bravo nor Lincoln Stryker is planning to stay in Valentine Bay. But when Lincoln moves in next door and needs a hand with his nice and nephew, cash-strapped Harper can't help but step in. They make a deal: just during the holiday season, she'll nanny the kids while he works. But will love be enough to have them both changing their plans?

#2805 HIS LAST-CHANCE CHRISTMAS FAMILY
Welcome to Starlight • by Michelle Major

Brynn Hale has finally returned home to Starlight. She's ready for a fresh start for her son, and what better time for it than Christmas? Still, Nick Dunlap is the one connection to her past she can't let go of. Nick's not sure he deserves a chance with her now, but the magic of the season might make forgiveness—and love—a little bit easier for them both...

#2806 FOR THIS CHRISTMAS ONLY
Masterson, Texas • by Caro Carson

A chance encounter at the town's Yule log lighting leads Eli Taylor to invite Mallory Ames to stay with him. Which turns into asking her to be his fake girlfriend to show his siblings what a genuinely loving partnership looks like...just while they visit for the holidays. But will their lesson turn into something real for both of them?

#2807 A FIREHOUSE CHRISTMAS BABY
Lovestruck, Vermont • by Teri Wilson

After her dreams of motherhood were dashed, Felicity Hart is determined to make a fresh start in Lovestruck. Unfortunately, she has to work with firefighter Wade Ericson when a baby is abandoned at the firehouse. Then Felicity finds herself moving into Wade's house and using her foster-care training to care for the child, all just in time for Christmas.

#2808 A SOLDIER UNDER HER TREE
Sweet Briar Sweethearts • by Kathy Douglass

When her ex-fiancé shows up at her shop—engaged to her sister!—dress designer Hannah Carpenter doesn't know what to do. Especially when former fling Russell Danielson rides to the rescue, offering a fake relationship to foil her rude relations. The thing is, there's nothing fake about his kiss...

HSECNM1120

*Brynn Hale, single mom widowed after an unhappy
marriage, has finally returned home to Starlight.
She's ready for a fresh start for her son, and what
better time for it than Christmas? But Nick Dunlap is
the one connection to her past she can't let go of...*

*Read on for a sneak peek at the next book in the
Welcome to Starlight miniseries,*
His Last-Chance Christmas Family
by Michelle Major.

"You sound like a counselor." The barest glimmer of
a smile played around the edges of Brynn's mouth.
"When did you get so smart, Chief Dunlap?"

"I was born this way. You never noticed before now
because you were too dazzled by my good looks."

Her eyes went wide for a moment, and he wondered
if he'd overstepped with the teasing. "I was dazzled
by you. That part is true." She rolled her eyes. "But I
guarantee you didn't show this kind of insight when we
were younger."

He should make some funny comment back to her,
keep the moment light. Instead, he let his gaze lower to
her mouth as he took the soft ends of her hair between

his fingers. "I might not have messed things up so badly if I had."

She drew in a sharp breath and he stepped away. This was not the time to spook her. "Come on, Brynn," he coaxed. "We both know it's not going to be good for anyone if you stay with your mom."

"She doesn't even want to meet Remi," Brynn told him, her full lips pressing into a thin line.

"Her loss," he said quietly. "All along it's been her loss. Say yes. Please."

She shifted and looked to where Tyler had disappeared with Kel. Without turning back to Nick, she nodded. "Yes," she said finally. "Thank you for the offer. I appreciate it and promise we won't disrupt your life." Now she did turn to him. "Very much, anyway," she added with a smile.

"Easy as pie," he said, ignoring the fact that his heart was beating as fast as if he'd just finished running a marathon.

Don't miss
His Last-Chance Christmas Family *by Michelle Major,*
available December 2020 wherever
Harlequin Special Edition books and ebooks are sold.

Harlequin.com

HSEEXP1120

CHAPTER ONE

Another Christmas over, another year about to begin.

Eli Garrett—sheriff of Wild Horse County, Montana—gazed out his office window at the gently falling snow. You could hardly describe it as *falling*, he thought, more like *floating*. It was a quiet time in the town of Painted Pony Creek and in the county, and he saw that as a Christmas gift of sorts.

This Christmas had been pleasant enough. Christmas Eve he'd spent with one of his longtime best friends, Cord Hollister, Cord's new wife, Shallie, and Cord's daughter, Carly. The wedding was just a week ago; he and J. P. McCall, the third member of their triumvirate as he liked to think of it, had been the best men. At the moment, J.P. was out of town, visiting family in California, with his service dog, Trooper, technically retired, along for the trip.

Carly was Eli's—and J.P.'s—honorary niece. All three of the men had been in love with Carly's mother, Reba, during their late adolescence. Then she'd disappeared, and as they'd found out from another friend, Brynne Bailey, Reba had died two years ago. But Carly had shown up last June, claiming one of them was her father.

DNA testing had eventually revealed that it was Cord.

Eli would've been delighted if he was her father. And as thrilled as he was for Cord, for his newfound happiness, he also felt a touch of envy. Even some dissatisfaction with his own life. He hated to admit that. But what Cord had, Eli wanted, too. Love, family…

How to achieve it, though? But he already knew…

He'd have to ask a certain woman to go out with him. And that woman was Brynne Bailey—which wouldn't be news to his friends.

He wondered if Cord would have anything to say on the subject. Knowing Cord, he would.

It hadn't come up during their Christmas Eve dinner. But he hadn't expected it to. This was meant for a private conversation, like today's.

Christmas Eve he'd brought them expensive wine and good-quality beer to go with their dinner. And gifts. An expensive new cell phone for Carly; she hadn't needed any help setting it up. A book of photographic art and subscriptions to a couple of photography magazines for Shallie. And for Cord? Nothing.

Except his friendship.

Don't miss Country Proud,
coming soon from Linda Lael Miller
and HQN Books!

HQNBooks.com